THE MAGICIAN'S WIFE

First published in 2025 by Vanish Publishing, a trading name of
Ellie Jay Ltd.

Company Number: 14984900.

ISBN: 978-1-918251-01-2

vanish
PUBLISHING

THE MAGICIAN'S WIFE

LORA JONES

March, 2014

PROLOGUE

I knew how the trick was supposed to be done. I'd seen similar illusions on TV before.

It had always gone like this...

A sudden flare of lights. A burst of music. A magician striding out to meet his audience, while a large box, black as a club, sits on a raised platform stage right.

A magician who beckons flamboyantly, his wife shimmying towards him from the wings, her blonde hair a halo, the sequins of her leotard dazzling, sheathing her body like she is something mythical; a luminous-skinned fairy, a mermaid with wet shining scales.

The woman climbs the stairs and into the waiting box and, as the front is closed up before her, she waves a silk handkerchief over the top of the box, a handkerchief the startling red of a fresh heart. She continues to wave it as she is fully enclosed within the box, as the stairs are moved away. As a second box, identical to the first, is wheeled to fill stage left. As this new box is also shown to be empty and both boxes are hoisted in the air.

The soundtrack swells then, and, like a conductor, the magician gives his signal, commanding two things to happen together, as quickly as the blinking of an eye. The waving hand disappears. The first box shudders apart. Yet now it is empty. The woman is no longer inside.

As the music reaches its crescendo, the magician gestures at the second box, wand blurring towards it like a baton. High above the stage, the box collapses, its base and sides dropping away, and in a cloudburst of glitter the magician's wife is revealed. She is perched upon a trapeze, her tapered legs crossed, slender feet pointed, white smile wide and ravishing as her sequins. And in that moment it becomes apparent: it is this woman who really holds the magic. Her reappearance is the climax. The story cannot end without it.

And so, I knew this is how the trick was supposed to be done.

But on Saturday, the 15th of March 2014, that wasn't what happened. Because that night, in front of the blazing lights and the gazing lenses, the glare of the audience and the scrutiny of the unseen millions watching on TVs and tablets and smartphones, something went very wrong. For when the sides of the second box waterfalled apart, the trapeze was unoccupied.

The magician's wife was not there.

She had suddenly, inexplicably, completely... vanished.

1.♠

As the man talked, my mind drifted to the message burning a hole in my pocket. The message that had been hand-delivered through my letterbox the previous morning. The message I'd read a hundred times already.

> **Very well, Clare, let's meet. I'll be at HMP Ferndon this Saturday. Come between 3-5 pm. Signed, a well-wisher.**

The words had been neatly hand-inked on a sheet of writing paper; the creamy, expensive kind. The paper was bordered purple and embossed with the initials "M.K." which, though I didn't realise it at the time, rendered the anonymous signature redundant: "a well-wisher". Despite the very nice paper and the very elegant handwriting, each time I read that signature I couldn't help but wonder what on earth I might be getting myself into.

M.K. Mara Knight.

I suppose I never expected her to answer me at all.

I had contacted Mara the previous day, five days after Angel Devereaux — the wife and assistant of magician Dex Devereaux — had abruptly vanished in front of millions on the first round of the TV show Talent Quest.

Nobody seemed to care at first, despite Angel Devereaux having disappeared on live TV. But as the week had gone on, with still no sign of Angel, the local paper I worked for was very keen to cover the story. The Devereauxs, it turned out, also lived in Morden, the same area of south London as me.

It was exactly the kind of case I had always wanted to cover. A sudden, baffling disappearance with zero leads. Maybe my coverage of the story could spark that lead, that memory. Maybe I could be the one to help bring this woman back. It was the very reason I'd worked two jobs and a night shift to fund my journalism diploma a few years earlier. To try to make a difference. So other people didn't have to go through the same thing I had.

But my boss at the Morden Mercury had other ideas.

'Not only are the Devereauxs local, but that Angel's a fine figure of a woman... for her age,' Jeff Tych said, crossing his legs. 'No, think I'll follow this one up myself, Clare. You take the story about that graphics place down the road. The owner's about to go to print on his hundredth pet birthday banner. You like dogs. And you're good with nutters.'

So, that is where I found myself the Saturday everything changed. Sitting behind the counter of Presto Print, nursing a cold mug of tea, while its owner pondered aloud whether a satin finish was more popular amongst corgis or cockapoos. Mr Chen was certainly a little eccentric, but it was unkind to call him a nutter.

I smiled politely and glanced at the clock on the wall. I should have left Presto Print thirty minutes ago. It was well past one, which didn't leave long to run back to the flat, grab my car keys and negotiate the perils of the M25. Especially if I was to be in with a chance of making it to HMP Ferndon in time to spend a good hour with Mara Knight.

My gaze wandered from the clock to the pinboard below it, across the mass of overlapping order slips tacked there, all jostling for position and stamped in red: "COMPLETE". Little records of lives and loved ones: birthdays, stag nights, retirements. "I ♥ HAPPY WOMEN", one order read. Strange, the things some people wanted printing onto banners. As my eyes traced the handwriting on the slips, I thought about the note in my pocket again.

Mara Knight hadn't been easy to track down. She had no social media and no website. In fact, I wouldn't have known about her at all if it wasn't for her husband, Travers. Like Dex Devereaux, he was a professional magician. Unlike Dex Devereaux, Travers had performed at most of the world's biggest venues, had had a residency in Vegas, entertained royalty, supported a host of good causes and, for a time, had even worked with the Metropolitan Police in an advisory capacity, with the job title: "Forensic Illusionist".

Then, nearly five months ago, in the middle of a magic show no less, Travers Knight had mysteriously vanished. He'd been performing his famous *"Buried Alive"* trick on a live TV special shot on location in Highgate Cemetery. The cameras filmed him going into an ordinary wooden coffin, from which he was meant to escape. But he didn't escape, and when panicked crew members dug the coffin out... it was empty. This wasn't supposed to happen.

To date, Travers Knight had never been found.

Just like Angel.

Despite what Jeff had said about me not working the story, I couldn't stop thinking about Angel. I couldn't stop thinking that there were others out there, too, who couldn't stop thinking about Angel. The consensus from Talent Quest was that she had simply run away, albeit in the middle of a live performance on national television. But as the days ticked by, I couldn't help thinking there might be more to it than that. So, I decided to go ahead and investigate Angel's disappearance. See what I could find.

I wanted Mara's help as what had happened to Dex Devereaux had happened to her. Not only that, but she'd been married to Travers for years, even worked with him for a while, according to an old version of his website. She knew all about magicians, illusions... how distractions are created, how people can be made to disappear.

Or perhaps there was something more, pulling me to Mara, even then. I just didn't know about it at the time.

What I did know about was HMP Ferndon. I'd come across it in my newspaper work before. It was a high-security women's prison in Hertfordshire, and I kept asking myself why Mara had suggested we meet *there*, of all places, before the notion grabbed me. When a woman disappears, the first person of interest to the police is her husband. So, does that mean when a man disappears, the first person of interest to the police is his wife?

Although it seemed utterly impossible, and there'd been nothing about it in the papers, the thought buzzed incessantly around my head. Is that why Mara Knight had suggested meeting at HMP Ferndon? Because she was now *in* HMP Ferndon?

'I'm terribly sorry, Mr Chen,' I said, swallowing down the rest of the stone cold tea and trying not to retch. 'Thank you very much for your time, but there's somewhere I really must be.'

2.♠

Racing out of Presto Print, I puffed my way up the hill to the flat. I cursed at the wet patches seeping under my arms when I let myself in, despite the cold spring. There was no time to change.

I dumped my bag in the "entrance hall", which was how the small square of floor between the front door, the bedroom and the living room had been described in the estate agent's brochure. In reality, the area barely accommodated a doormat. "My Clarey-Bird", that doormat read. A present from my boyfriend for my thirtieth last year, not long after we moved in.

'A mat from Matt,' he'd told me, gesturing from the floor to himself and grinning puppyishly.

Clarey-Bird was the title of one of Matt's songs, which he'd written in my honour. I didn't have the heart to tell him I'd never been sure about the song, much less the doormat.

All of a sudden, the door to the living room nosed open and a familiar shape came bounding towards me. My dog, Jasper. A cocker-terrier mix with the pinkest tongue known to man and a pale creamy-beige coat; a stark contrast to the oily grey it had been when I'd rescued him, not long after my birthday.

I rubbed Jasper's cheeks, kissing his head before turning to the hall mirror to give myself a once-over. I cringed at the mess looking back at me more than I'd cringed at the doormat. My chin-length brown hair was tangled and my cheeks flushed; a film of sweat sheening my face. Cursing again, I dipped into my bag, hurriedly swiping a bit of powder over my forehead and nose. The action caused a memory to rise, and I shivered, despite the sweat—

'Cla?'

It isn't really possible to shorten my name, but that didn't stop Matt from trying.

Pretending I hadn't heard, I dashed into the bathroom, where everything dripped with steam and damp towels littered the floor. I rolled on some deodorant, scrabbled around for my perfume. I couldn't find it. Unsurprising, given the state of the place.

'You off out again?' Matt said when I cut into the living room for the car keys.

I supposed I didn't look like I was. I glanced down at my nondescript cardigan and jeans, at the black and white Converse I'd been wearing since uni.

'Where are you going anyway?' Matt said, absentmindedly plucking a couple of strings on his guitar. 'That paint shop?'

'Print shop. And I've been already.'

Tentatively, Matt strummed a succession of chords. '*In the paint shop... where love takes flight,*' he started to sing. '*Brushstrokes dancing... in the soft moonlight. With every colour, our hearts unite...* Hey, I need to write this down...'

'I'll see you later—'

'*In the paint shop, girl everything just feels so right...*'

'Bye, Matt!' I called. 'Don't forget to walk Jasper!' I shut the door, hoping he'd be finished by the time I got back, since the next round of Talent Quest was on and I wanted to watch it live. See if there would be any mention of Dex or Angel Devereaux.

In the hall, I picked up my bag again and noticed something was lying next to it on the floor. I guessed it must have been there when I arrived.

Lifting up the square of card, I read the words printed across the top of it in bold black letters.

This is your final reminder. We have your parcel from...

Below this, someone had written "Luxe Lumina" in biro. "Please collect by 5pm."

I frowned. I certainly hadn't ordered anything from Luxe Lumina, a well-known luxury cosmetics brand. One of their eyeliners alone would probably have cleaned out a week of my wages. Then I remembered. I'd entered a promotional giveaway a few weeks ago on social media, to win a bottle of their new perfume, Parma Violet. My luck must be changing, I thought.

The parcel needed collecting that day, and the collection point given was the off-licence next door. Still self-conscious of the sticky patches now drying on my top, I decided to pick up the parcel straight away. I gave Jasper a final cuddle, then left.

I tore the box open as soon as I got in the car and, after giving myself a liberal spritz of Parma Violet and chucking the bottle in my handbag, I set off for Hertfordshire.

3.

By the time I reached the junction for the M25, my eyes had just about stopped watering, though I still had to make the rest of the journey with the windows down. Luxe Lumina's new perfume was not good. No wonder they were giving it away.

The visitors' car park at HMP Ferndon was pretty full when I arrived, but I managed to find a space not too far from the barriers, which were raised. I grabbed my handbag and locked the car, and as I followed the signs to the Visitors' Reception Centre, I could feel the pulse start to kick in my neck. I had never visited a prison before and had no idea what to expect.

Whatever it was, it wasn't the scene that greeted me inside. The reception was cheerful, welcoming even. Filled with children's tables and soft play, variegated pot plants and piles of glossy magazines. A wall-mounted TV was playing a rolling news channel. I joined the queue to sign in as the headline summaries scrolled across its screen. *Met Police investigate another large-scale drugs racket on the Harrowbrook Estate... First same-sex marriages in the UK to take place in a week's time... Champion race horse stolen from stables...*

When I finally reached the desk, a kindly lady with a grandmotherly hairstyle at odds with her snakeskin manicure directed me through a series of forms. Who I was, who I was there to see. She took a copy of my driver's licence and, once I'd filled out all the relevant papers, asked me to take a seat.

I glanced behind me. More chairs had been filled in the five minutes or so that I'd been at the desk. 'Thanks very much, but I'll stand.'

The woman looked mildly apologetic. 'Ms Knight is being brought over from B Wing, and the director's instructed that you see her in one of the closed rooms. Room Three.' She gave an ominous pause. 'I'm afraid there might be a bit of a wait.'

Could I have been correct in thinking Mara *was* incarcerated here? But for what, exactly? And was that why she'd told me to come between three and five, because these were the prison's visiting hours?

I checked my watch. It was after four, and I hoped there wasn't going to be too much of a wait or I'd never get through everything I wanted to ask Mara before the visiting time was up.

'Okay, thank you,' I told the woman, who obviously hadn't noticed that every chair was now full and the only vacant seats were a row of small patterned stools. As I neared them, it became apparent that these weren't for adults at all.

I ventured a look at the desk where the woman was still watching me with concern. Not wanting to disappoint her, I cautiously lowered myself into a sort of semi-balanced half-squat. At least I was small enough for the thing to accommodate me, one of the few times my size has ever come in handy. I issued an awkward smile to the woman, who seemed satisfied I was seated and continued with her work.

On the table before me lay a stack of colouring-in sheets. Beyond that, a row of faces tilted in my direction, multiple pairs of eyebrows raised. I was in one of the highest security women's prisons in the country, perched on a children's seat in the shape of a toadstool and feeling like the caterpillar from Alice in bloody Wonderland. At least my embarrassment quota for the afternoon had hit its limit. Things surely couldn't get any worse.

I checked my watch again, praying I wasn't going to have to stay in this position for very much longer — my backside already growing numb — when I heard a woman's voice behind me.

'Oh, love, have you run out of crayons?'

I felt a hand on my shoulder and tensed. It was blatantly obvious that the question was intended for me.

I turned to see a reddish blush creep its way up the woman's neck. 'I'm sorry,' she said. 'I thought you were... well...'

Sensing a few sniggers bubbling up around me, I murmured to her not to worry, and she scuttled away.

I was clearly wrong. I was in one of the highest security women's prisons in the country, perched on a children's seat in the shape of a toadstool while being mistaken for an actual child. Of course things could get worse.

I willed whoever was bringing Mara Knight from B Wing to hurry up, ran my mind back over what the woman at the desk had said. The prison director had been very specific. Rather than us meeting in the same area where all the other prisoners received their visitors, I was to be speaking with Mara in one of the closed rooms. Why? Was she not only an inmate here but a dangerous one at that?

In an attempt to steady myself, I took a breath, sensing my legs had begun to tremble. But whether that was down to the ridiculous way I was seated or what was about to happen, I had no idea.

4.♠

Another ten minutes passed before my name was finally called, by which time I had lost the feeling in both buttocks.

Sitting on that toadstool and being reminded of the caterpillar and his hookah had caused the nerves rippling in the seat of my stomach to intensify. A couple of nights ago, I'd returned to the flat after work to witness Matt furiously attempting to fan clouds of musky-smelling smoke through the living room window. Though I'd tried not to breathe, I once read that cannabis, even from passive smoking, can stay in the system for up to ninety days. Not only was I apparently visiting a dangerous criminal detained in one of Her Majesty's harshest penitentiaries — a place swarming with officers — I was potentially doing it with a banned substance in my system. I tried not to breathe again, in case anyone could still smell it on me.

The woman who had mistaken me for a child led me across to the main building, unable to meet my eye. A sturdy set of glazed double doors slid apart ahead of me as the woman left, revealing a much more austere room than the last. The floor was covered with mottled linoleum, an energy-sapping shade of grey, the walls an off-white and heavily scuffed. And the air was thick with that particular, pervasive disinfectant you only seem to get in institutions.

A warden sat just inside the vestibule. He checked through the forms I'd completed in the Visitors' Reception Centre, squinting silently between me and the papers on his desk, like he couldn't make sense of why I should be there. I almost felt the same and shifted my feet uncomfortably.

'Right,' he declared brusquely after a few moments had passed. 'Your bag, please.'

'Oh... yes.' I slipped it from my shoulder and handed it over. 'That way.'

He indicated to an airport-style metal detector and, as I walked through it, a second warden took my handbag away.

'You can have this back after it's been scanned,' the man explained. 'But you'll be asked to store it in a locker before you enter Room Three.'

I attempted a smile and told him that was fine, finding myself in a short corridor. While the bottom half of one of its walls was solid, the upper half was made from toughened glass, and through it I could see the second warden, rummaging amongst the chaos of my bag.

Once the warden had finished, he handed my bag back to me and lightly patted me down, then led me towards an airlock comprising two hefty sets of doors.

The man touched the pass that hung on a lanyard around his neck to the panel positioned at the side of each door. A green light flashed, and he pressed the pad of his finger to the biometric reader beneath. With each action he performed, my heart pounded harder, as though it would be impossible for me to ever get back through those doors again. The air between them seemed heavy, drained of oxygen, and I realised just how rapidly I was breathing.

'Carry on to the officer at the next desk,' the second warden directed, his voice startling in the confined space. 'Down to the right.'

He retraced his steps as the doors to the airlock sucked sharply closed behind him, and I started to edge in the direction he'd pointed.

'Madam!'

Something about the tone of the voice, brittle but self-assured, a little upper-class, pulled me up short.

Come on, Clare, I told myself. *Get a grip. You're supposed to be a hardened journalist, an investigator of crime, a seeker of truth. You're supposed to be a grown woman, despite the episode with the toadstool.*

My best efforts to quash my nerves dwindled, and I turned shakily.

'Left is right, Madam,' the warden said, smiling yet completely contradicting what the other warden had just told me. 'Bag check.'

'But it's just been...'

Her smile vanished instantaneously, and she glared at me as though issuing a challenge. A challenge coloured with the faintest trace of... *amusement*? This woman was odd, I thought, her quick-change demeanour more fickle than the weather.

'Of course.' I passed her my handbag and watched as she unzipped it, the cluttered contents threatening to disgorge themselves once more.

'Organised,' she muttered sarcastically, cocking her head.

I didn't have the chance to respond as, even if I'd dared, at the far end of the corridor there suddenly came a piercing shriek.

'I told you, it wasn't!'

'Liar!'

I looked up to see two women, each clasping the other's hair, ferociously grappling back and forth and flinging insults between them. I stood and watched open-mouthed. This shocking hand-to-hand violence all appeared to be down to a missing vape. Or not so much that the vape was missing, rather than whether its flavour was *Infinite Tangerine Bliss* or *Celestial Peach Symphony*. The whole thing was simultaneously disturbingly vicious and utterly ridiculous.

I forced down an uneasy laugh. If the visitors could get that heated over something so innocuous, what on earth were the inmates capable of?

Seconds later, several wardens rounded the corner, and together they wrestled the women apart. Of course, I realised. These women *were* inmates. I'd forgotten that prisoners at HMP Ferndon were permitted to wear their own clothes.

The two of them were still screaming at each other as they were taken away. In all the furore, I didn't even realise the warden had finished checking my bag and was impatiently jiggling it out to me.

'Not right to have left it here,' she said. 'Right?'

'Er... right,' I replied. Feeling myself gaping like a goldfish again at the fight I'd just witnessed, I took my handbag and slowly turned to continue down the corridor. I bore right, as the last warden had instructed, and saw another ahead of me.

'You here for Mara Knight?' he asked.

'I... yes,' I answered, no longer certain what I was doing there.

'This way.'

I glanced behind me, but the woman who'd checked my bag had gone.

'Mara Knight,' the warden remarked, clicking his tongue like he couldn't believe it.

'You know her well?'

He wheezed a laugh. 'Nah, not well. But whenever our paths do cross, she keeps showing me card tricks.'

'Oh?'

He laughed again, fuller this time. 'Did one for me a while back. Absolutely amazing, it was. She gave me the whole pack of playing cards to hold. Next thing I know, the cards have gone and I'm holding a block of glass instead!'

I crooked an eyebrow, unsure how else to respond.

'Swear to God. She did another one for me just this afternoon, as a matter of fact.'

Temporarily forgetting my nerves, I wondered whether I really was in some kind of Wonderland. Toadstools, a fracas that seemed to blow up out of nowhere, a warden speaking in riddles, and now a magician's wife with a constant supply of tricks up her sleeve. So Mara Knight really *did* know a lot about magic.

'She sealed the queen of spades inside a card box, nice and secure. You won't believe what happened next!'

'What happened?'

'Sorry, no bags past this point.'

'Yes,' I replied. 'The warden who did the first bag check already told me.'

He frowned at this. 'The *first* bag check?'

'Though I do have permission to—' I thought back to the day before, when I'd received that message from Mara. I'd phoned the number on the prison's website and explained I was a writer, asked if I could take my mobile in with me so I could record our conversation. No phones, I was told, but a small recording device was fine. So I'd bought a secondhand dictaphone instead. I fished it out of my bag and held it up for the warden to see.

'Yeah, you can take that in with you,' he said. 'And I'll pop your bag in the Room Three locker.'

'Nice and secure—'

'That's right.'

'No, you said it a minute ago — about the playing card. Nice and secure inside the box. So what happened next?'

A wave of recognition crossed his face. 'Oh, I see,' he chuckled. 'Well, she'd vanished.'

'Vanished?'

'The queen of spades. Turns out she was never in there at all.'

5.♠

The warden pointed amiably at a chair that was bolted to the floor. 'Take a seat,' he said, leaving the room. 'Won't be long.'

The fact the chair was adult-sized would have been a comfort, if my pulse hadn't at that point been hammering through my body. Would Mara be able to help shed any light on the Devereauxs? Would she be hostile? Dangerous, even?

I didn't know why I thought that. I was there at her invitation, after all. But being inside a high-security prison is oppressive. It makes you paranoid, even as a visitor. Maybe that's what she'd intended. Maybe she wanted to scare me away from the case for some reason, throw me off the scent?

Yes, I concluded. Paranoid.

I looked nervously around. Room Three was as claustrophobic as the airlock I'd passed through earlier: a tight, square box; walls, ceiling and floor the same cheerless grey and peppered with stains. There was a table before me, also bolted down, and another chair facing mine, with a second door into the room just behind it.

I stared at that door for some long seconds, presuming Mara Knight would be escorted through it from her cell. I preempted the sound of her footsteps, her jangling chains, but heard nothing. *Her jangling chains?* She wasn't Jacob Marley. I was letting my thoughts run away with me again.

In an effort to distract myself, I fiddled with the dictaphone. I checked the chair opposite. I smoothed down my clothing. I checked the chair opposite again. I didn't know why I kept doing it, since I was well aware nobody had entered, let alone sat down. Yet I had the distinct expectation that, each time I looked up, Mara would be sitting there watching me, as though she'd materialised from thin air.

Then the door did open, giving me a start. I took a breath.

A new warden entered this time, his arm bent behind himself as though leading someone by the hand. He drew level with the table, and the woman emerged from behind him, her own arm hanging from his in cuffs.

This, at last, was Mara Knight.

And my suspicions were confirmed. She *was* a prisoner here.

The warden released the handcuff from her wrist and took his place by the door. Mara sank into the chair opposite, her head slightly bowed, lank sections of loose black hair falling forwards to partly obscure her face. Though I'd seen only a handful of photographs of her, she looked rougher around the edges in person. Her nose was a little larger and less straight, her eyebrows sharper and thinner. Her complexion was the white of raw pastry rather than the light olive I'd seen in the photos. It was difficult to age her, also. From the photos, I'd have put Mara around her mid-thirties, but this woman could have been anything from twenty-five to forty.

Mara's eyes remained cast down to the edge of the table, where her fingers worked at a loose flake of veneer. I observed her pick away at it, the nails on each hand bitten to the quick. A tattoo peeped from just below the cuff of the hoodie she wore: two crisscrossing initials bordered by a heart. *T.K.*

Travers Knight. Her husband.

'Mara Knight—' I blurted, the single syllable of the woman's surname veering rather embarrassingly upwards in pitch.

Very slowly, she angled her face towards me, like a sunflower finding the light. Or rather more like something nocturnal finding the moon, so dark was her expression. She held my gaze boldly.

'I'm Clare,' I stammered. 'It's very nice to meet you. Thank you for agreeing to talk to me.' I partially extended a hand, intending to shake hers, before considering it too formal. And so my forearm was left hovering in the space between us like a spare part.

She did not move, and her expression remained unchanged.

I grasped my dictaphone, vaguely aware that I was gripping it far tighter than necessary, and held it up to her.

'I'll be recording our conversation today. I hope you don't mind?' It was a somewhat pathetic attempt at a breezy tone, as I internally pleaded she didn't. I wanted to remember every detail of the conversation to come, in case I noticed something important in it later that might have escaped me at the time.

Mara shrugged, like she wasn't bothered one way or the other.

Grateful, I pressed record, watching as the tiny blinking circle appeared on the dictaphone's screen. 'I'm here with Mara Knight,' I said. 'Mara, would you be able to please say something so I can check you can be heard?'

When the woman opposite moved her chest like she might be trying to regurgitate part of her lunch, I knew what was coming. Craning her neck forwards, she parted her lips and gave an ungodly burp.

An excruciating silence ensued. This was not how I'd expected the interview to start.

Recognising she wasn't going to say anything else, I stopped the recording and, flustered, rewound it. I pressed play, and the burp rang out emphatically for a second time.

'Thank you. I can definitely hear that.'

Snickering to herself, the woman went back to picking at the tabletop.

For the past few days, I had been mentally running over all the questions I wanted to ask Mara. But I realised now I was ready to start the interview, I couldn't recall a single one of them. *Ask her about the Devereauxs,* I willed myself. *Open your mouth and ask: do you know Dex and Angel Devereaux?*

'Do you—' I began, looking up to see Mara Knight had once more fixed her eyes on mine. Her irises were much murkier than I'd expected, even under the room's strip lighting, her expression half-nonchalant, half-threatening.

'Do you want to see a magic trick?'

It was the first time she'd spoken, and it struck me how low her voice was, a touch gravelly. A smoker's voice, carrying with it more than a hint of Cockney. I didn't know where Mara was from, but had expected something more neutral, less accented.

I thought back to what the warden had told me in the corridor, that this woman was always showing him tricks. I wondered whether, like the tattoo on her hand, it might have been some memorial to her husband. I wondered whether being in HMP Ferndon had actually driven her mad. The grin that was spreading across her face hinted it was a distinct possibility.

'Okay... yes,' I mumbled. 'Of course.'

I recalled the film *The Dark Knight*, how the Joker asked this very same question before skewering someone's eyeball on the end of a pencil. I held my breath as Mara jammed a hand in her pocket, and was relieved when the item she pulled out revealed itself to be a deck of playing cards.

She removed them from the box clumsily. 'Think of a card,' she said, as though delivering a script. 'Any card.'

'Er... The queen of spades?' I immediately knew that I should have picked something less obvious. My brain must have instinctively leapt back to what the warden had said, about Mara making this particular card disappear.

Suddenly, she slammed the entire deck down on the tabletop with such force I almost left my skin.

'Now!' she announced, nodding at it. 'Take a look through the pack. See if it's there.'

Aware of the time slipping by and the multitude of questions backed up inside my head, I hastily picked the cards up and sifted through them. The three other queens peered back at me sullenly. But there was no queen of spades.

I shook my head, confused. This woman didn't handle the cards like someone adept at doing tricks. Yet the card I'd chosen was missing. There was a pause.

'It's not there!' she declared, dropping back in her chair and folding her arms triumphantly.

'It isn't, no...' I answered, waiting for the rest.

'What?'

'Aren't you going to make her appear? The queen of spades?'

'Oh, that not enough for you?' she replied, with genuine surprise. 'I can't bring her back, can I? Don't work like that.'

I opened my mouth to ask what she meant, before deciding it made more sense to try to get on with my questions. 'Mara, I'm here to talk to you about the Devereauxs. Dex and Angel. I assume you know them?'

'You know what assume does?' she said.

I tried to mask my disappointment. Why couldn't anyone in this place seem to give a straight answer? 'Makes an ass of u and me?'

'Nope,' she replied, looking pleased with herself. 'It lands you in the shit.'

'So you *don't* know Dex and Angel?'

She blew out a sigh. 'Never heard of them.'

The Devereauxs had been performing together for nearly twenty years. How was it, then, that this woman — who'd been around the world of magic for almost as long — had never heard of them? 'Okaaay,' I said slowly. 'Have you been watching the latest series of Talent Quest?'

'Nope,' she repeated unhelpfully.

I glanced between her and my dictaphone. 'As I mentioned when I emailed you, I'm investigating the disappearance of Angel Devereaux. She vanished on live TV a week ago. On the show Talent Quest. And I'm here because I thought that with your knowledge of stage magic, you might be able to help.'

'Not me,' she said, just as unhelpfully.

I pressed on, my frustration rising. 'The trick the Devereauxs were performing the night Angel vanished was a teleportation. Angel got into a box on stage and disappeared. She was supposed to reappear in a second box, but never did. I'm sure you're familiar with teleportation?'

She chewed the side of her thumbnail. 'I am.'

'Great. So you know how it works?'

'Yeah. You say, "Beam me up, Scotty," then some bloke presses a button and it sods you off somewhere else.'

I looked at her agape.

'*Star Trek,*' she clarified, as though I was an idiot.

I understood the reference, of course, but not what was happening. Either Mara Knight was being deliberately evasive — which was odd, given she was the one who'd asked me here — or incarceration really had done something awful to her mind. 'So you don't know the Devereauxs and you don't know anything about the teleportation illusion?'

'Like I said.'

'But your husband performed that same illusion himself, didn't he?'

She stiffened at this. 'Did he?'

I had no clue how to continue. All I knew was how exasperated I was. That I had rushed around and driven all the way to Hertfordshire to chase a complete dead end. That I must have been a fool to ever think I could help to get to the bottom of something that was nothing to do with me.

'Why are you in here, Mara?' I said, shocking myself with my directness.

'This and that.'

A pregnant pause.

'Is it to do with the disappearance of your husband? Is it to do with Travers?'

She fixed her dark eyes on me, and her forehead buckled into a mournful scowl, making me instantly regret the question.

'I'm sorry,' I added quickly. 'But what I mean is, I can help. Find your husband. It's what I'd like to do, what *I like* to do. To help. Would you want that?'

Mara lowered her head to her chest, and again her hair fell forwards. Though I couldn't see her face, I was sure she was weeping, and was overwhelmed by guilt. I should never have asked her about Travers; I should have stuck to the Devereauxs, to what might have happened to Angel.

A long silence stretched between us.

'I'm sorry, Mara,' I said. 'I think this may have been a mistake. I shouldn't have bothered you.' I pressed the stop button on the dictaphone. 'I'll leave you in peace now. Thank you.'

I caught the warden's eye to indicate I had finished and checked my watch. Although I'd only been in there for fifteen minutes, there wasn't much time to make the drive back to south London through the evening traffic before Talent Quest started.

To my surprise, as I did this, Mara leant across to me, studying my watch too. Her demeanour, I noticed, had totally changed. I thought my last questions had upset her, but I now saw she was wearing a self-satisfied smile.

The guard steered her to her feet, securing her wrist back inside the cuff.

'Bye, Clare,' she said, as she was escorted through the door. 'Mara Knight is glad you came.'

6.♠

The woman continued to talk about herself in the third person as she was led away, my mind turning the strange exchange that had just occurred over and over until the door behind me opened.

It was the same warden who'd shown me into the room fifteen minutes earlier.

'Ready?' he asked.

I followed as he drew a key from his belt and twisted it into the front of the locker in which he'd stored my handbag.

'So, Mara Knight,' he said, guiding me towards the two sets of sliding doors that formed the air lock. 'Quite something, isn't she?'

That's one way of putting it, I thought. 'Mm-hmm,' I said instead.

'She show you a card trick?'

'She did, yes.'

'Good, isn't she?'

He reached for the security pass hanging around his neck and lifted it to the reader mounted next to the door. No sooner had I opened my mouth to respond to his question than it issued a flat, defiant beep, flashing red.

Pulling a face, the warden tried again. The same thing happened. When the reader failed to show a green light for a third time, he attempted to clean the card's barcode against the front of his shirt.

'Well, I'll be...' His voice faded.

I glanced towards him as he shook his head and held the security pass aloft. There was no barcode. In fact, the pass wasn't a pass at all. Though it was a card. A card I recognised.

The queen of spades.

'How the hell's she done that?' the man asked himself, running his fingers along his jaw.

Behind the glass of the furthest sliding door, one of the other wardens from earlier came into view. The man next to me signalled to him, and slid the queen of spades out of his lanyard.

Using his own pass — which evidently still worked fine and *hadn't* been replaced by a playing card — the other warden approached us through the airlock.

He accompanied me back the way he'd just come, and we left the victim of Mara's card trick hovering at the reader. He held the queen of spades between his thumb and forefinger, studying first the front and then the back as though awestruck.

In the half-glazed corridor, the warden indicated for me to walk back through the metal detector, which I did. The air was thick with a strange smell. The man who'd checked my paperwork when I entered the building was still sitting at the front desk. But this time he looked like he'd been crying.

I made my way back to my car, along two thinnish bands of well-tended lawn. "Keep off the Grass", a sign read, and my thoughts briefly returned to Matt's illicit joint as I dived a hand into my bag to rootle for the car key. I pressed the button and got in, swinging the bag onto the passenger seat before pulling the door closed. It slammed more loudly than usual, but the noise was completely eclipsed moments later when, as I drove towards the car park barrier, an ear-splitting series of peals echoed from all around. I jabbed a foot onto the brake, realising a noise such as that could mean only one thing.

A prisoner had escaped.

I began to panic, finding that no matter how hard I willed myself, I could not move. My heart was racing, knuckles whitening on the wheel, feet stiff above the pedals.

Then, the barrier up ahead started to lower as the prison was plunged into lockdown.

'Well?' said a voice from the back seat. 'What are you waiting for? Drive.'

7. ♠

I jammed my foot on the accelerator, but it was too late. The barrier was closing fast, and there was no way the top of the car was going to clear it. I either needed to stop, or—

At the last possible second, I yanked the steering wheel into a swerve, flattening the "Keep off the Grass" sign as my tyres sank into the pristine green areas that bordered the road.

'A woman who isn't afraid to break the rules,' the voice from the back of the car said. 'I like it. Though why they have a barrier when there's enough room for a car to drive around it is anyone's guess. I shall have to mention that.'

'Who the hell are you and what are you doing in my car?' I cried, her last sentence scarcely registering.

'Nice to meet you, Clare.'

Hands still gripping the steering wheel as though my life depended on it, I stole a glance in the rear-view mirror. 'Hang on a minute. You're... you're...'

'Yes,' she replied calmly. 'I'm sorry about all this, but it really was the only way.'

'You're the bloody warden! The one who checked my bag! The one who was spouting riddles about left and right!'

'I am. Well, I was. And those weren't riddles, they were a

pattern interrupt. A psychology technique. I was bombarding your brain with peculiarities to deter you from thinking about what I was *really* doing.'

I looked at her again, the strip of face reflected in the mirror meeting my eyes. Dark, thickish brows. Fairly light irises that most definitely weren't a murky brown. Pale olive skin. The prison wasn't the only place I recognised her from.

'It's you!' I sputtered. '*You're* Mara Knight!'

She gave a single, sudden exclamation, as if my conclusion had entertained her. Yet it was not quite a laugh.

'Which means... that woman in Room Three *wasn't* you!'

'Correct.'

'It also means... oh, my God—'

'Yes,' she replied. 'It means you've helped me to escape from prison.'

'No, no, no,' I moaned, eyes frantically scanning for a safe place to turn the car around. 'This isn't happening. I'm taking you back. Right now.'

'I wouldn't advise it,' she said. 'It's all there in the Prison Act, section nine. Technically, you're an accessory now. Your sentence, if convicted, could be up to ten years.'

'Ten *years*—?'

'It'll be alright,' she continued, 'trust me. Just give me a lift home.'

'A lift home? You're mad!'

'Not at all. I don't live that far from here, so it shouldn't take you too much out of your way. But please keep your speed down. Driving like this will only attract the wrong sort of attention.'

'I've just helped someone escape a high-security prison

— the highway code's the last thing on my mind!' Peering in the mirror again, I saw a trace of amusement in her eyes.

'Turned out not to be so high security.'

I glared at her askance, incredulous at what was unfolding. At what I had somehow managed to unwittingly get myself into.

From not too far behind us, sirens blared, my mirrors spilling over with a blaze of blue lights. A police car was fast approaching.

'This cannot be happening,' I exclaimed. 'Tell me this isn't happening!'

'I can't do that, I'm afraid,' Mara answered flatly. 'I told you to slow down.' Inexplicably, she turned and waved at the police car through the rear window, its bumper only inches from mine. 'I suppose you'll just have to do what they want and pull over.'

'How the hell can you be so calm?' I said, drawing the car in to the verge. 'You might be used to all this, but how do you think *I* feel? Christ, I—' My heart felt like it was moving into my mouth, with the contents of my stomach not far behind. 'I've never been in trouble before, never broken the law...'

'Are you sure?' came Mara's reply. 'I thought I could smell pot on you earlier.'

'Oh, God...' I buried my head in my hands and tried to keep breathing, aware that as I did the car door was being opened.

'Get out.'

When I looked up, I was astonished to realise it wasn't me the policeman was addressing.

'What's your name?' he said, extracting Mara from the back of the car and clamping a set of handcuffs around her wrists.

'Your name?' This time, it *was* me the question was directed at, as a second police officer approached the driver's door and told me to join him at the side of the car.

I hastily reeled off my details, scrabbling in my wallet for my driving licence.

'You appear to be a little on edge... *Clare*,' the man said, checking my licence details.

At this point in the proceedings, it seemed to be the understatement of the year.

'Sorry.'

'Did you know you were speeding?'

'Sorry,' I repeated. 'I really am. I've never been pulled over before. Nothing like this has ever happened to me—'

He held up a hand, a signal that I should stop talking. 'Fifty-four miles per hour in a fifty mile per hour zone. One mile an hour faster and I could give you a ticket. Ten per cent rule.'

'I really am terribly sorry—'

The man cut me off. 'Looks like I'll have to arrest you for assisting an escaped prisoner, instead.'

My heart was thundering so hard in my chest I didn't think I could bear it any longer. But then I heard Mara's voice sounding from the back of the police car. 'Before either of you go any further, you might want to radio DI Paulson at the Met. Explain who it is you've just cuffed.'

After a little more back-and-forth, the man reluctantly pressed the button on his radio, and a crackling discussion followed. I couldn't hear anything of it, but after a minute the officer ended the conversation and returned to Mara.

'Alright,' he said to her, a little sheepishly. 'If you'd like to stand up, I'll get those cuffs off.'

'No need.' Mara got to her feet, extravagantly displaying her wrists. To the amazement of both myself and the two men, the handcuffs were already off. 'You ought to fasten them tighter next time.'

Exchanging a baffled look, the two policemen got back into their car.

I returned to mine on legs that felt ready to buckle any moment. 'I don't understand,' I said, mainly to myself, as I crumpled into the driver's seat. 'What is going on?'

'Give me a lift home,' replied Mara, letting herself in next to me. 'And I'll tell you what I know about the disappearance of Angel Devereaux.'

8.♠

'I'm afraid I'll have to insist you drive blindfolded. I don't like strangers knowing where I live.'

Mara absorbed the look that crossed my face and, though she didn't smile, her eyes glinted. I decided she was probably joking. Though given the events of the past hour, I couldn't be certain.

I'd been in such a state of panic when the police stopped us I hadn't fully taken in what Mara Knight looked like in the flesh. Though everyone's tall to me, she had equalled the height of the police officers who'd pulled us over. She was slender, with dark hair pulled back into a large low bun. Light green eyes, which gave the impression they were taking in much more than they actually saw, were set high on her oval face, above well-defined cheekbones. But despite her beauty, her demeanour was infused with an air of something else. Cynicism? Standoffishness? I wasn't sure. But it created a peculiar tension about her, like being in her company made you mildly uncomfortable, but at the same time you couldn't imagine being anywhere else.

She was wearing tightish black jeans and a short-sleeved white shirt, topped on each shoulder by objects that resembled folded-up socks, black in colour and printed with silver stars.

Noticing me studying them, Mara removed the items. Weirdly, they peeled away as though they'd been held there by tape.

'Do you have a satnav, or do you want me to give you directions?'

After everything that had just happened, I thought it was me who should really be asking the questions. Like how on earth had she managed to get out of prison? Why had those policemen cuffed her and then released her? And just what did she have to tell me about Angel Devereaux?

I took my smartphone from my bag, connecting it to the car's Bluetooth and inserting it into the phone holder on the dashboard. The same questions were still swirling in my head as I punched in Mara's postcode. She lived somewhere in the far north of London. A forty-five minute drive away.

A silence followed. I wondered whether Mara had already forgotten that, only moments before, she'd promised to tell me what she knew about the Devereauxs.

'So,' I ventured. 'Angel and Dex. You know them?'

'Not really. I've run into them once or twice.'

There was another silence while I waited for her to elaborate. But she did not.

'I thought you said—'

'Put it this way, Angel Devereaux isn't well liked in some quarters.'

I narrowed my eyes, considering her words. Through the windscreen, the car taillights ahead of us curved into the distance, a line of fuzzy red diamonds in the gathering murk. Could Mara also believe what I suspected from the start? That Angel hadn't just run away mid-performance?

'You think that somebody who didn't like her wanted to harm her, then? That somebody *took* her?'

Mara's face shadowed. 'It is a distinct possibility that what happened to Angel wasn't—'

At that precise moment, my phone started to ring, making me jump. Every time I thought I was getting a little closer to the truth of Angel Devereaux's disappearance, there was some interruption.

I checked the screen. A mobile number was calling me, but not one I recognised.

'Aren't you going to answer it?' Mara said, a wry note of mirth in her voice. 'Put us out of our misery?'

Only then did I register the unfamiliar ringtone, the lyrics sounding from the speakers. *"One way to fly, my Clarey-Bird. But two ways to hear my three words."* It was the Clarey-Bird song again. Matt had been messing about with my phone the previous night; he must have altered it.

Cringing, I hastily shoved in the hands-free cable and picked up the call. 'Hello?'

'Hello, Clare Deyes? I understand you're with Mara Knight. I'd like to speak to her, please.' The woman's voice had a velvety timbre but a no-nonsense edge. They were statements rather than questions.

'I—?' I was so thrown — not only by this woman knowing I was with Mara, but actually ringing my mobile to speak to her — that I didn't know what to say.

'Ms Deyes?'

Falteringly, I tugged the hands-free line out of the phone and signalled to Mara, 'It's... for you.'

'Hello Dhita,' Mara said, before the woman even had the chance to speak again. 'I thought I might hear from you.'

'I knew you'd do it!' the voice replied, with more than a hint of excitement. 'Does Paulson know yet?'

'I should think so. Two officers pulled us over, and I told them to radio him.'

'God, I bet he's as annoyed as hell. This might just tip him over the edge!'

'We live in hope.'

The woman — Dhita — laughed. 'So, come on then...'

'You *are* on speakerphone,' Mara replied.

'Even better,' said Dhita. 'I bet Clare Deyes is just as desperate to find out how you managed to escape one of the highest security women's prisons in the country as I am, especially since she helped.'

I opened my mouth to respond by telling her I hadn't a clue what she meant, or, indeed, what I was doing providing a lift home for an escaped convict. But before I could say any of that, Mara cut in.

'It was simple,' she said. 'Just a series of methods and effects.'

Dhita gave a fruity sort of laugh. 'Simple? Come on! Start from the beginning. I have to know *everything.*'

I squinted at the battery icon on the phone. I couldn't decide whether I was irritated that they were using up the remaining 27% to conduct their conversation, or desperate for the battery to last long enough for me to hear everything.

'First up,' Dhita went on, 'how the hell did you get through the biometrics? I've no doubt you pickpocketed the pass—'

'In a manner of speaking,' said Mara. 'I showed the warden

a card trick earlier. Made the queen of spades disappear from the deck and switched it for the pass in his lanyard. A classic transposition. I did think he might have noticed sooner.'

'Okay,' Dhita said. 'But how did you get the biometrics? You can't pickpocket a finger.'

'I got a copy made.'

'A copy—?' Dhita spluttered.

'Of the warden's finger, yes,' Mara returned. 'His name's Richie, by the way. When you and I visited HMP Ferndon a fortnight ago, I showed Richie a card trick. And in doing so, I obtained a very good impression of his fingerprint.'

I cast my thoughts back to earlier. What had that warden told me about Mara? That she'd done a card trick for him some time ago. *She gave me the whole pack of playing cards to hold. Next thing I know, it's changed into a piece of glass.*

'You deliberately turned those cards into glass so you could get a good fingerprint!' I exclaimed.

Mara raised her eyebrows and slowly nodded at me, impressed. 'Glass is one of the easiest surfaces to extract fingerprints from. As Dhita knows.'

'Amazing!' whooped Dhita.

'I used the print taken from the glass block to create a silicone replica of Richie's finger. That's how I made it through the biometric scanners.'

'And how did you get that finger into prison?' Dhita asked. 'Or do I not want to know?'

I snorted at this, then felt Mara's gaze boring into me from the passenger seat. 'What?' I said. 'It was funny. Or am I missing something?'

'So *that's* what you wanted Clare for?' said Dhita. 'To get the finger into prison?'

'But I've never heard of this... this *finger* before! I didn't take anything into that prison other than the stuff I always keep in my handbag.' Then it struck me. 'Oh, God. It was the perfume!'

'What perfume?' asked Dhita. 'I don't understand.'

I didn't understand it myself. 'I entered a giveaway,' I muttered, trying to work it out. 'A few weeks ago, on social media. With Luxe Lumina, the cosmetics brand. To win a bottle of their new Parma Violet perfume.' I turned to Mara. 'But you couldn't possibly have known that.'

'Your social media profiles *are* public, Clare,' Mara replied. 'When you got in touch about the Devereauxs, I had a little look at your accounts. Came across your comment on the Luxe Lumina post to enter their giveaway.'

'No,' I said, shaking my head. 'I only collected that parcel earlier today. The collection card arrived just as I was leaving for HMP Ferndon.'

'I paid someone to watch your flat,' Mara replied, as though it was the most normal thing in the world. 'A TaskRabbit, funnily enough. The bunny I hired popped the missed delivery card under your door when they saw you arrive home. Obviously, we'd been corresponding by then, so I already had your address. Which was how I knew where you lived to get the other message to you as well.'

I straightened in the driver's seat, trying to push away the notion that I had not only been completely used, but spied upon too. In my own home, no less.

'It still doesn't make sense,' I said. 'Yes, I put the perfume bottle in my handbag and took it to prison with me. But again, you had no way of being sure that I wouldn't leave it in the car.'

'Correct,' answered Mara. 'If you had, then my plan wouldn't have worked. I would have just had to think of something else. But having you collect the parcel on the way, rather than having the parcel delivered straight to your flat, significantly increased the chances.'

I remembered how confused the warden, Richie, had looked when I told him I'd already had not one but two bag checks. 'I took the bottle of perfume into prison, and you slipped it out of my handbag when you pretended to check it,' I said, playing over the series of events from earlier. 'And I didn't see you do it as I was distracted at the time. By those women arguing in the corridor about a vape.'

Without warning, Mara clapped her hands together. 'They did a fine job! For a couple of boxes of cigarettes apiece, ironically.' She huffed out a breath. '*Celestial Peach Symphony!* Presented with a flavour like that, I'd also be ready to tear someone's hair out.'

'So, the fake finger was concealed in the perfume bottle, somehow?' Dhita asked.

'It was,' Mara confirmed. 'It fitted inside the glass from the bottom. I had a friend of mine make the bottle. He works quickly.'

'And once you had Richie's pass and biometrics,' Dhita continued, 'how did you actually get out — past the scanner and the front desk?'

'That was the other thing about the perfume,' Mara replied. 'It wasn't actually perfume.'

A hint of the disgusting smell from earlier still lingered in the car, and I recalled the way the liquid in that bottle had stung my eyes and burned my throat. 'No, it wasn't *perfume*, was it?' I asked pointedly.

'I'm sorry about that,' said Mara.

'Sorry? I was coughing for the best part of half an hour.'

'I did put enough actual perfume in the sprayer for a couple of pumps, in case you wanted to try it. But I'm afraid the rest was PAVA.'

'*PAVA...?*' I blurted.

'Well, yes. An incapacitant, like pepper spray. As in *PAVA Violet*.'

Dhita gave another low laugh. 'You do love a good pun.'

'So does my editor,' I said, even more annoyed than I had been before. This Dhita must be some sort of criminal too. Why else would she be impressed by such an unhinged plan as this, I thought, doing my best to ignore how impressed I was myself. This was the kind of scheme a hero and his team undertake during the climax of a Hollywood movie, not the kind of scheme a lone woman carries out from a prison in an ordinary corner of Hertfordshire.

'To answer your question, Dhita,' said Mara. 'Once Clare had gone into Room Three, I used the fake finger and stolen pass to open the first double door. I sprayed the PAVA through that door and waited for a warden to open the other one. The air currents between the double doors and the outer door caused the PAVA cloud to travel past the airport scanner to the front desk. It carries in a fine mist, similar to a PAVA grenade.'

Dhita whistled. 'A PAVA *grenade*? Aren't they only allowed

in a few states in America?'

'There are ways to get your hands on a similar substance in this country,' said Mara. 'If you know who to ask. Anyway, all I did was wait until the mist had travelled to the front desk, then make my way through. It's not as if I was carrying anything to set the scanners off. I spoke to the wardens as I went, complaining about the smell. They didn't recognise me. Of course, it helped that, like them, I had my mouth and nose covered.'

'So that's why the warden at the desk looked like he'd been crying when I left.' I said.

Dhita went momentarily quiet. 'Probably best not to mention the PAVA,' she said. 'We might get sued.'

Mara's story, of how she'd managed to break out of HMP Ferndon, seemed to me to be nothing short of outrageous. I still had no idea why she was even in prison in the first place, let alone why she'd engineered such an escape. And in the course of it all, she had wasted my time, almost poisoned me with PAVA, and made me look like a complete and utter idiot.

'Can I just point out that there was no way I could have known that woman in Room Three wasn't you,' I piped up defensively. 'She looked similar enough.'

'Of course,' Mara replied. 'That was the point.'

It certainly explained why the woman had left the room speaking about herself in the third person. *Mara Knight is glad you came.*

'Who was she, then?' I said. 'She burped into my dictaphone.'

Mara gave an exclamation of delight. 'That was Kelly. I told her to keep you busy for fifteen minutes minimum to allow me to get out.'

Which must have been why she'd made a point of checking my watch before the warden led her away.

'*Kelly?*' said Dhita. 'As in Kelly Keogan? You asked Kelly Keogan to be your stand-in? Most women in there are too scared to be in the same room as her.'

Discomfort bristled through me, before I recollected what the warden had said as he'd led me into that interview. *The queen of spades. Turns out she was never there at all.*

How right he was. Mara had never been in Room Three. This whole thing — her elaborate breakout from prison — it had all been an extended magic trick, with me the unwitting stooge. I made a promise to myself that I would hear her out in the car — since there was no doubt this would make an excellent story — but that once I'd dropped her off at her house, I would never have anything to do with Mara Knight ever again.

'Very clever,' I mumbled sulkily. 'It was a nice touch giving her that tattoo as well, to really make her look the part. *T.K.* On her wrist, inside a heart. Your husband's initials?'

My eyes darted to the passenger seat to see Mara's face tighten. She turned abruptly to the opposite window. A few seconds passed.

'That T stands for Tayte. He's Kelly's seven-year-old nephew. They're very close. She's missed him, I think.' Her voice had changed. It was taut and dull now, her expression still hidden.

I shifted in my seat, feeling guilty for bringing Travers Knight up for the second time that day.

Mara cleared her throat. 'And that reminds me, Dhita. In my opinion, Kelly's conviction is unsafe. You should have Luke handle it.'

'We can talk about that later,' Dhita replied. 'Right now I want to know what you're wearing.'

Though I tried to keep my expression neutral, my eyes widened.

'No need to blush, Clare,' Mara returned. 'Dhita just wants to know which clothes I could possibly have taken into a high-security women's prison to allow me to break out of it. The answer, Dhita, is black jeans, black trainers and a white t-shirt. That combination sufficiently passed for a warden's uniform. From a distance, at least. And I sticky-taped a couple of black and silver hairbands to my shoulders to serve as epaulettes.'

There was a pause.

'The prison service has serious problems,' Dhita said.

'Nevertheless, it worked,' Mara went on. 'I think I've told you everything—'

'Not everything, actually,' I cut in. 'When I started to drive away from the prison, you were already in the back of my car. You obviously didn't take my keys from my handbag, as I still had them. So how did you get in?' Given everything I'd heard so far, my brain was already ticking through the potential methods she might have used: picking the lock on the car door, forcing the latch mechanism, stealing and replacing the key at some earlier point I wasn't aware of—

'I simply opened and closed the back door of the car at the same time you opened and closed the driver's door,' said Mara. 'Do it quietly enough and the other person tends not to hear, allowing you to slip inside.'

'You want to watch that in future, Clare,' said Dhita.

'How did you know which car was mine, then?'

Mara tilted her head towards me and raised her eyebrows. 'I told you. Your profiles—'

'My social media profiles are public, yes,' I finished, bringing to mind the numerous photos on Facebook that Mara could have looked through in order to identify my car.

At that moment, my phone flashed red. Low battery.

'Dhita, I must go,' Mara announced. 'Clare's phone is running out of battery.'

They said goodbye and hung up, and Mara went back to staring through the passenger window as if the conversation that had just taken place — a detailed description of a prison break — was nothing out-of-the-ordinary.

'Who was that, another friend of yours?' I asked Mara, the thought that I'd been used as a pawn in said prison break still rankling. 'Another shady character, I expect. Like Kelly?'

'Not quite,' Mara replied. 'That was Detective Chief Inspector Adhita Anand of the Metropolitan Police.'

'Detective *Chief Inspector*—?'

'An old friend of mine. It was Dhita who recommended to the prison service that I be brought in to test their security. Obviously, it was lacking. My husband used to work for the Met...' Her voice grew strange again, a shade unsteadier. 'And now I, on occasion, do the same. Dhita's currently on maternity leave. Her replacement—'

'DI Paulson?'

'Yes, DI Graham Paulson. Let's just say he leaves a lot to be desired. It's the next left, by the way.'

We were somewhere on the leafy northern fringes of the capital by this point, though it was getting dark. Mara indicated to an unobtrusive-looking gap in the trees, and I turned the car into it, through an impressive set of iron gates.

I found myself in a tunnel-like lane, branches arcing around it so snugly it was almost a rabbit's burrow. The car headlights bobbed slowly along, illuminating dense swells of dark-leafed laurels. Then, suddenly, the vegetation swept apart like a conjuror's reveal, and a large building loomed into view up ahead.

The building's facade was uplit by a series of outdoor lights. Their glow was warm, but the effect was a little like someone pointing a torch upwards below their chin in a horror film; it gave the faintest sense of foreboding. The building itself was a curious juxtaposition of architecture: the classical pediments and balustrades you might see in an old church, mixed with the unwieldy dark gothic of a mansion from a Brontë novel. A round tower at the rear jutted into the swirls of a black velvet sky. Like Mara, it combined the oddly beautiful and the distinctly uneasy, and the result was something you couldn't stop looking at. Added to this was the fact that the place was absolutely huge.

I followed the expansive area of gravel around several sweeps of topiary, wondering where on earth to stop the car.

'Here is fine,' said Mara.

I drew to a halt in front of not one but two vast pairs of double doors, set behind a succession of eight great stone pillars guarding a porch. I peered inside it. Two pairs of double doors, but only one doorbell. Surely this wasn't really all one house—

'Appreciate it,' said Mara, breaking my thoughts. 'Nice to meet you, Clare.'

As she got out of the car and closed the door behind her, I

checked my watch. Not only was my phone nearly dead, but it was already well after half-past six. Talent Quest started in less than twenty minutes, and it was still a ninety-minute drive to the flat.

Mara reopened the passenger door and leant inside. 'You'll never make it back to Morden in time for the show now,' she said. 'So I suppose you'd better watch it with me instead.'

9.♠

I locked the car and followed Mara inside. We passed through one of the sets of enormous double doors and into an atrium. On an expensive, smooth-stoned floor sat two doormats, each almost as large as the rug in my living room. The mats were printed with a tasteful black design, I noted. Not a song lyric in sight.

I fretted about Jasper and whether Matt would remember to walk him. He adored the dog, but when he was busy with his guitar, a bomb could take out the entire street without him noticing. I concluded that I should probably ask Mara if she had a charger I could use for my phone, when the thought was completely snatched from my mind—

Opening the hefty door before her, Mara rotated a switch to her left. A bright sphere swelled above us, extinguishing the darkness and flooding the space we stood in with clear golden light. It was a vast chandelier, hanging on chains from the ceiling.

We were in an entrance hall, black-and-white tiles stretching out across the floor like the glossy squares of a chessboard. The walls were part-panelled, part-painted; a deep midnight-blue. A large wooden staircase opposite the front doors wound up into blackness, its chunky carved balusters dark and shining, as though they'd been dipped in syrup. A glass cabinet big enough to accommodate a person was prominently positioned close to the foot of the stairs. I squinted, certain I could make out a human form lurking within it.

Almost as unbelievable as the things I could see were the things that I couldn't. There were no pigeonholes for post, no communal coat rails or meter cupboards. And none of the doorways leading off from this hallway were numbered. So this really *was* one house.

Mara stepped towards an antique mirror as large as a shop window, a long console table nestled beneath it. She opened one of the drawers, withdrew a card from the pocket of her jeans and placed it inside. I took in the text printed across the top. *HMP Ferndon.* Below was a photo of Richie, the prison warden, accompanied by his name. *Richard Radley.* It was his pass, the one she'd swapped earlier for the queen of spades. Mara caught me staring.

'They've probably deactivated it by now,' she said. 'But still. You never know when these things might come in handy.'

I peered into the drawer and was amazed to see it was full of nothing but security passes, each bearing a different company logo, employee name and photograph. Mara shut the drawer. On the glass top of the console, she set down an item that I recognised as the bottle of perfume I'd "won" earlier that afternoon. I re-read the name scrolling in elegant italics across the glass. *Pava Violet.*

'How did you do it?' I asked Mara. 'How'd you change the writing? It said *Parma* earlier, I swear it did. *Parma* Violet.'

'Are you sure about that?' Mara replied. 'Or did you merely see what you wanted to see? When the warden fetched Kelly from my cell to Room Three, he saw a woman about the same height and build as me, with hair the same colour, playing with a deck of cards like I'd asked her to. He was expecting to see me, and so he did. Same with the writing on that perfume bottle.'

Leaving me still frowning at the bottle, Mara continued into a room off to the right. I trailed after her, passing the glass cabinet. As I neared it, I saw there was indeed a human form inside, a freakish-looking automaton dressed in the clothes of a butler. A brass plaque on the lower part of the cabinet was engraved with the name: "Montgomery". It gave me the creeps, and I quickened my pace. But when I reached the doorway to the next room, I froze once more.

The space was vast, topped with a ceiling that must have been eight metres high. Around three of its walls, about halfway up, ran a galleried walkway; the woodwork the same treacly-brown as the staircase. Wooden carvings and panelling also covered the back wall of the room, as though it might once have been an altar.

'This part used to be a church,' Mara clarified, switching on an assortment of lamps.

The room was filled with a host of strange and stunning objects, both ancient and modern, objects that shouldn't really have gone together but somehow did. Day-glo neons hung side-by-side with framed vintage magic posters — sporting names such as *Maskelyne* and *Blackstone*. An Edwardian gramophone neighboured a Bang & Olufsen speaker. There was a snowy taxidermied dove perched under the dome of a bell jar. A circular black rug on the floor gave the optical illusion of it being a hole that might swallow you any second. But most incredible of all was the collection of furniture. A bizarre host of cupboards, tables and boxes, some painted with Chinese lettering, others with openings cut out of them the exact diameters of necks, wrists and ankles. One even had a circular saw jutting menacingly from its side. And, most extraordinary of all, against one wall stood a gilded, three metre-high Egyptian sarcophagus.

'Jesus...' I exclaimed.

'Tutankhamun, actually,' said Mara.

I gazed around in awe. 'Are these *all* magic props?'

'Some are. I hire a lot of them out. For the right price.' She gestured to an expansive sofa. It was modular in style but Victorian in shape, deeply buttoned and upholstered all over in a rich, damson-coloured velvet. 'Take a seat. Can I get you a drink?'

Mara crossed to one of her many peculiar cabinets. It was the kind a person might get into in order to be sawn in half and divided into three sections. She opened two of them up to reveal shelves crammed with enough bottles and glasses to supply a good-sized cocktail bar.

'Er... no. I'm driving.' I answered, wondering if it had already escaped her mind. 'Thanks.'

Mara noticed me eyeing the cabinet. 'It came from a magician working in the '60s,' she said. 'It killed him in the end.'

I shuddered at the gaps slicing across the cabinet, gaps into which a lethal series of blades must have been thrust as part of the magician's act. And here was this woman, using it to store her booze. 'He *died...* from...' I started.

'Cirrhosis of the liver,' she clipped, extracting a large glass tumbler from a shelf. 'He used it as a drinks cabinet as well.'

Mara pointed some sort of remote at another vast mirror mounted on the wall. To my surprise, it launched itself into life. It wasn't a mirror at all, but a giant TV screen, bearing what looked like the views from about eight different CCTV cameras.

Mara switched channels. 'Tea, then? Juice? Water? There's tonic, sparkling, flavoured...'

'Erm, tap water is fine.'

Mara swivelled neatly on her heels and disappeared back out into the hallway.

Resisting the temptation to investigate every single object in the room while she wasn't watching, I instead took my phone from my bag and typed a text to Matt.

Something's come up. Will explain later. Just watching Talent Quest with a...

My thumb hovered above the phone. How on earth to describe Mara? An acquaintance? Someone I'd just met? That woman I went to visit in prison? It all sounded too weird. I settled on—

... a friend. Be back after. Don't forget to take J out for an hour.

I pressed send on the text seconds before the battery died altogether.

The adverts preceding Talent Quest were playing on the TV

screen now, and I again glanced around the space I was sitting in, stuffed with its many fantastical objects. But my gaze hooked on one of the simplest things in the room. I picked it up. It was a picture in a plain ebonised frame, a candid photo of a young couple on a hillside. Their hair was being fiercely licked by the wind, but their arms were entwined, their heads together and their faces lit by smiles. They looked genuinely happy. It was Travers and Mara—

'Here you are.'

Her voice was too loud at my back. It gave me a start, the frame I was holding very nearly skidding from my fingers.

'S— sorry,' I sputtered, quickly replacing the photograph.

Mara's expression was unreadable as she set down my water on a side table, a bottle of red wine and empty glass in her other hand. She had swapped the white t-shirt she'd been wearing for a long-sleeved black ribbed top with a scoop neck. She'd untied her hair, too, and it fell down her back in thick dark waves.

Pouring wine into the glass, Mara took a generous swig and positioned herself in a wingback chair. The rings on her left hand glimmered in the light from the floor lamp next to her. They were the only jewellery she wore, the broad gold band of her wedding ring snug against what I presumed was an engagement ring below. This ring was gold too. Finer, with a dusty purple stone set into it, cut in an odd shape, like a straight-edged teardrop.

What had happened to Travers? Why had he disappeared from that coffin, to leave his wife rattling around in this huge secluded house on the outskirts of London? She'd taken over his job at the Met and was clearly now making a considerable income hiring out his props, given the size of house she was maintaining. And that was without the royalties coming in for the tricks he'd devised and sold. Could Mara *really* have been behind his disappearance—?

'Well, this is it,' she commented, cutting across my thoughts. The insipid synth-rock of Talent Quest's theme music blasted from the speakers surrounding us. 'Let's see what they say about Angel.'

'When you said she wasn't liked in certain quarters, what did you mean exactly?'

Mara took another sip of wine. 'Just that. Magic's a man's world. Angel Devereaux's a skilled woman within that world. She isn't afraid to suggest improvements to material.'

'You mean she's difficult?'

Over the rim of her glass, Mara raised her eyebrows. 'If that's what you call a woman with talent.'

Her words hung in the air.

Talent Quest usually opened with a brash, edited-together recap of the previous week's show. But tonight, as soon as the opening music faded, the programme cut to a different type of recap. The colours were muted, the background music tense.

'*Our last show gave us a dose of the unexpected,*' the voiceover began, in a tone so overly-serious it sounded sarcastic. '*And when a teleportation trick turned into a vanishing lady trick, our judges were left <u>dis</u>-illusioned...*'

The recap playing on screen was an edited version of the trick the Devereauxs had performed the week before. There was Angel once more, shimmying across Mara's giant TV screen, her blonde hair billowing at her shoulders, the sequinned leotard she wore hugging her body. I watched as she climbed the stairs into the first box, and it was closed behind her. The last time Angel had been seen for a whole week.

The footage next cut to the two boxes, simultaneously being hoisted in the air. The first box opened, revealing it to be empty. Then, as the music built to a climax and a burst of glitter showered the stage, the second box dramatically juddered apart. Angel Devereaux was supposed to be inside that box, perched on a trapeze. But the box was empty.

From there, the footage cut to a crash-zoom into Dex's face. He looked shocked. I'd forgotten how shocked. His mouth had dropped wide, and you could almost see the sweat forming in beads across his forehead. If *he'd* somehow been behind all this, his acting was top-notch. But then again, he was a performer.

'Tonight, Dex Devereaux is back!'

There was a pause, a shot of the two black boxes from the previous week's show.

'God. He's actually going to perform the same trick he was doing when his wife disappeared,' Mara said bitterly, downing a glug of wine.

'Yes, tonight — live on Talent Quest — Dex Devereaux returns, with a lovely new assistant by his side. He will be performing his now-famous teleportation trick again. And he's assured us that, this time, everything will go according to plan.'

10.♠

'Why does that sound like a case of famous last words?' said Mara ominously.

On the TV, the presenter emerged from the wings to a surge of audience applause. He began an interview with Shane Sinclair, head judge on the Talent Quest panel. Shane was ludicrously tanned, with dyed black hair, eyebrows, eyelashes, and even matching stubble. It was an unusual look for a man approaching sixty.

'Listen, it's not for us to speculate on what's going on in the Devereauxs' marriage,' Shane drawled superciliously. 'But we felt it was only fair this week to give Dex another bite at the cherry...'

'Only fair to boost his ratings, he means,' Mara muttered. 'Repulsive the show's even back on this week with Angel still missing.'

It was Shane's own company, Proactive Productions, that made Talent Quest, and I thought of all the press coverage that Dex's "trick gone wrong" had garnered for Shane so far. Mara was right; it was great PR to have Dex back on the show.

Another piece of video footage was played. In it, Dex Devereaux was talking square-on to the camera, like he was addressing the viewer directly. Dex was around fifty years old but looked a little older. He had a stocky build, with a modest middle-aged paunch he tried to hold in. His hair was highlighted and back-combed into a fluffy '80s-style quiff. In the video, he was wearing his classic stage costume: a black satin shirt with a few too many buttons left undone, black leatherette trousers and slightly heeled shoes.

'Angel, if you're watching, please come back,' he pleaded down the camera lens, wringing slim-fingered hands. 'I want you to know, honestly, that I miss you. I'm dedicating this performance tonight to you.'

His face bore an uneasy expression. Like he was nervy, but also enjoying the limelight while trying to pretend that he wasn't.

'He's lying,' Mara announced.

'How do you know?'

'His eyes flicked off to the side at the end of his last sentence.'

'He might just have been distracted.'

'He was overly gestural. He used the word "honestly" when there was no need, something liars tend to do in an effort to authenticate what they are saying. And his voice also changed pitch.'

'You seem to know a lot about psychology.'

Mara snorted. 'You could say that. I also know that they won't have Dex Devereaux perform until the end of the show, to maintain their viewing figures and keep the advertisers happy.' She picked up the wine bottle and began refilling her glass. 'So I'm having another. It's the only possible way to get through it.'

No sooner had Mara spoken than it was time for the first act of the night: Josie the Chihuahua. A woman took to the stage with a tiny dog that was dressed as Elsa from *Frozen*, complete with a gauzy mini shawl and wig. Blonde plait dangling over its forepaw, the animal proceeded to yowl along to a *Let It Go* backing track, as its owner looked proudly on.

'See what I mean.' Mara groaned, peering despondently into her glass. 'I should have chosen a stronger Merlot.'

Fifty-five minutes later and, as well as Josie the Chihuahua, we'd sat through a topless pensioner thrashing out a hard rock medley on his air guitar, plus a ginger-haired man armpit-farting his way through ABBA's *Waterloo;* an act Mara had branded "utterly insidious".

I could feel my stomach grumbling by this point. It was nearly 8 p.m. and I hadn't eaten a thing since before I'd left for Presto Print. I wondered whether to ask Mara for a biscuit or something once the show had ended, realising how strangely comfortable I had grown on the sofa over the past hour. That was even despite the dodgy succession of acts on the television. And despite the fact that I didn't know this woman I was sitting with at all; this spiky, shadowy woman with her massive, magical house, her missing husband and her mysterious past. I was almost a little sad that I would have to leave soon to make the drive back to my ordinary flat in Morden.

'*And now,*' announced the presenter, '*after a sensational appearance — or should I say <u>dis</u>-appearance last week — please welcome back to the Talent Quest stage, the Master of <u>Dex</u>-ception... Dex Devereaux!*'

'*Fi*-nally,' Mara declared, as Dex's music started.

I sat up straighter, focus glued to the TV screen to see what would happen next.

The lights dipped and flared to reveal a large black box positioned to the right of the stage, its front hanging open. Out strode Dex, beckoning to the wings extravagantly, from where a woman danced to join him. Angel's replacement. From a distance, the two women did look similar. The replacement was blonde, too, and wearing the same sequin-encrusted leotard as her predecessor. But this new woman was also about twenty years younger than Angel, even more petite, and with straighter, longer hair than Angel's trademark bouffant.

She pouted and postured as Dex slipped up behind her, fondling the narrowest part of her waist before caressing the stockinged leg she extended towards him. She tipped back her head as though in ecstasy, hair flicking down her back.

'What a lovely dedication to Angel,' commented Mara sarcastically, referring to Dex's words of only moments before.

Once they'd finished posturing, the woman climbed the stairs into the waiting box and, as the front was closed up to seal her inside, she began waving a vivid red handkerchief over the top. I sensed Mara glancing at me at this point, but didn't know why. A couple of stagehands removed the stairs and wheeled a second box into position stage left. This box was also shown to be empty before Dex closed up the front of it, just as he'd done with the first.

As both boxes were lifted on wires into the air, the woman's hand and the waving red handkerchief were still visible at the top of the first box. The soundtrack rose, and Dex gave a signal, commanding two things to happen together.

'DO IT!'

The woman's hand and the handkerchief both vanished in an instant, the first box shuddering apart. Yet now it was empty. The woman inside it had already gone. The studio audience applauded and whooped.

'No!' Dex shouted back. 'She's not gone, she's just travelling!' He raised both arms like a conductor. His face was strained this time, intense. He thrust out his wand, and a shower of glitter erupted from the end of it. 'Yeah!' he screamed.

'Christ,' said Mara.

With both boxes hanging around six metres above the stage, I shifted to the edge of the sofa. This was the exact point in the trick when, last week, everything had gone wrong. This was the point at which Dex's new assistant should reappear, sitting on the trapeze inside that second box.

Shining with sweat, Dex gave his final signal. 'DO IT!'

There was a collective intake of breath from judges and audience alike. And then, the sides and base of the second box started to tumble apart.

The first thing I noticed was the empty trapeze.

In a flash of white, like something unfurling, the box's sides dropped open and a limp form plummeted to the floor. At first, it looked like a mannequin. A mannequin dressed in the same sequinned leotard as Dex's assistant, like it was part of the act. But then the mannequin landed; the sickening thump-crack of flesh and bone when it hit the stage audible even above the music. It was, of course, not a mannequin at all.

For a few protracted seconds, the camera caught the woman lying there; her skewed limbs, the unnatural crick of her neck, the line of blood escaping her lips. It caught, too, the familiar bouffant of blonde hair.

The woman who had unexpectedly reappeared to lie lifeless on the Talent Quest stage wasn't Dex Devereaux's new assistant.

The woman was Angel.

11.♠

There was a beat. Not of silence, exactly, but that peculiar vacuum of reaction time; those slow seconds before anyone can make sense of what they've seen or knows what to do.

On Mara's TV screen, Dex and a couple of members of the Talent Quest production crew rushed towards Angel. And it was then that I saw properly what that unfurling of white had been in the moment the box fell apart. A pale banner was hanging like a sail from the bottom of the box. As I read the words printed unapologetically across it, my blood ran cold.

I ♥ HURTING WOMEN

So this was deliberate. Some sadistic exhibitionist had taken a woman's life live on prime time TV. And, judging by the plural chosen for the banner, he had either done it before or would do it again. *Women.* I felt sick to my stomach.

The camera abruptly cut away from the stage and onto the studio audience. A few people were on their feet, craning their necks for a better view of what was going on. Some were pointing, talking urgently amongst themselves, while others sat stock-still, hands clamped to their mouths.

As the studio descended into chaos and the cameras

carouselled between different shots of the audience, the onstage microphones were still audible. They picked up the sounds of bodies scrambling, shouts to call an ambulance, and then, in an eerie lull in the commotion, two very distinct words.

'*She's dead.*'

A few people in the audience started to scream. There was an extended bleep, and a test card appeared, together with the words: "Talent Quest will return shortly".

'Oh my God,' I breathed, spiralling to face Mara.

She was sitting forwards in the wingback, pale and completely motionless.

I couldn't believe what I'd just witnessed. Despite my suspicions that there was more to Angel's disappearance than met the eye, I don't think I really believed it until then.

My thoughts cycled between devastation for Angel's family and despair that I hadn't been able to help. I thought how horrific it would be to see someone you loved appear dead in that way on a programme you were casually watching on television, how it would colour the rest of your life. I thought I had failed. Failed myself, failed Angel, and failed the families of the other women who went missing. If only I'd got involved earlier, had been better at uncovering information, maybe I could have prevented what had just happened. Or maybe I was being naive. I couldn't make sense of it.

Moreover, what the hell had happened to Dex's new assistant?

'Where's that other woman gone? Angel's replacement? What, she vanishes, just like Angel did last week, and then Angel's body shows up in the very place the other woman's meant to reappear, at the exact same moment?'

'My thoughts exactly,' said Mara. She tipped back her head and drained the wine in her glass. 'We must go to the studio. Right away.'

'But surely it's going to be a crime scene, we can't just—' I stopped myself, her words sinking in. 'Hang on a minute... *We?*'

'Of course,' she returned. 'I can't drive. I've been drinking. You don't mind, do you? You did say in your conversation with Kelly this afternoon that you like to help. Just don't tell them you're press.'

'Well, yes...' I paused. 'Hang on, though, how could you possibly know what I said to Kelly—?'

Mara ignored this and crossed to the door. She stepped into a pair of boots and snatched up an overcoat from the back of a chair, flinging it around herself. It was woollen, almost floor-length and fitted at the waist. A rich bottle-green.

I followed her into the hall, an unfamiliar sensation thrumming in my chest. Hoping Matt had received my earlier text, I headed to the car, having not the slightest notion where the night would take me next.

It actually took me to Buckinghamshire, an hour's drive from Mara's. We turned off the main road, where an illuminated sign with chrome lettering denoted the entrance to Shinetree Studios. Mara directed me to stop beside a security kiosk, for her to flash a pass at the man inside. From what I could tell, it was some sort of police pass this time, bearing her name, and not one pickpocketed from a prison warden.

I'd never been to a TV studio before and hadn't expected it to look so industrial. Shinetree comprised a series of enormous, boxy buildings made from corrugated metal, with various trucks and portacabins clustered on the expanses of tarmac surrounding them. It gave the place the appearance of a colossal haulage depot.

Mara guided me into a parking space close to a large opening in the side of one of the buildings. A collection of emergency vehicles had already assembled there, and taut strips of police tape cordoned off the area. As we got out of the car, a stretcher was wheeled past and into a waiting ambulance. A long black zipper-bag shrouding a human form. I guessed it must have contained Angel's body, and a wave of nausea overcame me.

'Mara Knight,' said Mara, addressing the constable behind the tape. 'I'm here for DI Paulson. Is he around?'

The constable said nothing, but appraised us impassively.

'It's okay, constable, she's with us.'

We turned to see a man of around my age approaching. He was plain-clothed in a burgundy sweater, dark trousers and brown jacket. He had neatly cut, mid-brown hair, and when he smiled, I noticed the faint dimples that showed in his cheeks. I also noticed that he was holding a steaming hot dog swaddled in a napkin, slathered in the most delicious-smelling onions my nostrils had ever encountered. My mouth watered.

Mara looked between us, taking in my expression. 'Clare, this is Detective Constable Luke Taylor.'

Luke. This was who Mara had told Dhita to have check Kelly

Keogan's files.

Transferring the hot dog to his left hand, Taylor extended his right for a handshake. I opened my mouth to say hello, but found I couldn't speak, so offered a tight smile instead.

'Amazing work this afternoon,' DC Taylor told Mara, looking genuinely awed. 'We had a book running in CID. On how quickly you'd get out. There was a box of doughnuts in it for the closest guess.'

'Really?' asked Mara. 'Who won?'

'I did, actually,' DC Taylor replied proudly. 'I guessed ten hours.'

'Not bad,' said Mara. 'My exact time was nine hours and thirty-seven minutes, I believe.'

'Amazing,' DC Taylor repeated. 'Though there's a rumour going round that you might have had help?'

My cheeks reddened. Once again, I felt like a total idiot to have been used for a high-security prison escape whilst remaining completely unaware of what was happening. I suddenly experienced a flood of self-consciousness, standing there next to this woman who had managed to engineer said escape with all the aplomb of it being nothing more than a day's work. This tall, confident woman wearing her expensive coat, while I was dressed in my jeans and old Converse. On the drive to Shinetree, Mara had somehow even applied a little makeup.

Rather than admitting it was me who'd been the unwilling participant in Mara's breakout, I attempted a joke. 'CID will think that help came from you,' I said to DC Taylor. 'After all, you did win those doughnuts.' In my head, the line had sounded slick. Out loud, it was about as slick as a length of flypaper.

Mara raised her eyebrows.

'Do you work with Mara?' asked DC Taylor, grinning.

'Actually, I work for—' I started, intending to impress him with the fact that I still worked in a relatively junior role for a local newspaper. It was misguided on multiple levels.

'For me,' Mara cut in, shooting me a glare. 'Well... *with* me.'

Embarrassed, I looked away. I realised that the building we were standing by was the studio in which Talent Quest was filmed. That the opening led, through a pandemonium of boxes and equipment, directly onto the stage. I shifted uneasily at what had happened on that stage a little over an hour ago, just metres from where we were standing.

In an effort to assess what was going on, Mara stepped further inside the studio, leaving me hovering with DC Taylor. Despite my unease, I was once more reminded how long it had been since I'd eaten when a fresh waft of fried onions from his hot dog hit me. Without warning, my stomach gave an unholy and extended wail. I shifted my handbag to my middle to stifle it, hoping DC Taylor hadn't heard.

Venturing a glance, I caught the hint of a smile still playing on his lips.

'Here,' he said, holding the hot dog out. 'It was meant to be for the DI, but sounds like you need it a lot more than he does.'

'Oh, no... I couldn't. I don't want to get you into any trouble.'

'I won't tell him if you don't,' he replied. 'Here.'

I thanked him and accepted the hot dog, feeling awkward when his fingertips brushed mine.

'Ah, here's Graham now.'

Following Mara's voice, I saw a man in a grey-brown suit

advancing towards us. He was in his mid-forties, and taller than DC Taylor. His hair was brown but netted with grey at the sides, largely combed back and lying a little too long over his collar. He was clean-shaven apart from a thickish moustache, which was of a shape last fashionable in the '80s. For a senior detective, there was an untucked kind of shabbiness about DI Graham Paulson.

'Who called *you* in?' the man asked Mara uncomfortably.

'Nice to see you again too, Graham,' she replied. 'And who else would you call in? A missing woman is now dead, having fallen out of a teleportation illusion, an illusion I know like the back of my hand. I just saved you the trouble of dialling my number.'

Paulson scowled and shifted stiffly, eyes zeroing in on the remains of my hot dog. 'I thought I'd told you to get *me* one of those?' he asked DC Taylor.

Mara proceeded inside, through the jumble of cabling and equipment, towards the Talent Quest stage. Rows of empty audience seating confronted us and, before them, another circle of police tape separated the stage from the rest of the studio. I stopped behind it while Mara continued on.

'Mara!' came a muffled voice.

A figure in a white crime scene suit met Mara at the tape, tugging down her hood and face mask. The woman was in her fifties, with a wiry build and numerous ear piercings. Her hair was short and spiky and dyed a brilliant orange. Because of the way she was dressed, I presumed she must be a CSI. A crime scene investigator.

'Hello, Lindi,' said Mara. 'Any obvious cause of death?'

'We won't be sure until the autopsy comes back. But it looks like the fall from the box probably broke her neck.'

I flinched. So Angel Devereaux's death literally had gone out to millions on live television.

'Anything else obvious at this stage?'

'Nothing that particularly stands out. Somewhere like this, big crew and lots of people traipsing around... forensics could all amount to nothing. But be my guest.' Lindi unzipped her suit and reached inside, retrieving a packet of cigarettes. 'You'll have to excuse me a minute though, Mar. I'm gasping for a fag.'

Mara lifted the police tape for Lindi, who ducked under it and headed outside. I watched her go, unsure what else to do, wondering if I might soon be asked to leave the studio altogether.

'You can stay here,' Mara said, registering my expression. 'Just make sure you keep to that side of the tape.' She turned in the direction of the stage.

'Wait!' I called. 'Aren't you meant to wear a white suit to go over there?'

'Yes,' Mara replied, moving towards the potential crime scene, regardless. 'But if you've seen the detective shows, you'll know that, for the likes of me, the white suits are optional.'

I glanced around. DC Taylor had joined Mara on the stage, but I couldn't see DI Paulson. There was no sign of Dex Devereaux either, but the two large black boxes that he'd used for his teleportation trick had been lowered and were sitting on the floor, a few feet from where Angel fell. Their sides were closed now. The threatening white banner was curled beside them, its words obscured.

'Have you spoken to Angel Devereaux's replacement yet?'

Mara asked Taylor. 'The woman who did the trick with Dex earlier?'

'Katarina Riley,' Taylor replied. 'And no, we haven't. The DI got the audience and crew into one of the other studios so we could speak to them all. We assumed she'd be among them. But nobody remembers seeing Katarina since she got into that first box.'

So, one week ago, on live TV, Angel Devereaux had climbed into the first box and disappeared. And tonight, instead of reappearing in the second box, her replacement had vanished just like Angel, while Angel had reappeared in the second box dead. It was crazy. How could grown women appear and disappear from two boxes in front of multiple cameras and a studio audience of several hundred people?

The words concealed in the folds of the banner came back to me. Someone was hurting women. *Women*. Angel was dead. Did that mean Katarina was next?

'In that case, the first box is a good place to start,' Mara said, while I looked on, puzzled. Did she really think Katarina Riley might be found still inside that first box? There didn't seem enough space in it to conceal a rabbit, never mind a person. And why hadn't the police already searched it?

My thoughts were quickly answered, as Mara began her examination of the box. What she'd told DI Paulson was right: she obviously knew this prop like the back of her hand. She swung each of the box's sides open from the top like a succession of dishwasher doors. Without warning, a dismembered human hand bucked lifelessly up over one of the sides, its wrist gushing blood. I jumped and looked away. Heart racing, I assumed Mara had indeed discovered the remains of Katarina Riley. But when I dared to look back, I saw the blood gushing from the hand was just a red handkerchief.

'Well, now you know how that bit was done,' Mara said, pointing at it.

So the hand waving the handkerchief was a fake, never belonging to Angel *or* Katarina. It was just a ruse, a distraction to allow the assistant to do something else whilst appearing to still be inside the box.

Satisfied with her investigation of the box's sides, Mara moved on to its base, pressing her hand around it. I was astonished to see it pop apart. The base was not solid at all, but a shallow box of its own, with a top that lifted like a lid. A secret, human-sized compartment. It was a compartment that only someone intimate with the world of magic would have known about. Someone like Mara.

'Empty,' said Mara. 'No Katarina.'

Mara then turned her attention to the second box, scrutinising the sides and lifting open the base as she had done with the first. But she spent far longer on this one, peering inside of it and bobbing her head up and down, frowning to herself. Had she found something? And if so, what?

Mara withdrew the index finger of her right hand and held it up. The tip was stained red. But it wasn't a handkerchief this time. It *was* blood.

Mara stared solemnly at DC Taylor. 'Get Lindi back in here. And contact the pathologist.'

'The pathologist?'

'Get them to thoroughly examine the right side of Angel Devereaux's head. The fall from the box might have killed her, but I strongly suspect she sustained another injury before she died.'

12.♠

In an attempt to stop myself from bursting through the police tape and across to Mara, I clutched it tightly. I was desperate to see exactly what she'd found inside that second box. But the area of staging around both boxes was being cleared again, so the CSI Lindi could conduct an examination of those hidden compartments. After exchanging a few more words with DC Taylor, Mara joined me at the cordon.

'You think Angel sustained another injury before she died?' I asked her. 'But how do you know that for sure? How do you know the injury was to her head, even? Couldn't that blood have come from something innocent, like a cut on her finger?'

'Unlikely,' Mara replied. 'When an assistant conceals themselves in the base of that box, they have to lie in a very specific position or the trick wouldn't work. The right side of their head would be at the exact point where the blood was.'

'So you mean... someone hurt her before she crawled inside the compartment?'

'It's possible.'

Was it also possible that Angel hadn't *crawled* into the base of that box at all? Maybe someone had hit her on the head, knocking her unconscious. Maybe they thought she was dead and hid her body there, not knowing the box would spring apart in such a dramatic fashion live on prime time television.

'Or maybe they knew that's exactly what would happen,' Mara answered, and it was only then that I realised I'd been talking out loud. 'But yes, she must have been unconscious when she hit that stage.'

Mara stared back at the stage, where Lindi was now busy swabbing the second box. For a brief moment, the other sounds from the studio dulled, and I was sure that I could hear something. A faint ticking, perhaps. I listened harder. Nothing. It must have been my imagination.

A good portion of the studio was crammed with kit. Barrel-sized coils of cabling and chunky metal stands were dumped next to all manner of cases and holdalls that I presumed belonged both to the crew and performers. It was chaos. In places, the stuff must have been stacked metres high.

I stepped towards the holdall nearest to me and opened the zip.

'I don't want any of this crap touched!' DI Paulson's voice boomed. 'This all needs to be done by the book.'

I hastily re-zipped the holdall, pretending to fiddle in my handbag instead. A few paces away, Mara was also nosing around the heaped-up equipment.

'What's happening about the CCTV?' she asked, in no hurry to move away from the kit.

'The team's on it,' replied Taylor.

Paulson rolled his eyes. In the time it had taken Mara to examine the boxes and find the blood, he'd got himself another hot dog. Though he hadn't started eating it yet, a blob of mustard had somehow settled itself on the knot of his tie.

'There are a couple of dozen cameras at Shinetree,' Paulson barked, using the hot dog to gesture around the studio.

'Finding Katarina Riley would seem to be a priority,' returned Mara. 'And you have mustard on your tie.'

'We're on it,' Paulson cut back, flustered, scrubbing at the mustard with a paper napkin. 'We're police officers, not *magicians*.'

With Paulson distracted, Taylor leant towards me. 'The DI's not always like this,' he murmured. 'Between you and me, I think Mara winds him up.'

I wondered whether Paulson's pride had also been dented a little. After all, Mara had just found a clue in a murder investigation that his team had missed, albeit one that would have been impossible for someone with no prior knowledge of the prop to uncover—

'Oi!'

We turned to see a woman in a catering uniform marching towards us through the piles of equipment. She made a beeline for Paulson, stopping merely inches away from him. 'Who told you you could have that?'

'I beg your pardon?'

'That hot dog. Catering's for film crews only. You're not a crew member.'

Paulson lowered the hot dog and puffed out his chest. 'No, madam, I'm a little more important than that. I'm a detective inspector. Here to investigate a potentially very serious offence.'

He angled himself away, obviously assuming this would bring an end to the matter, but the woman continued.

'That's as may be, but if you're not filming, then you're not eating. Like I said, catering's for cast and crew only. There's a very strict policy.'

In defiance, Paulson took a large bite of the hot dog.

'How dare you!' the woman exclaimed, tugging the sleeve of the closest uniformed officer. 'This man should be arrested. He's technically stealing—'

During the small gaps of outraged silence in the catering lady's tirade, I swore I could hear that strange, faint sound again. Not so much a ticking this time, but a tapping.

'Can you hear something—?' I started to whisper to Mara.

'*She* had a hot dog too, but she's not crew!' I looked up to see Paulson jabbing a finger in my direction. 'In fact, what *are* you doing here?' His eyes slipped to my hip and narrowed.

I glanced down. My handbag was still open, from when I'd pretended to fiddle in it earlier; my press pass from the Morden Mercury balanced perilously atop the rest of the contents. I quickly shoved it inside and closed the bag up.

As Mara pulled me back to the door and said her goodbyes, I listened for the tapping noise again, but heard nothing.

13.

It was after midnight by the time I turned onto the gravel driveway to Mara's house, an unfamiliar jumble of emotions roiling inside me. Shock, foreboding, exhilaration — all cut through with complete exhaustion. Added to this, my phone was still dead. With everything else that had happened, I'd forgotten to ask Mara if I could charge it.

'Thanks, Clare,' she said, as the car drew to a halt.

Mara gazed distractedly at the towering building before us, still washed from below in its pale orange light. She remained like this for about a minute, then jarred herself into action, getting to her feet.

'It's late,' she called over her shoulder. 'If you want to stay, you can.' She shut the car and set about unlocking one of the vast double doors into the atrium.

I wasn't sure how to respond. I didn't have the energy for the drive back to Morden, nor did I have a working phone if I got into an accident. So, I switched off the ignition and followed Mara into the house.

Back in the living room, she was using some sort of remote control to close the curtains across the triple-height windows, which covered two of the walls. They were scarlet and thick, and looked more like stage curtains than anything you'd be likely to find in somebody's home.

'Er, it would be great to stay over,' I ventured, realising I'd trudged inside without responding to her offer. 'If you're sure you don't mind?'

'Of course.'

I thought about Jasper, thought I should ring Matt to let him know I wouldn't be back at the flat until morning.

'Would you mind if I used your phone quickly?' I asked. 'Mine's still dead.'

'Feel free.' Mara indicated to a high round side table, on which there sat a large ceramic fruit bowl. Having removed her boots in the hall, she again dropped into the wingback chair, still wearing her coat.

Another wash of tiredness hit me, and I wondered whether I'd just asked the question I thought I had.

'That *is* the phone,' Mara remarked, noticing me dithering.

Like everything else in the house, the bowl of fruit wasn't what it seemed. I stepped forwards, picked up the banana and put it to my ear. There was no dialling tone.

Several seconds passed before Mara's voice sounded from the chair. 'Try the apple.'

Feeling like an imbecile, I swiftly replaced the banana. A number of apples were nestled in the bowl, each as red and shiny as the next. I lifted up the only apple that had a wire coming out of it, thinking it most likely *this* one was the phone, but beginning to understand that, in Mara's house, anything was possible.

Nevertheless, the apple parted in the middle, opening to

reveal a keypad. I punched in Matt's number and shot Mara a smile that did its best to convey I had known it was the apple all along. But she wasn't looking in my direction.

Since Matt didn't pick up, I left him a message, explaining that I was staying the night at a friend's house and would see him in the morning. When I'd finished, I turned to see Mara, motionless in her chair. Her chin was tilted upwards, and her eyes were closed. Although she didn't look particularly relaxed, I assumed she had fallen asleep.

'Do you want a drink?' she asked suddenly and leapt from her seat.

Mara proceeded to the bizarre cabinet in which she kept her bewildering array of bottles. She extracted an ornate cut-glass bottle filled with a mystifying pink liquid and waved it at me. I couldn't even guess what spirit it held, but given I didn't have to drive home, I thought it couldn't hurt to try.

'Yes. Please.'

Mara took a slender drinking glass from the cabinet. She poured the pink liquid from the bottle into it and, as she did, let go of the glass and reached back inside the cabinet for a second one. My mouth fell open. The first glass was left hanging in mid-air, levitating even as it filled with liquid.

She finished pouring and handed the glass to me. I shook my head, concluding I must be even more exhausted than I'd realised. It was just as well I wasn't driving home.

As Mara poured her own drink, I took a cautious sip of mine. The liquid was nothing more than a little sweet at first. Then the full force of it struck the back of my throat, inflaming my gullet. I spluttered, coughing violently.

'That's... that's...' I gasped, 'much more... potent than I expected.'

Mara continued to drink from her glass quite serenely, as though it contained nothing stronger than water. She examined the bottle's label impassively. 'Hmm. Seventy per cent proof, apparently.'

'Seventy—?'

As my coughing subsided, I thought about what an unlikely turn of events this was, to now be spending the night in this vast house with this woman. I took a couple more tentative sips from my glass, starting to enjoy the fire tracking its way down my gut, the giddy buzz building in my skull.

'My boyfriend's going to wonder what's going on,' I reflected aloud. 'Me not going back tonight. He might think I've met someone else.' I swallowed another small sip of the drink, adding absentmindedly, 'Suppose I have, in a way.'

Mara, once more installed in the wingback, observed me silently.

'I mean,' I went on, fuelled by the pink liquid in my hand, 'before I met Matt, I was definitely more spontaneous. But when you start living together... I don't know, you sort of fill each other's shoes, without even realising they don't really fit.' Glancing at Mara, who was now studying the contents of her glass, I continued to drink, waffling on misguidedly. 'In the year Matt and I have been living together, I've never stayed out all night, actually. I mean, maybe that spark between us isn't what it was, but still... it's probably the longest we've been apart...'

My eyes meandered to the photograph in the ebonised frame. Mara and Travers, smiling together on that windswept hillside. 'What's the longest you and your husband have been apart—?' The words were out before my brain had the chance to catch them, but by that point it was too late.

A torturous silence ensued.

'Four months, three weeks and two days,' Mara replied.

There was another beat of quiet.

'God, I'm sorry. I shouldn't have—'

'It's fine.' Mara drained her glass of the pink liquid and pulled a face. 'The 31st of October, 2013. It was the last time I saw him. We'd been together fifteen years. He would never have left without telling me. Never have stayed away without getting in touch.' She cleared her throat. 'So I can only conclude that he's... well...' Mara's face twisted into an involuntary contortion of anguish, and she turned aside.

Dead, I thought. She assumed Travers was missing because he was dead.

It was the same succession of thoughts I'd had about my own situation, all those years ago.

Since I'd met her, hours earlier, I hadn't seen Mara display much real emotion at all. But that moment, fuzzed though my mind was from the drink, I began to understand the almost constant restlessness she exhibited, the way her demeanour shifted like the elements of the high Alps. She thought Travers was dead, but there was no certainty to that notion, no closure. A feeling I was all-too-familiar with. I experienced a sweep of guilt that the possibility she'd had any part in her husband's disappearance had ever crossed my mind.

Swilling the liquid around in my glass, I narrowed my eyes and spoke into the loaded silence. 'My boss doesn't know about me investigating Angel's disappearance. I took it upon myself to do it. You see, when I was ten, my mum disappeared. My dad... well, he had problems of his own, and I left home early.' The burning in my throat intensified, but this time it wasn't the alcohol. 'Knowing there's someone out there who's vanished from your life, it leaves a hole. Sort of an open loop that needs putting right.'

Hands gripping the sides of my glass, my knuckles whitened. I focused hard on those little knolls of bone, trying not to cry, bracing myself for Mara to ask what happened to my mum.

But she didn't.

'That's exactly it,' she said instead. Her voice was different, somehow. Mellower, less commanding. 'Audiences expect vanishes to be temporary. An object disappears, then that same object is brought back, the equilibrium restored. When the object doesn't reappear, a state of profound and constant psychological tension is created. In my opinion, there are few things more agonising.'

I took in the wisdom of Mara's words, which seemed to cut to the quick of everything, transporting me right back to the years after my mother's disappearance.

When I summoned the courage to glance up again, I saw that Mara was looking directly at me. She held my gaze for a long moment, something kindling in the lower part of her face which I later recognised as a smile.

14.

I woke up on the damson velvet sofa on top of a pile of pillows. A couple of lambswool blankets in a tartan weave had been draped over me in the night. The curtains were still closed, but a watery lemon light was seeping in around their edges. I checked my watch. It was just after seven.

As I lifted my head, a delicious smell caught in my nostrils. I peered around the room and saw a steaming mug of coffee on the nearest table. Next to it was my phone, plugged in and showing a full battery. There was also a reply from Matt.

OK. CU tomoz. Jasp sends boops & wags.

'Did you sleep alright?'

The voice came from a pool of darkness behind me. I turned to see a figure sitting at the enormous dining table positioned before the elaborate wooden wall that had once formed the old church's altar.

Though it was early — and not only had I had a late night, but that late night had followed one of the maddest days of my life — I felt surprisingly rested.

'I did,' I answered. 'Thank you.' I took a sip of coffee, piping hot and smokily delicious.

'You were dead to the world after that drink.'

I cast my mind back and recalled the cocktail glass, floating of its own accord. 'That pink stuff. What was it?'

'Some sort of trendy gin. Hideous, really. I much prefer vodka.'

Taking the mug of coffee with me, I decamped to a seat opposite Mara. She was fiddling with a series of objects that were lying on the table. Several folded napkins, a box of matches, a small candle, salt and pepper pots in the shape of dice, a carved wooden box, and the cork from the wine she'd had the evening before; a distinctive burgundy stain around its base.

'About last night...' I started, unsure what I was trying to say.

Mara said nothing. She balanced all the things on the table in a large heap in front of her, with the exception of the cork. This she held between thumb and forefinger, then gave a rapid, elegant sweep of her hands. The cork vanished.

'I've been thinking about that girl who was assisting Dex with the trick,' she said, as though making something disappear was completely unremarkable. 'Katarina Riley. I need to find out whether she's been reported missing. And we'll have to see what the police say about the CCTV. There must be footage of her leaving the studio. Either alone or with someone else. You read that banner. Finding her is urgent.'

I agreed. To make sure the man who hurt Angel hadn't done something terrible to Katarina too. And at the very least, to speak to her as a witness. 'She must also have been one of the people closest to the stage when Angel fell.'

Mara nodded, gesturing to the heaped-up objects before her. 'You may dismantle them now. See what you find.'

Without considering what an odd request it was, I began to remove the napkins, condiment pots and other things, until the only item left was the carved wooden box which had been at the very bottom of the pile. Mara gave a nod, so I picked the box up and looked inside. There it was. The exact same cork she'd made vanish moments earlier, with its peculiar burgundy stain.

I laughed out loud. Not just at the impossibility of this, but at the crazy sequence of events that had unfolded in the past twenty-four hours. Card tricks, a levitating drink, a prison break, spending the night in this vast house amongst all these fantastical possessions—

I stopped laughing abruptly. A woman was dead after having disappeared, another now missing. What had happened to Angel Devereaux? And where was Katarina Riley? Was she really in danger?

That cork inside the box, under the heap of items on Mara's dining table. It reminded me of something. The disorder at the back of the Talent Quest stage, those teetering stacks of equipment—

'I heard a noise!' I exclaimed. 'Last night. In the studio...'

'A noise?'

'I tried to tell you. But then it stopped. I just thought it was nothing.'

There was a pause.

'Go on,' said Mara.

'Well, what if it was Katarina? What if she was still there last night? Somewhere in the studio, amongst all that stuff? What if the man who hurt Angel concealed her somewhere? There were so many boxes and bags, plenty large enough for...' I realised how silly it sounded and my words dwindled.

I looked over at Mara. She was resting her head on interlinked fingers, her eyes closed, brows drawn in concentration.

'I'm probably wrong,' I said. 'It was a stupid idea. I was just thinking out loud—'

Mara's eyes sprang open. 'Not at all. In fact, it was a perfectly sensible suggestion.'

In one fluid movement, she pushed back her chair and stood up. She was already dressed, in much the same kind of top and trousers she'd been wearing the previous night. Mara completed her outfit with that long green coat, whipping it around herself like a shadow.

'Do you have any plans for this morning?' she said, crossing to the door. 'Because if you don't, then I think we should go back to the studio.'

'What, you mean... *now*?'

'Now.'

15.

Since it wasn't much after eight on a Sunday morning and still quiet, we were back at Shinetree Studios within the hour. I'd driven again, and Mara had pressed a fistful of notes into my hand to cover the petrol. She said me driving would save her getting her car out, though I couldn't think where her car was actually kept. The gravel driveway narrowed too much at the sides of the building to get a car around from the rear, and there was no sign of a garage.

Even though it was early, the studios were already open. Or perhaps they'd been open all night, especially since one of them was now a potential crime scene.

I slowed the car at the security guard's kiosk, and again Mara showed her police pass to the man inside. She continued to flick the card between her fingers as we drove the rest of the way to the studio and parked the car. I glanced towards it.

'Oh, I almost forgot. Here.' Mara reached into her pocket and flung a second pass in my direction. The words "Proactive Productions" were printed across the front, together with the name "Cece Sutherland". The passport-sized photograph that accompanied this name showed an attractive woman in her twenties, with long, waving brown hair, a glazed pout, and a bold, come-hither expression. It looked more like a modelling headshot than a picture that might have been taken for a security pass.

'What's this for?'

'For when you need it.'

'Need it when?' I returned, aware I was sounding like a parrot.

She pursed her lips, pointedly darting her eyes between myself and the studio. 'In case anyone questions why you're here.'

It didn't seem to have crossed Mara's mind that I looked nothing like the woman in the photograph. I wondered whether she'd used some sleight of hand trickery to get hold of this pass too. Just like she had Richie's at the prison.

'How come you have this?' I asked.

'Cece can be very indiscreet,' she replied, without really replying at all. 'She's Shane Sinclair's ex, you know.'

I began to protest that if Mara thought I was comfortable being in possession of a stolen security card, she was quite wrong. But before I could finish, she got out of the car.

'Fix it in your work lanyard is my advice,' she called perfunctorily as she made her way towards the studio door.

I remembered how DI Paulson had almost seen my press pass the day before, and grudgingly followed her advice, clipping the Proactive Productions pass in front of the one for the Morden Mercury.

The studio was far quieter than I'd anticipated, given a murder had occurred on the premises just twelve hours earlier. With the exception of a small handful of vehicles and a couple of patrol cars, the car park had almost completely emptied out.

We approached the police tape cordoning off the large doors in the side of the studio. One of them was fully closed now, with the other ajar just enough to let someone through. A single female officer was stationed next to it.

Mara flashed her police pass. 'She's with me,' she said, and the officer lifted the tape for us both to proceed inside.

The studio was far gloomier than it had been the previous night. With only one or two lights on, the place had a deeply unsettling ambience, the stacks of equipment looming ominously in the shadows. It was cold, too, as the early morning March air seeped in through the opened door. I shuddered. The place was eerily still, and I became painfully aware of the point on the studio stage where tragedy had struck just hours before. I kept involuntarily turning my head towards it, somehow convinced Angel would be there, even now.

Mara trod silently amongst the tombstone-like stacks of piled-up equipment and paused. There was no noise at all. None of the ticking or tapping I'd heard the last time I was in here. I started to feel stupid that I'd ever raised the idea of Katarina Riley still being trapped somewhere amongst all this mess.

'Where were you standing when you heard the noise last night?' Mara whispered. 'About here?'

I tried my best to retrace my steps of the previous hours. 'Maybe... around here?' I replied uncertainly. The space had looked so different the night before, lit and bustling with police and CSIs. It was really just a best guess that I had been standing in this same position when I'd heard the tapping. I couldn't be completely sure.

Mara moved beside me, and together we strained our ears through the studio's chilly darkness.

'Hello,' said Mara. 'Hello?'

Still nothing.

Once again, my attention was caught by the part of the stage above which those boxes had been hanging, seconds before Angel's appalling reappearance. I screwed shut my eyes, focusing hard on bringing to mind the sound I'd heard the preceding night, and which direction it may have been coming from. Perhaps it *had* been nothing out of the ordinary, but if there was even a slim chance that the missing Katarina was still here, then we had to do everything we could to find her.

'Is anybody there?' I called, trying to summon an authoritative, enquiring tone, but sounding more like I was conducting some sort of seance. My blood pulsed through my body with such forceful expectation it gave my voice a tremulous, theatrical edge. More Madame Arcati than respected investigator.

Mara frowned. We both glanced around, listening again.

BEEP-HISSSSS!

At the door, the police officer's radio suddenly spluttered violently into life, making me jump. Then it went quiet again.

'Congratulations, you made contact,' quipped Mara.

She took a few steps forwards and called out once more. I followed, listening while twisting my head like an owl. But there was still nothing to be detected. Nothing whatsoever.

Just as I was growing certain that our return to Shinetree

had been a complete waste of time — and that the noise I'd heard the previous night was nothing to do with Katarina Riley or the events surrounding her disappearance — it happened. I finally heard it again.

Tap... tap...

I stopped dead, craning my neck in an effort to determine the direction the sound was coming from.

Tap... tap... tap...

Its exact location was difficult to pinpoint, but it seemed as though it was coming from the door.

When I realised what it was, my heart sank. The radio again. The noise I thought might have been Katarina attempting to attract somebody's attention was just a slow bit of static on the officer's radio; a crackle so intermittent it sounded like a tapping. So that's what I'd heard last night. One of the police radios.

Mara picked up on this too. 'Don't be disappointed, Clare,' she said. 'An easy mistake to make.'

But I was disappointed. Shoulders slumped, I plodded back towards the door, ready to leave. The closer I got to the exit, however, the quieter the noise became. It was strange.

I swivelled to alert Mara, but she was some distance away, poking around one of the many mountains of equipment. The location of the sound *was* difficult to pinpoint, but as I backtracked my route to the centre of the studio, I became adamant it wasn't the police officer's radio after all. For the noise grew louder. Louder, until the tapping became distinct; a more determined knocking, regular in rhythm. And then another sound joined it.

'*Mmm-mmm!*'

A few feet in front of me stood a large black case, its top obscured by the bags and coils of cabling heaped upon it. Plastic, with chunky metal edges and bulbous reinforced steel corners, it looked like a flight case: the type of thing I'd seen musicians wheel kit around in at the deafening gigs I'd been to with Matt. He'd always said I had overly-sensitive hearing.

'*Mmm-mmm!*'

A wave of adrenaline coursed through me. It was a voice, a human voice. Muffled, but unmistakable.

'Mara!'

I yelled her name, shoving the stuff off the top of the flight case with an increasing sense of urgency, as the whimpering coming from inside it grew louder. Mara joined me, and together we cleared an area around the case and located its two hefty clasps, prising them apart with clanks that rang across the studio.

The front of the case swung open like the door of a fridge. Then there came a rapid intake of breath, and a woman's form tumbled out, crumpling onto the floor. She began to weep uncontrollably.

At first, I scarcely recognised this woman as the Katarina Riley I'd watched sashay across the Talent Quest stage. Her blonde hair was knotted, her cheeks stained with mascara, her sequinned leotard rucked around her body.

But Katarina Riley it was. We had found her.

'Thank God,' I murmured.

I struggled to help Katarina to her feet. Her legs were weak, thighs trembling from the near twelve hours she'd spent cramped inside the case.

As I steadied her, I saw that Mara was busy examining one of the case's clasps, stroking a short piece of cut string between her fingers, string that was knotted around the clasp itself.

'Officer!'

Finally abandoning the clasp, Mara shouted for the police constable, who came hurrying over from the door.

Katarina was shivering feverishly, so I removed my cardigan and draped it across her shoulders. As I did, I noticed faint oval marks around her wrists, a patination that continued up each of her arms.

The police officer radioed for backup and a paramedic, and before long a second officer had arrived. Together, they assisted Katarina from the studio, as Mara explained they'd also need to call a CSI to examine the flight case properly. That it looked like there were fingerprints all over it.

When they'd gone, Mara turned to me. 'I take it you saw those bruises on her arms?'

I replied I had. 'You don't think she might have got them from struggling inside that case?' I asked. 'From trying to get out?'

'I doubt it. They looked like finger marks to me. Large ones. Fresh too.'

There was a pause. And as Mara held my gaze, I knew what she was thinking. That those bruises were made by whoever had forced Katarina Riley inside that case in the first place.

And then another thought struck me. That I'd been right

when I feared Katarina was in danger. That those bruises on her arms had been made by Angel's killer.

I ♥ HURTING WOMEN.

Just as I'd suspected, the man who'd killed Angel had locked Katarina in the case to come back for her later.

We had found her just in time.

16.♠

We stayed with the flight case until the CSI Lindi Wilcox
arrived. It was little wonder Katarina Riley hadn't been able to
make much noise inside that case to alert someone's attention.
Its interior was covered in a thick layer of egg box-like foam, to
protect the fragile camera equipment it would usually hold. The
foam had acted as a layer of soundproofing. Thankfully, the case
wasn't airtight, but the restricted air available to Katarina whilst
trapped inside of it would have made her woozy, and even less
capable of struggling or calling out.

By the time we exited the Talent Quest studio, the coffee
Mara had made me earlier had well and truly worn off, and
I was ready for breakfast. With the catering truck from the
previous night closed, Mara, seeming to know exactly where she
was going, headed around the maze of buildings and through a
small blue door tucked down an alleyway.

'You know this place well?' I asked.

'I do.'

Positioned just inside the door were a couple of vending
machines. Mara inserted some coins into the first of them, and a
few seconds later handed me a chocolate bar and a cup of coffee.
Her fingers hovered again over the machine's keypad. There

was an almost imperceptible shake to them, and I wondered whether my question about Shinetree had upset her.

Though Mara hadn't elaborated on how she knew these studios so well, I presumed it was because she had been here with Travers during some of the big-budget magic shows he'd filmed. I had so many questions about it all, especially after spending the night in their extraordinary house amongst those extraordinary magic props, and seeing that single photo of them both in the ebonised frame. But I worried Mara would suspect I might be gathering details for some sort of story, so I kept my questions to myself.

She finally settled on a coffee from the machine, as I wandered along the corridor examining the succession of glossy photos hanging behind glass on its walls. A gallery of the many TV shows that had been filmed at Shinetree over the years. Candid behind-the-scenes shots of celebrities and crews on the studio stages.

'Wow, look, it's *Bangers and Cash*!' I exclaimed, smiling at the photo of the popular afternoon quiz show on which contestants answered questions to win the opportunity to trade in their old car for the cash equivalent of a brand new one.

'I get the distinct feeling they came up with the title for that show before agreeing on a format,' Mara remarked.

I pointed at the host, an older man with a striking tan and pearly smile. 'Ha! Marty Diamond! My nan loves him. He seems so genuine.'

'Yes,' Mara replied. 'As genuine as the photos he sent of his own Cash and Bangers to a woman on Twitter.'

My mouth fell open. 'No way! But he's always so...

enthusiastic.'

'The three court injunctions against him are testament to that.'

Her sentence went largely over my head, as my attention was caught by the next photograph.

'And this is *Ladies Let Loose*!' I cooed, studying the picture of the five female presenters on the set of their chat show, a longstanding mainstay of lunchtime television. 'It always seems like they have so much fun. Not afraid to offer an opinion, though!'

'Mmm,' Mara returned drily. 'I don't know how Studio Four manages to contain all that sass.'

I gazed at her, incredulous. 'You don't like them?'

'I never said that.'

'You didn't need to.' I tapped a fingernail to the glass. 'But Pamela Dooley looks great, doesn't she? She must be... what, about sixty now?'

'Forty-eight, I believe.'

'*What?*' I peered more closely at the picture. 'She's only *forty-eight*?'

Mara made a faint, strangled noise in the back of her throat.

'Oh my God,' I uttered, dropping my voice to a whisper. 'She's right behind me, isn't she?'

I spun around, readying myself to apologise to Pamela Dooley. But nobody was there.

Puzzled, I followed Mara's line of sight, returning my attention to the wall and registering what it was she'd been looking at.

The photograph showed a large studio stage illuminated by

two purplish-blue lights, the rest thrown into dramatic shadow. This lighting gave the scene a portentous, almost melancholic feel. Two men stood in the centre of the stage, both smartly dressed in deep green three-piece suits and white shirts. However, whereas the expression of the first was open and genuine, the other man's body language was totally different. The shorter man's demeanour, and the way he'd angled himself away from the other, made it look like he was irritated about something.

I didn't immediately recognise this second man, but the first was Travers. Judging by his matching outfit, I assumed the shorter one was probably Travers's double act partner. I knew from the articles I'd read about Mara's husband that their partnership had dissolved just weeks before Travers started performing on his own, about a year prior to his disappearance. It was a strange photo to be displayed here, especially compared to all the others, which were markedly more cheerful.

Mara cleared her throat and turned away from the wall. 'Well, that was unexpected. Though I should have known he'd be here somewhere.'

It struck me how poignant her words were after what had just happened. We'd found Katarina Riley, a previously missing person, only metres from where we were standing. Yet Travers's whereabouts remained a mystery, still.

'We should go,' Mara said, discarding her barely touched cup. 'I don't think there's anything more to be gained here. And that coffee really is disgusting.'

Outside, an ambulance was parking up not far from where we'd left the car. A door opened in the nearest building, and we saw Katarina Riley being helped through it by two police officers, wrapped in a silver blanket. As we neared, she glanced up at us and caught Mara's eye, saying something to the officers and making her way over.

Understandably, Katarina was still jittery and dishevelled, her cheeks heavily splotched with the remnants of last night's stage makeup. But she had recovered herself enough to speak.

'I... I just wanted to thank you,' Katarina told Mara, her voice a little hoarse and faraway. 'If you hadn't come back, then...' she shuddered. 'Then I dread to think what could have happened to me.'

'Ah, well that was all Clare,' said Mara generously.

I held up my hands as though it was nothing. 'Apparently, I have very sensitive hearing.'

Katarina smiled weakly at me before turning back to Mara. 'Wait a minute, I know who you are. You're that... *magician's wife.*'

Mara's face tightened. 'I am.'

'I've seen you around before, at shows and stuff. You must know Dex. That why you're here?'

'Not exactly,' Mara replied. 'I came because of Angel.'

Katarina adjusted her silver blanket uncomfortably. 'Yeah, I heard. She wasn't an easy woman to be around at times, but... Well, she didn't deserve that.'

Mara had already mentioned Angel Devereaux's reputation. But in the moment it was an odd remark for Katarina to make, given the circumstances.

'Did you know Angel well?' I asked.

Katarina shifted her feet. 'Yes and no,' she replied vaguely.

Mara's eyelids flickered slightly as she registered the curious reaction to my question. I wondered if I should surreptitiously take out my dictaphone and record the conversation. Then I remembered what Mara had said about concealing where I worked. So I left it in my bag.

'Do you remember anything about how you came to be in that flight case, Katarina?' Mara asked.

Katarina scanned the car park briefly, almost as though she was anxious that someone might be listening. 'Well, once Dex closed the first box up, I climbed out and into the back of the stairs...'

'So you were inside them when they were wheeled offstage?' Mara said. 'As you usually would be?'

Katarina nodded.

Suddenly, it all became clear. How a woman could enter that first box and — with the aid of the fake hand waving that bright red handkerchief, a red too bright to be ignored — appear to vanish from it. By slipping out and into the back of the small set of steps she'd ascended to get into the box in the first place. As well as being on wheels to allow for their easy removal from the stage, the steps were also hollow.

I recalled how I'd sensed Mara glancing at me when we were watching Talent Quest. She was trying to gauge whether I'd realised that Katarina was hidden inside those steps. But the thought hadn't even crossed my mind. I was quite blown away by how clever it all was, that something could be so fully hidden like that, in plain sight. What you believed was a completely inconspicuous object — the set of steps — was, in fact, the very essence of how the trick worked. While the audience's attention was drawn away by something that wasn't at all what it seemed.

'Once the stairs were offstage, I climbed out of them. Again, as planned. But I was just about to get into position inside the second box when someone grabbed me.' Her eyes shadowed. 'At first I thought he was a stagehand, just trying to help me get out of the steps more easily. It all happened so quickly.'

'And he put you into the flight case?' I said.

Katarina nodded shakily. 'I tried to fight against him. To scream too. But he covered my mouth.'

Katarina Riley was small, like me. Nevertheless, it must have been some feat on the part of her kidnapper to wrestle her into a flight case like that. I looked at Mara.

'Did you see the man who did it?' Mara asked. 'Would you be able to recognise him again?'

Katarina shook her head. 'Everything happened too quickly. All I was thinking about was how to get free.'

'Could you tell if he was tall, short?' said Mara. 'Thick-set? Skinny?'

'I don't know...'

'How about his hair — did you notice what colour it was?'

Katarina shrugged. 'I didn't see.'

Mara's brow furrowed. It was pretty dark in the space behind the studio stage when the lights were off — as they would have been when the show was being recorded — but not pitch-black.

I believed what Katarina was saying, but it was bad luck she couldn't give any details that might lead to the identification of the man who had done this to her. The same man who had potentially also killed Angel.

'And that's everything? There's nothing else you can remember?' asked Mara.

'I don't think so,' Katarina answered.

'You're sure? Nothing at all?'

'Erm...' She paused awkwardly. 'I think he smelt of cigarettes... maybe?'

'But you can't be certain?'

'Not really.' She lifted a hand to signal to the waiting police officers. 'If you'll excuse me, I'm very tired. I'd like to be checked over properly. At the hospital.'

The officers began to assist Katrina into the ambulance when a familiar voice boomed across the car park.

'TRINA!'

I recognised the voice before looking up, the words *"DO IT!"* echoing in my mind from the previous night's show.

Dex Devereaux was striding towards us. And rather than looking relieved that Katarina was alive, there was a tinge of annoyance on his face. Annoyance, I realised, that she was talking to Mara. Like he was worried she might be saying too much.

17. ♠

As Dex Devereaux neared the ambulance, his expression altered a little, masking his earlier annoyance. He stretched out his arms.

'Trina!' he declared again. 'Thank God.'

Dex's dated brown leather jacket creaked as he pulled Katarina into an embrace. He closed his eyes, moaning contentedly as he squeezed her. Perhaps it was nothing but relief that she was safe, but it made my skin bristle a little. Especially given his wife had just fallen to her death from one of his magic props live on national television.

'Careful,' Mara warned him. 'Katarina's feeling a little delicate. As would you be if you'd spent the night where she had.'

Mara fixed her sharp green eyes on Dex, and I wondered whether her last sentence had been deliberate. Was it a test to catch Dex out? To gauge whether he *had* been aware of Katarina's whereabouts?

But, unsavoury though the man appeared, Dex couldn't possibly have had anything to do with his assistant's disappearance. Or his wife's death, for that matter. It was difficult to think of a more watertight alibi than performing live on TV in front of millions of people. And why would Dex jeopardise his own career like that, by having Katarina disappear on one of the biggest shows in the country, when the same thing had happened to his wife just the previous week? For one thing, it made him look like a bad magician.

'Where was that?' Dex asked uneasily. His natural accent was more pronounced than it was on stage. Something northern.

Katarina took an unsteady breath. 'I'll tell you later.'

He shot her a look that implied she shouldn't have said this, and Mara noticed it too. So, Dex and Katarina were going to see each other later that day, I thought. But surely they couldn't be rehearsing, not after everything she'd been through over the past twenty-four hours?

Dex, this time registering Mara's gaze, once again shifted his expression. 'Well, jeez,' he crooned to Katarina. 'I'm just so relieved you're okay.'

Katarina offered a watery smile in response, and the waiting paramedic helped her into the ambulance. The vehicle pulled off, and several stiff seconds of silence ensued.

'I'm sorry about your wife.' I said. 'It must have been a terrible shock.'

Dex seemed to become aware of my presence for the first time then, peering down at me as though examining an insect. I tucked my hair behind my ear self-consciously, once more feeling drab in comparison to Mara.

'Yeah...' he said. 'Of all the things to happen, eh?' He blew out a breath. 'That's twice I've tried to do that trick and twice it's been sabotaged. Not sure Shane will have me back again.'

I was instantly thrown by the crassness of the remark.

'Yes, that must be very worrying for you,' said Mara.

'Well, yeah, it is,' Dex replied, Mara's sarcasm flying over his head. 'Thank you.'

At this point, a large silver minibus pulled up, close to where we were standing. The heads of about twenty passengers clustered behind its dark windows.

Still preoccupied by his own self-pity, Dex's mobile beeped, and he removed it from the pocket of his jeans. 'This thing's been going off all morning.'

'People wanting to offer their condolences about Angel,' Mara said. 'It's understandable.'

'No, it's not that — it's the bloody press and social media,' Dex returned. 'I'm a laughing stock. Last night's fiasco's trending all over the internet.' He shook his head. 'And that's without what happened two weeks ago. Bet Shane's lapping all this publicity up.'

'*Fiasco?*' I couldn't keep my surprise to myself any longer. 'That's a strange way of referring to your wife's death.'

Dex snapped his attention from his phone and glared at me. 'It's the frickin' trick I was talking about, love,' he said, with genuine animosity.

My cheeks flushed, and I felt even smaller than I usually did. 'It's—' I managed, after a few seconds had gone by. 'It's just... that you don't seem particularly cut up about it.'

Dex snorted. 'Of course I'm cut up about it,' he countered, not looking cut up about it at all. 'I *needed* her, didn't I? Anyhow, we'd been together almost twenty years.'

The unexpected confrontation with Dex was clouding my thinking, but doing a slow mental calculation I worked out that meant Angel must have been in her very early twenties when she'd started seeing him. I hadn't realised she was quite so young. There again, most of the information I'd been able to find about the couple was all about Dex. Every time Angel was referred to, it was as "the assistant", "the magician's assistant", or "the magician's wife".

'Mind you,' Dex went on, 'she'd made enough of my money vanish over the years.' He jabbed a finger at me. 'Bet you're the same. Straight from daddy's money to hubby's money. Women, eh?'

Dex seemed completely oblivious of how tasteless his remarks were in the immediate wake of his wife's death; a woman who had been missing and then reappeared murdered. I hadn't been able to find out whether Angel had had much of a family, but I couldn't stop thinking about how those who loved her were feeling this morning. Dex clearly didn't fall into that category.

'Actually, for your information, I've been self-sufficient since I was a teenager.'

The voice was mine, but with an edge that was hard and alien. Hearing it, I realised how much Dex's remark had got to me, how gutted I was that I hadn't been able to help Angel. My face flushed again, and I turned away before he had the chance to respond.

Across from us, the minibus doors had slid open, and its passengers were beginning to disembark. Surprisingly, given what had happened at Shinetree over the past twenty-four hours, the lithe young men and women now assembling in the car park were dressed in police uniforms. Though theirs weren't regular police uniforms at all. Their clothes were tight-fitting and spangled with diamante and glitter, the women's skirts short and flaring out from the thigh. I guessed they were dancers, here to film a segment for the popular weekly dancing show that went out at the same time as Talent Quest on a rival channel.

Mara, still studying Dex, apparently hadn't noticed the people milling around the minibus. When I glanced back at him, I saw he was gawping at the female dancers in wonderment.

'So the last time you saw Angel alive was when she climbed into that box on Talent Quest, a week last Saturday?' Mara asked him.

'Yeah...' he replied distantly.

'Nothing since?'

Dex, attention still fully on the dancers, didn't answer.

'Nothing since?' Mara repeated.

'No!' Dex finally tore his focus away from the women, a note of anger in his voice.

'Did you check that second box last night before you went onstage?' Mara continued, unperturbed.

Dex stiltedly adjusted his weight. 'No.'

'You *didn't*?' asked Mara, astonished.

'Well, it was usually Angel's job, wasn't it?' Dex said. 'And if you must know, Katarina and I were late getting to the studio yesterday. The props were brought here a few hours earlier. When we did arrive, there was no time to check anything.'

Mara made a face, which Dex caught.

'I suppose your husband never had anything like that to deal with,' Dex sneered, the bitterness in his tone impossible to miss.

'Not with the kinds of big-shot gigs he was doing.'

'He always had to check his own props, yes,' replied Mara coolly.

'You don't understand,' Dex protested. 'It was madness. As soon as I arrived, the production crew were telling me I had to do a piece to camera as though I was talking to Angel, asking her to come back.'

I remembered the prerecorded video that had gone out on the show the night before, in which Dex earnestly addressed the camera. I also remembered Mara's reaction to it. She thought he'd been lying.

'You didn't have a rehearsal?' asked Mara.

Dex gave a hollow laugh. 'There wasn't time, even if they'd wanted one.'

'*They?*'

'Shane's lot. They told me a rehearsal wasn't needed. That since we'd been doing the same trick the week before, the cameras and everything were already blocked.'

It sounded like Dex might be lying again, trying to pass the buck. As Mara said, it was a magician's own responsibility to check their equipment.

The dancers filed past us on their way into one of the studios and Dex ogled the last of the blondes admiringly. 'I gotta say, those WPCs take a lot better care of themselves than the real thing,' he commented, eyes trailing the young woman as she disappeared out of sight. 'Anyway, it's been lovely chatting to you ladies, but I only came here in the first place to collect my props.'

So he hadn't come to the studio because he'd heard Katarina

had been found, after all.

Mara snorted. 'I think they're still needed.'

'*Still?*' Dex looked at her agog. 'Some ginger woman was poking around them last night. She must be finished by now.'

'You'd have to check that with Detective Inspector Paulson,' Mara retorted. 'And, ah — here he is. Just the man!'

I turned to see DI Paulson and DC Taylor making their way towards us, becoming increasingly aware that I was still in the same shabby clothes I'd been wearing the previous night.

'We're here to speak to Miss Riley,' said Paulson, bypassing any niceties.

Dex, visibly relieved, shuffled backwards.

'You just missed her,' said Mara. 'The paramedics have taken her to hospital.'

'That's a shame,' replied Paulson. 'We'll have to catch up with her later.'

'Well, since you *are* here, perhaps you could let Mr Devereaux know whether his props are still wanted,' said Mara, gesturing to Dex.

But when Paulson, Taylor, Mara and I looked to where she pointed, where he'd been only moments before, Dex had gone.

'Something deeply fishy about that one,' Paulson commented. 'Not a fan of his work, either.'

'Neither is the rest of the country,' Mara replied.

18.

I dropped Mara off at her house on the way back from Shinetree, and we bid each other a slightly awkward goodbye.

As she went inside, I idled a moment before the huge edifice of her converted chapel, watching one of the twin double front doors draw gently to a close. The sound of it clicking shut was like the final full stop of a story. It marked the end of what, over the last day or so, had seemed to me to be the wildest adventure of my life.

As I steered the car down Mara's long, tree-lined drive, the grand facade of her house diminished in the rear-view mirror before disappearing altogether. I made the remainder of the journey home in silence, the leafy, village-like scattering of Mara's area of north London giving way to the sprawling density of the city the further south I went.

By the time I reached the outskirts of Morden, familiar though it was, it felt oddly akin to crossing a border into a different country. There was a new unfamiliarity to it, somehow, like it had changed. The heightened jumble of emotions I'd experienced over the past day — the roller coaster prison escape, the excitement of watching Talent Quest in Mara's phenomenal house, the tragedy of Angel's reappearance, relief at finding

Katarina and the confrontation with Dex — they all began to leach away, replaced by an overwhelming sense of anti-climax. A little over twelve hours ago, I'd been helping a woman break out of one of the highest-security prisons in the country. Now I was crawling along behind a number 45 bus en route to my poky flat and a boyfriend who probably hadn't remembered to take the rubbish out.

I knew I had a lot to be thankful for, but tomorrow morning it was back to my job at the Morden Mercury. Maybe I'd deluded myself that I could ever make a difference as a journalist, especially when I was only ever allowed to cover the neighbourhood's most trivial goings-on. I was struck by a dreary vision of an unending succession of local businesses — key cutters and massage parlours and fast-food outlets — all run by their own versions of Mr Chen, with schemes as endearingly insignificant as his pet birthday banners.

I reached the flat and pushed open the door, and was immediately hit by a burst of stale air. Old shower steam mingled with beer and a chicken and mushroom Pot Noodle. Then an energetic bundle of calico-coloured fur barrelled towards me. I dropped to my knees as Jasper's tail beat a euphoric rhythm against my leg. Squeezing the dog in my arms, I inhaled the comforting, animal smell of his coat, an immediate balm to my rather gloomy frame of mind.

'Hello, Jaspie,' I murmured, planting a kiss on his head. Jasper dropped onto his side and lifted his paws, revealing the soft cream underbelly he wanted petting. I gave it a scratch, and he thumped his tail contentedly.

Getting to my feet, I called Matt's name.

No reply. He was clearly out, the flat empty.

Jasper bounded after me into the living room, which, on second thoughts, could hardly be described as empty. The nondescript flat-pack furniture, white rental walls and worn laminate flooring were almost entirely obscured behind conurbations of dirty crockery, discarded clothes and scrunched pages of notepaper covered in spidery, experimental song lyrics.

As I moved into the kitchen to fill myself a glass of water, the bowl of fruit on the counter caught my attention. I took in the red apples nestling within it, recalling the enchantment of Mara's house and how nothing had been quite what it seemed, including her. My world felt suddenly small. Depressingly predictable.

Not far from the fruit bowl was propped a torn piece of cereal box on which Matt had scrawled a message.

Got gig @ Red Lion. Back late. Pizza in fridge. Jasp fed + watered. Frankie's gonna rock it 2nite!

"Frankie" was Matt's stage name. Frankie Eden, to be exact, since he insisted Matthew Lewis wasn't a rock and roll enough name to perform under. Though why he'd opted for a moniker that sounded like a middle-of-the-road '60s crooner, I'd never been able to work out.

Though Matt had filled Jasper's bowls, I decided to take him for some fresh air before bed. Hearing me remove his lead from the kitchen drawer, the dog instantly bounced towards me. In his mouth was his favourite toy: an extendable ball-launcher, the ball part shaped like a squashy red tomato. Jasper plonked himself at my feet and dribbled, wide-eyed with anticipation.

My world might have shrunk again, but it was still the bigger for containing Jasper.

I was exhausted by the time we returned, and it was all I could do to summon the energy to shower and change into my PJs. Two floppy slices of Margherita awaited me in the fridge. I ate them standing and straight from the box, Jasper enjoying the scraps of cold pizza a lot more than me.

Painfully aware that I really should tidy the flat ready for the week ahead, I instead switched off the lights on the chaos of the living room, and retreated to bed. Bundling my way under the duvet, Jasper nuzzled at my side, I closed my eyes.

Tired as I was, however, sleep would not come. I wondered what Mara was doing, how she whiled away her time alone in that massive house. Her restlessness appeared so constant I just couldn't imagine her settling on the sofa in front of a box set, or curling up in bed with a good book.

I wondered what Katarina was doing too. Whether DI Paulson and DC Taylor had spoken to her, whether she'd been discharged from the hospital. Were Katarina and Dex together even, as she'd hinted they would be? It was likely I'd now never find any of this out.

Nonetheless, the questions swirled around my head for hours, increasingly replaced by visions of Angel Devereaux, plunging from that box suspended above the Talent Quest stage.

The heavy limpness of her form plummeting down; sequins flashing past the camera as she went; the stomach-churning noise her body made when it hit the studio floor.

The more my mind cycled through those horrible scenes, the more I became aware that I had no idea what kind of person Angel actually was. Jeff had described her as "a fine figure of a woman". Katarina had said she was difficult, Mara that some people hadn't liked her, that she'd been a woman in a man's world. It seemed wrong that Angel's legacy consisted of these snatches of one-sided opinions: about her looks; her reputation; her being Dex's wife; her sensational, tragic demise. What, I wondered, was Angel Devereaux *really* like?

Giving up on sleep altogether, I extracted my laptop from beneath the bed and plugged in the charger. Not really knowing what I was looking for, I again typed "Angel Devereaux" into my web browser, finding largely the same assortment of online newspaper articles and magic forum posts about the Devereauxs that I had before.

Clicking onto the video platform Clipster, I re-watched a few recordings of the Devereauxs' stage act. These mainly comprised videos filmed at local theatres, corporate events or private functions. Whilst some were professionally shot, others had been recorded on phones and camcorders, the handheld footage shaky or low resolution. But the more clips I watched, the more apparent it became. That, although Dex's stage demeanour was cheesy and a little forgettable, Angel was dazzling. She performed with a fluidity and panache evident no matter how unsteady or grainy the footage.

The same could be said about clip after clip. Then I came

across a video that was a couple of years old. It looked like it'd been filmed in the lobby of a theatre after a show, as the Devereauxs were signing programmes for their audience. A young boy asked Dex to show him a trick and so, holding his pen between his fingers, Dex gave an extravagant flick of his hands and the pen completely disappeared. As I'd noticed on Talent Quest, Dex had surprisingly slender fingers for his stocky frame, fingers you'd assume would have been perfect for sleight of hand. But seconds later, the same pen slid out of Dex's sleeve and clunked to the floor, prompting his expression to darken with irritation.

When Dex's back was turned, Angel flawlessly performed the same trick for the boy. And the extraordinary thing was, as she was still dressed in the leotard she'd been wearing on stage, she didn't have any sleeves. Her hands were empty apart from the flimsy, dinted gold wedding band on her ring finger.

The video continued, and I observed Angel greeting every audience member with an easy amiability. She had time for them all, with an openness that betrayed nothing of her supposedly "difficult" personality. But when she moved to leave the lobby with Dex, I was certain I detected a sadness in her expression, her smile straining at the corners in a way it hadn't before.

Jasper snored, and the minutes ticked by, and I clicked onto another video. It had been uploaded in 2006 but, according to its caption, recorded years earlier. I must have missed this particular video when I'd first looked up the Devereauxs online. Or perhaps I'd been more focused on their recent shows. The video was entitled "Dex Devereaux Fire and Water — AMAZING Illusion!"

The view count on this video was significantly higher than any of the others of Dex and Angel. I clicked play. In the centre of the stage stood a platform, on which Dex was positioned beside a large, long glass tank full of water. The tank was bathed in blue light and bookended by several burning torches mounted in holders.

With a flamboyant sweep of his arm, Dex summoned Angel from the wings, and she appeared in a body-skimming leotard of aquamarine sequins. After a couple of super-fast spins in his arms, Dex dragged a heavy length of chain from behind the tank, binding first Angel's wrists, and then encircling her torso and waist, so her arms were pinned to her front. As the music built, Angel climbed up the stairs at the side of the tank and stepped into the water. Taking a deep breath, she sank beneath the surface until she was wholly submerged.

Dex took up a metal petrol can and, as Angel writhed inside the tank, he emptied its contents onto the surface of the water, drawing gasps from the audience which were audible even above the music. Dex next withdrew a torch from its holder, touching its burning end to the water. It caught with an almighty *whoosh*, causing the whole top of the tank to be sealed by a seething layer of orange flames, while Angel thrashed below them, bubbles escaping her mouth.

As the illusion escalated to its thrilling conclusion, Dex, standing before the tank now, drew up a length of black velvet from his feet. The stage became an inferno as pyrotechnics flared in a blazing arc around the tank. In the blink of an eye, the velvet was dropped again, and — miraculously — Angel was standing right where Dex had been merely moments before, soaking wet, while Dex was submerged in the water, bound by the chains.

The whole illusion was truly spectacular, not least due to how dangerous it seemed, but also because of the speed with which Dex and Angel switched places. I didn't have the first clue how any of it had been done. And neither did anyone else, judging by the hundreds of comments underneath the video.

His best trick ever!

How did they DO that??!!!

Wow. Just WOW.

I wondered why the Devereauxs hadn't performed Fire and Water on Talent Quest, given it was not only their most impressive illusion, but by far their most popular. I searched the name of the illusion itself and scanned the handful of results. Although the Devereauxs were the first to do the trick — judging by the video upload details stretching back to the early 2000s — Fire and Water was now regularly performed by the famous American illusionist Kaelen Volt in his nightly Vegas show. In fact, the Devereauxs hadn't performed the trick since Kaelen had started doing it. Or that's what it looked like from the videos.

I petted Jasper awhile, in awe of what I'd just seen. When I drew my attention back to Clipster, I noticed the next recommended video was the Devereauxs' performance on the latest episode of Talent Quest. Without thinking, I clicked play, reliving the anticipation, then abject horror, of the previous night. I watched again how Katarina had started the trick with

Dex. I watched Angel fall. I watched the camera cut back to the second box, which was open and swinging slightly from its cables. And directly below it, that pale banner had unfurled. I quickly hit the pause button.

I ♥ HURTING WOMEN

The starkness of those letters and what they meant seared the screen, a tingle of recognition coursing the length of my spine. There was something about the sequence of those capitals that was undeniably, naggingly familiar—

From the top of the bedside cabinet, my phone suddenly sounded the tinny lyrics of its ringtone, startling both myself and Jasper.

"...my Clarey-Bird. But two ways to hear my three words."

I frowned at the clock. It was approaching midnight. I hadn't realised I'd been looking through the Devereauxs clips for quite so long.

At first, I wondered if it might be Matt calling, but it wasn't his number. The number was unknown. Half expecting it to be some sort of prank, I reluctantly answered the call.

'Hello, Clare.'

My heart kicked. I recognised the voice instantly.

'I have a theory about that flight case, but I shall need somebody's help to test it out.'

I squinted at the time again. 'What... *now*?'

Mara gave a small exhalation of amusement. 'That would be ideal. But I think it can probably wait until morning.'

I sat up straighter in bed. 'Hang on, do you mean... that you have a theory about the flight case we found Katarina in?'

'The very same. I have one just like it in my garage. We can use it to stage a reconstruction if you'd care to come over and assist. Shall we say 11 a.m?'

'Of course,' I replied, not stopping to consider I was due in the Morden Mercury office long before then.

'Excellent. In that *case*, so to speak, I shall see you in the morning.'

Jasper looked up drowsily, as if to answer Mara, before replacing his chin on my leg.

'Oh, wait!' I said suddenly. 'Do you mind if I bring Jasper along?' With me having been out for most of the weekend, it wasn't fair to abandon him in the flat for the third day in a row.

The line went quiet, as though the name didn't register. 'No, that's fine. I'll see you tomorrow—'

'Wait!' I cried a second time. 'This theory of yours. Do you mean you know how the man put Katarina in that case?'

There was another pause.

'It's entirely possible,' said Mara, 'that she might have put herself there.'

With these words, Mara hung up, leaving me wide awake and open-mouthed, staring disbelievingly at the opposite wall.

19.

At eleven the next morning, I pulled up before the gothic grandeur of Mara's house for the third time in as many days. On the passenger seat beside me, Jasper panted contentedly, oblivious to the fact he was about to meet the owner of the strangest — and probably largest — house he'd ever sniff.

A stitch of guilt tweaked my stomach. I'd called Jeff before I left the flat, telling him some urgent personal issue had come up and that I'd likely be a few hours late for work. He wasn't happy but seemed to believe me. As I'd ended the call, I breathed a sigh of relief that I'd bought myself a few hours off writing four hundred words of copy on the problems a local bakery was having with a particularly persistent pigeon. And not only that, but I was back in the world of the Angel Devereaux investigation, back with Mara Knight.

I clipped on Jasper's lead, and together we approached Mara's double front doors. I buzzed the bell and waited. No one answered. Jasper's ears pricked, and he twisted a little impatiently. I went to push the bell again when, all of a sudden, the dog uncharacteristically bolted away from me, snatching the lead clean out of my hand.

'No!' I called after him. 'Jasper!'

His little pale backside was fast disappearing at the furthest end of the building. I shouted for him again, more frantically this time. But when I reached the point where I'd last seen him, I was astonished. There, in the earth before Mara's house, was a vast hole. An opening into what looked like some type of underground bunker.

'Arghhh!'

The scream sounded from within.

'Mara?'

I raced down the ramp and into the peculiar bunker, where I was confronted by the sight of Mara, marooned atop a flight case identical to the one at Shinetree. A few feet in front of the case lay Jasper, who had rolled onto his back to expectantly await a tummy tickle.

'Clare, you're here!' Mara breathed, looking genuinely unnerved. 'God knows where it's come from, but could you please remove that animal?'

Assuming she might be allergic, I crossed to Jasper and regained a hold of his lead. The dog stood and gazed cheerfully at Mara, wagging his tail.

'Mara,' I said, 'this is Jasper. He's very pleased to meet you.'

Mara's eyes moved between me and my dog.

'*That's* Jasper?' she said. 'I assumed you were referring to a child on the phone last night.'

I couldn't help but laugh. 'I don't have a child! And you're the one who told me you'd gone through my social media with a fine-tooth comb. Surely you saw the photos of him?'

Mara appeared confused by this. 'Well, a dog wasn't relevant to the objective,' she said in her oddly formal way. 'Neither was a child, for that matter. So it didn't register. In any case, I'm more of a cat person.'

Then it dawned on me. 'Don't tell me you're frightened of dogs!'

She coloured, ever-so-slightly, and folded her arms. 'They bark and they bite. I've no wish to be on the receiving end of either.'

I encouraged Jasper away and tethered him to a built-in metal shelving unit by the entrance. 'Is he okay here?'

Still eyeing him suspiciously, Mara nodded.

'He really just wanted a tummy rub,' I said. 'They're his favourites...' The words petered out as, for the first time, I properly took in the space around me. 'Whoa.'

It was like a subterranean garage-cum-workshop, one of its walls lined with expanses of boarding onto which hand tools of all kinds were hooked. Against another was a vast assortment of power tools, while a huge alcove at the rear housed floor-to-ceiling shelves, holding various storage boxes with labels such as "DOVE THROUGH DUCK PANS" and "HEAD SHRINKERS". Numerous other black flight cases were there, too, lined up neatly in front of them. Finally, to the right-hand near side were what looked like three separate vehicles under tarpaulins.

'What a garage,' I uttered.

'My husband used it to devise some of his illusions. It's a handy space,' Mara said, referring to an area many times larger than my flat without irony. 'Anyhow, shall we begin?'

She was wearing another long, deep green garment over her black top and jeans today, rather than her woollen coat. It was something between a cardigan and a kimono, and billowed lavishly as she moved around.

I followed her over to the flight case, with its solid black resin sides, chrome wheels, chunky metal edges and reinforced steel corners.

'Right,' said Mara, tapping the top of it with her fingernail. 'Point one on the agenda: the case. You'll see it's pretty much exactly the same as the one at Shinetree. Point two: the theory. That Katarina Riley somehow managed to lock herself *inside* said case. She had, after all, worked as a magician's assistant, and had experience of concealing herself in confined spaces. And finally, point three: her motive for doing so. Which we shall come to presently, if our test proves successful.'

When Mara had first mentioned this theory of hers on the phone, I'd thought it was crazy. But then I remembered how warily Katarina had glanced around the studio car park before speaking to us, as though someone might be listening. How she couldn't give any details of her kidnapper whatsoever. Did Mara suspect Dex had been behind his wife's death, perhaps getting Katarina to act as a distraction?

Mara produced a ball of thin, strong cord from her pocket. 'Now, if you remember, when we found the case at Shinetree, there was a short piece of string looped around one of its external clasps—'

I cast my mind back to the previous morning, when I'd seen her fondling the string as I'd helped Katarina from the case. That string had been threaded through the clasp itself. The more I mulled Mara's theory over, the more plausible it seemed.

'Like this,' Mara went on. She cut a generous length of the cord, threading it through the case's exterior clasp mechanism and securing it there with a series of knots. 'So if Katarina was inside, could she have pulled both clasps shut using the string, then somehow cut through it?'

'How would she have been able to pull the clasps shut using the string, though?' I asked. 'As the door in the side of the case closed, the string would have been pinched in place.'

'Exactly,' replied Mara. 'But two small holes may have been drilled in the case's door, which the strings could have been fed through. I drilled a couple in the door of this one before you arrived.'

I studied where she pointed and saw two tiny holes, just wide enough for the cord to pass through.

Mara swung the flight case open and gestured inside.

'It's the same,' I observed, 'just with slightly different lining.'

'Yes.' She held her position.

A beat or two passed. I assumed she was waiting for me to make some further observation about the case. I opened my mouth, grasping for what that observation might be.

'You'll probably want to take your shoes off.'

The penny finally dropped. When Mara had asked if I wanted to help test her theory, what she really meant was did I want to spend the morning I'd bunked off work cooped up in a sealed flight case. Though I supposed it was a better use of my time than investigating the pigeon pastry thief. And in fairness, Mara was too tall to try out the hypothesis herself.

I eyed the case's interior. It looked uninvitingly snug. From the door, Jasper pulled back his ears and whimpered out a warning.

'I'll be just here,' said Mara.

She passed me the ends of the strings and, feeling more than a little ridiculous, I folded my body into the foam-lined box. It was as cramped as it had looked from the outside. I'd no idea how Katarina had lasted so many hours in the case, and that's before its door had even been closed. Then again, as Mara said, Katarina was used to being confined inside magic props, and I wasn't.

'Now, pull both strings and see if that will close the door,' said Mara.

Knees tucked to my chin, I did as she instructed, and the door successfully drew closed. But before it could seal itself completely shut, the strings became jammed.

'I thought that would happen,' I said, shoving it open again with my foot.

'Yes,' Mara agreed. 'That particular method's a no-go.'

I handed her back the strings, and she carefully fed their ends through the two pre-drilled holes.

'Have another try.'

Readjusting my position a touch, I tugged again on the strings. This time, the flight case's door drew fairly smoothly shut, until I was entirely sealed within its pitch-dark interior. My heart began to beat faster. I fumbled with the top string first, trying to manipulate the external clasp into its final position. It was awkward, the cord slicing into my fingers. Then, just when I thought my efforts were in vain, I heard a metallic *click*.

'No way!' I exclaimed. 'I did it!'

I tried the lower clasp next and, after a few more minutes, it made the same clicking noise as the first. So that proved it. Katarina *could* have locked herself inside the case. And all she would have needed to do next was cut the strings from the inside, as close to the holes as possible, and hide the excess.

As I was considering all this, the flight case opened. Mara was kneeling down, frowning at the clasps.

'So that proves it, right? Katarina locked herself in! She *must* have been in cahoots with Dex... he killed Angel and then used Katarina to create a diversion... to make his wife's death look like the work of a serial killer, maybe? I bet she just made up that detail about the man smelling of cigarettes. She ended the conversation pretty quickly when we pressed her about it—' I extricated myself from the flight case and stood blinking in the light as Jasper gave a triumphant bark.

Mara, however, didn't reply.

'What do you think?'

'I think you've proved it, Clare,' she said.

I smiled broadly.

'It would have been *impossible* for Katarina to lock herself inside that case.'

'What—? But I heard the clasps shut, I'm sure I did.'

'Take a look.' Mara indicated towards the two chrome fastenings. 'They're surprisingly complicated. They consist of two butterfly clasps, which have to be turned anti-clockwise to cause these hooks to engage and pull the whole clasp together.'

I watched as she demonstrated, with an increasing sense of disappointment.

'What you heard was the butterfly part clicking flat. But the hook was never engaged. So the case was never properly fastened.'

'And when we found Katarina in that studio, both clasps

were definitely properly fastened,' I said.

'Exactly.'

I went over to Jasper and gave him a rub. 'Then the string you saw on the clasp must have just come from a label?'

'Most likely,' said Mara. 'We shouldn't be too disheartened. We've tested out an effect and eliminated a potential method. That's not bad for half an hour's work.'

'I suppose.' Perhaps she was right. We now knew for sure that Katarina had been put into that flight case by somebody else, as unlikely as that seemed. 'I can't believe someone was able to wrestle her in there, though.'

Mara gave a nod. 'But just like the theory that Katarina locked herself inside the case, the idea of someone else forcibly putting her there is improbable, but not impossible.'

I recalled a Conan Doyle quote from school. 'When you have eliminated all which is impossible, then whatever remains, however improbable, must be the truth.'

Mara made a face, like she'd just tasted something sour. 'Yes. Though that maxim's used far too much nowadays to explain away complete and utter bollocks. From ghosts to Bigfoots to God knows what else.'

I pondered her words a moment. 'Perhaps people just need to start eliminating more.'

Mara issued a single, loud laugh. 'You're right about that.'

'So, who can we eliminate in Angel's murder?' I asked, stepping back towards the flight case. 'Katarina. She did have those bruises on her arms, remember?'

Mara made an utterance of agreement. 'Large ones. If Katarina had put herself in that case, then we could have assumed Dex had made them before the show started, as part of the facade. But now I think we can safely say that they were made by her attacker.' This notion set her off pacing the garage floor. 'Dex Devereaux. What exactly did you make of him yesterday?'

I recalled how Dex had indulged in that inappropriately lengthy embrace with Katarina, how he'd been more concerned about us speaking to her than her being safe and well. And that wasn't to mention him ogling those dancers, only hours after his wife's death. I remembered, too, how small he'd made me feel. What he'd said about women relying on their father's or husband's money. I decided I didn't just dislike Dex Devereaux, I actually loathed him.

'I wouldn't trust him as far as I could throw him,' I declared. 'He didn't seem to care about Angel at all. He was just worried his trick had gone wrong. What kind of man calls his wife's death a "fiasco"?'

'Indeed,' replied Mara. 'But if he intended to harm Angel and had Katarina kidnapped, then why call it a "fiasco" at all?'

She had a point. If Dex *was* behind all this, why hadn't he at least pretended to be upset about Angel's death?

'And, of course, he has the best alibi in the book,' she continued. 'So now we just need to work out if it was possible that he could have killed his wife and put Katarina in that case whilst he was live on stage. And if not, eliminate him from—'

At that moment, Mara's mobile rang. She withdrew it from the pocket of her jeans and glanced briefly at the screen.

'Hello Dhita,' she said, pressing the speakerphone button. 'Clare's here as well. She's been helping me test out a theory.'

'Hello again, Clare,' said Dhita. 'I'm surprised you want

anything more to do with her after Saturday.'

'Me too,' I replied, at which Mara lifted the corners of her mouth.

'Good work yesterday, Clare,' said Dhita. 'Having the nous to go back to the studio to look for Katarina like that.'

I thanked her, flushing with pride that I'd been able to help.

'Any updates today?' asked Mara.

'Afraid not,' Dhita replied. 'I'm bored silly waiting for this baby to arrive. I rang to ask you the same.'

'Nothing, as yet. Apart from that there is no way Katarina Riley could possibly have locked herself in that flight case.'

'Why would you have thought that?' asked Dhita, before answering her own question. 'Ohhh, you suspect *Dex* might be behind all this?'

'I don't trust him,' I chipped in. 'So we're working to eliminate him.'

Dhita chuckled. 'There might be a job at the Met for you yet, Clare.'

'You don't happen to know whether there's anything new on that banner, Dhita?' asked Mara.

'Luke tells me the police are still trying to trace where it might have come from, who printed it, et cetera. But I'll let you know.'

Who printed it.

Something about those words clanged in my skull. The hard black letters of the banner burned behind my eyes, just as they had on the screen of my laptop.

I ♥ HURTING WOMEN

There was a definite familiarity about them, about the way the "I" and the heart icon preceded the word "women". A vision flashed in my mind. I *had* seen that same succession of letters before. The red "COMPLETE" stamps. The jumble of order slips, all overlapping each other. One particular slip, half-hidden beneath the next. My pulse picked up pace.

'Mara!' I exclaimed, grabbing her arm without thinking. 'I know where that banner came from.'

20.♠

After driving around the block a few times, a parking space finally opened up just across the road from Presto Print. Beside me, Mara's gaze was fixed somewhere beyond the windscreen, the rich fabric of her kimono-cardigan incongruous against the worn grey seats of my little Ford Fiesta.

Once I'd persuaded Mara that Jasper didn't pose any danger, and that it was perfectly safe for the two of them to be in the same vehicle, she'd reluctantly got into the car. Still, Jasper had been relegated to the blanket I laid out for him in the boot, the back shelf removed.

'Here we are,' I announced unnecessarily, as we exited the car to be faced with the unassuming frontage of Presto Print. Its sign was slightly sun-bleached, the window display crammed with examples of Mr Chen's handiwork — baby shower announcements and personalised posters and, inevitably, several brightly coloured banners featuring beaming canines. Nevertheless, the place looked a shade drabber than I remembered it being, just two days ago. I lifted Jasper from the boot.

The bell above the door jangled as we entered, the air inside thick with the not-unpleasant tang of ink and vinyl. Rolls of paper stood propped in corners, and half-finished banners lay across the large workstation behind the counter like incomplete crosswords of unknown lives. And there, grinning at me below the printed bunting that crisscrossed the ceiling, was Mr Chen.

He greeted me warmly. 'Ah, Miss Deyes! Come back for another newspaper story? I had a breakthrough with the Schnauzer Silhouettes range! Much more definition around the beard, you see...' He brandished a small, square banner sporting a surprisingly detailed dog profile against a fetching lilac background.

'It's lovely, Mr Chen,' I nodded.

'Ooh, and who is this handsome fellow?' Mr Chen asked with outright glee as his eyes fell on Jasper. 'Let me guess... part-cocker spaniel, part-terrier. Now, when's his birthday?'

Since Jasper was a rescue dog, I had no idea, though the vet estimated he'd been about two when I adopted him. 'The first week of April,' I lied, not wanting to disappoint Mr Chen.

'Then he'll be wanting a banner!' the man proclaimed. 'Very popular to pin on railings outside Tesco. Then, when dog drives past in car, he will see it. What year was he born?'

'Erm... 2012?'

'Ah, so he's a dragon, even though he's a dog!'

At that point, clearly growing bored by the exchange and still giving Jasper a wide berth, Mara stepped forwards. 'We came to ask about a banner you printed recently. Nothing to do with dogs, I'm afraid.'

Mr Chen appeared a little crestfallen by this.

'Your banner put in an appearance on television last Saturday,' Mara went on.

'Really?' said Mr Chen, impressed.

'Did you see Talent Quest?' I asked.

Mr Chen's expression darkened. 'British TV,' he muttered. 'Not good.'

'I can't disagree with you there,' said Mara. 'Anyway, the banner in question had black text on a pale background. Plain capitals—'

'*Plain* capitals?' Mr Chen enquired. 'Oh yes, we do those too, of course. Very popular for... well, making a statement, though there are far better examples of our work.'

'It was about four foot wide.' I gestured vaguely, approximating the size as being the same width as the box I'd seen in the Talent Quest studio. Though the box had looked bigger in real life than it had on the television.

'And the words printed across it were "I heart hurting women",' added Mara.

'With a picture of a heart, rather than the word,' I clarified, recalling how the half-hidden jumble of slips I'd seen on Saturday made the words look as though they were spelling: "I ♥ HAPPY WOMEN".

Mr Chen's eyes slowly broadened in recognition. 'Ah, that one! Yes, yes, I remember now. Unusual wording... I heart hurting women.' He tutted. 'Not nice, I thought. But the customer is always right, eh? You want another one the same?'

'Not exactly,' I said. 'We were just wondering if you still had the order slip?'

'Order slip?' Mr Chen looked momentarily flustered, gesturing towards the pinboard I'd noticed on my last visit, at the chaotic collage of papers stamped "COMPLETE". 'Of course.

I keep them all. Good for the accounts. And sometimes people come back. Want the same again. Saves time!'

How on earth he'd manage to relocate an order slip should such a thing happen, given the sheer number of them pinned to the board, I couldn't imagine.

Mr Chen bustled over to it and began riffling through the slips, dislodging pins and paper as he went. They dotted the floor around him. 'Let's see... "Happy 40th Kev!"... "Emma's Hen Do Hullabaloo"... "World's Best Dad"... Ah, here! Plain capitals, pale background.' He unpinned one of the slips and scratched his cheekbone thoughtfully. 'Yes... "*I heart hurting women*". I thought there was something off about this at the time. Very off.'

'What date was the order placed, Mr Chen?' I asked.

'Late last Wednesday. Wednesday the 19th of March.'

So, the banner was ordered just under a week ago. Four days after Angel first vanished.

'And is there a name on the order?' asked Mara. 'Of the person who placed it? Or a phone number?'

Mr Chen shook his head.

'There *isn't*?' I said.

'There is, but this is confidential information. If my customers knew I was giving out their details, my reputation would be ruined.'

Mara and I exchanged a glance.

'I tell you what,' Mr Chen said, his eyes glinting impishly. 'You order a birthday banner for Jasper's big day, and I'll share the order details.'

Mara gave a noise of amusement. 'Done.'

Mr Chen, seeming satisfied with this, chortled. 'I don't have the number of the person who placed this order. But the name here is...' he squinted, as though unable to make sense of his handwriting. 'Dood...? No, *Dodd*. Definitely Dodd.'

My heart sank. It wasn't a name I recognised.

'And how was the order placed?' Mara asked, unperturbed.

'By phone,' Mr Chen confirmed. 'It says here. But like I said, no number.'

'Do you remember if it was a man or a woman who called?' I pressed, brightening a little. Maybe Mr Chen could remember the voice, the accent?

Mr Chen looked from me to Mara and back again, then shook his head apologetically. 'I'm sorry, Miss Deyes, I'm really not sure. So many calls, you see. And last Wednesday was madness! The new glitter finish for the Poodle Pretties line had just come in. That's why it was annoying the customer who ordered the banner wanted a rush job. They were very strict. It had to be done by Saturday morning. Latest.'

This was interesting. It suggested the banner was a last-minute decision.

'If you don't have any phone details,' said Mara, 'was that because the order was collected in person?'

'Yes, yes,' Mr Chen replied emphatically. 'In person.'

I straightened, instinctively glancing around the shop at the CCTV cameras mounted below the ceiling. There would be a recording of whoever placed that banner, a recording of them coming in to pick it up. A recording that would surely lead us to Angel's killer. 'And do you remember who that was? What they looked like?' I asked.

Mr Chen screwed his face in concentration. 'No, sorry. We're always so busy, especially Saturdays. I thiiink,' he went on, drawing out the word as he dredged his memory, 'it was a man. Can't be sure. But the banner was paid for when it was ordered. Over the phone. So he just came and went.'

There was a pause. Mara narrowed her eyes. Had she picked up something in the information Mr Chen had given us that I hadn't?

'Now,' she declared, clapping her hands together. 'This birthday banner for Jasper. Mr Chen, what would you recommend? I'm thinking something suitable for an indoor party. Do you have any thoughts, Clare?'

She steered me further towards the counter as Mr Chen promptly launched into an enthusiastic explanation of finishes, and the relative merits of vinyl versus nylon. He withdrew various sample books from under his counter.

Simultaneously, Mara took out her phone and began scrolling through bookmarked social media posts; flawless shots full of pretty party inspiration. It was... surprising. The last thing I could imagine was the Mara Knight I'd become acquainted with over the past few days taking tips from social media influencers.

'How about a banner along these lines?'

She leant forwards to show the photo to Mr Chen, angling her phone above the counter, with its clutter of samples and order slips.

'Excellent!' Mr Chen replied, slamming his hand down decisively. 'One hundred per cent doggy satisfaction guaranteed. Or your money back!'

Back outside the shop and — as Mr Chen had observed — Jasper was indeed excited by the prospect of a customised birthday banner. I, by contrast, was not.

'*Seventy-five pounds?*' I shouted to Mara over the traffic as we crossed back to my car. 'Do you know how much I get paid at the Morden Mercury?'

She waved a hand impatiently. 'I'll reimburse you.'

'Ten foot by six? Where the hell am I even going to hang it?'

'Don't worry about that. In any case, it was all worth it.'

I glared at the back of her head as I settled Jasper on his blanket. Getting into the car again, I wondered how to tell Mara she'd lost her mind. She swivelled to face me.

'Dodd,' she said gravely. 'The name on that order. It's Dex's real name. Dexter Dodd. Devereaux's his stage name.'

I hadn't entertained the possibility that Devereaux wasn't Dex's real name, and nothing I'd found about him online had mentioned it either. But if even Matt wanted to make himself sound glitzier on stage, then it made perfect sense Dex did too.

My stomach lurched as the significance of this sank in. So Dex *had* ordered that banner. While Angel was still missing. And he'd collected it as well. Last Saturday. Was that why he was late to the studio?

Hot on the heels of these questions, however, came others, tangling the whole issue further. Why had Dex gone to the trouble of bothering with a banner at all? To lead everyone into thinking his wife's death was the work of some showboating serial killer? Was this the same reason he'd "kidnapped" Katarina?

'So he chose the live Talent Quest show as the time to do all this because he knew he'd have the best alibi going. And it would look like someone else's handiwork,' I said, thinking aloud. 'But still, how did he get Katarina into the case?'

Mara took out her phone and proceeded to tap the screen.

'Even so... Dex's name on the slip, that banner being ordered while Angel was missing...' I shook my head. 'And you said he was lying on that piece he did to camera. It has to be him.'

'There's only one way to find out.'

'Check Presto Print's CCTV,' I said.

'No,' replied Mara. 'Those cameras were all fake. Mr Chen doesn't have any CCTV.'

I smothered a groan.

'We can find out by having Dhita check the credit card number on that order slip.'

I opened my mouth to say in that case, we should have asked Mr Chen for it. In my opinion, seventy-five pounds was more than enough to cover both a ten-foot pet birthday banner *and* someone's credit card details.

Mara showed me her phone. 'And here it is.'

Impossibly, there on the screen was a photograph of the very order slip for the "I ♥ HURTING WOMEN" banner, complete with the credit card details of the person who'd ordered it. I couldn't believe what I was seeing. 'Wait, how did you—'

Mara pressed some more buttons before putting the phone

to her ear. 'Dhita? Yes, I'm with Clare again... Listen, if you're still bored, I need a favour. A credit card number check. Can you see who the following details belong to?' She read them out. 'Let me know as soon as you can.'

Being back at Mara's house, attempting to lock myself into a flight case, and now lifting someone's credit card details. It had been another outlandish day, and it was only just past lunch.

Dex Devereaux might have been trying to get us to look in the wrong direction, but I was sure we were starting to see right through his illusion.

21.

It took ten minutes to drive to my flat through the traffic as we waited for Dhita to call back with the news about the credit card. The thought of whether DI Paulson would mind Mara always relaying potential new evidence to Dhita, and not to him, briefly flitted through my mind. Surely he'd be annoyed? Though Dhita was technically Paulson's superior. And every new clue we unearthed made me more and more certain that we were closing in on the truth about Angel's death.

Mara hadn't said much since we'd left Mr Chen. She gripped her phone in her hand, seesawing her gaze between its screen and the view through the window.

I'd tried to encourage her into a coffee shop to wait for the call at first, not wanting her to see the flat. It was late for lunch, and we popped into the Costa on the high street for some sandwiches. Mara had initially asked the barista for a Pinot Grigio and been confused when he said they didn't sell it. So, she and I had eventually left with a pain au raisin and a ham and cheese toastie, respectively. I'd reluctantly agreed that we take them to my flat to eat, as by that time my hour of free parking opposite Presto Print was up.

As Mara followed me along the cracked concrete of the short

front path, I became acutely aware of the peeling paint on our communal front door, the overflowing clutter of bins plonked next to it. Leading Mara into my poky, probably still-messy flat felt like ushering royalty into a garden shed.

'Well, this is it,' I said blandly, fumbling with my keys.

Jasper gambolled inside and up the stairs to the first floor. He disappeared through the door to the flat before I'd scarcely nudged it ajar. The same stale smell from yesterday hit me once more, overlaid this time with a fug of Lynx Africa. I braced myself.

Mara's eyes scanned the entrance hall, which, aside from an errant pair of Matt's trainers, wasn't in too bad a state.

'That's a very unusual way of welcoming people,' she remarked.

'Er, yes... it's from a song,' I muttered, realising she was referring to the doormat. *My Clarey-Bird.*

'Of course,' she replied. 'Your ringtone.'

Making a mental note to change it as soon as I'd eaten, I hastily gathered up the discarded pair of trainers and replaced them neatly beneath the coat pegs.

Speaking of Matt's songs, the unmistakable electronic whine of an effects pedal sounded from the living room, stopping abruptly at the sound of our voices.

'Cla?' The living room door swung inwards and Matt appeared framed in the opening. His blonde hair was mussed, and he was dressed in the same faded band t-shirt he'd been wearing on Saturday. Behind him, a steaming, half-eaten Pot Noodle was balanced precariously on the arm of the sofa, together with the rest of the mess I hadn't bothered to clean up the previous night. I now regretted that decision.

'Oh, hi.' He offered Mara a nod, unplugged headphones dangling around his neck. 'You're back early,' he told me.

Jasper nosed his way to Matt's ankles, and Matt bent down and rubbed his head. 'Hey boy, you missed me?'

'Hi Matt,' I said, forcing cheerfulness. 'This is Mara. Mara, Matt.'

Mara inclined her head. 'Hello.'

'Right,' Matt said, already gazing back at his guitar. 'Cool. Well, I've just made food if you want any.' He gestured towards the steaming container of plastic. 'Anyhow, I'm trying to nail this riff...'

With that, Matt disappeared back into the living room, and a discordant chord sequence commenced. He was playing his electric guitar through headphones, which always sounded awful.

Settling Jasper in his dog bed, I turned back to Mara and waved apologetically towards the kitchen area. 'Tea? Coffee? Though we might have run out of milk, actually.'

'Water will be fine,' Mara replied, picking her way around a pile of Matt's laundry near the washing machine as I tried to mask my embarrassment. 'Impressive work back there, Clare. Remembering the relevance of those order slips in Presto Print.'

Perhaps she'd noticed me squirming at the state of the flat — and the state of Matt — as her words eased my humiliation. But only slightly.

I slid two plates from a cupboard for our food. 'Oh, well...' I hesitated. 'I guess it was just luck, really. Please.' Painfully aware of the weedy strumming issuing from Matt's un-amped guitar, I pulled a chair out for her from under the breakfast bar, which was all we had in lieu of a dining table.

Mara picked at her pastry as I took a bite of my sandwich, my mouth suddenly dry, the bread chewy. It sounded as though Matt was trying to work out a chord sequence with disastrous results. But despite being desperate to drown out the noise, I had no idea what to say to Mara. I wracked my brain for something to break the non-silence. When nothing was forthcoming, I decided to just ask the question that'd been bugging me since we left the print shop.

'That photo you took of the order slip and those credit card details... how did you manage it? Mr Chen was right there.'

Mara gave the ghost of a smile. 'Do you have any thoughts on that?' she asked, inserting a raisin into her mouth.

This threw me a little. I had almost become used to Mara telling me how various magic tricks were done. The prison escape and teleportation illusion, if not how she was able to make the cork disappear and that glass float of its own accord. I took another bite of my toastie, considering. The picture must have been taken when Mara was showing Mr Chen her party inspiration photos. But I clearly saw her phone screen, and the camera app was not open.

'There had to be something in your hands when you were showing Mr Chen those party shots,' I said, continuing my train of thought out loud. 'Something as well as your phone.'

She raised her eyebrows and took a tiny bite of her pastry, the voluminous sleeves of her coatigan falling to her elbows.

'Aha! You had something up your sleeve!' I declared through a mouthful of cheese. 'Some kind of... periscope! With mirrors!

You dropped it into your hand, which enabled an image of the order slip to be reflected to a camera further up your sleeve and then photographed.'

Mara cocked her head. 'That would have required me to come prepared. I don't rig myself up like a suicide bomber every time I leave the house.'

I mused on a potential method for a few more minutes, though it was difficult to focus over the whiny *glinging* of Matt's guitar. First chord, second chord, third chord... and then an awful, jarring fourth. Rather than being "nailed", his riff seemed to be falling apart.

'Okay, so if you didn't come prepared, then you must have taken the photo with something you had on you already,' I said.

'Warmer,' Mara replied.

I scanned her hands, clasped beneath her chin as she watched me deliberate. They were bare, apart from her two rings. That thick gold wedding band and the ring with the purple stone.

'Your ring!' I said. 'That's not an amethyst, it's a tiny camera. It took a picture of the slip and then sent it to your phone. Probably by Bluetooth.' I folded my arms, satisfied with my deduction.

Mara twisted the purple ring restively and moved her hands below the countertop. 'I can assure you it's just an engagement ring,' she said. 'I'm not James Bond.'

After a few uneasy seconds had passed, Mara's gaze flickered towards Matt, who was still engrossed in his composition. She pulled out her mobile. The sleek reflective device looked exotic on my beige laminate worktop.

'It's simply an app,' she told me, clicking on what looked like an icon for an ordinary smartphone note-taking app. 'A friend of mine coded it. You open the app up, navigate to whichever other app on the phone you'd like to use as a front — Instagram was the one I went for earlier — and then double tap to take a photograph. There is no flash and no shutter sound.'

Of course. A covert photography app. Another piece of completely unpredictable technology in Mara Knight's arsenal. Despite her protestations, she was beginning to seem more like James Bond by the second.

'It also records video,' she added, looking pleased.

The method Mara had used to take that photo was also, I realised, a classic piece of misdirection. By engaging Mr Chen on a subject he was passionate about, she'd created a blind spot, distracted him too much to recognise what was actually going on right under his nose. Though I never did ask why she had all that party inspiration saved on an Instagram account.

Oblivious to our talk of custom-coded phone apps and covert photography, Matt continued to strum his guitar, only stopping occasionally to shove forkfuls of noodles into his mouth.

Mara's phone, still on the worktop, emitted a low ping. She glanced at the screen.

'Dhita,' she said, her voice dropping.

Typing a quick reply to let Dhita know it was okay to call, Mara rose from her seat. 'I'll take this in the hall,' she announced.

Matt lifted one ear of his headphones. 'Huh?'

'Nice meeting you, Matt,' Mara declared. 'Good luck with your riff. Try F for that last chord, rather than G major. And you might also want to experiment with drop A tuning.'

She swept towards the front door, leaving Matt open-mouthed

on the sofa.

I didn't have the chance to ask how Mara also seemed to magically know about guitar chords before her phone buzzed. She answered and put the call onto speakerphone.

'Got a few things for you,' Dhita's voice said. 'Firstly, the credit card used to pay for that banner at Presto Print?'

There was a pause.

'It's registered to one Dexter Dodd, same address as the Devereauxs' house in Morden.'

My breath hitched. So it *was* him. The confirmation sent a shiver across my skin.

I looked at Mara. She said nothing and was totally still, but I could feel her mind whirring.

'So he ordered it under his real name, using his credit card—' said Mara, in a way that implied this was odd.

'Hold on, there's more,' Dhita continued. 'The path report on Angel came back. You were correct about the blow to the side of the head – right temporal region. There was only a small nick in the skin. But there was bruising. Subdural haematoma starting. Consistent with being struck by a blunt instrument.'

'So Dex struck her,' I whispered, picturing the awful chain of events that must have unfolded backstage, unbeknownst to everyone else in the studio. 'Before putting her in that box.'

'But,' Dhita cut in, 'that wasn't the cause of death. C.O.D. was a fracture-dislocation of the upper cervical spine. A broken neck. Consistent with a fall from height, just as Lindi suspected. Otherwise, there were no signs of her having been held anywhere beforehand... like in a flight case, for example. Angel wasn't dehydrated or malnourished. And there were no traces of sedatives, alcohol, or anything else untoward in her system.'

I frowned, trying to piece it together. 'So Dex attacked Angel. But he didn't drug her, he instead knocked her out before the show started, to hide her inside that box... and she was alive until she fell.'

It sounded convoluted, and I still didn't have the first inkling why this was the plan Dex had chosen. Nevertheless, it was horribly plausible.

'Dex certainly had means and opportunity before the show started,' Mara murmured, more to herself than to Dhita and me. 'But it still doesn't explain who locked Katarina in that flight case. Dex must have had help with that. And why on earth...'

'Why on earth would Dex have chosen to do things *this* way?' I offered, completing Mara's sentence by voicing my thoughts of a few moments before. But even as I said this, the notion made a little more sense to me. 'Dex hit Angel on the head to get her inside the box, knowing that if she was unconscious a fall from that height would prove fatal.'

'Not necessarily,' returned Mara. 'It was likely, but he couldn't have been absolutely certain that the drop would kill her.'

'But the way an assistant has to lie in the compartment of the box... maybe he knew that specific position would ensure the best chances of that happening.' I countered. 'Of her unconscious body falling headfirst. And it does make more sense that he chose to do it live on Talent Quest, despite what he said in the studio car park about the whole thing having ruined his career.' I was in full flow now, convinced we were reaching the truth. 'Dex knew that if his plan was successful, which it was, then he would have the best alibi in the world. And just to direct attention away from himself even more, he ordered that banner, making it look like it was all the work of some maniac serial killer.'

'He could also have figured that the fall from the box would be enough to conceal the wound he made when he struck Angel,' said Dhita. 'The blood from the blow could well have been missed — it very nearly was — and so the bruising could have passed as resulting from the fall.'

'Why not simply drug her in advance?' said Mara.

'So no drugs were found in her system postmortem?' I said.

'Yes, that would have been more damning,' said Dhita. 'More suggestive of foul play.'

'Okay, but what did Dex do with Angel the week she was missing?' Mara went on. 'That part doesn't make sense either.'

Though I have to admit her doubt was a little irritating, especially in the face of what appeared to be such solid evidence, Mara did have a point.

'Anyway,' said Dhita, 'we have the banner ordered with his card, under his real name... That's enough. Paulson's getting a warrant to search the Devereauxs' house as we speak.'

22.♠

Surprisingly, some hours later I wasn't back at my flat, at Mara's mansion or even at the Devereauxs' house. I was back on the Talent Quest stage. But this time the studio lights were blinding, the gazes of Shane Sinclair and his team of judges were boring into me and, behind them, sat a full studio audience. The atmosphere was heavy, expectant. It was so quiet you could hear a pin drop. Or Shane Sinclair's designer stubble grow.

And then I realised. All these people were waiting... for me.

I was instantly seized by panic. I have never performed in my life. My mouth was parched, sweat trickled down my breastbone, and my knees felt like they were about to give way altogether. I didn't have a clue what to do next. Being in front of an audience absolutely terrified me, but the wings were blocked by crew members, the stage hemmed in by judges and audience. There was no escape.

So, I did the only thing I could. I opened my mouth and shakily started to sing a cover of the first song that came to mind.

Clarey-Bird

The trouble was, I could only remember a tiny handful of the words. So I sang them again and again, my voice growing weaker and more uncertain with every pathetic repetition. Then it registered. The lyrics weren't coming from my mouth at all—

I jolted out of the dream and sat bolt upright in bed, my heart still racing. On the bedside table, my phone screen was lit, the ringtone jabbering into the silence of our bedroom. I ran a hand across my face and tilted the mobile towards me. The time was 5.55 a.m. The number Mara's. Beside me, Matt moaned and turned over.

What on earth did Mara want at this hour? In my still-discombobulated, post-nightmare state, I wondered whether it might be about the warrant. But Mara hadn't mentioned getting in touch again when I'd left her the day before. Nor had she mentioned whether she'd be attending the search at the Devereauxs' house. And I assumed that, even if she was, I certainly wouldn't be. Perhaps it had happened already. Perhaps that's what she was ringing about.

I picked up, waiting for Mara to tell me the latest findings on Dex. But what she actually told me was that she was standing outside our communal front door, staring up at our bedroom window.

Mara explained that, around midnight, Dhita had messaged to say the police would be beginning their search of the Devereauxs' house imminently. And that, due to the potential magic paraphernalia kept there, it would be useful if she could be on hand in case she was needed. I again pondered the question of when Mara slept.

'I've been in Morden for the past hour,' she clarified.

'You've been watching our bedroom window for an hour?'

'Not exactly. I've sort of been between here and there.'

'*There* being Dex's house?'

'Yes,' Mara confirmed. 'I didn't call earlier as I didn't want to wake you.'

'You've just woken me now.'

'Mmm,' she replied vaguely. 'Anyway, I'm about to head back there. The police should be nearing the end of their search, so I shall see if there's anything for me. You may come too. If you want.'

I told Mara I'd be ready as soon as I could and buzzed her in. She claimed she was happy to wait downstairs, but I suspected she was trying to avoid Jasper, of whom she was still irrationally wary. I drafted a text to Jeff, explaining that I was sorry, but the same personal issue was going to keep me away from the office for a second day. I hoped that sending this text at 6 a.m. rendered the story a little more believable.

I tugged some clothes from my wardrobe, dragged a comb through my hair and swiped on a bit of lip gloss. Yet again, there was no time for a shower. Lastly, I refilled Jasper's bowls. Throughout the whole of this process, my brain had been humming with what might already have been uncovered at the Devereauxs' house. Could they have found more evidence of Dex's guilt, concrete proof that he really *had* murdered Angel?

Twenty-five minutes after Mara's unceremonious wake-up call, I was about to find out. She and I turned into Chelford Close, a quiet residential street a relatively short walk from my own, and fairly similar in appearance. Rows of early twentieth-century semis stretched either side of the road. While some of these had seen better days — their wooden window frames rotten, gutters broken and bowing — others had been newly extended, their pebble-dashed facades painted a brilliant white.

The Devereauxs' house was one of the semis that fell into this latter category. They were obviously doing better from magic than I expected. A cluster of police vehicles blocked the drive, and personnel in uniform streamed in and out of the front door. As we neared it, my eye was caught by movements in the windows of neighbouring houses. Horizontal blinds twitched, gauzy nets stirring across the double glazing. One woman, clad in a shocking pink dressing-gown, had positioned herself squarely in the open doorway of the property opposite, to gawp at proceedings.

'Well, a police search is certainly more entertaining than breakfast television,' said Mara, noticing the woman too. 'Though so is a crisp packet blowing along the pavement.'

On the road outside the Devereauxs' house, DI Paulson stood talking, through a mouthful of bacon sandwich, to DC Taylor. I found myself once more cursing Mara for not leaving me enough time for a shower.

Hearing Mara's voice, Paulson glanced up at us and bristled.

'Good morning,' she said. 'Have you only just arrived, Graham? You weren't here earlier.'

Paulson's complexion grew a touch ruddier at being addressed by his first name. 'Knight. Someone said you'd been sniffing round. Anand fill you in again, did she? I'll remind you it's *me* who's the Senior Investigating Officer on this case. Not her.'

'DCI Anand merely informed me that a search warrant had been granted,' Mara replied. 'Given the potential magic props inside — and my involvement with the case thus far — she felt my presence here this morning might prove useful.'

Paulson snorted. 'Civilian involvement. Investigations like this should be left to the professionals.'

'It's thanks to a civilian — Clare — that a missing young woman was found locked inside a flight case,' Mara cut back, raising a hand in my direction.

'We'd planned to make a full search of the stuff in that studio on Sunday,' snapped Paulson. 'We'd have found Miss Riley then.'

'And it's because of Clare's recollection of where that banner was printed that you're here this morning.'

This momentarily silenced Paulson.

'That was good work,' said Taylor.

'Thank you.' I shifted, glancing away.

'So, how far along are they?' Mara gestured inside.

'Almost finished,' said Taylor.

'Found anything of interest?' asked Mara.

'Wilcox!' Paulson shouted through the Devereauxs' front door.

Seconds later, Lindi Wilcox appeared. 'Oh hello, Mara,' she said. 'Clare.' She was holding a clear evidence bag in her hand. It looked empty. 'Yeah, there's nothing much, aside from what you'd expect. The place is remarkably clean. Hardly any prints that aren't likely to belong to the occupants.'

The place is remarkably clean. Was that evidence in itself?

That Dex had cleaned up in an effort to hide something?

'We did find this, though,' Lindi went on. 'Caught on the back of the sofa. Could well be nothing.'

She passed the evidence bag to Mara and, as Mara pressed it between her fingers, I saw there *was* something inside: a single strand of long, fair hair.

'Interesting,' mused Paulson. 'Likely from a woman, but not the victim's colour.'

'Not the victim's colour?' I whispered to Mara. 'But it's blonde.'

'Angel wasn't blonde,' Mara replied. 'She was dark. She performed in a wig.'

I couldn't believe it. Angel's trademark bleach-blonde bouffant had looked so real.

'How about having Mar look over that item upstairs while she's here?' Lindi asked Paulson.

He snapped his attention from the bag to Mara. 'Suppose,' he said reluctantly. 'But *she'll* have to stay outside.'

'Oh… yes,' I mumbled, realising he meant me. 'Of course.'

'I'm afraid Clare is needed,' countered Mara brusquely. She unwrapped something from beneath her coat and pushed it into my hands. It was a brown leather buckled pouch; similar to a bum bag, but far chicer. 'She's assisting me today and is a vital handler of my equipment.'

Before Paulson could object, Mara took hold of my arm and sailed inside.

Despite having been full of police personnel for the past few hours, the Devereauxs' house did look clean — just as Lindi had said — and smelled faintly of air freshener. Considering

Dex had been living there on his own for a week, it was also surprisingly tidy. The decor, comprising pale carpets, neutral walls and modern furniture, was almost minimalist. Compared to the brimming, eclectic opulence of Mara's house — or even the mess of my flat — it felt oddly sterile, nothing like a happy marital home. Although the Devereauxs were performers, there was little personality here. And unless I was missing something, I didn't spot a single magic prop.

Mara paused at the top of the stairs, becoming aware she hadn't asked the location of the item the police wanted her to see.

'It's in the master bedroom. At the front,' came Lindi's voice from below.

We made our way into the room, followed by Lindi, Paulson and Taylor. The Devereauxs' bedroom was dominated by a king-sized bed topped with a plain cream duvet. It was bookended by simple ashen nightstands, while mirror-fronted wardrobes covered the entirety of one wall. In the lee of the bay window stood a modern black dressing table, on which was propped a framed print showing the constellation Leo. This object aside, the decor in here was as anonymous and functional as the rest of the house.

Anonymous, that was, with the exception of one piece.

Mara had frozen in front of the item: a large and ornate chest of drawers. It was constructed in a reddish-coloured wood, with four intricately carved, well-spaced drawers finished with heavy brass handles. The piece was totally out of keeping with the other furniture.

'Yep, that's it,' Lindi told Mara. 'It reminded me of something you've looked at for us before. Even so, sure as hell none of us can work *this* one out.'

Mara didn't respond immediately. She circled the chest of drawers slowly, running her fingertips along its carvings, rapping her knuckles gently against its sides. It all sounded perfectly solid. 'It's possible there's something similar going on here,' she murmured mysteriously.

Mara pulled open one drawer and then another, first revealing stacks of women's tops and woollens, and then a jumble of men's socks and polo shirts.

'It just seems to contain both their clothes,' said Taylor. 'Dex's and Angel's. And nothing else.'

'That's how it appears,' Mara replied.

Behind Lindi, Paulson cleared his throat impatiently.

Removing the drawer of Dex's socks and shirts altogether, Mara placed it on the carpet. Then she passed her hands along the inside surfaces of the cavity.

'Aha!' she said after a few moments had elapsed. She extended a hand. 'Clare, my lancets, please.'

It took me a minute to realise she was referring to the contents of the pouch she'd given me. I unbuckled it, the leather unfurling like a manicure kit. The kind of manicure kit that might have been used by a high-end safe breaker. Inside were several orderly rows of various metal and wooden tools, all held in place with loops of elastic.

I hadn't the faintest idea what a lancet was, so I reached for the only tools in the kit which appeared to be a pair. They consisted of short metal handles with slim pointed steel ends, like very thick pins.

Mara gave me a reassuring nod. They were indeed the lancets.

Taking one of them in each hand, sharp tips raised, she inserted them into the top of the drawer cavity. There came a muted click and then a thud, as though a little hatch had opened and something had fallen out.

My breath caught. A secret compartment.

Paulson stepped forwards, peering into the chasm between the drawers, as Mara withdrew an object. A jeweller's box, covered in velvet. Nestled inside, on a bed of ivory satin, were two elegant gold wedding bands, one sized a little larger than the other. A tiny sapphire was set into the first of them, and an orange stone in the second. Both the rings and the box looked brand new.

'Well, well,' muttered Paulson. 'What do we have here?'

But Mara wasn't finished. She reached back into the cavity and extracted something else. It was a piece of white paper. Heavier than ordinary note or printing paper, and folded quite distinctly into thirds, with an additional strip tightly turned over at one end.

Mara unfolded the paper. The inside was covered in handwriting in a dark blue ink. I craned my neck around her, catching fragments of the sentences.

> **"...when we can finally be together... properly, legally..."**

> **"...it doesn't seem like your divorce will ever happen..."**

> **"...that money will set us free..."**

"...my heart, always..."

It was a love letter.

The handwriting was upright and controlled. But there was no name, signature, or even initial, at the bottom.

'Bloody hell!' exclaimed Paulson, snatching the letter from Mara's hand and scanning the lines of ink. 'An affair! And I'm willing to bet good money that the woman who wrote this is the same woman that blonde hair belongs to. Dex Devereaux – Dodd – whatever he calls himself, bumps off the wife cos she won't give him a divorce. So he can marry his bit on the side. Takes his wife's money while he's at it, by the sounds of things. Motive. Clear as day. And old as the hills.'

We can finally be together... properly, legally.

Paulson was right. Dex had planned to marry whoever had written that letter. And what had he said when we spoke to him at Shinetree?

She'd made enough of my money vanish over the years.

I remembered how Katarina had disclosed Dex and her would be seeing each other last Sunday. I remembered how tightly he'd held her in the studio car park. And I also remembered how he'd fondled her waist on Talent Quest as she tipped back her head, shaking out her blonde hair.

Hair the very same colour and length as the strand Lindi found downstairs.

Practically bouncing on the balls of his feet, Paulson wielded the letter triumphantly. 'We've got him!'

23.

I stared at the letter, still in DI Paulson's hand. I stared at the two new wedding rings in their velvet box.

'Right then,' Paulson declared, as Lindi carefully photographed the chest and bagged the newly discovered items. 'Where'd you say Devereaux was now?'

'Local Travelodge, Sir,' DC Taylor replied.

'Let's get over there, then. Arrest the creep on suspicion of the murder of his wife.'

They followed Lindi back downstairs, leaving Mara still scrutinising the chest of drawers.

A sense of vindication settled over me. The banner; the rings; the letter mentioning divorce, money and marriage; the strand of Katarina's hair: it all painted a picture. A deeply unpleasant picture, but generally a coherent one. Dex had wanted Angel gone, had wanted their earnings to himself. Dex had wanted Katarina. She must have been in on it, or at least agreed to being locked inside that case, to make it look like Dex wasn't culpable. He had surely paid someone to help him with that part. And this was where Dex had hidden his motivation for it all. In an elaborate piece of antique furniture in his own bedroom.

'That chest is incredible,' I muttered to Mara.

My voice seemed to break her thoughts. 'It is,' she agreed. 'I examined a similar piece of furniture for Dhita a few months ago. Also with a secret compartment.'

Secret compartments, just like the bases of those teleportation boxes. Dex had hidden the wedding rings and Katarina's letter in the same way he'd hide something if he was performing a trick.

'Strange place to conceal proof that you murdered your wife... in the most conspicuous item in the whole house.' Mara's voice had lowered to almost nothing. Yet it carried an unmistakable undertone of doubt, suggesting she saw something everyone else was missing.

'But he had the means and opportunity to kill Angel,' I said, feeling the need to reinforce the obvious. 'And by finding those things we can now be sure of his motive. He was having an affair with Katarina. He wanted to marry her. But Angel wouldn't consent to a divorce. You saw how shifty he was at Shinetree. Plus, there's also the banner, ordered in Dex's name and paid for using his credit card. He even collected it himself.'

'The evidence certainly *appears* to be compelling,' Mara conceded, replacing the drawer. She glanced around the Devereauxs' bedroom, then back towards the landing. 'All I'm saying is, if I were Dex, I would have used a false name to order the banner. And chosen a different hiding place for evidence that implied I'd murdered my wife. Somewhere less prominent.'

Mara's words hung in the air. She did have a point. I again thought how impersonal the Devereauxs' house was. That carved chest of drawers would have looked much more at home at Mara's, amongst her cabinets of curiosity, fantastical props and other bizarre contraptions.

'Yeees,' I agreed slowly. 'Then again, I can't imagine that any of the other stuff in this place has secret compartments.'

A flicker of understanding crossed Mara's face, the type of quicksilver shift in her expression that was becoming familiar.

'Of course,' she breathed, shooting off along the landing. 'Right again, Clare!'

I raced after her. 'What are you thinking?'

'Thinking? Just that if Dex is guilty, there has to be more. Signs as to where he kept Angel for the week she was missing.'

Again, I thought it was obvious. 'He kept her here. That's why the house is so clean. And even if he hadn't cleaned up so well, finding traces of Angel in her own home isn't exactly incriminating.'

'Then there'll be other signs,' Mara returned. 'Minute traces of blood or skin cells on whichever implement he used to strike her, to knock her out.'

Mara had caught up with Taylor and Paulson now, who had reconvened on the Devereauxs' front path. 'Dex will have a lock-up,' she told them, 'to store his magic equipment. There's no equipment here whatsoever, and it must be somewhere. He'll be hiring some sort of storage unit. Nearby.'

'Storage unit?' Paulson repeated sceptically. 'We already have enough to make an arrest. I'm off to get Devereaux now.' He paused, thinking. 'But if there's more we can build our case with... Taylor, you go check out this lock-up.'

With that, Paulson strutted over to his car. It was parked in front of the house opposite, where the woman in the lurid pink dressing-gown was still stationed in her doorway. But rather than merely gawping at the scene, she now looked seriously annoyed.

'Hey, you!' she shouted. 'Bloody cheek!'

A beat passed before Paulson realised she was talking to him.

'I've been wondering who this thing belonged to,' she went on, thrusting her index finger towards his dusty BMW. 'You've been blocking me in.'

'Blocking you in?' He readjusted his tie, glancing uneasily around in the hope that none of his colleagues had heard. 'This is a potential murder investigation, Madam—'

'Blocking a driveway's still a civil offence. I've a good mind to report you to the police—'

As the woman across the road continued her tirade, Taylor made a call to the station. He asked them to check the bank statements of Dex's they'd pulled yesterday, when they had verified his credit card payment to Presto Print.

'You were right again,' Taylor told Mara as he ended the call, gazing at her as though impressed. 'Dex pays a regular monthly amount to a self-storage facility just outside Morden.' His phone pinged. 'And I've got the address and number of his lock-up right here.'

The facility was a drab affair, around a ten-minute drive south of the Devereauxs' house. Rather than being one of those new places with rows of well-lit secure rooms arranged on various floors, these units were more like garages, their slightly battered metal doors lining the sides of a small maze of alleyways. DC Taylor, Mara and I, accompanied by two police constables, negotiated our way around these alleys until we located Dex's lock-up.

Taylor had a copy of the key, obtained when he'd brandished his badge at the security guard in the front kiosk. He inserted it into the unit's lock, turned the handle, and hauled up its door.

'Lights!' Mara announced, reaching for the switch.

A single plastic strip light, its casing clustered with dead flies, droned slowly into life. The space it illuminated was crowded with equipment. There were lengths of velvet printed with crescent moons, wheeled suitcases and clothing bagged in plastic, hanging on portable metal rails. There were piles of ropes and black bin bags. The two large boxes against the right-hand wall looked very much like the ones Dex had used for his teleportation illusion. There were also stacks and stacks of misshapen cardboard boxes, their outsides scrawled with labels hand-written in black Sharpie.

Hand Chopper

Assistant's Revenge

Daggers and Spikes

'Whoa,' said Taylor. 'A killer who labels the evidence.'

I laughed a little too hard. Especially given the circumstances. Mara raised one of her perfectly shaped eyebrows at me.

'Let's start at the front and work towards the back,' Taylor said. 'We can stack the stuff we've gone over out here.'

We stepped inside the unit, where the air smelt

overwhelmingly damp. The constables began methodically moving objects and opening boxes as I hovered next to Mara, feeling like I shouldn't be touching anything. Clutching her leather pouch of tools, I tried to look useful.

Everyone worked meticulously for over an hour, and a collection of top hat boxes, glow-in-the-dark paint, and wooden components of varying colours amassed just outside the lock-up's door. The middle of the space had been cleared, with the remainder of the stored equipment stacked around the edges. I watched as the younger of the two police constables made his way towards a tower of solid-looking boxes nearer the back of the unit, decorated in starburst-shaped stickers.

The constable opened the topmost box first. It was empty, its interior a yawning black hole. He began probing around inside this space with a gloved hand.

'Last one looked empty,' he muttered to his colleague. 'Turned out it contained two mirrors, a fake dove and a string of sausages—'

All of a sudden, the man issued an almighty shriek and leapt backwards as a truly horrible spectacle unfolded before us. Inside the once-empty box, a large ovoid mass swivelled rapidly to face us. Literally *face* us.

It was a human head.

Its glassy eyes were wide and fixed, its deathly pallor bearing a corpse's clamminess. And its hair, like Angel's... like Katarina's... was *blonde*.

'Oh my God,' I gasped, my stomach lurching.

'Sir!' The constable yelled to DC Taylor, who had gone outside to take a call. 'You need to see this!'

'No need to panic,' Mara said, stepping calmly forwards to peer at the contents of the box, 'she isn't real.' She reached inside and carefully lifted out the head. 'Moulded latex. And an extremely good likeness of Angel. Specially made for one of the Devereauxs' illusions, obviously.'

Mara upended the prop, showing the hollow cavity at the neck where the mechanism fitted to allow the head to rotate.

'You look like you need a drink,' Taylor said, patting the still-rattled constable on the shoulder.

Mara spun away to continue searching, but Taylor gently touched her arm. 'That was the station on the phone,' he said. 'They've started to question Dex, but he isn't talking. He's already denied knowing anything about the rings or the love letter, and he says the hair could have come from anywhere. Which, in fairness, it could. He's now started to "no comment".'

'No Commenters are *always* guilty,' I said, forgetting my knowledge of police procedure came primarily from Netflix box sets, when I was standing with people who did this for a living. I felt my cheeks colour.

Taylor smiled. 'Well, we've a limited time we can hold Dex for, before deciding whether we have the evidence to go ahead and charge him. If we could find anything concrete amongst the stuff left here, it could really help.'

Mara moved in the direction of the large black boxes. 'I'm going to check the teleportation trick again,' she said.

I followed, as she began tracing a fingertip along the box's metal framework.

'So Dex got the boxes back, then?' I asked. 'Like he wanted?'

'He was certainly very keen to have his props returned when we spoke to him at the studio,' Mara confirmed. 'Though every magician's protective of their equipment, naturally.'

'I think they were dropped off here late Sunday. Lindi had finished with them by then,' said Taylor, as he determinedly pulled what looked like a never-ending length of bunting from a tube.

Mara paused and glanced towards him. 'Flags of the World,' she remarked. 'Just to warn you, Luke, there are two hundred and fifty-four of those things. With the last one being a Union Jack shaped like a pair of underpants.'

Taylor shrugged, and I watched him continue to withdraw and examine each flag. When, after a few moments, I transferred my attention back to Mara, I saw she was preoccupied by a very specific point on one of the boxes.

'Is that...?' I murmured.

'Yes,' she said. 'It's the box Angel fell from. Torch?'

I was getting used to this now. I hurriedly unrolled her leather pouch and located a slim Maglite, the same green as Mara's coat.

She flicked it on and aimed its light at one of the vertical edges of the box. 'Do you see that?'

I knelt beside her, seeing nothing. Then, as Mara ran the torch beam along the dark metal, my eyes registered a small indentation. It was no bigger than a fingernail.

'It's a chip,' said Mara. 'It's been painted over. And recently, by the looks of it.'

She was right. It wasn't completely flawless, but whoever had touched up the damage had done a pretty good job, matching the hue of the new black paint to the original almost exactly.

I assumed it must have been Dex, that his prop had somehow got chipped and he'd filled it in with a drop of enamel paint. But a quality to Mara's voice tightened a small knot of unease inside me.

'This has been done deliberately. To try and cover something up.'

24.♠

'I should have noticed this when I was at the studio,' said Mara, shaking her head.

The box's painted-over chip lingered under the torchlight, a tiny imperfection marring the otherwise smooth framework.

'But as soon as you came across the blood in the base, Lindi had to step in and swab it,' I countered.

Mara, however, was still annoyed with herself.

'You think it was Dex who covered the damage?' I asked. 'It must have been—'

'Sir!' The older of the constables called to DC Taylor, who was still patiently unfurling the Flags of the World bunting. 'What's the betting the Guv would make short work of these, eh?' The man rattled the can he was holding. It was labelled: "Roasted Peanuts".

Although DI Paulson wasn't overweight, it was true that whenever we saw him, he did always seem to be eating.

The constable flipped the lid off the can and almost left his skin as, with a loud and comical *boing*, a four-foot long spring snake was unleashed into the air. The snake whizzed across the lock-up and arced dramatically downwards, disappearing behind a stack of boxes which nobody had yet searched.

Still positioned by the teleportation illusion, I was the closest to where the errant snake had landed, so I nudged myself into the gap behind the boxes to retrieve it. Bending down to gather up the spring and paper reptile in my hands, an object lying crookedly across the floor snagged my attention.

I pulled the sleeve of my jumper down over my hand to avoid contaminating the item with my fingerprints and picked it up. It was a smartphone, its dark screen blank. A black leather case fitting snugly around the phone was the kind that also held bank cards. Taking in the name printed across the top of these, I swallowed hard.

Discarding the snake on the lid of the nearest box, I held the phone up. 'Er, I just found this. When I got the snake. It was on the floor, behind those boxes. It looked like it'd been dropped down there.'

The Hungarian flag dangled limply from Taylor's fingers. 'Could it be Dex's?'

'No,' I replied, trying to keep my voice even. 'I think it's Angel's.'

Taylor and I exchanged a look. I passed the phone to him.

With gloved hands, he turned the mobile over, then briefly depressed the power button. 'It's off,' he said. 'Or else the battery's dead.'

'Given how long Angel was missing, it's likely been off for a while,' Mara commented. 'Which explains why trying to track her phone signal was a dead end.'

So Angel's phone had been here the whole time, hidden amidst the multitude of Dex's magic props. Were Mara's earlier suspicions correct... was *this* where Angel had been kept the week she was missing? And did that also mean the weapon Dex had used to strike her was here somewhere too?

Taylor pressed the power button again, for longer this time, and the phone's screen flooded with light. After a few seconds, a prompt showed, asking for the pin to be entered.

'Damn, it's protected,' said Taylor, frustrated. 'Not surprising, but having Digital Forensics unlock this may not be quick.'

Mara stepped closer to him, peering at the screen with its patterning of smudges and fingerprints. She read out the words showing across the bottom of it. '"Unlock using biometric data".'

There was a pause.

'I can unlock it for you now,' she said.

A thought rippled through my head: that she must have somehow got hold of one of Angel's fingerprints, too, just like she had Richie's at the prison. It wouldn't have surprised me if Mara Knight was a one-woman, mobile fingerprint database.

Taylor appeared momentarily thrown, contemplating Mara's offer. 'Without Angel Devereaux's fingerprint, I don't see how you can,' he said.

'"Unlock using biometric data",' Mara repeated. This time she let the sentence hover there.

It was only when she strode towards the box covered in its starburst-shaped stickers that I realised what she was about to do.

The latex head.

Just when you thought Mara's methods couldn't get any more ingenious, she would come up with something totally left-field. It was certainly one up on using a fingerprint.

Mara extracted the latex head from the box and brought it

over to where Taylor and I were standing.

'Switch it on again and hold it up,' she told Taylor, who was still clutching Angel's mobile.

He did as she instructed and, as the constables looked on in astonishment, Mara positioned the head — the exact replica of Angel — face-to-face with the phone screen.

Despite the object being fake and the phone potentially containing evidence that could prove vital to the investigation, it was a morbid thing to watch. I couldn't help but think that the last person to unlock the phone this way had been a living and breathing Angel, and I was caught by another wave of despondency that we'd been too late to prevent her awful demise. Perhaps I should have focused more on Dex all along.

For a heart-stopping fraction of a second, nothing happened. Then the lock screen disappeared and the home screen took its place, playing a generic animation on repeat. A swirling pattern of blue waves and orange flames.

'Huh, incredible!' Taylor remarked, impressed by Mara once more. He began swiping through the contents of Angel's phone.

The apps installed on it all looked to be pretty standard: messaging, news, banking, a calendar. The social media apps weren't particularly illuminating, either. They were logged in to Angel and Dex's joint work accounts, which police had already trawled. The direct message folders of those accounts were a mixed bag. Some followers wrote to the Devereauxs in amazement, having just seen them perform a certain trick and swearing they had witnessed real magic. Others begged Dex to tell them how such-and-such an illusion was done, adamant they couldn't rest until it was revealed to them. Then there was the last camp: the people who'd got in touch with the sole purpose of informing the Devereauxs they'd worked out *exactly* how their tricks were done.

'Typical magic fan mail,' tutted Mara. 'They're always wrong.'

'Those people who claim to know how the tricks are done?' I asked.

Mara looked at me askance. 'No,' she returned. 'All of them.'

Taylor clicked in and out of a few more apps and folders, but there appeared to be nothing on Angel's phone that offered a definitive clue as to who was responsible for her death.

'How about checking her photos?' I suggested.

Taylor gave a nod and navigated to Angel's gallery. It was surprisingly sparse compared to my own, stuffed, as mine was, with photos of Jasper demonstrating his wide repertoire of frankly adorable poses. Indeed, there was only a handful of pictures in Angel Devereaux's gallery in total.

Taylor tapped on the first photograph, and a shot of two portions of fish and chips filled the screen, the edges of the paper that held them bending as though being blown by the wind. Accompanying this image were several others that seemed equally unremarkable. A photo of the stubs of two theatre tickets, placed side-by-side. A photo taken in a park, of two takeaway cups of hot chocolate laden with whipped cream and sprinkles. And a pair of metal funfair tokens, cupped in Angel's hand.

They looked like typical "couple photos", snapshots of shared moments in the lives of two people. Yet there was an odd formality about them, a sense of restraint.

'Must be from dates that Angel went on with Dex,' said

Taylor.

He clicked through the remaining pictures. There were a few shots of performance venues, close-ups of costume details, props and equipment. The last image of them all had been taken far longer ago than the rest. It was a photograph of Angel at school.

Though she couldn't have been older than sixteen in the picture, Angel's lithe, slight frame and heart-shaped face were unmistakable. But it was odd to see her with her natural hair colour, her signature bleach-blonde bouffant replaced by a curly dark mane spilling over her shoulders.

She was dressed in school uniform: a flared skirt, white shirt beneath a v-neck sweater, blazer embroidered with a bird emblem. But whereas the girl in the background of the picture wore her blazer straight and buttoned-up, Angel's was tied by its arms around her middle. Her white shirt was untucked, her jumper askew on her shoulders. She was posing exuberantly for the camera, hips tilted, one hand on her waist, the other extended into the air, fingers splayed across a fanned deck of playing cards in a curving "*ta-da!*" It was as though she was on stage, even then.

I felt a sudden surge of grief at how her life had ended; that child with the entire, yawning span of hopes and dreams ahead of her.

The other girl looked on as the sun shone down on them both, leaking into the camera lens and hazing the scene.

After a few moments, Taylor exited the gallery. 'I'll just check her videos as well.'

Aside from a few videos of Angel proudly displaying

numerous props and demonstrating illusion parts, there was nothing striking. Lastly, Taylor clicked onto Angel's voice notes.

A couple of files were listed here, mostly with the names of the tricks the notes related to, or else saved under a default date and time stamp.

One of the files, however, stood out from the rest.

Mara spotted it first. '"TQ convo",' she read.

'Talent Quest convo?' I asked, my pulse quickening a little.

Taylor's finger tapped the play icon.

The recording was clearly covert; the two voices on it initially muffled by background noise. Even when they weren't, the sound quality indicated that, as the recording was made, the phone was concealed. Or maybe held discreetly.

'...remarkable, Angel. Truly.' It was a man's voice, oily and familiar.

'Thank you,' Angel replied. Her words were louder than the man's, as though she was right on top of the phone. She also sounded guarded, forcing brightness.

'No, I mean it,' the man continued. 'You have a... natural talent. Something *very* special.' His words drawled, becoming louder. Perhaps he was edging closer to the phone. To Angel.

A beat passed.

'Proactive Productions is always looking for fresh talent,' the man said.

There was a creak, as though someone had sat down. A shuffle, like the other person was inching away from them. Or was I imagining it?

'We could do great things together, you and I. If you play your cards right.'

'What are you suggesting?' said Angel, her voice enquiring but tinged with unease.

'Just that... opportunities arise. For those willing to grasp them. A woman like you... you deserve more than him... and nobody need ever know. Certainly not your husband...'

'Well, I...' Angel responded, laughing awkwardly.

The man echoed her with a low, smooth laugh of his own. 'All I'm saying, sweetheart... is that if you *don't* do what I'm suggesting, you may find you regret it... A performer... dying on stage. It's always superb for the ratings—'

The recording ended abruptly, its closing words weighing the lock-up's musty air, heavy with menace. Everyone was completely still. Even the two constables had stopped searching to listen. Taylor let out a low whistle.

'*Shane Sinclair,*' I breathed. 'That was Shane Sinclair propositioning Angel, *threatening* her. Threatening to kill her if she didn't... what, sleep with him? God, I wonder if Dex knew?'

Taylor's eyes narrowed in thought.

I felt sick. Not only had Angel been married to a chauvinistic sleaze, here she was having her life threatened by one too. And Shane Sinclair wasn't just a slimy misogynist; he was one of the most powerful men in the British media. It was little wonder Angel was deemed difficult. What other agency could she possibly clutch at, when it was being eroded on all fronts by the men she came up against?

It was then that I noticed how pale Mara had become, how detached and pained her expression as she stared off into the distance, at a point beyond the lock-up doors.

'Mara, you okay?' Taylor asked.

Mara gave an extended, controlled exhale, regaining a little of her composure. 'Angel recorded this for a reason,' she said slowly. 'Shane Sinclair has a reputation.'

'Angel recorded it because she felt threatened,' I blurted, not stopping to absorb her last statement. 'So she had evidence of what Shane was really like. Of the threats he was making. What else could she do?'

'It does sound like the two of them were alone when this was made,' Taylor chipped in, picking up the thread. 'But did Sinclair then act out on those threats? By murdering Angel and framing Dex?'

'He's always been a master of controlling the narrative,' Mara said gravely. There was the tiniest break in her voice.

So,' I started, looking between them both. 'Are we now saying it's Shane Sinclair? That *he's* Angel's killer?'

25.♠

Since there was nothing else of interest at the lock-up, Mara and I left while the police stayed on to ensure that Angel's phone was bagged, the Devereauxs' stuff replaced and the unit secured. Although the phone was a crucial find, it was frustrating that something more hadn't been unearthed among the magic paraphernalia, something else that could have helped definitively fill out the missing pieces of this increasingly bewildering puzzle.

'Annoying there was no sign of any weapon,' I said to Mara, as we emerged from the alleyways of the lock-up facility and onto the main road. I'd parked down a side street off this road, but as we started back towards it, a shower of spring rain began beating down around us.

I increased my pace in order to reach the car quicker. But when I turned around, Mara was no longer with me. Ducking out of the rain, she was swinging open the door of the nearest pub.

Inside, Mara still seemed a little off. She asked for a large vodka tonic, downing it quickly before ordering food. We took some more drinks from the bar and settled ourselves at a table in the corner. Despite it being lunchtime, the place was fairly quiet.

'Are you alright?' I asked, repeating Taylor's question. The change in Mara, which she was clearly trying to hide, appeared to have been brought about by that recording on Angel's phone.

'Mmm,' she murmured noncommittally.

'It's just... you don't seem yourself.'

Mara didn't reply.

I shifted in my seat, glancing through the window at the rain streaming down the glass. A few minutes passed.

'I know we just discovered quite an incriminating recording,' I said, at last. 'But I was hoping there would have been more at the lock-up. The object used to knock Angel out. Traces of blood or skin cells on it, like you said.'

Mara took a long swig of her wine. 'Not to mention fingerprints,' I continued. 'The fingerprints left behind on that object by the person who used it to strike Angel.'

'But was that person Dex or Shane?'

Rather than the contents of Angel's phone filling out the investigation with new and vital details, it felt like it'd been fractured instead. There now appeared to be *two* suspects. Two men with means, motive and opportunity.

Could Shane Sinclair have orchestrated Angel's disappearance and death, ensuring that it happened in the most public, ratings-grabbing way possible, while simultaneously framing Dex? If we *had* found a weapon at Dex's lock-up, Shane could well have planted it there. Mara had said he was a master of controlling a narrative. And he was a media mogul, motivated by popularity and turnover, and the power both those things brought him. A power that came only from people watching his shows.

A performer dying on stage... superb for the ratings.

Dex had said it himself. *Bet Shane's lapping all this publicity up.*

But Shane also took great pains to come across in the press as a loving family man, a loyal husband and devoted father to his two teenage daughters.

Nobody need ever know. Certainly not your husband.

'That thing you said in the lock-up, about Shane having a reputation,' I exclaimed, suddenly remembering. 'What did you mean?'

Did Mara have some insider knowledge about Shane Sinclair that I wasn't aware of? Had he made a pass at *her*, even, in the past? Threatened her in some way?

Mara said nothing for a moment, as though attempting to formulate an answer.

'Oh, just that it's an open secret in the entertainment world,' she responded eventually. 'The man's known for trying to have his way with every attractive woman who crosses his path.'

I still didn't think this fully explained Mara's reaction in the lock-up. And as damning as that recording of Shane Sinclair was, there remained aspects of Angel's death that didn't make sense. The banner being ordered by Dex on Dex's credit card, for one thing.

'If Shane framed Dex,' I said, 'then could he have got Dex's credit card details when the Devereauxs were at the studio filming Talent Quest? Maybe he snuck into their dressing room or something?'

'Shane Sinclair's famous,' Mara countered. 'And he has a

very distinctive look. A little too distinctive to go creeping into dressing rooms unnoticed. Especially in a busy studio.'

'Then perhaps he had one of his crew get Dex's card details when the Devereauxs were busy? An assistant?'

'Plausible,' Mara replied. 'But the more people involved in the details of a murder, the more layers of complexity are added. The more scope there is for things to go wrong, for the perpetrators to be discovered, for secrets to be revealed. Sinclair must have engineered it some other way.'

We sat in silence awhile, as the revelations of the past few days clicked through my brain.

'Do you think Dex really did want to marry Katarina?' I asked Mara. 'Might he have wanted a divorce, only for Angel to refuse?'

But this line of thought led us straight back to Dex Devereaux being our primary suspect. And given the recording we'd found on Angel's phone little more than an hour ago, Dex's guilt didn't now seem quite as clear-cut.

From the depths of my handbag, my phone's text notification sounded. I ignored it.

'But would Angel have refused a divorce?' Mara took another large throatful of wine and closed her eyes. 'There's something in that.'

'Yes, and Dex hiding those rings and that letter in the most obvious piece of furniture in his house does feel *too* convenient,' I tacked on.

The case was becoming frustratingly, maddeningly confusing. I desperately wanted to help work out what had happened to Angel, and so far, I thought, I had. I'd helped to find

Katarina; had figured out that banner came from Presto Print; had also located Angel's missing phone. These all felt like key pieces of the investigation that could yet lead to Angel's killer. Could provide a resolution to the case of a previously missing woman, a resolution I hadn't been able to find following my mum's disappearance—

A woman arrived at the next table and, apparently oblivious to my proximity to her, shook out her umbrella. Droplets of rain soaked my leg. I slammed down my glass harder than I intended and swore under my breath.

Across the table, Mara opened her eyes, observing me coolly before addressing the woman. 'Do you mind?'

'Oh, sorry,' the woman replied, realising what she'd done. She squinted at us through a long, thick fringe. 'Didn't see you there, love.'

Mara grabbed a handful of serviettes from the neighbouring condiments station and passed them to me.

I dabbed my jeans sulkily. 'I don't... I don't know what to make of it all now,' I mumbled, once a few minutes had elapsed. 'I thought we had a clear suspect in Dex, were getting close to discovering what happened to Angel. But with that recording, I'm not so sure...'

'A lot of the evidence pointing to Dex feels like misdirection,' Mara said quietly. 'Like the real action is happening elsewhere. And for different reasons entirely. And right now I'd say that action was with Shane Sinclair.' Her expression darkened. 'Take it from someone who knows.'

It was Mara's unique understanding of the art of deception that had prompted me to reach out to her in the first place, had led me down this path. But I couldn't help feeling she knew more about Shane Sinclair than she was letting on.

Another phone notification sounded. This time, Mara fished her mobile from her pocket and studied the screen.

'Bingo, they've taken Sinclair in for questioning,' she said. 'Let's go to the station and see what he has to say for himself.'

26.♠

'Go to the station? We're allowed to just waltz in there and oversee a murder investigation, then?'

Mara's eyes scanned me, a faint trace of amusement returning to them following our regrouping in the pub. 'Well, *I* am.' She began walking in the direction of my car, her posture less tense than it had been earlier. 'Come on,' she called over her shoulder. 'I'm sure we can work out a way to get you inside.'

As I followed her along the pavement, dodging in and out of other pedestrians as I went, I reached into my bag for my phone. The earlier notification had been a message from Jeff.

Clare, need you back here pronto. Big story breaking – local cat stuck up council Christmas tree (in March!). Cat's called Tinkerbell. This is priceless. Needs your touch.

I sighed, shoving the phone back in my bag without replying. Cover the story of a cat stuck up a tree or continue to assist with the investigation into a previously missing woman's murder; a murder that had gone out live on television? It wasn't much of a choice, but still, I tried not to think what Jeff would say if he realised what I was up to. He was covering the Angel Devereaux story himself. If I approached him with what I now knew about the case, it would feel wrong. And not just since I was certain he would take those details, those potentially vital clues, and splash them across the Mercury's pages as part of his own story. This wasn't about simply covering a story to me. It never had been.

The rain had eased to a drizzle before we left the pub, and the drive to the station was accompanied by the intermittent swing of my windscreen wipers. As I crawled along in the midweek, midday traffic, Mara told me more about the message she'd received. It was from DC Taylor, and DI Paulson had asked him to send it.

I wondered why Paulson suddenly wanted Mara around when, despite the progress she — and I — had made over the past few days, her presence seemed to irritate him so much.

'Graham's interviewing Shane Sinclair as we speak,' said Mara.

'But he's not been arrested?'

'No. Dex is the one under arrest. Sinclair is merely assisting the police with their enquiries,' she replied, adding enigmatically, 'at present.'

In the station reception, the man on the desk buzzed through to tell Paulson that Mara had arrived. As I still didn't have a clue whether I'd be allowed any further, I began preparing myself for a disappointing return to the office. I thought I should come up with as many cat/tree-related puns for Jeff's latest story as possible. Could *"Feline Fir-asco"* work? Or perhaps *"Local cat needs de-tree-ment"* was better? Or how about *"Cat pines for solid ground—?"*

'Hi, both.'

My mental spiral of awful wordplay was broken by Taylor's voice.

'The DI wants to see you after he's finished with Sinclair,' he told Mara. 'That okay?'

'Of course,' Mara replied, flashing him an unusually vibrant smile.

Taylor appeared temporarily dazzled, and I felt the dimmest tinge of resentment that *I* didn't have that effect on anyone.

'I hope you don't mind if Clare comes too?' said Mara. 'She's continuing to work with me on this one.'

'Sure,' Taylor replied. 'I'll just arrange a pass.'

'I'll help with Shane Sinclair any way I can,' Mara told him. 'You know that.'

Her words threw me slightly, again hinting that something else had gone on — was *going on* — between Mara and Shane than met the eye. What did she mean?

Taylor fiddled about for a second, attempting to insert my printed-out visitor's pass into its little plastic wallet. 'It's actually not about Sinclair,' he said. 'It's about the CCTV from Shinetree. One or two interesting things came up when our team went through it. It was recommended to the DI that he ask your opinion.'

'Recommended by DCI Anand?' asked Mara.

Taylor smiled. 'Yup.'

He handed the pass to me, and I pinned it on my jacket.

'Bet that pleased Graham,' said Mara.

Taylor sucked in his breath. 'To be honest, things aren't going great with Sinclair.'

'He's not talking,' Mara stated.

'Nope. And he has a high-powered lawyer in tow as well.'

'High-powered lawyer.' Mara scowled. 'Why am I not surprised?'

We were led down a corridor smelling faintly of disinfectant and instant coffee, stopping outside a door marked "Observation Room One".

'In here,' Taylor said, holding the door open for us.

The room was dim and windowless, dominated by a large pane of glass set into the far wall; a two-way mirror onto the interview room. I'd assumed that if we watched Shane's police interview at all, it would be on monitors, so I was slightly stunned at this kind of set-up, which I'd only ever seen on US crime dramas before. It was a little eerie, voyeuristic to be observing Shane Sinclair on the other side of the glass, drenched in the harsh fluorescent lights of the interview room. He was unnervingly composed, dressed in an expensive-looking cashmere sweater, his tan rendering his teeth a startling and unnatural white.

Shane sat mostly unmoving, a sharp-featured woman in an equally high-end outfit occasionally leaning across to confer with him. His lawyer, presumably.

Opposite them, Paulson was hunched over the tabletop, his rough-and-ready air contrasting sharply with Shane Sinclair's polish.

Taylor switched on the speakers. 'Not sure how much you've heard from DCI Anand,' he whispered to Mara, picking up from earlier. 'But the DI's getting nowhere fast. Not with Dex and now not with Sinclair. It's a high-profile case, and he's the SIO.

You can imagine...'

'He wants an arrest that sticks, and soon,' Mara commented.

As she said this, Shane Sinclair glanced up at the glass and smirked, his eyes landing directly on mine. Unsettled, I looked quickly away.

In the interview room, Paulson angled himself forwards. 'Mr Sinclair, I'll return, if I may, to that recording I played to you earlier, the one found on Angel Devereaux's phone. On that recording, Mrs Devereaux appeared to sound uncomfortable, threatened. While you seemed to suggest that her life would be in danger if she failed to cooperate with you.'

Before Shane could answer, his lawyer cut in smoothly. 'Detective Inspector, my client has already stated that his words have been taken entirely out of context. He was purely expressing professional admiration for Mrs Devereaux and suggesting potential career avenues.'

'*Potential career avenues?*' Paulson scoffed. '"A performer dying on stage... superb for the ratings." That sounds pretty specific to me.'

'A figure of speech,' Shane's lawyer clipped back. 'Nothing more. The recording's muffled, with huge gaps missing where it's inaudible. I would suggest that both of those things prevent an understanding of the actual context of the conversation.'

There was a silence.

I hadn't expected Shane Sinclair to say anything during the interview, but he opened his mouth then, voice oozing a practised charm. 'As my lawyer says, it was simply a figure of speech. Show business is a dramatic world. Angel understood that. She was a talented woman, far more so than her husband, frankly. I saw potential, offered guidance. Perhaps she misinterpreted my intentions, just as you are doing now.' He spread his hands, a gesture of injured innocence.

Misinterpreted or not, Angel still felt threatened enough by Shane to make that recording in the first place, I thought.

His lawyer shot him a look, as if to convey he shouldn't be speaking at all. Sinclair missed it, however, meeting my eye through the glass for a second time, an expression of seedy admiration on his face.

'And the timing?' Paulson pressed. 'Of your private meeting with Angel Devereaux—?'

'You've no way of proving it was private,' interrupted the lawyer. 'My client has informed me there were members of his production staff present.'

The corners of Paulson's moustache twitched irritably. 'Even if that was the case, your "guidance",' he bent his fingers in the air as if to indicate speech marks, 'happened just days before Angel Devereaux disappeared, little more than a week before she turned up again dead on your biggest show. Given what we *can* hear being said on that recording, you have to admit it's quite a coincidence?'

'Exactly that. A dreadful *coincidence*,' said the lawyer, answering Paulson's question.

Sinclair looked at me yet again and gave his creepy smirk.

'Why does he keep doing that?' I muttered to Mara. 'Smirking at me? It's freaking me out.'

'It's a two-way mirror,' Mara retorted, reminding me what I'd already forgotten. 'He's not casting you admiring glances, Clare, he's admiring himself.'

Mara's words were sharper than usual, sharper than they needed to be, and I felt silly to have misconstrued the action. Why would Shane Sinclair be looking at me? He was a man intoxicated by himself; his image, his power. A man bold and unpleasant enough to make the kinds of threats we'd heard on that recording.

The interview room lapsed into silence again.

'I can't see us getting much more out of him,' Taylor whispered.

Just as he said this, Shane opened his mouth. 'I can't clarify this matter any more than I already have. Dex was a middle-of-the-road performer. Tired. Dated. And I admit it, I only invited him back on the show after his wife disappeared since I thought it would be good for the ratings. When I said "a performer dying on stage", I didn't mean it in the literal sense. I meant "dying on stage" as in a performer messing up, their act going badly, unexpectedly wrong. You must have seen my shows. Public embarrassments, unforeseen happenings. Car crash television. It's what my audiences tune in for.'

So Shane hadn't literally been threatening Angel's life; was that what he was now claiming? That he'd instead threatened to make her look like a bad performer on Talent Quest if she didn't succumb to his advances?

It was at this point that I became aware of Mara's increasingly erratic breathing. Her hands, I saw, had formed rigid fists at her cuffs. Taylor reached out and touched her arm, causing my attention to snap back to Shane.

'I'm in the media, Detective Inspector. It's what I do. I provide entertainment,' Shane went on. 'There's no law against giving the public what they want to see.'

'I hardly think they want to see a woman falling to her death while they're chowing down on their Saturday night takeaway,' Paulson snapped.

'Obviously, I had no idea that was going to happen,' said Shane. 'Angel's death was a complete tragedy. I told you. Dex was old hat. He had minimal talent in his field, and what he had passed its sell-by-date in the nineties. Angel was the real star of that double act. She performed with far more skill than her husband. I'd watched her—'

'What my client means is that he was present at some of the Devereauxs' rehearsals,' the lawyer clarified hastily.

Shane Sinclair, realising it wasn't in his interests to keep talking, ran a hand through his hair and checked his watch. It was the manner less of a man being questioned about a murder and more like one waiting for a tedious meeting to end.

She performed with far more skill than her husband. I'd watched her.

27.♠

'Interview ended at 16:34,' huffed Paulson, stopping the recording.

On the other side of the two-way mirror, Shane Sinclair's face radiated a smug self-assurance.

'Looks like that's it, then,' said Taylor, flicking off the speakers. 'The DI will have to let him go now. We don't have enough to make an arrest.'

'Yet the recording seemed so clear-cut,' I said. 'That Shane was making a threat on Angel's life. The recording proved he'd followed through with that threat.'

Taylor's lips tightened. 'Yes, but... inaudible sections, figures of speech, words potentially taken out of context... It's all plausible deniability, as Sinclair's lawyer pointed out. In addition, he's claiming there were production staff present when he had the conversation with Angel. It wouldn't be difficult for him to find someone willing to back that up. It does feel like there's currently more evidence against Dex...'

I didn't know what to think. A man who'd killed his wife so he could marry someone else, or a man who'd engineered a woman's death to boost his ratings? It seemed like we were dangerously close to being back at square one. Like the real action, as Mara had said, was happening elsewhere.

Speaking of Mara, though she continued to claim she was fine, she hadn't uttered a word since we left the observation room.

'You alright to come see that CCTV footage from Shinetree?' Taylor asked her, to which she nodded in response.

He led us down a succession of corridors until we ran, headlong, into Paulson. The DI was pacing up and down, taking out his post-interview frustration on a substantial packet of Monster Munch.

'Knight,' Paulson said. 'And you again,' he added, registering me hovering beside Mara.

'Where's this CCTV footage?' Mara clipped, cutting straight to it.

Paulson indicated to Taylor, who swung open a large door at the end of the corridor. We passed through it into a sizeable office, dotted inside of which were about ten plain-clothed detectives. Some were on their phones, while others juggled manilla files, or else sat studiously clicking away on computers.

Paulson led us between one of the many rows of desks in the office. He gestured again to Taylor, who took a seat in the furthest chair and typed something on the keyboard in front of it. His computer screen brightened, displaying two separate folders.

'All the clips recovered from the CCTV cameras at Shinetree,' Taylor clarified. 'On Saturday the 15th and Saturday the 22nd of March, the two nights the Devereauxs performed on Talent Quest.'

Mara took a seat next to Taylor, with Paulson flanking his

other side. I tried my best to crane for a view of the screen in between their heads, desperate to see whatever it was the police had found on that footage.

Taylor navigated to the folder dated the 22nd of March. Last Saturday. 'First interesting thing was this—'

But Paulson cut him off. 'That's *not* why we asked Knight to come in,' he barked. 'You're in the wrong folder.'

Taylor's finger hesitated above the mouse button. 'I just thought... that being familiar with Proactive Productions and knowing the kinds of people who hang around the variety scene... well, that Mara might recognise him?'

So they'd found someone on the footage. Someone new. A man, at the studio, the night Angel died. A man behaving suspiciously, by the sounds of it. Why else would they want to identify him?

Then the rest of Taylor's words sank in. 'Wait — you know Proactive Productions?' I asked Mara, surprised.

She toyed uneasily with a stack of letterheaded paper on the desk next to her, her face shadowing. 'I do.'

'Then you know Shane Sinclair?'

'For my sins.'

On some level, it seemed like I'd known Mara forever, and I had to remind myself that it had only been four days. I hadn't a clue who she was, not really, even though I felt as if I did. She was like a lagoon; ancient yet newly discovered. And though the water's surface might be smooth, it was utterly impossible to see into its depths. Occasionally, you might catch a glimpse of something, but before you had the chance to understand it properly, it was gone.

I recalled what Mara had told me in the pub. When she'd mentioned Shane's reputation, she hadn't just been speaking from the point of view of a stranger; she actually *knew* him.

Take it from someone who knows.

I wondered again whether she'd ever been on the receiving end of his advances, his threats—

There was an awkward silence. Taylor darted Mara a concerned glance.

'Shane Sinclair knew my husband,' Mara muttered, apparently uncomfortable at having to explain herself. 'Proactive Productions made a number of Travers's TV specials.'

'Including the last one—' Paulson began, before stopping abruptly. He faltered for a moment, then shoved the last couple of maize monster feet into his mouth.

In an instant, it all became clear. Why Mara had been so out-of-sorts since listening to that recording in the lock-up. Why she'd made a beeline for the pub. Why her tongue had been so sharp as we watched Shane Sinclair's interview, heard those things he was saying.

Public embarrassments, unforeseen happenings. Car crash television. It's what my audiences tune in for.

That's what Mara had really meant by Shane's reputation: that he was notorious for pursuing ratings above all else. And his company had made Travers's final TV special. *Buried Alive.* It was the last time Mara's husband had ever been seen. Travers was supposed to have been inside that coffin, but it was empty... one of Shane's "unforeseen happenings".

I shakily let out a breath I hadn't realised I'd been holding. Did this fact alone imply that Shane Sinclair was still our prime suspect for the murder of Angel Devereaux? Travers. Angel. Katarina. Three performers who had gone missing on Shane's shows. And now one of them was dead.

'Shall we get on?' Mara forced unsteadily.

Paulson's chewing slowed at Mara's tone. 'Well, go on, then,' he garbled to Taylor through his mouthful of crisps. 'Show it to her.'

His detective constable finally double-clicked the mouse button. A new window opened, and a grainy clip began to play. 'This was recorded at 20:19 precisely,' said Taylor. 'Little more than a minute after Angel fell to her death.'

It was dark by 20:19 last Saturday, so the monochrome security footage was illuminated from above by a single electric light. It had been taken from a camera placed high on the side of the building, its lens focused on a plain wooden door. With Talent Quest in progress, the outside of the studio appeared deserted.

'That's the left far side entrance into the Talent Quest studio,' murmured Mara.

'It is,' Taylor replied. 'Watch what happens next.'

Suddenly, the door burst open, swinging back on its hinges and crashing into the wall, as a figure darted from the studio, vanishing out of shot in the bottom left corner of the screen. Only perhaps "darting" was the wrong way to describe how that figure moved. It would have been more accurate to say the man lurched forwards so clumsily it looked like he might at any moment trip over his own feet.

I watched as Taylor replayed the couple of seconds of footage. A man, making off at such speed, less than a minute after Angel's fall. 'He *has* to know something about Angel's death,' I said. 'Doesn't he?'

After he'd let the short clip run a few more times, Taylor pressed pause and zoomed in. The unknown man filled his computer screen. At that size, the image was incredibly pixelated, blurring any distinguishing features. He could have been anything in age from eighteen to forty. His hair was bulky and appeared fair, and his trousers sat low on his hips, as though on the point of falling down. His t-shirt had parted company with them altogether and, in the man's haste to remove himself from the studio, had ridden up over his belly.

I squinted at the screen. Something was printed across the front of that t-shirt. A single word in white capitals.

'Does that say "crew"?' I asked.

'It does,' replied Taylor. 'We were thinking he must have been employed that night by either Sinclair's company or the studios. Thing is, our team's contacted both Proactive Productions *and* Shinetree. But neither seems to recognise him.'

'Do *you* recognise him?' Paulson asked Mara.

She frowned. 'Afraid not. Image quality's too poor. Other than he's youngish, a little below average height, fair hair...'

'Could be a member of the crew legging it because they saw something they shouldn't have,' said Paulson, tossing his empty crisp packet into the bin. 'Or,' he added, 'someone who knows more than they're letting on.'

Perhaps that man in the clip really had been working at Shinetree in some capacity, but the studio and production company didn't recognise him due to the grainy recording. Perhaps he'd been so freaked out by witnessing a woman fall to her death that he needed some fresh air, which explained why he tore with such urgency through that studio door.

'We're working on identifying him,' said Taylor.

'And the other footage?' Mara asked, her gaze still fixed on the ungainly running figure.

Taylor closed the window and clicked into the second folder, containing the clips recorded on the 15th of March, the Saturday Angel vanished. He selected about eight of these clips and started them playing simultaneously, the screen splitting into views of the various doors in and out of the Talent Quest studio.

'We've been through every second of this footage, from every camera, covering every one of the exits,' Taylor said. 'But there's no sign of Angel Devereaux leaving that studio. Not of her own volition and not being forced out by someone else.'

'Remember where we found Katarina?' I said. 'Couldn't Angel have been taken from the studio in a flight case?'

'We still can't be completely sure that Katarina didn't agree to being put inside that case,' answered Mara, studying the clips on screen.

'Also, we checked the footage,' Taylor said. 'No cases left the studio that night — via *any* of the exits — that were large enough to hold a person.'

Mara's lips pursed doubtfully.

'Dex's props, then?' I asked. Paulson glared at me in a way that implied I didn't have the right to be chipping in, but I continued anyway. 'Could Angel have been inside one of them? Could she have been loaded into the hire van and then driven back to his lock-up?'

'Nope!' tooted Paulson.

'A couple of Shinetree staff helped Dex load the van after that first show,' Taylor offered, by way of explanation. 'They swear all his stuff was empty. The van was a little smaller than the one hired last Saturday, so the teleportation boxes had to be open in order to fit everything in.'

'Even the bases?' asked Mara.

'Even the bases,' Taylor replied.

'She didn't leave that first Saturday night,' Paulson announced, emphasising every word. 'With Dex or anyone else.'

'I very much doubt that,' said Mara, in direct contradiction.

'Well, if she didn't walk out, and she wasn't taken out in a case, then what are you saying?' Paulson demanded. 'That Dex Devereaux's powers of illusion are real, and he *teleported* her out of there?'

Mara, Paulson and Taylor got to their feet.

'We don't even know Dex was responsible for any of this,' Mara returned. 'And anyway, you couldn't keep someone in the studio all week. There are far too many people about. How would you explain going back-and-forth to them, for one thing? For another, the pathologist said there were no signs on Angel's body of her having been confined anywhere tight. No malnutrition or dehydration. None of the bruising Katarina had.'

'Well, there are no signs of Angel coming in the following Saturday, either,' Paulson countered. 'Her remaining at Shinetree for the week is the most logical explanation.'

'Logic doesn't always apply in cases like these,' said Mara.

'But evidence does. And there's no evidence to suggest Angel left that studio,' said Paulson.

'You simply haven't found it,' Mara shot back.

'We've checked every frame!' Paulson insisted, his face flushing. 'My team are professionals. They know what they're doing.'

Mara's gaze bored directly into Paulson, unwavering. 'Your team might be professionals, but they're not in the business of deception. And I'm telling you now, deception is exactly what's been used here.'

'Which means it's definitely Devereaux, then!' crowed Paulson.

'No!' snapped Mara, the heat of the argument escalating.

'You forgotten all the evidence we already have, Knight? The banner, the stuff found at Dex's house—'

'All far too obvious. Far too indicative of someone trying to set him up. Someone like Shane Sinclair.'

Hearing Shane's name, Paulson's expression altered.

'Sinclair could have done anything to those studio cameras,' Mara went on. 'Doctored the footage, kept some of it back. Even ensured the cameras were pointed at very specific angles, to give the views from them he needed to cover his tracks that night. You might think — because you cannot see any proof of it on these CCTV recordings — that it's impossible Angel left the studio between shows. But that's not true.'

Paulson's jaw tightened, his moustache vibrating with indignation. A moustache, I noticed, that was faintly dusted with tiny crumbs of Monster Munch.

'You're so convinced of Dex's guilt,' said Mara, 'that you're failing to take into account the bigger picture.'

'And you're so convinced Shane Sinclair was behind what

happened to your husband you're bringing a very unhealthy bias to this investigation—'

'How dare you,' Mara seethed, stepping towards Paulson and almost matching his height. 'You wouldn't even have an arrest right now if it weren't for Clare and me. How dare you suggest—'

'That's enough, Knight!' Rattled by Mara's proximity, Paulson finally exploded, slamming a hand on the desk. The computer monitor juddered, and a folder of papers flopped to the floor. 'I've had it with your interference. Continuously showing up at every potential crime scene... trying to influence this case with your own agenda... conferring with Anand behind my back. She might be a DCI, but while she's away, *I'm* the SIO around here. And I'll be going over her head with this. Right now. To DCS Shenton.' Puffing out his chest, Paulson broke towards the door. 'You think you know better than seasoned detectives? Well, you can take your second-hand knowledge and your husband's magic tricks and get out. You're off the case. Officially.'

A stunned silence ensued. Several of the other detectives in the room, who had for the last few minutes been listening to the exchange open-mouthed, dragged their attention back to their work.

Mara's expression was unreadable as her gaze followed Paulson from the office. The door swung shut behind him; the noise cutting through the echo of his words, still thickening the air.

28.

DC Taylor ran a hand through his hair, a gesture somewhere between remorse and exasperation.

'God Mara, I'm so sorry about that,' he murmured, attempting to move towards her.

For a moment she was perfectly motionless, as though sculpted, her face indecipherable. Then, without a word, she strode towards the office door, dark coat surging behind her like a storm cloud.

For a handful of long seconds, I didn't know what to say. I eventually mumbled a hasty goodbye to Taylor and scurried after Mara. But already there was no sign of her in the corridors, or in the reception where we'd waited together earlier.

I decided to dawdle near the front desk for a while, to see if Mara materialised. But when she didn't appear after fifteen minutes, I handed in my pass and left the station, not knowing what else to do.

The automatic doors sighed closed at my back. I crossed the station compound, passing my parked car, and headed through the gates, from where I could scan the main road. Dipping into my handbag, I remembered I still had Mara's leather pouch of tools. I clutched it impotently as I continued to look left and right, a small wave of dismay washing over me. Although it had stopped raining now, puddles still slicked the pavements, reflecting the monochrome skies like molten pewter. But Mara was gone.

I made the short drive back home and let myself in, the familiar mugginess of the flat hitting me like a damp flannel.

'Alright?'

Matt looked up from the sofa, where he was slumped beside his guitar, tangled headphones askew. Jasper sat next to him as they shared a half-eaten plate of what looked suspiciously like chicken chow mein. He'd gone from noodles in a pot to noodles on a plate. Still, I supposed, progress was progress.

'Good boy.' Matt patted Jasper's back affectionately and noticed my eyeline. 'Late lunch,' he said. 'You finished work for today?'

'Sort of.'

Jasper jumped from the sofa, pink tongue polishing the last remnants of soy sauce from his jaws as he bounded towards me.

'By the way, I followed that woman's suggestion,' said Matt.

Forgetting to answer, I bent down to pet Jasper, burying my face in his fur.

'I switched out the G for an F chord and whacked the tuning down to drop A.'

'Huh?'

'It really improved the riff,' Matt went on. 'She in a band or something? That coat's certainly a look.'

It took me a second to realise he was talking about Mara. When I did, I wanted to laugh, since the notion of her being in a band was so absurd. Then I was caught by the same wave of dismay that'd hit me outside the police station. Given what had happened to her husband on one of Shane's shows, Mara must be finding the Angel Devereaux investigation as difficult as me. And Paulson seemed to have a knack for tactlessly bringing the conversation back to Travers, whether he meant to or not.

Take your second-hand knowledge and your husband's magic tricks and get out.

It was probably obvious to a lot of people, but Detective Inspector Paulson often spoke with his foot in his mouth. Literally, in the case of his Monster Munch. Of course he wanted to do his best with the Angel Devereaux investigation as its SIO. But it was thanks to Mara's input — and mine — that he'd amassed enough potential evidence of Dex's guilt to arrest him. As Mara had pointed out.

I could see what he meant about that evidence against Dex appearing damning, but at the same time I couldn't help but think Mara was seeing something about all this that the rest of us couldn't. Yes, she had a bias against Shane Sinclair and, from what I could piece together, understandably so. But that recording on Angel's phone did make me think that rather than Dex killing Angel, it was more likely he'd been framed by Shane. Shane had far more power than Dex, after all. Had that figure we'd seen sprinting from the studio on the CCTV footage been employed by Shane to carry out some part of Angel's murder, despite Proactive Productions saying they didn't recognise him?

'You in tonight?' I asked Matt.

'Yeah,' he answered, picking up his guitar. 'Now the riff's nailed, I gotta work on the rest of the album. Only got until Friday 'til I leave for Mum and Dad's. Be away for the weekend.

That okay?'

'Yeah,' I answered, not really listening again. I went into the kitchen and grabbed Jasper's lead and ball-launcher. 'I'll just give the dog a quick walk.'

Outside the rain had kept off, but the clouds still crowding the sky meant it was already getting dark. Jasper and I crisscrossed the streets that surrounded ours, heading towards the park. Once through the gates, we started along our favourite path, skirting the trees at the border of the vast green space before heading across the grass towards the tumulus. I extended the ball-launcher, and with an accurate flick of the forearm, sent the bright red tomato spinning into the air. Jasper woofed happily, careering after it time and again with unbridled glee.

A little while later, with my dog back on his lead, we made for the path once more. Jasper knew this route like the back of his paw, but we'd only been walking ten minutes or so when he began behaving oddly. He strained at his lead, pulling me sharply down a much quieter, more concealed route. This track was dark; the gathering dusk and the trees huddling densely along it rendering it darker still. I didn't like it one bit.

'Jasp, no,' I warned, tugging him to a standstill. 'This way.'

The dog remained planted to the spot, staring at the track ahead until he gave a single, determined bark.

I edged closer, thinking I would let him go a few paces further before turning back. But Jasper took this as a signal to continue and forged single-mindedly ahead, nose firmly to the ground. What could he smell? I knew from my work at the paper that the secluded area of the park we were moving towards was regularly used by dealers and addicts. I wished I'd kept a hold of that PAVA spray of Mara's, but all I had of use in my bag was her pouch of tools. I pondered whether to remove one of those lancets, just in case.

After about twenty feet I'd had enough, and was on the point of steering Jasper back the way we'd come when he started to bark insistently, focused on a very specific point in the distance. Something was there, and he could see it. No, not something. *Someone.*

I peered through the massing gloom and saw them too. A dark figure crouched ahead of us on the snaking lee of the track, its form broken by the branches clustering densely around it.

'No... shush!' I hissed at Jasper, hoping they hadn't heard. 'Come. On!'

But Jasper wouldn't budge. And it was too late, in any case. For they *had* heard him.

A voice drifted towards me through the murk.

'I told you before, Clare. A barking dog is not to be trusted.'

I couldn't believe it. 'What the hell are *you* doing here?'

With a jubilant yap, Jasper trotted towards Mara, tail threshing with delight. I pulled him to a halt a few feet away from the fallen tree trunk on which she sat.

'He really likes you, you know,' I said. 'He wouldn't have bothered leading me to just anyone. You must be special.'

She gave a low laugh and sipped from the water bottle she was holding. The evening chill was beginning to bite and, despite me now having company, I still wasn't keen on loitering in one of the most secluded areas of the park.

'This path's slightly dodgy,' I warned Mara. 'Bit of a haunt for druggies.'

'Oh, I just met one,' she replied calmly. 'He seemed friendly enough.'

Mara was, I noted, looking surprisingly serene given what had just occurred with Paulson. Her extravagant coat was buttoned high against the cold, and her manner was a lot easier than it had been when I last saw her sweeping out of the police station. She didn't flinch quite so much at Jasper's proximity to her, either.

'I waited for you. In the station reception,' I said. 'I didn't know where you'd gone.'

'I just needed some air,' she replied, taking a long swig of water.

'About Paulson...' I said, feeling the need to apologise on the man's behalf.

She waved a hand dismissively. 'Forget it.'

'For the record, I think you were right to suggest they look more at Shane.'

She tilted her head from one side to the other, like she wasn't sure. 'I am biased, I admit,' she conceded.

'Totally understandable,' I replied, deliberating whether to ask the next part. 'Did you ever seriously consider that Shane might have been responsible for... you know... what happened to your husband?'

Mara took another glug from the bottle and screwed her face. 'Directly? I don't know. There's never been any evidence to suggest he was. But I strongly suspect… that he knows more than he's letting on.'

Overhead, a magpie gave a series of harsh, rattling calls. There was a pause.

'In fairness to Graham, it's a complicated case. As I said before, there's some kind of greater deception at work here. I just don't know what it is…' her voice dwindled despondently.

'Yet,' I said. 'But you will.'

She gave the slightest smile.

'Aren't you cold?' I asked, drawing my jacket around me. 'Want to come back to ours to warm up…? Or go get some food somewhere?' I tacked on, recalling the state of the flat.

Hearing the magic word "food", Jasper responded with an emphatic bark.

Mara silently got to her feet, and we proceeded back along the path.

'What on earth is that?' she asked after we'd emerged from the trees and out into the open. She was pointing at Jasper's ball-launcher, which I was holding. It was just like Mara to have no trouble levitating a glass or cracking a biometric code, but be completely unable to identify a dog toy.

'I'll show you,' I replied, picking up a crumpled drinks can that lay discarded on the path. I inserted one end of it into the plastic cradle of the launcher. 'Keep an eye on that bin over there.'

Squinting to gauge my aim, I drew back my arm and discharged the can into the air. It flew the intervening seventy feet with ease, landing squarely in the bin's open mouth.

'A crack shot,' Mara applauded, impressed. 'So it's a litter picker?'

'Not quite, I answered. 'It helps me throw Jasper's ball further.' I held the tomato up before her and gave it a squeeze. It squeaked comically.

Since Mara gave no further reaction, I slipped the launcher into my bag. 'Ah, I have your pouch—'

Before I could finish, a discreet buzz sounded from the depths of Mara's clothing. She withdrew her mobile and examined the screen.

Tapping out a reply with alarming speed, Mara replaced the phone in her pocket. 'Text from Dhita,' she explained. 'She heard about Graham's tantrum.'

We walked awhile in companionable silence, though I had the impression Mara's thoughts were elsewhere. At the park gates, I paused. 'You didn't say whether you wanted to come back to the flat or stop off somewhere for food?'

Mara's expression changed like she'd only then remembered. 'We're going to Dhita's,' she replied. 'She's invited us for dinner. At her house.'

'Us?'

'That's what she said. If you're free?'

I hadn't spent much time with Matt for days. Weeks, probably. But he'd said he was working on his album, and I was intrigued to meet Dhita, and hear her latest thoughts on the Angel Devereaux investigation. Did she think, like Paulson and Taylor, that the evidence still implicated Dex? Did she suspect Shane? Or had the man seen running away from the studio on the CCTV footage been identified, pointing to someone new entirely? With Mara off the case, we were unlikely to hear anything from anyone else.

'Yes,' I said decisively. 'I'm free.'

Mara gave a nod. 'Good,' she answered. 'Though it's a bit of a drive.'

29.♠

I installed Jasper back in the flat and told Matt there'd been a change of plan, that I had to go out to follow up on a story. Mara stayed downstairs as I grabbed my car keys, having somehow volunteered myself for driving duties again. During almost the entire journey, her hands fidgeted restlessly with a sheet of paper as she directed me through the outer reaches of west London.

Dhita's house was situated in a small town just outside the suburbs. It was after eight by the time Mara issued the last of her directions, and I parked up before a decent-sized detached new-build, halfway down a well-kept street. An attractive garden faced the road, with a double garage to the right of the house. In front of this garage, a sensible charcoal people carrier was parked, along with a smaller, sportier car in a vibrant shade of cherry red.

We made our way up the block-paved drive, and Mara pressed the doorbell. From the depths of the house, a cheerful, melodic chime rang out.

'Oh no!' I cried, the lack of a gift for Dhita suddenly becoming apparent. 'I haven't brought anything.'

I'd been invited to dinner at a Detective Chief Inspector's

house, only to turn up completely empty-handed.

'Don't worry,' Mara declared, reaching into her coat and extracting an entire, unopened bottle of wine. 'I have.'

I couldn't think where she'd got it from — there certainly hadn't been time in the two minutes it'd taken me to pop into the flat for my keys. So my mouth was still open as the door swung inwards to reveal a woman in her mid-thirties, whose demeanour put me at ease immediately, despite her rank.

DCI Adhita Anand was only a little taller than me, her dark hair flowing almost to her waist. Between the scarf she wore as a headband and her pair of arty, stonewashed dungarees, she was dressed more like a bohemian than an off-duty senior police detective. The dungarees were stretched taut across her middle, revealing a significant baby bump.

'Mara! Come in. Good to finally meet you, Clare. But please excuse the chaos.' She laughed and gestured behind her, to a hallway strewn with multicoloured toys and miniature shoes.

'You should see my place,' I replied awkwardly, trying to make a joke. 'No kids, though, just a boyfriend who makes as much mess as one.'

From somewhere at the rear of the house came a peal of children's laughter. A man appeared then, in the threshold at the end of the hallway, wiping his hands on a tea towel. He was average height with light-brown hair and an open, friendly face. A face that seemed the tiniest bit familiar.

'Clare, this is my partner, Jake.'

At the very moment he took my hand in greeting, a tiny blurring form in a nightie sped out into the hallway, clamping itself to Jake's leg.

'And this is Lila,' Jake said.

'She's supposed to be in bed,' said Dhita. 'But she wanted to see her Auntie Mara. And meet you, Clare.'

Jake lifted the pretty, hazel-eyed toddler into his arms. 'Please, come through.'

I followed the others into a generous open-plan living area at the back of the house, where a glazed wall comprising two large sliding doors offered a view of a garden sparkling with fairy lights. A rustic dining table in the centre of the space had been set for three, and to its side were several squashy sofas.

On one of these was curled a small boy in pyjamas, who I guessed couldn't have been much older than six. When we entered, he was watching a laptop screen, circus music and cartoonish sound effects drifting from its speakers.

'And Dillon's up too,' Mara said. 'Good evening, Sir.'

As soon as he heard her voice, Dillon put aside the laptop. He moved towards Mara, regarding her hands expectantly.

'Oh!' Mara uttered, pressing her palm to her forehead like she'd just recollected an important fact. 'Of course. I have something for you.' She extravagantly withdrew the bottle of wine from behind her back and held it out to the surprised little boy. 'Here you are. Please tell me you drink wine?'

The child giggled, and so did Dhita, who took the bottle from Mara's grasp. 'Maybe when he's older,' she said.

'Quite right,' replied Mara earnestly. 'Give it another year.'

Dhita rubbed her stomach and examined the bottle's label. 'I hope this is alcohol-free.'

'Don't worry, I'll drink it,' said Mara.

Intrigued by the exchange, Lila wriggled from her father's

arms. She puttered over to join her brother, who, rather than being eager to get back to his cartoon, continued to stare at Mara.

Mara crouched down to meet the children's eyes. 'Now,' she said, bringing her palms together, one on top of the other. 'Blow on my hands.'

They advanced slowly as one, Lila's pudgy fingers steadying herself on her brother. Leaning forwards, the children blew gently on Mara's skin.

'Watch closely,' Mara whispered. 'And be very quiet.'

Mara carefully opened her hands, which were no longer empty. In the centre of her left palm, sat a beautiful origami dove. She wiggled her fingers above the paper bird and, very gradually, it began to hover in the air.

'Whoa!' exclaimed Dillon, as Lila's face popped wide.

Mara brought the bird back to her hand and picked it up. Accompanied by the sudden, shocking sound of ripping paper, she tore the dove clean in two.

Only the bird wasn't torn at all. But there were now two, as a second origami dove had appeared from nowhere to join the first, Mara holding a paper bird in each hand.

'For you, Dillon,' she said, presenting him with one of the doves. 'And this is for you.' She held the second out to Lila, who took it with as much reverence as if it were holy.

Jake cheered Mara's performance while Dhita laughed again. 'Why do I have a feeling that paper is police property?' she said.

So that's where it had come from — the paper Mara was playing with in the car. The police station.

'Because you saw it was letter-headed?' Mara answered. 'Very shrewd, Detective Chief Inspector.'

Dhita rolled her eyes dramatically as Jake ruffled his son's hair. 'Come on, you guys and your doves are late to roost,' he said, lifting Lila into his arms.

I didn't know what I'd expected of Dhita's house, but it wasn't this. Perhaps I thought the home of a senior police detective would be more sterile or serious than the happy, welcoming family space it was. It couldn't have been more different from the house in which I'd spent my own childhood. Especially after Mum vanished. But instead of making me sad, or envious of the children, I could feel an unfamiliar warmth seeping along my veins.

Clutching their paper doves, and still enraptured by the impromptu magic show, the children retreated up the hall with their father. Mara glanced at me and winked, and only then did I realise I was smiling as wide as Dillon and Lila.

Jake didn't join us for dinner, explaining he'd eaten with the children already and had some work to finish. Despite being dressed in clothes that had clearly seen some wear and tear, I expected him to head to a home office to spend the next couple of hours with a spreadsheet. So I was surprised when Dhita said Jake was a self-employed carpenter and was actually heading out to the double garage, which had been converted into his workshop. I'd supposed a police detective's other half would have a desk job, when the reality was he was making desks for a living.

While Mara uncorked the wine, I helped Dhita transfer an enormous dish of risotto to the table, accompanied by a bowl of salad as big as my kitchen sink.

'All thanks to Jake,' Dhita said, holding up her hands.

As the contents of the bowls diminished, talk inevitably turned to the Angel Devereaux case.

'Luke said after he spoke to you, Paulson went straight to Shenton,' she said, referring to DCS Shenton, her superior officer. 'Paulson wasn't happy.'

'That sounds... bad?' I ventured.

Dhita waved a hand. 'Not really. I gave Shenton a call after I heard—'

'God, you really are bored waiting for this baby to come, aren't you?' Mara cut in.

Dhita chuckled. 'You're not wrong there. Anyway, Shenton just advised we let Paulson get on with it for the time being. He'll be in touch soon enough, cap in hand, when he wants something.'

Mara swilled her wine and shrugged. 'I've never seen Graham go cap-in-hand for anything. Except maybe a bacon sandwich.'

'Paulson's his own worst enemy,' Dhita sighed, rubbing her bump. 'He means well, deep down. He's a good guy. But he hates feeling undermined. Especially,' she added, with a twinkle in her eye directed at Mara, 'by someone demonstrably better at the job.'

Mara gave a narrow smile. 'Graham's so convinced Dex murdered Angel he's taking every potential piece of evidence as confirmation he's correct. It's a classic distraction. And could be precisely what the killer wanted.'

'And that recording of Sinclair was very incriminating,' mused Dhita. 'Now, in my opinion, he *isn't* a good guy.'

'You think it's Shane then?' I asked.

'I couldn't say,' Dhita sighed. 'Not from this distance. Look, off the record...' She plucked a toasted almond from the remnants of salad. 'The case has benefited hugely from your perspective. Both of your perspectives. Look what you've achieved so far, the potential evidence you've discovered. Plus, I think it's fair to say you saved Katarina Riley's life.'

'I'm worried about the CCTV footage from Shinetree,' Mara said, her focus shifting. 'Graham's convinced Angel never left, because his team couldn't see her leaving on the recordings. But they don't know what to look for. They see objects. Not the potential deception behind them.'

Dhita nodded thoughtfully. 'You think she was missed?'

'I think it's highly likely. It would be too risky to keep a kidnapped woman at Shinetree for the week, whoever our perpetrator is. And if I wanted to get someone past CCTV cameras, I could come up with a hundred ways to do it. I was missed leaving HMP Ferndon, after all.'

Dhita grinned. 'Point taken.' Pushing back her chair, she hauled herself to her feet and retrieved the laptop from the nearby sofa. 'Right. Let's take a look, shall we?'

Mara drained her glass and brought her hands together. 'Now you're talking.'

Placing the laptop at the head of the table, Dhita proceeded to tap at its keyboard while Mara looked on. As they worked, I busied myself with clearing the table.

'Those the files?' Dhita asked Mara. 'Two folders. Saturday the 15th and Saturday the 22nd of March?'

I guessed she must have logged on to the police computer system remotely, accessing the security footage from Shinetree. The footage we'd seen on Taylor's computer that afternoon.

'They are,' confirmed Mara.

'In that case, if you can find something relevant to the investigation on that footage, then go for it. You have...' Shuffling along the table, she checked the clock. 'Ooh, about ninety minutes before Jake and I get back to our re-watch of Game of Thrones. New series starts soon.'

'I love that show,' I said.

'All those dragons and fairies... now that's *real* magic,' Dhita returned, throwing a cheeky glance in Mara's direction.

The remark, however, didn't register. Or if it did, Mara didn't show it. She was already totally engrossed in the studio's security footage, brow furrowed with concentration.

'Oh, leave that,' Dhita told me, as I stacked the dirty crockery on the counter. 'Jake's very good. He'll sort it in the morning.' She topped up my water glass.

'He seems lovely. Have you been together long?'

'Yeah, since our early twenties,' she replied. 'About fifteen years.'

'Wow,' I said, musing that the two years I'd spent with Matt felt just as long. I pushed the thought from my mind. 'How long have you and Mara known each other?'

'God, donkey's years,' Dhita replied. 'Longer than I've known Jake. We met at university.'

I glanced over at Mara to see if the mention of her past would prompt her to look up, but she was still too absorbed in the footage.

'We were both reading psychology. Well, Mara was. It was one of the modules of my philosophy degree. That was long before I decided to join the Met, obviously.'

That explained Mara's analysis of Dex's mannerisms during the Talent Quest interview. 'She told me she knew a bit about psychology.'

'She's being too modest,' Dhita replied. 'Highest graded student in the country.'

'In England,' came Mara's voice from the end of the table. 'I may be hard at work, but I can still hear you gossiping about me.'

'She then went on to a doctorate,' Dhita continued. 'On the psychology of deception. Which is how she met Travers.'

'A doctorate which never—' Mara started, then quickly fell silent.

Dhita and I turned towards Mara in unison to observe her nose almost touching the laptop's screen.

'You've found it?' I urged. 'A clip of Angel leaving?'

Mara peeled her attention from the computer and rested her chin on her hand. 'No,' she replied. 'But one mystery's been solved.' She got up and repositioned the laptop in front of Dhita. 'I decided to work backwards, starting at the footage from last Saturday. Check that nothing had been overlooked.'

On screen was paused a clip of the Shinetree Studios loading bay, its timestamp showing 17:48 on the 22nd of March. A large transit van was parked in the bay, and two men were unloading it, carelessly flinging the stuff between them. They were clearly in a hurry.

The men wore black t-shirts printed with the word "CREW" — the exact same type of t-shirts as that other man had been wearing. The one on the footage we'd seen at the station, running away from the studio the night Angel died.

Between the ground and the open back of the van, a metal ramp had been precariously balanced. A trolley was waiting at the top of this ramp, and the men lifted a large black box from the back of the van, placing it on the trolley. As nondescript as this object was, I recognised it immediately. It was one of Dex's teleportation boxes. Which meant the van must be the one that was hired to transport Dex's props from his lock-up to Shinetree, ahead of his Talent Quest performance.

Having set the box down, the men wheeled the trolley forwards. But no sooner had they started to do so than the entire thing slipped from their grasp; box and trolley both hurtling down the ramp before crashing against the studio wall.

'That explains the repainted chip,' said Mara. 'Unsurprising given their unloading technique.'

Dhita cocked her head enquiringly.

'When Dex's lock-up was searched, I found a chip on one of his teleportation boxes,' Mara said. 'It looked like it had recently been touched up. And now we know why. The props team must have panicked and tried to cover the damage they'd caused. They did a pretty good job of it too. Of course, they'll be doing specialist paint jobs all the time working at Shinetree.'

'Then the repainted chip was nothing,' I said, a little disappointed it hadn't been more of a clue. 'Just careless handling on the part of the studio guys?'

Mara didn't answer, reclaiming the laptop and returning to the footage.

At least an hour passed, Dhita and I making coffee and nibbling biscuits, chatting to each other while Mara carried on combing through the CCTV clips. I occasionally glanced over at her while she clicked furiously on the keyboard, thumb anchoring the side of the laptop as she worked.

Finally, Mara shut the laptop decisively and leant back in her chair.

'I don't understand it,' she muttered. 'There's no sign of Angel leaving Shinetree the Saturday before last. There really was nothing removed from the studio after the first show that could have accommodated her.'

'So Paulson was right?' I asked, confused and a little incredulous at the possibility. 'Angel was at Shinetree the whole week she was missing?'

The question lingered between us, unanswered.

30.

'We found Katarina inside a flight case in the studio,' I said, a long beat of silence later. 'So could Angel's killer have done the same to her? Locked her in a case with the intention of having it removed from Shinetree on the Sunday instead, perhaps?'

'It's definitely worth nudging Luke to get the team to go through the footage from Sunday the 16th,' said Dhita. 'Monday the 17th, as well. Won't be quick, though.'

Mara made a face as though sifting through the possibilities.

As we'd all fallen quiet, I began gathering up the coffee cups for Dhita, the clink of china the only sound against my thoughts. I wondered if this was it, if the trail of how Angel had been taken from Shinetree the week she disappeared had now gone completely cold.

'New text message!' a child's voice called suddenly.

I twisted to the doorway, expecting to see either Dillon or Lila there. But it was empty.

Dhita chuckled and picked up her mobile. 'Good text alert, isn't it? Though I'll have to change it before I go back to work. Having my child shout across CID every time I get a new message might be considered unprofessional.'

'You should hear Clare's ringtone,' quipped Mara.

I made another mental note to eradicate the birdy song from my mobile as soon as I got home.

'Message from Luke,' said Dhita, her eyes skimming the text. A moment later, she looked up, first at Mara, then at me. 'They've identified him.'

I froze for a second, thinking she was referring to Angel's murderer.

'The man running away from the studio on Saturday night?' Mara asked.

Dhita nodded. 'His name is Lenny Finch. Twenty-five years old. Employed in a succession of menial jobs.'

Mara leant forwards, elbows on the table. 'Lenny Finch,' she repeated. 'So now they have a name, could the police get back in touch with—'

'They already have,' replied Dhita, preempting Mara's question. 'Luke contacted Shinetree Studios *and* Proactive Productions earlier this evening. But both still insist that Lenny Finch has never worked for them.' She replaced her phone on the tabletop. 'Nobody seems to have any idea why he was at the studio last Saturday, let alone wearing the same uniform as the rest of the crew.'

'Could one of them be lying?' I suggested. 'Shane's company, for example? Trying to cover something up?' If this Lenny Finch wasn't crew, then what was he doing there? And why run? It seemed too convenient that a man who had no reason to be at Shinetree in the first place just happened to be there the same night a woman was murdered.

Dhita shrugged. 'It's possible. Though by all accounts a filming studio's a pretty chaotic environment.'

Mara agreed. 'Easy for someone to slip in through the cracks, either officially or unofficially.'

Easy for Mara, maybe. A woman who could break out of prisons. I'm not sure I'd have had the faintest idea how to get all the way into Shinetree by myself. I doubted I could make it past the entrance kiosk.

'But also, yes,' Mara added. 'Proactive Productions could be lying. It's second nature to Shane Sinclair. And fish stinks from the head.'

Dhita shot Mara a concerned look. 'Though Lenny Finch could even have been a temp the studio has forgotten about. Hired through an agency as extra help that night,' she said.

'Lenny Finch...' pondered Mara. She reclaimed Dhita's laptop, her fingers flying across the keyboard. The laptop screen, angled away from me, glowed the telltale blue and white of a popular social media interface.

'Jesus!' Mara cried, recoiling from the screen.

'What is it?' I shifted for a better view, convinced she'd discovered something shocking about Lenny.

'Let me guess,' said Dhita, not in the least bit anxious to see what it was. 'You're logged into my Facebook account and the first thing you saw were the pics from Sergeant Cooper's hen do?' She turned towards me. 'It's company policy to hire a police strippergram. That way, when they're finished, we can tell them they're under arrest for impersonating a police officer.'

'Under arrest for committing a public decency outrage, if these photos are anything to go by,' said Mara.

Opening up an incognito window, Mara logged back into Facebook, this time using details that didn't appear to belong to anyone. An anonymous profile opened up, and she typed Lenny's full name into the search bar. Mara clicked onto the only account listed in the results.

'Lenny's Finch's profile,' she said, swivelling the laptop slightly so Dhita could see.

The page that loaded showed the Facebook profile of a young man with thick sandy hair that looked too heavy for his head. His face almost completely filled the shot he'd chosen as his profile picture, to the extent that viewing such an extreme close-up was a little discomforting. It sounds unkind to say so, but Lenny Finch was far from conventionally handsome. He was chubby with small and fairly close-set eyes, a smattering of acne between his brows, and a prominent, fleshy nose.

This profile image was odd in another way, too, in that it appeared to be the only photo on Lenny's Facebook account that didn't feature magic. Or rather... *magicians*. As Mara scrolled down the page, the feed that was revealed was a veritable deluge of magician-related content.

Almost every photograph showed Lenny Finch with various figures from the magic scene, some I vaguely recognised, others I knew to be magicians only from the fans of playing cards they held, or the way they were dressed. Black suits and red cummerbunds were paired with satin top hats; crow-black hair dye with a slew of silver emo jewellery; and flamboyant, blow-dried mullets with tight-fitting leatherette trousers and open shirts. The kind of tight-fitting leatherette trousers and open shirts worn by Dex Devereaux. Because many of these photos of Lenny had been taken *with* Dex Devereaux.

'He certainly seems to be a big fan of Dex's,' said Mara,

underlining the fact. She slowed her scrolling, pausing on each of the pictures of the two men standing together, presumably following magic shows. In every one of them, Lenny's smile was wide and desperate, like in being there he was fulfilling a fantasy. And yet the photos had been taken a little haphazardly, with strange croppings, as though they hadn't been framed carefully enough.

A series of comments had been posted under the photos, written by an older woman called Jean Finch, who I assumed must be Lenny's mother.

My boy! He's definitely got the magic touch!

Gorgeous in this one!

So handsome.

Trawling through these images, one loomed larger than the rest, as cropped out on its right-hand edge stood a sliver of a figure. I followed Lenny's eyeline in the picture. His gaze was glued to that figure, as though fixated on it, his whole being distracted by its presence, expression illuminated by a fanatical adoration.

That figure was Angel.

Surely it wasn't merely a coincidence that Lenny Finch was at Shinetree the night Angel was murdered; a place he otherwise had no business being? In my mind, I replayed that clip of him bolting through the studio door moments after her death, with the panic of a man who knows he has just done something unspeakable. Had he also been at Shinetree the *previous* Saturday, when Angel disappeared...?

Dhita, who had been quietly observing the contents of Lenny's profile, picked up her phone, which was flashing with another notification. 'The police are on their way to speak to Lenny Finch. At his home address.' She paused and uttered an exclamation of surprise.

'What is it?' I asked.

'Lenny Finch,' Dhita replied, '*also* lives in Morden.'

31.

A groan of pure exhaustion escaped me as I dragged my eyelids apart. It felt like I'd only just closed them, for the first time since Friday; the day before I stepped out of Presto Print to head to HMP Ferndon where this whole thing began.

It was difficult to believe that was only four days ago. Four whirlwind, draining days of prisons, magic paraphernalia, television studios and police interview rooms. A night spent at one of the largest and downright most surreal houses I'd ever entered; dinner with a Detective Chief Inspector and — as Jeff might have put it in one of his Morden Mercury articles — more twists than a contortionists' convention.

It was the noise of my phone that had woken me. It was plugged in beside the bed, pulsing with a faint light. A new message. And, speak of the devil, it was from Jeff.

Deyes. You're too late on the cat Christmas tree story. Mrs Higgins coaxed cat down with a bit of fish and the Merton Gazette ran a full-page spread. Headline was: Cat Dreaming of a White-*bait* Christmas. That story had huge potential, but boat missed. Anyway, the Morden Pothole Vigilantes are staging a "decorate a crater" protest on the high street this

**aft using garden gnomes. Get on and speak to the
organiser once you see this. Goes by the name of
Captain Crater. You actually coming in later?**

A heavy sense of resignation settled over me. With no idea
when — or if — Mara would be in touch with more information
on the Angel Devereaux case, it was back to reality this morning.
Finally time to face the music at the Morden Mercury. Or rather,
the pothole gnomes.

Only then did I notice the time. It was already 9.36 a.m. After
the excitement of the past few days, and not getting back from
Dhita's until well after midnight, I had spectacularly overslept.

And so had Matt, who remained a gently snoring lump
beneath the duvet beside me.

'Hey,' I mumbled, prodding his shoulder. 'It's nearly ten.'

Matt grunted and burrowed deeper under the covers,
clinging to the mentality that, in order to write good songs, it
was essential to shun any semblance of a conventional schedule.

I dragged myself from the bed. My body ached, my brain
feeling like over-kneaded dough. I showered quickly, hoping
it would perk me up, but I was still half-asleep when I forgot
about my toast. As I was scraping the burnt patches from the
first incinerated slice, my phone rang.

It was probably Jeff, I thought, chasing up his earlier
message. I blearily picked up, not stopping to check the number.

'Morning, Clare.'

The unexpected crispness of the voice caused me to lose
my grip on the toast, which landed squarely in Jasper's food
bowl with an accuracy that could only have been achieved

accidentally.

'Mara, hi,' I replied, recalling I'd last seen her disappearing into an unmarked cab outside Dhita's house late the previous night. 'Did you get back okay?'

'Fine. Listen, I find myself with an unexpected hour or two free at lunchtime. And, funnily enough, I'll be in Morden. Fancy a drink around one-thirty? We could walk Jasper.'

Still drowsy, I didn't immediately think to ask what was bringing her to Morden. Nor did I question why she'd gone from being terrified of Jasper to volunteering to take him out for a walk in the space of forty-eight hours. Or maybe because she hadn't mentioned the Angel Devereaux investigation, I inadvertently followed my subconscious and assumed, in my sluggish state, that Mara Knight and I were now friends.

'Oh. Um, yes. That sounds... lovely,' I managed. 'One-thirty is fine.'

'Great. See you then. I'll text you a place.' With that, she hung up.

I instantly felt a little less resigned to the day. Maybe this investigation — this foray into a world far removed from dog birthday banners, cats up Christmas trees and gnomes protesting about potholes — had forged some connection between Mara and me. Though at the same time I couldn't deny the deep-seated compulsion to know more; about Dex Devereaux, Shane Sinclair... and now Lenny Finch. About what had really happened to Angel, and why a woman who'd disappeared from a magic prop one week had turned up dead from inside of it the next.

I quickly tapped out a text to Jeff, telling him I was running a little late. I said that I'd speak to the pothole people and then pop into the office for an hour, but that I might need to leave just after 1 p.m. to chase another story.

In a way, it was completely true.

To my relief, during the thirty minutes that I managed to squeeze in the office between interviewing Captain Crater and leaving to meet Mara, Jeff was out covering a story of his own. I assumed it was the Angel Devereaux case. But at least his absence avoided having to make something up about why I wouldn't be in the office again that afternoon. Or why I hadn't been at work for the past two days.

Jeff had left me a note suggesting a potential headline for the pothole story based on a statement he'd just received from the council. He also told me he wanted the story finished and on his desk by the end of the day. Given my failure to deliver the Tinkerbell exclusive, there was no way he'd let me off the hook if Captain Crater went to the Merton Gazette too.

I flew from the office to the flat to collect Jasper, looking forward to a leisurely lunch with Mara, dissecting all the details of the investigation we'd gleaned so far. She'd texted me the name of a new dog-friendly bistro off the high street, one I'd been meaning to try since it opened. But when Jasper and I arrived there, we saw Mara standing outside, already clutching two takeaway cups.

'Flat white. Two sugars,' she said, holding one of the drinks out to me.

Jasper sat down, raising a forepaw expectantly in the hope there was something for him too.

'Oh... right,' I replied, taking the coffee. 'You want to do the dog walk first and then lunch?'

Mara took a sip from her cup, her eyes unreadable. 'Listen,' she said. 'I might have had an ulterior motive when I asked you to meet me here today.'

I wasn't sure I liked the way this was going.

'I conducted a little research last night.' Her voice lowered, green irises glinting. 'Lenny Finch.'

'What about him?'

'After seeing all those Facebook photos of him with various magicians, his surname rang a distant bell. So I went through my husband's old fan mail requests.' She paused, a flicker of something briefly crossing her face. 'Travers kept almost everything his fans sent him. Letters, gifts, artwork... Anyway, it turns out that Lenny Finch wrote to him about four years ago, requesting a signed photograph.'

My irritation at her real reason for inviting me to lunch warred with my curiosity about where this was heading. 'And?'

Mara took a long sip from her mug, strong fumes wafting from its lid.

'Lenny included his address in the letter.' She pulled a square of paper from her pocket and held it up. 'Maybe you know where the street is?'

My eyes widened. I knew where it was alright, and so did she. 'That's...' I began, my pulse speeding up. 'That's the very next street over from the Devereauxs' house.'

My little corner of south London suddenly felt uncomfortably small and tangled. Lenny Finch, apparently a magic super-fan, lived practically on the Devereauxs' doorstep.

Mara's eyes clamped themselves to me. 'I thought,' she said, 'that we could pay him a visit? He wasn't under arrest last night, so I'm betting the police will have finished with him by now.'

A knot of annoyance and trepidation tightened in my chest. 'For one thing,' I said, 'Paulson would go berserk if he heard about it. You may not care about getting into trouble with the police, but I do. Also, we've no idea if this Lenny Finch had something to do...' I checked myself and dropped my voice, 'something to do with a woman's death. What if he's dangerous?'

She snorted. 'I can take care of myself. Anyway, he may not even be at home.'

'So you want us to trespass instead?' I cut back. 'I think that wine last night must have gone to your head.'

'It wouldn't be trespassing,' she replied. 'We'd just be walking your dog. It wouldn't be our fault if, when let off the lead for a second, he scampered down a driveway he shouldn't.'

'So you asked me to lunch so you could make use of my dog, by sending him into a stranger's garden?'

'Technically, I asked you for a *drink*,' said Mara, taking another sip of her coffee and ignoring the question altogether. 'Which is what we are having.'

'This is the third day in a row I will have taken off work. Do you want me to lose my job? I'm supposed to be writing up a story this afternoon.'

'About what?'

I expected her to keep pressing her point about what a good idea it was for us to go poking around Lenny Finch's house, so the question threw me a little. 'What do you mean?'

'What's the story about, the one you have to write up?'

I gazed off into the distance, trying to mask my exasperation with both Mara and the subject of the story. 'Potholes.'

She gave one of her single syllable laughs.

'Look, I already lost the paper a story this week. If I don't cover this one, my boss is not going to thank me. He even has a headline he wants to use.'

She fixed me with a stare, not needing to ask the question.

'"Morden potholes: the council says they're looking into it."' I sighed, attempting not to cringe at the cliché.

'That headline doesn't work,' said Mara.

'I'm well aware of that. Because there are pot*holes*. Plural.'

'It doesn't work,' she went on, 'because the council never actually looks into anything.'

A beat passed.

Then, despite myself, I started to laugh. I looked at Mara and saw a smile flit across her lips.

'What do you say? Worth chasing a story I know you, like me, care about... by taking a peek at Lenny's house?'

I took a few steps before answering, knowing the lure of potentially getting closer to discovering what had happened to Angel was ultimately too strong to resist.

'I suppose it's not against the law to walk down Lenny's street,' I said. 'But Jasper stays on his lead.'

Jasper, oblivious to the moral quandaries still plaguing me as we made our way to Lenny's house, trotted happily ahead of us down the pavement.

When we were only a couple of streets away, we saw two schoolgirls heading in our direction. I guessed they were around fourteen and probably on their lunch break, engrossed in something on a mobile phone. As they grew level with us, I took in their navy blazers, embroidered with their school's crest and name: Arden Lake Grammar. Peeling her attention away from the phone screen, one of the girls spotted Jasper.

'Oh my God, he's gorgeous!' the girl exclaimed. 'Mind if we pet him?'

'Go ahead,' I smiled.

The girls crouched down to lavish praise on Jasper, who lapped up the attention, rolling onto his back and thumping his tail.

As they gushed over my dog, Mara scanned the street, as though calculating something internally.

'Is it okay to take a photo with him?' the second girl asked, still brandishing her phone.

'Sure.'

With Jasper ecstatic at the fuss, I offered them the handle of his lead. The first girl proceeded to take a photo of the second with Jasper, before they swapped places and pored over the results.

'Look!' they cooed, returning the lead and flashing the phone screen at me. 'How cute is that?'

I smiled again, noticing that Mara had moved away. 'Very,' I nodded, only half-registering the pictures. The girls had been so focused on taking photos of my dog they'd almost cropped themselves out of them entirely, while Jasper remained front and centre.

Thanking me, the two girls hurried away, identical schoolbags bouncing on their backs, enthusing over Jasper's ears, coat and tongue, and how sweet-natured he was.

'See?' I called to Mara as I caught up with her. 'Jasper is perfectly harmless, and may even be considered "sweet"...'

My voice tailed off as I realised we were walking along the Devereauxs' road. With Dex still in police custody, there were no signs of life at the house. The curtains were drawn across every window; the cars in the driveway parked behind firmly bolted gates.

'It's literally over the next junction,' said Mara, referring to Lenny's.

We left the Devereauxs' street and crossed onto the adjoining road. A quarter of the way along it, Mara paused.

'Just there,' she said, giving a subtle inclination of the head.

I glanced at where she'd indicated. Like the Devereauxs' road, this street was also a hotch-potch of properties in varying states of repair. But Lenny Finch's house, even from this distance, appeared to be the worst. It was one in a row of mud-coloured brick terraces almost at the far end of the road, its frontage unkempt, window frames rotten and roof bowing in places. The concrete slabs that formed its short front pathway were cracked and riddled with weeds.

'What now, then?' I asked Mara.

'Now we proceed along the road as though we were merely out for a dog walk,' she said.

I peered at the route ahead. 'But it's a cul-de-sac. Why would we walk a dog down a cul-de-sac unless we lived there?'

'That doesn't matter,' Mara replied, draining her cup and casting it into the nearest wheelie bin. 'I doubt anyone will notice.'

We continued along the pavement, the Finch house looming closer and closer until we found ourselves right in front of it. Mara stopped and stared down at Jasper.

'What?'

'He looks like he needs to relieve himself,' she said.

I wondered whether she was now an expert in dog behaviour, as well as magic, crime, psychology, guitar riffs and everything else. 'Nooo,' I replied. 'I don't think so.'

'Just tell him to, then,' she said, more quietly. 'That way we can linger here for a while to take a look at the place, and it'll seem less suspicious. He's a dog, they take commands. Tell him to...' she circled a hand. 'Make a mess.'

I looked at Mara agape. 'They don't take *those* kinds of commands. What if somebody hears?'

'They'll just think you're telling him to *sit—*'

Before I had the chance to respond, the front door of Lenny Finch's house was promptly opened. A woman stood framed in the threshold. She was about fifty and as thick-set as Lenny. Though she looked nothing like her profile picture, I presumed she was Lenny's mother; the woman who'd written those comments under his Facebook photos.

The woman's hair was bleached to such an extent it looked like great chunks had snapped off, with what was left forming dry clumps around her head. Her mouth had a downwards turn to it, enhanced by the vertical smokers' lines which crossed her lips.

Keeping one hand braced against the door, the woman extracted the stub of a lit cigarette from her mouth, an inch of ash dangling from its end.

'What do you want?' she rasped, smoke pluming from her nose and mouth.

'Merely out for a dog walk,' I replied affably, following what Mara had said minutes before.

'Down a dead end?' the woman scoffed.

I shot Mara a glare that said *I told you so*, but she was already moving towards the open door.

'Good afternoon,' she said, her tone disarmingly pleasant. 'We were wondering if Lenny Finch was in? We're friends of a friend.'

The woman's eyes — the same colour as her cigarette ash — narrowed, flicking from Mara to me to Jasper.

'Lenny's not here.' She took a long drag and tossed the cigarette to the ground. 'He's at work.'

'That's a shame,' said Mara.

The woman reached into the pockets of her hoodie and removed a packet of cigarettes and something silver. She turned her back, and I heard the sound of a fresh cigarette being lit. 'What do you... want with him... anyhow?' she said between puffs.

'As I say, we're friends of a friend,' Mara replied. 'Of Dex

Devereaux.'

Facing us again, the woman's countenance twitched almost imperceptibly.

'We were hoping to ask Lenny about his work at Shinetree Studios last Saturday evening,' continued Mara.

The woman shifted her weight defensively, hand still on the door. 'My Lenny wasn't working at any studios last Saturday evening. And he told the police the exact same thing.'

She had to be lying. 'Do you know where he was in that case?' I asked.

The woman squinted at me, indulging in another long draw of her cigarette. 'Not that it's any of your business,' she said, blowing smoke at my face. 'But he was working that night as well. He's a hard worker, my Lenny.'

She nodded her head at this, as though vindicated. I began to cough.

'Really?' said Mara. 'It's just that there's a CCTV clip of your son that puts him at Shinetree last Saturday. During the recording of Talent Quest, in fact. In the very same studio.' She let the implication hang there, along with the assertion that this woman was Lenny's mother, which the woman didn't correct.

'Must just be someone who looks like him, then. Lenny was at Sonny's off-licence down on the high street last Saturday. He's got a job there. Go and ask the owner if you don't believe me.'

'Mrs Finch… Jean. I'm sure you'll have heard that Dex's wife, Angel Devereaux, was murdered at Shinetree Studios last Saturday,' said Mara.

The woman's jaw quivered for a fraction of a second before

stiffening. Her eyes, hard as two chips of flint, bored into Mara. Mara didn't move and didn't break eye contact.

Then, all of a sudden, Lenny's mother took a step back and, in one swift motion, slammed the door.

We stood there as the noise echoed down the quiet street, its abruptness startling. Jasper whined softly, wondering what would happen next.

'Well,' said Mara, turning away. 'That was interesting.'

I coughed again, a little outraged at having smoke purposefully blown into my face. Just like the smell of Matt's joint, I'd probably stink of cigarettes now for days—

And then something clicked.

When we spoke to Katarina in the studio car park, she'd only given us one potentially useful detail about her kidnapper. I'd doubted whether it was even true at the time, or whether she'd been mistaken, or else made it up to cover herself or Dex. But in that moment, as we walked back along the road, I remembered exactly what she'd said, and it didn't seem so random, after all.

'Mara,' I breathed, grabbing her arm. 'Remember what Katarina told us about the man who put her in the flight case?'

Mara stopped dead on the pavement, her expression altering as the understanding dawned. 'I do.'

'She said the man who put her there... smelt of cigarettes.'

32.♠

We walked a few streets in silence, mulling the detail over. Katarina says she thinks the man who forced her into a flight case smelt of cigarettes. A clip is then found of a man running away from the studios, a man who shouldn't have even been there that night. And when we go to that same man's house, it stinks of cigarettes...

It felt as though it might be another step forwards, but like all the details in the Angel Devereaux case so far, I wondered whether it would actually lead anywhere. Each new piece of information that came to light at first seemed clear-cut, but the only thing any of our discoveries had led to so far was confusion.

Fifteen minutes after having the Finches' front door shut in our faces, Mara, Jasper and I were back on the high street, heading towards the bistro at last. I was starving by this time, and desperate to finally sample the delights of the lunch menu.

When we were a few steps away from the bistro's chic navy frontage, Mara's phone buzzed. She retrieved it from the inner pocket of her coat with one of her characteristic quicksilver motions.

'Lindi,' she told me, picking up the call.

'Hi Mara,' came Lindi's voice down the receiver. It was loud enough for me to hear, but I found myself leaning towards it regardless, eager to find out what she had to say. 'I'm at work at the mo, just called for a catch-up.'

'How nice,' said Mara. 'I've been meaning to speak to you about the barcode.'

Clearly, this wasn't going to be as interesting a conversation as I'd first hoped.

'Right,' replied Lindi.

'Do you have the results of the DNA test on the hair?'

'Come on, Mar,' Lindi said. 'You know I can't tell you anything about that.'

'Is it Katarina's?' asked Mara, undeterred.

Lindi didn't reply.

'Then it *isn't* Katarina's?'

'Mara,' Lindi repeated, a note of frustration in her voice. 'You know I can't tell you anything about that. You're off the case.'

'Thanks, Lindi,' said Mara calmly and, to my surprise, ended the call.

'Not much of a catch-up,' I remarked. 'Looks like we'll never get to the bottom of who that hair belonged to.'

The corner of Mara's mouth quirked upwards. 'On the contrary. Lindi just told me everything I needed to know.'

I hadn't a clue what she meant by this.

'Thanks to that phone call, I know whether the hair was one of Katarina's,' responded Mara enigmatically.

'How the hell could you?' I asked. 'Did Lindi just say something I didn't catch?'

Like Lindi during the phone call, Mara didn't reply.

'So, what — you're telling me you can actually read minds

now?'

Mara remained silent.

'If I didn't know better, I'd assume Lindi was just speaking in code or something.'

'You know I can't tell you anything about that.'

I did a double take. She'd ignored my first three questions only to trot out the same line that Lindi had used a minute ago.

All of a sudden, it made sense. Four days spent in this woman's company must have been rubbing off on me.

Not a barcode, but a *bar code*.

'It was a code!' I rushed, recognising the pattern. 'Lindi kept saying, "You know I can't tell you anything about that". It sounded like she wasn't answering your questions at all, but she was. She was answering in the affirmative. Using that response to mean yes. And when her answer was no, she stayed silent altogether.'

Mara nodded proudly. 'I taught Lindi the code in a bar one night,' she said. 'So we could discuss the people I didn't like the look of without them knowing.'

It was so simple, though I had to admit, pretty ingenious.

'So, the hair,' I continued. 'Based on the code, Lindi told you that hair is *not* one of Katarina Riley's.'

'Correct,' she confirmed. 'It's *not* one of Katarina Riley's.'

'Which means it could have come from anyone.' A sliver of disappointment crept into my voice. If the hair wasn't from Katarina, then it was one less piece of evidence against Dex. 'Another dead end, then.'

'Not necessarily,' Mara mused. 'Dex has denied all knowledge of how the hair got into his house, claiming it could have been transferred from anywhere. Which is perfectly true. And even if it had been proven to be one of Katarina's, it could still have been present at the Devereauxs' house quite innocently. Katarina was working with Dex, after all.'

'Transferred down the back of their couch, though?' It seemed unlikely. But since the hair wasn't from Katarina Riley, the finer points of how it'd found its way into the Devereauxs' house no longer mattered. Mara was right; it could have come from anywhere.

Half-nodding, half-shrugging, Mara swept inside the bistro. We chose a table in the window from where we could people-watch. A smorgasbord of shows flashed from the screens of the TV shop directly opposite. Jasper sat at my feet, his mouth watering as much as mine at the divine smells wafting from the kitchen.

The waiter brought us olives, bread and water and, for the first time in four days, I felt myself starting to relax. I took a deep, steady breath as I perused the menu. Time to enjoy a leisurely lunch before dragging myself back to the Morden Mercury.

When the waiter returned, I ordered Chicken Provençal with fries and salad, plus a complementary bowl of dog biscuits for Jasper. As I poured out the water for Mara and myself, my mind once more circled back to Angel.

'So, are we now juggling three suspects?' I asked. 'Dex, with his banner and the wedding rings. Shane Sinclair, with his unsavoury background and compromising recording. And lastly, Lenny Finch, the magic super-fan who lives a stone's throw from the Devereauxs' and was seen running away from the studio the very same night Angel died.' As I spoke, I ticked them off on my fingers. 'I can see why the evidence against Dex looks persuasive. He had the motive, he ordered that banner…'

'But Sinclair had motive too,' Mara countered, 'however perverse. Maybe Lenny Finch did as well. We just don't know what it was yet.'

'Could Shane really have planted the love letter and rings at the Devereauxs' house, though?' I supposed it was possible. 'He did know when it was going to be empty, I guess. When Dex and Angel were at the studio.'

We sat awhile in silence. With the olives and bread diminishing, I glanced towards the kitchen to see if there was any sign of our lunch. The last time I was this hungry was when we were at the studio on Saturday night. With the following morning coming a close second. I recalled the vending machine coffee and chocolate bar, eaten in the studio corridor before we spoke to Dex in the car park.

'Remember what Dex said to us on Sunday?' I asked Mara, the words suddenly hitting me afresh. 'He said, "That's twice I've tried to do that trick and twice it's been sabotaged." *Sabotaged.* Why use that word in particular? Did Dex suspect someone else? Did he suspect Shane? Or was he just trying to deflect attention away from himself?'

'Deflect attention—?' Mara stopped. 'The CCTV footage,' she murmured, as though considering it all anew. 'Of course. That morning, in the studio… I need to see the footage again.'

She straightened, looking around as if the waiter would at any moment appear bearing Dhita's laptop, rather than our lunch orders. Then she began patting down her coat.

'But that would mean going back to Dhita's house,' I reminded her. 'Since we can't just turn up at the station and ask Paulson if he wouldn't mind us logging on to Taylor's computer for an hour.'

Mara ceased patting herself as abruptly as she had started, a faint, almost indiscernible smile touching her lips. 'We don't need to do either.'

She dipped in and out of a coat pocket and jubilantly held up her hand. It was empty.

'I don't get it.'

Without answering, Mara gave me a thumbs-up.

When I continued to look blank, she slid the forefinger of her other hand up the side of her still-raised thumb and, to my astonishment, a silver USB connector emerged from its tip.

'What the—' I uttered, baffled by the bizarreness of the gesture. It took another second to realise what she was showing me. Mara didn't have a bionic digit; she was holding up a thumb drive.

A literal *thumb* drive.

My jaw dropped. 'Oh my God, are you saying the CCTV footage from Shinetree is on—?'

'You know I can't tell you anything about that,' she interrupted and, with a theatrical flourish, snatched the fake thumb into her fist and put it back inside her coat.

I recollected Mara on Dhita's laptop the previous night, clicking furiously on the keyboard, thumb anchoring the side of the laptop as she worked. Only that wasn't her thumb. It was the thumb *drive*, a latex replica thumb. She must have had it plugged into the laptop before copying the CCTV files onto it. Like a lot of things Mara did, I didn't know whether to be impressed or appalled.

'That footage is confidential,' I said. 'Copying it off a police system... surely that's against the law?'

'Technically,' Mara replied, completely unrepentant. 'Though I'm hoping that solving Angel's murder might offset the consequences. Now, shall we take this back to your flat and have a look?'

'Oh no,' I said quickly, well aware that Mara had now tried to encourage me to break the law twice before I'd even had lunch. And that was without all the other stuff that'd taken place over the past few days. 'You're not doing it on *my* computer. I'm not going to be an accessory.'

The legs of Mara's chair squealed on the floor as she pushed it back. 'You already are,' she returned, flicking her coat behind her and moving in the direction of the bistro door. 'An accessory in solving this case! Come on, we'll go back to mine to look at those files instead.'

'The Chicken Provençal, fries and salad?' came the waiter's voice at my shoulder.

I looked impotently between the plates of mouth-watering, freshly prepared food in his hands and the bistro door, where a final glimpse of Mara's green coat was disappearing into the street.

Since I couldn't take Jasper to Mara's with me, I left him with

Matt. At least he'd enjoyed his bistro biscuits. Jasper, that is, not Matt. When I rushed in and out of the flat, my boyfriend was hunched over the tuning pegs of his guitar, a half-eaten Big Mac balanced on the end of his knee.

A few hours later I was back in Mara's entrance hall, clutching a takeaway myself.

'Mind if I heat up my Chicken Provençal?' I asked Mara.

'Sure.'

She led me across the gleaming tiles of her chequerboard floor and through another doorway off the hall. The sheer scale and theatricality of every room I'd seen in Mara's house so far had taken my breath away, and the kitchen was no exception.

The same deep, treacle-coloured floorboards stretched out beneath my feet. What felt like acres of polished marble counters topped kitchen cabinets the same shade as the floor. A brushed chrome fridge, capacious as the entrance hall in my flat, occupied a large section of one wall like some sort of parked spacecraft. A breakfast bar for six with high, luxuriantly padded chairs formed part of a huge island in the middle of the room. And above it hung another giant shining globe of a chandelier. The light outside was dimming, and little pools of colour from the stained glass set high in the windows bled across the cabinets and countertops, giving the space an enchanted, mystical feel.

Mara gestured to the oven and pulled a tin from one of the nearby drawers. My stomach howled as I took the lid off the foil takeaway container. I couldn't wait to eat, and decided to cut the chicken in two so it could heat through quicker.

Behind me, Mara was busy pouring two generous glasses of wine and booting up her laptop. So I located a knife myself, reaching across to a sturdy knife block and extracting a lightweight chef's-style knife. I dug it into the chicken.

'Whoa—!'

The knife gave and wobbled beneath my fingers, springing back on itself. The blade wasn't metal at all, but rubber, the type of knife you might buy from a joke shop. Only far more realistic.

Mara came over to me and hummed out a laugh, taking the rubber knife from my hand and making it vanish up her coat sleeve. She then passed me a steel version from the knife block.

After popping the food in the oven, I joined her at the breakfast bar.

'Right,' she announced, taking a slug from her glass. 'CCTV files from Shinetree Studios. Saturday the 15th and Saturday the 22nd of March.'

Still unsure of the legal implications of what we were about to do, I indulged in a long sip of wine myself.

Mara inserted the thumb drive, her laptop screen showing the two yellow folders that contained the CCTV footage. 'Remember what you said to me in the bistro?' she asked.

'There's no way I'm letting this Chicken Provençal go to waste?'

She eyed me over the rim of her glass.

'Erm...' I recalled our earlier conversation. 'I asked why Dex chose to use the word *sabotage* as a way of describing Angel's disappearance and death.'

'No,' Mara replied. 'Well, yes, you did. But you also said, "Was Dex trying to deflect attention?" Deflect attention though, or do the opposite — *that* is the question.'

'Either you're misremembering *Hamlet* or I'm not following.'

Mara clicked into the folder of CCTV clips from Saturday the 15th of March. 'Last Sunday, when Katarina was found. When we were at Shinetree and spoke to Dex... What else do you remember going on that morning?'

I remembered seeing the photos on the wall of the corridor, speaking to Paulson and Taylor in the car park. I remembered the paramedics, the ambulance, Katarina being helped into it, sheathed in a silver blanket. I remembered Dex in his leather jacket, scowling at me before his tongue lolled from his mouth like Jasper's when those dancers walked past...

'The dancers!' I blurted. 'They were dressed as police officers. Well, sort of. Their outfits weren't exactly authentic.'

Mara carried on clicking through the clips from the studio's security cameras. She selected one that appeared to show the very same door out of which Lenny Finch had bolted. Then she began scrubbing through it.

A thought struck me. Was Mara implying that the man who'd kidnapped Angel was dressed as a police officer... a *real* police officer? That *this* was the method he'd used to get her out of Shinetree? Furthermore, I wondered, had that man been Dex? Once the show had finished, could he have donned a very different set of clothes in order to sneak past the studio's CCTV in plain sight? Had Shane hired someone to impersonate a cop to take Angel away? Or was the "policeman" Lenny? Had he been there that first Saturday as well as the second?

Mara suddenly hit pause. She leaned into the screen, squinting at it for many long moments. Then she fell back in her chair and shook her head.

'What?' I urged, barely able to contain my curiosity. 'What?'

She'd found something, I could tell. But all I could see on the screen was a fairly ordinary-looking man. A beanie was pulled over his head, and he was dressed in dark clothes: trousers, jacket, boots, gloves, t-shirt. A t-shirt printed across the front with a single, familiar word in white capitals: "CREW".

But this man wasn't Lenny Finch. Nor was he Dex Devereaux, or even Shane Sinclair. This man was a stranger, an entirely new suspect.

'*That's* the man responsible for Angel's disappearance and death?' I asked Mara, a little aghast at what kind of person I was looking at.

'No, Clare,' she replied steadily. 'That *is* Angel.'

33.♠

'I don't understand,' I said. 'For one thing, that's clearly a man.'

Mara zoomed in, the black and white pixelated figure filling the laptop's screen. Although the individual was undeniably short, there were no characteristics of a woman's figure to be observed about their body whatsoever. In fact, the man even appeared to have a beer belly.

I brought Angel to mind, sashaying across the stage in one of her dazzling sequinned leotards. Her finely tapered legs and fingers, the way her slender figure nipped in at the waist, the swell of her bust and hips. Nothing like this person frozen in time on Mara's laptop screen. Moreover, there was an undeniable shadow across their chin.

'That's stubble,' I pointed out. 'And a monobrow.'

Mara let the footage play for another fraction of a second, as the face on screen repositioned itself slightly. Then she hit pause again.

I retrieved my phone from my handbag and searched online for a decent resolution image of Angel Devereaux. When I found one, I directly compared her face with the face on Mara's laptop. Angel's was heart-shaped, slim-nosed and almond-eyed. And this man's... was *also* heart-shaped, slim-nosed and almond-eyed.

'But hang on, aren't we getting ahead of ourselves here?' I asked. 'What if that's not Angel on the CCTV footage, but a relative? That would explain the resemblance. What if she had a brother, for example? They fall out for some reason, he comes back, abducts her to get something out of her... money, maybe? And when that's unsuccessful, he kills her. She could even have had a twin.'

'It's usually identical twins that are used in magic, not non-identical ones,' said Mara. She tapped the screen. 'Believe me, that's Angel.'

I still wasn't sure what to think. That this very masculine-looking figure on the screen was Angel seemed to be the most outlandish notion. Plus, it was nigh on impossible to gauge from that grainy footage whether Mara was indeed right.

I stared harder at the screen. The figure's small, granular face almost appeared to be etched with an expression I couldn't quite decipher. Resignation, perhaps?

If this one low-resolution video clip was supposedly proof that Angel *had* left the studio that first Saturday, then just where had she been for a week? And, most importantly, how had she ended up dead in that second box a week later? We still had absolutely no idea.

I studied the figure again. The man's clothes, the stubble, the look of resignation.

'Someone disguised her,' I said suddenly. 'To get her out of the studio without attracting attention.'

'It's possible,' replied Mara. 'They could have swiped a little dark powder over her chin, given her clothing a few sizes too big to disguise her figure. Hat, oversized gloves to make the hands and wrists appear larger, thick socks under boots to bulk up the ankles. I've done it myself to great effect in the past.'

Still considering the deception of Angel's enforced disguise, it didn't occur to me to ask Mara when she'd done this. Or why.

'My guess is she's still wearing her stage leotard under those clothes,' she went on. 'As soon as you mentioned deflecting attention in the bistro, it hit me. Whoever did this wasn't *deflecting* attention. They employed a more ingenious approach. By dressing Angel in such a way that *no* attention would be drawn to her.'

I pondered Mara's words. Could this person on screen really be Angel Devereaux? Mara had been convinced Angel would be here somewhere, on this footage, and now — apparently — she was. But was it simply a case of wishful thinking — a desperation to solve the puzzle of what had happened to a missing person — causing us to see things that were never really there?

I opened my mouth, wondering how to begin—

'I'm sure I can smell burning,' Mara commented.

'Oh no!' I yelled. 'My chicken!'

'God, look at the time,' I remarked sleepily, the salvageable remains of the Chicken Provençal a few feet away on the coffee table. 'I should get going.'

I hadn't realised it was already after nine, and I needed to make the drive back to Morden ready for work the next day.

I'd sunk into the plush upholstery of Mara's sofa to such an extent it was almost impossible to extricate myself. We'd been discussing the Angel Devereaux case in the living room for the past few hours, my head fuzzed with more theory, suspect and method variations than it could comfortably hold.

'Come on, Clare,' I muttered, willing myself to my feet.

Mara appraised me impassively from the wingback. 'Take one of the spare rooms for the night.'

'Are you sure?'

'Of course. I'll go up now and turn the heating on.'

The suggestion was music to my ears, but again I hadn't planned on staying out overnight, and all I had in my handbag were a few bits of makeup and a hairbrush. 'But I don't have any of my stuff.'

Mara huffed. 'There are clean pyjamas in the wardrobe, toiletries in the ensuite, and enough spare pillows, blankets and towels to stock a medium-sized branch of John Lewis.'

'You have a lot of guests, then?'

Mara looked affronted at the suggestion. 'No,' she replied. 'I can't stand them.'

She disappeared for a short while, returning to lead me back through the entrance hall and up the impressive main staircase, which seemed to continue forever. Passageways led left and right off the top of the stairs, their walls lined with a fascinating assortment of prints, photographs and paintings. Many of these — like the artwork on display downstairs — were vintage magic posters, while others were startling optical illusions. Infinite constellations, not dissimilar to Escher prints, dizzied the viewer. Stark black-and-white abstracts gave the solid upstairs walls the appearance of being alive and rippling.

Mara proceeded to the end of the passageway and pushed open a door. A pair of bronze bedside lamps illuminated a large bedroom, the upper parts of its walls and ceiling painted a deep, inky blue. The colour of this ceiling, plus its height, gave the impression the room was receding up into its own private stratosphere.

An undraped antique four-poster bed dominated the space, its carved uprights rising into the air from a scattering of richly-coloured floor rugs. The remainder of the furniture — lamps, ornaments and soft furnishings — followed the style of the rest of the house; a fusion of pieces that were either modern, or looked like they'd been pilfered from a stately home or museum of theatrical props.

'Bathroom's through there,' said Mara, gesturing to a door on the left. 'Help yourself to any toiletries, whatever you want. Ditto anything in the kitchen. Breakfast is... whenever you surface.'

I thanked her, thinking how nice a lie-in would be in this opulent space. 'I'll probably have to be up around six.'

Mara raised her eyebrows.

'To make it back to Morden in time,' I clarified. 'I'll be expected in the office.'

'See you at six, then,' she said, drawing the door closed behind her.

Just like Mara had said, there were several pairs of unisex pyjamas in the wardrobe, together with fleecy dressing-gowns and multiple piles of spare bedding.

The ensuite was another beautiful room, somewhere between a Dutch Golden Age painting and an Art Deco hotel. Dusky wallpaper with a dense pattern of insects and fruits covered large sections of the walls, with the rest decked out in sparkling black tiles. A white ceramic roll-top bath on brass feet jutted grandly from the wall, an orderly stack of fluffy towels on the shelves of the bamboo table beside it. And on top of the table was a cut-glass bottle with a large manilla tag attached to its neck. Written on the tag, in Mara's elegant handwriting, was a message.

To Clare. A little thank you for your help at HMP Ferndon. Best, Mara.

It was a bottle of Luxe Lumina's Parma Violet perfume, the real thing this time. I smiled, washed and cleaned my teeth, then sprayed a little of the sweet, expensive scent onto my skin.

Dressed in one of the pairs of pyjamas, I gave an involuntary exhalation of contentment as I got into the bed, pillows piled behind me like marshmallows, goose-feather duvet swaddling me like a cloud. I texted Matt, plugged my phone in to charge, and set my alarm for the following morning.

But despite the day's exertions, sleep once more felt like it was a million miles away. I tossed and turned awhile, my mind a relentless whirring projector. It replayed the scenes of the past few days, over and over: Angel plunging tragically from the box on live TV, Katarina's bruised arms, the words on that banner, the CCTV footage from Shinetree and what the hell it all meant. Then there were the police searches, the items found at the Devereauxs' house, Angel's recovered phone.

My brain ticked back through the phone's contents. There was the recording of Shane Sinclair. Had he really been threatening Angel's life, or was the true context of their conversation totally different from how it had sounded? Was he only threatening to embarrass her? There were the "couple photos"; inconsequential shots Angel had taken while out with Dex. Nothing unusual about those. And then there was the picture of the two schoolgirls.

Two schoolgirls.

The girls we'd encountered on the way to Lenny's house leapt to the forefront of my mind. They'd been on their lunch break, wearing school uniforms comprising long flared skirts, white shirts, navy blazers. Blazers embroidered with the name of their school, one I hadn't heard of before. *Arden Lake Grammar.* Above this name had been the crest. A flying bird emblem, long wings outstretched. The same emblem from the photograph on Angel's phone.

Giving up on sleep, I propped myself against the bank of pillows and grabbed my mobile off the nightstand. I opened the search engine and typed in "Arden Lake Grammar".

The school's website was a tasteful shade of mid-blue, its name and crest animating in white at the top of the page. At this resolution, the creature on that crest looked like a seabird. Presumably conveying that an Arden Lake education provided its students with everything they needed to soar.

Judging by the photos on the website, the school itself was

made up of a series of old buildings, surrounded by an oasis of leafy grounds, complete with the lake from which the school took its name. It was located just to the north-east of Merton, in the next borough, which explained why I'd never heard of it before, or come across it at work.

Arden Lake's website revealed the school was co-educational, teaching both boys and girls, and its pages were filled with sunny shots of smiling students, carrying folders or participating in various sports. I opened up the website's menu. About... Curriculum... News... Admissions... Alumni. *Alumni.* Could Angel be here somewhere?

The Alumni button navigated to a separate blog, which outlined the achievements of the school's previous students. There were posts, digitised school newsletter articles, and an assortment of press clippings, all featuring past pupils' successes in medicine, law, sport, the arts...

I searched for "Angel" within the page I was on, but the results highlighted — posts about angel investments, sculptures or charity work — did not relate to Angel Devereaux. Scrolling to the bottom of the screen, I saw the blog consisted of over a hundred pages in total. I had no idea whether these pages were even worth combing through; there might well be nothing of interest among them. But a little niggling sensation told me to give it a try.

I checked through one page and then the next, systematically searching for Angel's name on each. Though Mara had told me that Dex's real surname was "Dodd", and I'd heard on a news bulletin that Angel's original first name was "Angela", I had no clue what her maiden name was.

I'd waded through many years of entries by the time I eventually found it, dated September 1996.

<u>Arden Lake Alumna Conjures Festival Magic!</u>

The celebrated Edinburgh Fringe Festival bore witness to some true Arden Lake talent this summer, as recent alumna Angela Wood (Class of '92) took the notoriously competitive arts scene by storm with her spellbinding solo magic show.

Those of us who recall Angela's mesmerising performances in the drama department's productions won't be entirely surprised. However, to command a Fringe stage solo, and garner such enthusiastic acclaim in the process, is a considerable achievement for anyone, let alone a Festival newcomer.

Reviewers have described Angela's performance as a breathtaking display of classic sleight of hand, infused with a fresh, modern wit and an uncanny ability for clever misdirection. "She held the audience in the palm of her hand," one critic noted.

Arden Lake Grammar is immensely proud to see one of its own shining so brightly on such a prestigious international stage. We have no doubt that Angela Wood is a name to watch in the world of entertainment, and we wish her every continued success. We can't wait to see what she has up her sleeve next!

Included in the article was the publicity photo for Angel's Edinburgh show. Although she was performing magic here, too, her onstage look couldn't have been more different. There was no blonde bouffant in sight; her natural dark brown hair tamed into flattering ringlets, which fell about her shoulders. Absent, too, were the sequinned leotards and shining tights. She was dressed instead in an outfit that resembled a more feminine version of a classic magician's suit. A black jacket with satin lapels fitted snugly to her figure. A flattering pair of matching black trousers accompanied it, and the ensemble was completed by a stylishly knotted pale silk scarf, in place of the traditional bow tie.

The short paragraph below this article described Angel as a recent drama graduate of Lincoln University. And her talent for performing had obviously been evident even before then. I thought back to Shane Sinclair's claim that he'd only singled Angel out that day in the studio as he recognised the scale of her talent. Did this article add further weight to what he'd said?

I moved down to the very last part of the post. Another photograph of a young Angel, the familiarity of which registered with a jolt. It was the same picture that had been on Angel's phone.

From the screen of my own mobile, Angel beamed back at me charismatically. There she was again, in her Arden Lake Grammar uniform, blazer tied jauntily around her waist, arm flung up in that ebullient, exaggerated pose. And a little way behind her stood the other girl, Angel's friend. Her posture was more restrained, a trace of admiration very slightly animating her expression.

Beneath the photo was a caption. The two girls' names.

Angela Wood and Erin Grant.

34.♠

The clock on my mobile showed almost one in the morning, despite my brain fizzing like it was noon. I took in Angel's school photo once more; that single fleeting moment in her childhood flooded with pure golden light. Had Angel kept that picture on her phone because her school days were such a happy time? Because looking at it was like gazing through a portal, onto a sunny afternoon when her whole life shone brightly ahead of her, radiating with potential?

Crucially, did the presence of the photo on her phone imply she was still friends with Erin Grant? If so, then could Erin be aware of anything, however insignificant, that might lead us to Angel's killer—?

A noise, far-off in the depths of the house, interrupted my thoughts. At first I dismissed it, presuming a huge old house like Mara's was apt to make strange noises, but then the sound came again. It was like an odd, intermittent thudding, emanating from one of the rooms downstairs.

Mara must still be up. And I was seized by the urge to tell her what I'd just found.

I flung back the duvet and got out of bed, pulling on one of the dressing-gowns from the wardrobe. Mobile still in hand, I padded quietly across the archipelago of rugs. The room was lit only by the dimmer lamp on the nightstand, its low glow not quite reaching the door. I stood in the spreading pool of shadow awhile, listening again and hearing nothing. But as I pressed an ear to the door, there came a distant, unearthly wail.

My pulse quickened. The cry didn't sound like Mara. It didn't sound human.

I eased the bedroom door open and peered out. The passageway was pitch-black, its only illumination whatever light was filtering in through the window on the staircase. At the top of the stairs, I hesitated, clueless as to which of the many doors off the landings might be the one to Mara's bedroom. Although I was certain the noises I'd just heard had issued from the ground floor.

Not thinking to search for the light switch, I softly descended the grand staircase by feel alone, the substantial carved banister cool beneath my hand. The vast entrance hall at the bottom was hushed, the chequerboard tiles cutting a chill along the soles of my feet.

A meagre shred of light was showing in the slit beneath the living room door. I edged towards it through the powdery darkness and gave a tap on the panelled wood.

No reply.

Pushing the door ajar, I didn't see her straightaway. The living room was far darker than when I'd left it, several hours before. Only one small side lamp was on, its single electric bulb glowing as if by magic, from what looked like a completely transparent — and wireless — glass base. A log fire had, at some point, been lit in the hearth, but allowed to burn out. All that was left was a dissipation of dying embers, rippling orange. The heating must have gone off for the night down here, too, as the enormous room was almost arctic.

Mara was sitting cross-legged in her favourite wingback chair, staring so deeply into the crumbled remains of the faintly glowing logs it was like she was in a trance.

'Mara?'

She didn't move a muscle, as though she had no awareness of me being with her. It was a little eerie; her sitting there, inert and unblinking, the scant light in the room throwing the wall carvings into dramatic relief. The taxidermied dove beneath its bell jar looked like it might, at any moment, beat its wings. The Egyptian sarcophagus seemed to breathe.

I drew closer. 'Mara, are you okay?'

She was wearing her black jeans and a thin knitted top. I extended an arm and touched her hand, which lay limply on the arm of the chair. It was frozen to the bone.

I said her name again, and only then did her head creak to face me. There was a second when she didn't appear to recognise me at all, before apprehension dawned.

'Clare... You're awake.'

I removed my hand from hers. Was I seeing things, or was there a tint of redness to it?

I pulled a nearby footstool over to the wingback and sat down. 'I couldn't sleep,' I replied. 'Did you hear those noises? Thudding, and some sort of a... *wail*.'

'No,' she said, a little too quickly.

I offered to put some more logs on the fire, but she told me she was fine, apparently unbothered by the room's temperature.

So I decided to press on, holding my phone proudly aloft.

'I found something. That photo, on Angel's mobile. The one of her at school? In her uniform?' My excitement that this might somehow prove useful to the investigation began to build once more.

Mara nodded slowly.

'I remembered that those girls on the way to Lenny's house were wearing identical school blazers to the one Angel was wearing in the picture. So, I searched the name of the school. And their website has an Alumni section.' The words tumbled eagerly out. 'Anyway, not only did I come across an article about Angel there, but I found the *exact same* photo that was on Angel's phone. Remember the girl in the background? Her name is Erin Grant!'

'Erin Grant,' Mara agreed, her expression inscrutable. The remnants of the fire cracked loudly.

'Well, I figured it's got to be worth finding more out about Erin. Though Angel might just have had that photo on her phone because she liked it, there's a chance the two of them are still friends.'

'Erin Grant,' repeated Mara listlessly. Gone was her usual air of impatient, restive energy. It was like she was stupefied, ill. I wondered whether something awful had happened in the time I'd been upstairs. I started to ask her this question when she suddenly spoke again.

'Erin Grant has a chartered accountancy business. Near the park, as a matter of fact.'

She wasn't making sense. 'Park? What park?'

Mara fixed her eyes on me quizzically, as though the answer

was obvious. 'The park. In Morden.'

My bubble of enthusiasm at coming across Erin's name on the school's website popped. Of course Mara already knew. And she not only knew, she'd gone one step further. While I'd been congratulating myself on finding a name, Mara had probably already drawn up Erin Grant's entire employment history, plus a full psychological profile.

'Oh,' I said, the single word doing little to express the inadequacy I actually felt. 'Right. You already found her.'

'An hour or so ago,' Mara confirmed. 'The same way you did. Then, I conducted a few more online searches. It puts quite a number of our key players — the Devereauxs, the Finches, and now Erin Grant — all living within a surprisingly small radius in your patch of south London. I wonder if Shane Sinclair knows Erin Grant somehow?'

My deflation aside, the coincidence was striking. I considered how Morden, usually so unremarkable — literally the end of the line — was suddenly a hotbed of connections to a nationally televised murder. I wondered why Mara would think Shane knew Erin, other than she clearly still saw the man as our number one suspect.

When I looked back at Mara, she'd returned to gazing intensely into the dwindling fire.

'Listen, are you sure you're alright?' I asked her. 'Did something happen while I was upstairs?'

'While you were upstairs? No.'

'Because it must be hard, you know, this investigation, what happened with your husband—' I blurted the sentence out, not just to break the deafening quiet, but also because I knew it was true. Some part of Mara was broken, like me. The void left from which something had been ripped. And perhaps us pursuing the case of a previously missing person so obsessively wasn't filling that void, but making it more apparent. Stretching it wider.

'Clare, I'm fine,' Mara snapped back, her tone keen as a blade.

A minute of oppressive silence passed.

'Okay, well I suppose I should try to get some sleep,' I mumbled, feeling a familiar weariness wash over me. A weariness that wasn't just the result of lack of sleep, but always being two steps behind.

A few short hours later, I felt like I'd barely slept a wink. Dragging myself from the ridiculously comfortable four-poster, I headed into the bathroom.

I initially hoped the mirror was a trick piece of glass, and that it wasn't me but some other haggard individual gawping my way, her hair a tangled mess, dark circles blooming beneath her eyes. I felt every bit as crumpled as my duvet now was, after hours of my tossing and turning. Though it was only a couple of minutes after six, I knew I still had to get a move on to be in with a chance of making it back to Morden in time for work.

I splashed some water on my face, dragged the brush through my hair, and applied some of the moisturiser I found in the chic bamboo cabinet above the sink. The concealer I dabbed on next did little to disguise the bags under my eyes. I was applying some lip gloss to finish when a small, irrational spurt of annoyance rose inside me.

Despite Mara's manner last night, I supposed she was in the kitchen already, brewing a fresh pot of coffee and looking infuriatingly put-together. She didn't even seem to sleep. Maybe she just plugged herself into some sort of mains charger overnight, emerging perfectly restored and several intellectual leaps ahead of everyone else by the morning.

A burst of tinny lyrics sounded from the nightstand, where my phone was still plugged in. I crossed back into the bedroom to answer the call, assuming it was Matt. It wouldn't have surprised me if he was still up, having spent all night working on a song.

But glancing at my mobile, I saw it wasn't Matt calling. It was Jeff.

My stomach clenched. Not only had I spectacularly missed last night's deadline for the finished pothole story, I hadn't even started writing it yet.

As tempted as I was to ignore the call, I knew, deep down, that I had to bite the bullet. I took a breath. 'Hi, Jeff,' I said, in as breezy a manner as I could muster. 'You're calling early.'

'I have to call bloody early, don't I?' Jeff began. 'To be in with a chance of getting hold of you! What the hell happened to the pothole story? It should have gone to print this morning! I take it you saw the note I left for you? Or were you telling more porkies when you said you were coming into the office yesterday?'

'I'm really sorry, Jeff. I had every intention of writing the story. It's just... well, something came up.'

'Something came up?' he parroted, voice laced with suspicion. 'This is getting to be a habit, Deyes. And in the meantime, we're being made to look like thorough chumps by the Merton Gazette. I dread to think what headline they'll have come up with for this pothole story. We'll have lost out on a great pun for the second time in one week.'

'I know and I really am sorry,' I replied. 'I'm on my way in now. I'll see you in a few hours—'

It was only then that his words of moments earlier landed with a clang. I hardly dared ask. 'Hey Jeff, what did you mean when you said *more* porkies?'

'I've seen you, Deyes. Cavorting around Morden this week when you should've been in the office. Funny that everywhere I've been, trying to get the latest on the Angel Devereaux story, I've caught a glimpse of *you*. And who's that woman I've seen you hanging around with?'

My cheeks burned. How could I have been so stupid? I knew Jeff had been busy chasing the story of what had happened to Angel. Why had I thought I could bunk off work to do the same and he wouldn't see me?

'You're on thin ice,' Jeff continued. 'If you can't cover the stories I put your way, then I'll find someone who can—'

Bolstered by a sudden, reckless cocktail of exhaustion, embarrassment and irritation, I interrupted him. 'Actually, Jeff, that woman is Mara Knight. Wife of Travers Knight. The famous magician.'

'Travers... Knight?' Jeff went quiet for a second, the information percolating. Then he grew impatient again. 'A *magician's* wife? So that's what you've been doing the last few days? I thought I'd told you to leave the Angel Devereaux case to me?'

Hoping Mara wasn't outside, I lowered my voice, heart thrumming against my ribs. 'I haven't been talking to Mara about Angel Devereaux. I've been talking to her about... *her husband.*' I paused, swallowed hard. 'There's a story there, Jeff,' I said. 'And I think it might be big.'

A long beat of silence ensued, so long I assumed Jeff, still angry with me, had hung up. 'You think you're on to something, Deyes?' he murmured. 'About what happened to Travers Knight?'

I chewed my lip, considering how best to answer. 'I could be.'

'It's not strictly Morden news.'

'I know.'

'That said... jeez, if you think you can get to the bottom of the televised disappearance of a national celebrity when nobody else has, then it will be major for the Mercury. How long do you think you need?'

'Er, well, it's all... ongoing,' I managed. 'Maybe another few days?'

'Fine. Travers Knight, eh?' Jeff marvelled. 'This could be huge. Keep me posted.'

He hung up, and a wave of guilt came crashing over me, eclipsing my exhaustion.

35.

The conversation I'd just had with Jeff, about investigating Mara Knight and her husband's disappearance for the Morden Mercury, sat like a stone in my stomach. I tried my best to ignore the sensation. I'd bought myself a little more time. A couple more days to delve into the baffling, tragic case of Angel Devereaux, alongside the only person I knew who might actually be able to make any sense of it.

When I'd dressed and gone downstairs, Mara had indeed been in the kitchen, a fresh cafetière of coffee steaming from one of the silvery marble countertops.

'Morning, Clare.'

'Morning.'

'What can I get you? Toast? Cereal? There's muesli, granola, porridge...'

The thought surfaced that Mara's cheery tone might have been prompted by her manner last night. She was trying to make amends, and I again felt the heaviness weighing inside me. 'Just toast is fine, thanks.'

Mara fed slices of thick, artisanal bread into a café-style toaster and depressed the handle. She brought the coffee pot and cups to the table, along with sugar, honey and a little cream.

'Help yourself.'

I thanked her again, pouring out some coffee and feeling worse about my call with Jeff by the second.

'So,' she started, joining me at the breakfast bar. 'You're heading back to Morden this morning. Straight back to the office?'

Teaspoon in hand, I toyed with the dissolving sugar cube in my cup. 'Well, no, actually. My boss, erm... he texted to give me the day off.' I cleared my throat at the lie. 'Wants me to write up that pothole story.'

Mara appraised me, head tilted to the side. Could she tell I was lying?

'Right,' she replied. 'Or you'll be in a pot-*whole* lot of trouble?'

I gave a tight smile, forcing down a mouthful of coffee. 'Something like that.'

Mara got to her feet and popped the toast. 'Only...' she said, an appealing edge to her voice, 'since you're going that way, I was wondering whether you might give me another lift?' She placed the perfectly toasted bread in front of me, together with an assortment of jams, and a small ceramic top hat that lifted to reveal a diamond-shaped pat of butter.

'You're going to see Erin Grant?' I asked, taking a guess at what she had planned for the morning.

'I am.'

I thought back to the other girl in that sun-drenched photograph on Angel's phone. Was Erin another dead end, or a piece of Angel's past that might just fill out the holes in the present?

I layered butter and jam on one slice of toast and then

the next, hoping the food might pad out the hardness in my stomach. 'In that case, I'll come with you.'

And so, not long after nine, we found ourselves standing outside Keystone Chartered Accountants in Morden. The office was a tidy, unassuming Victorian semi on a quiet street to the west of the district. A resin-fronted plaque showing the company logo and names of its accountants reflected the green bank of trees bordering the park opposite.

'Shall we?' Mara asked, one eyebrow slightly arched.

I nodded, tempted to cross my fingers. Surely — given Erin was a school friend of Angel's and lived in the same area as the Devereauxs — she must know something useful?

The accountancy firm's reception area was hushed and understated. It consisted of an entrance hall with cream walls, muted abstract paintings, and a receptionist obscured by a substantial jug of lilies. We moved towards the desk.

'Good morning,' said Mara, her voice smooth. 'We'd like to speak with Erin Grant, please. We don't have an appointment, but it's rather important.'

A grey head meerkatted over the top of the lilies as the receptionist stood up. 'Oh,' she muttered. She moved the flowers aside and took off her spectacles, which swung low on a copper chain across her bust. 'I'm afraid Ms Grant isn't in the office this morning. Well, not until ten. She's starting later this week.'

'Can we wait?' Mara asked.

'You could,' said the receptionist, shoving her spectacles back on and magnifying her eyes to twice the size they'd been without them. 'But I doubt Ms Grant will have much time to speak to you. She has back-to-back clients from ten 'til lunchtime.'

My heart sank a little, and the woman must have caught my disappointment.

'If you need to speak to her urgently, well... she does like to take a coffee to the park,' she said, waving vaguely to the window. 'Before work. She has a regular spot by the bandstand.'

'By the bandstand,' repeated Mara. 'Thank you, you've been very helpful.'

'Not at all, but I can't guarantee she'll be there,' replied the receptionist, removing her spectacles again. 'She's been feeling a little off this week, hence the late starts. Hay fever. Shouldn't really be coming in at all if you ask me.'

As we turned away, a printed sheet of paperwork caught my eye. It was folded in thirds, and the top rows of numbers were visible, like it might be a client's tax return. At the top of the page, below an additional fold, was the name "Angel Devereaux".

Was Erin Angel's accountant?

Back out on the pavement, Mara scanned the park boundaries. 'Bandstand?'

'This way.'

We skirted Morden Park's outermost footpath, following it until we reached the tennis courts. Thinking that marching straight towards the bandstand may not be the best tactic, I stopped and pointed to the hexagonal, weather vane-topped roof further along the path. 'Over there.'

Mara leaned around the courts, head twitching left and right.

'I think I see her. Woman sitting alone with a cup of coffee. And reading... a magazine, by the looks of it. Come on.'

We continued around the tennis courts and along the path. Nearing Erin Grant, I saw that the bench she was sitting on was in a very pretty spot, nestled below an elm facing the bandstand. Despite the intervening twenty-five years, Erin appeared to have changed little since the photograph was taken of her at school. Her skin had a pale, almost translucent quality, a scattering of freckles visible across the bridge of her nose. Her fair hair was pulled into a sleek, neat chignon, held in place with a tortoiseshell clip.

Erin coughed, a dry, papery sound, and dabbed at her nose with a tissue. As Mara had observed, a magazine was lying open on her lap. A coffee cup was balanced on top of it, clutched in her other hand. From the ring finger of this hand, a plain gold wedding band caught the light. It was a curious thing. It looked simple in quality, somehow. Thinner and cheaper, more scratched than the other jewellery Erin wore.

As our shadows fell over her, Erin looked up. Her eyes, lightly bloodshot from her hay fever, widened slightly, revealing startling blue irises.

'Erin Grant?' said Mara.

'Yes?' she replied, a flicker of apprehension crossing her face. 'Can I help you?' Her voice was hoarse, a tad unsteady.

'We were wondering whether we could have a quick chat with you about Angel Devereaux?' I asked with a friendly smile. 'Don't worry, we're not police or anything.' I was trying to break the ice, but with hindsight it was a misjudged opener and seemed to have the opposite effect to the one I intended.

Erin stiffened. 'Why would I worry if you were police?' she said, gaze flitting off towards the tennis courts. 'I don't have anything to hide.'

I remembered what Mara had said about Dex avoiding eye contact during his Talent Quest interview. Erin's eyes had just done the same. Did that mean she was lying as well?

'Spoken like a true Piscean,' Mara cut in. 'A water sign, so honest, sensitive, intuitive...'

Erin awkwardly shifted her grip on the magazine, which I now noticed was open on the weekly horoscope section. 'How did you...?'

'Know you were a Pisces? Just a feeling. I believe your horoscope this week revolved around moving into a new phase in life... a romantic disappointment... and something that's been unsettling you financially.'

I could sense my expression had altered, and was set with a surprise and confusion that mirrored Erin's own.

Erin visibly bristled, clutching the top of the magazine tighter. 'Something unsettling me financially? I'm a chartered accountant. Most of my clients' tax returns unsettle me. It's all rubbish, anyway.' Erin wrenched the page over so hard it came free of its staples. 'So if you're not police, then why are you here? I suppose my receptionist told you where to find me?'

'Nice view of the bandstand,' Mara remarked randomly.

Erin, still avoiding eye contact, frowned.

'To answer your question, we're here because I knew Angel Devereaux through the magic grapevine,' said Mara. 'Via my husband.' She forced these last words out.

'Funny she never mentioned you,' returned Erin defensively,

only realising what she'd said a moment too late.

'So you *were* a friend of Angel's?' I asked.

Erin's face met ours then, her attention alternating between us. 'We went to school together. Then university. All a very long time ago.'

She must have studied at Lincoln too.

'We lost touch after that,' Erin went on, straining a false smile. 'So I'm sorry, but I can't help you.' She sipped her coffee and carried on leafing through the magazine, as though the matter was closed.

'Do you live in Morden as well?' asked Mara. 'Nice place.'

'I'm just up the road myself,' I added.

There was an uncomfortable pause.

'Look, I know what you're getting at,' Erin snapped. 'That Angela lived in Morden and here I am too.' She threw a hand into the air in a gesture of frustrated emphasis. 'But if you must know, I only moved back here last year. I grew up a few streets away.'

'Do you know Shane Sinclair?' Mara asked suddenly, in a complete change of tack.

Erin looked genuinely bewildered. 'Of course not,' she said. 'Why would I?'

'And what about Dex Devereaux?' said Mara.

The shift in Erin was instantaneous, her guardedness sharpening to a brittle anger. Her blue eyes, previously watery, turned to steel.

'Dex?' she hissed. 'She should never have married him.'

I recalled Angel had been with Dex since her early twenties. Which means she must have met him while she was still a university student, or not long after.

'Did you ever meet Dex?' I asked Erin. 'Angel and he must have got together not long after you were at university?'

'They met at the Edinburgh Festival,' said Erin. 'But yeah, he'd already been sniffing round her when she was performing at uni.'

It struck me then where Dex's accent was from, an accent that sounded northern but that I couldn't immediately place. Lincolnshire.

'Angela had a solo show in Edinburgh. Dex was already a known magician at the time. *And* he was in a relationship. But he was looking for a new assistant and decided to pursue Angela.' She spat out a bitter laugh. 'An assistant! Angela had been doing magic nearly her whole life by then. She had more talent in her little toe than he had in his entire body.'

I brought to mind the photograph of Angel in her stage outfit, her physical appearance so different to how she looked when she was with Dex. In her own show, she had stood out, an individual. When performing with Dex, she'd been the blonde and sequinned embodiment of a stereotypical magician's assistant.

Furthermore, this was the fourth time that Angel's skills as a magician had been lauded. Shane Sinclair had said it. *Angel was the real star of that double act.* Then there was the glowing feedback on her Edinburgh show. *She held the audience in the palm of her hand.* Dex intimated himself in the studio car park how the Devereauxs' act had relied on Angel. *I needed her, didn't I?* And now here was Erin, telling us exactly the same thing.

'Do you have any idea why Angel took Dex up on his offer and became his assistant?' I asked. 'It sounds like she was very talented. Couldn't she have performed alone?'

Mara answered for her. 'There were far more opportunities in the nineties magic world for men than there were for women.'

'Exactly,' Erin agreed, her voice rising. 'Like I said, Angela should never have been with him. Performing... magic... the limelight... it was an *obsession* with her. And...' She swallowed hard. 'Angela was attracted to the moron, I suppose. On whatever level.'

I thought of the photo of the two of them at school, the kindling of admiration in Erin's expression, whilst Angel postured flamboyantly, showing off for the camera.

'Angela thought... no, she was *convinced*, that being with Dex was the only way. For a woman to make it in that world. *His* world.' Erin's plastic coffee cup crackled in her hand. She was squeezing it so tightly her fingers were pink. Her voice dipped and grew unsteady once more, a quality to it like paper tearing as she uttered her next words.

'I'm certain that man killed her. He was jealous — pathologically jealous — that she was so much more skilled than he was. He'd resented her for years, and last week he finally snapped. He... he loved hurting women.'

The words from the banner screamed in my mind, the crude black lettering suddenly vivid against the green backdrop of the park.

36.

The sentence Erin Grant had uttered echoed starkly as we left the park bandstand and retraced our route to the gates.

He loved hurting women.

Its closeness to the words printed on that banner sent a shiver down my spine. It couldn't merely have been a coincidence, though when Mara had asked Erin why she'd said that about Dex — and used those words in particular, that he "loved hurting women" — Erin insisted it was true. Adding a little shiftily that it must just have been in her subconscious. I don't know if I believed her.

As I replayed our conversation with Erin, my steps slowed.

'How did you do that?' I asked Mara. 'That stuff with the star signs? You couldn't possibly have known she was a Pisces. Unless you looked it up beforehand. But I couldn't find anything about Erin online other than her LinkedIn profile, and I don't think your star sign is usually included on your CV.'

Mara, who had marched a few paces ahead, turned to me. 'A lucky guess, mostly,' she admitted, though there was a glimmer in her eye that suggested something more. 'Erin had the magazine open on her lap, yet not only was the top of the page turned over, but she was obscuring it with her right hand, like she'd been reading the bottom. Pisces is usually the last star sign, so the lowest on the page. And as for the rest...' She shrugged. 'A new phase in life, a romantic disappointment, something about money worries... Broad strokes, Clare. Most people can find something in their lives to fit those. It's a classic cold reading technique.' She paused for a second, brows drawing together. 'Her body language suggested I'd landed a few hits, though.'

It made sense. That Mara would be adept at reading people, at spotting their subtlest cues. Still, it felt like more than that. It felt, as many things with Mara did, a little like real magic.

'She seemed to know a lot about Dex for someone who claims she lost touch with Angel after uni,' I mused, recounting the vitriol in Erin's voice.

Mara didn't reply for a minute. 'Grief does strange things to people,' she said eventually. 'Old resentments can resurface.'

Erin clearly hadn't liked Dex when she'd first met him all those years ago. But how well did she know Dex and Angel now? She said she'd not long moved back to the area, and yet was certain Dex was behind Angel's tragic end, and that last week he'd "finally snapped". Did Erin know more about the Devereauxs' relationship than she was letting on? Did the paperwork at Keystone Accountants bearing Angel's name imply Erin was familiar with the Devereauxs' income? And wasn't it a little early in the year for hay fever?

We walked awhile in silence.

'Of course!' Mara exclaimed, breaking the quiet.

'What is it—?'

She tapped the side of an index finger to her mouth in thought. 'Several people now have been singing Angel's praises when it comes to magic. Shane Sinclair, Erin Grant. That's without the online videos showing Dex fudging some sleight of hand move, before Angel steps in to perform it flawlessly.'

'I was thinking the same thing.'

'So what if...' her eyes narrowed. 'What if it was *Angel* who invented the Devereauxs' most famous illusion? What if Dex had very little to do with it?'

I pictured Angel writhing in the tank of water, trapped beneath that boiling layer of flames.

'Fire and Water?' I blurted. 'You think it was Angel's trick?' The idea was startling. It reframed everything I thought I knew about the Devereauxs' dynamic.

'It was so much more spectacular than anything else in their repertoire,' Mara mused, her gaze distant. 'A set piece, with an underlying theme. Whereas all their other tricks were more off-the-peg. Standard. Unimaginative. The speed at which Dex and Angel changed places during Fire and Water was technically superb. There was no air supply to the tank, no trapdoor, and no signs of wet footprints on the stage. It was flawless. And for an effect to be flawless, its method must be exceptional. Too exceptional for Dex's brain to have come up with.'

'So why not do it on Talent Quest?' I asked. 'Given it was their best trick? The Devereauxs haven't performed Fire and Water since the early two-thousands.'

We turned out of the park and along the road that flanked one side of it, heading towards the high street. Building sites rumbled with activity; young mums with pushchairs navigated their way along busy pavements; the scent of a fry-up drifted from a nearby café.

'Kaelen Volt performs Fire and Water every night in Vegas,' said Mara. 'Which suggests the Devereauxs sold it to him. Years ago, most likely. The ongoing royalties from the sale of an illusion like that would be substantial.'

This sounded like Mara speaking from experience.

It made sense, though. That there was no evidence of Angel and Dex performing Fire and Water for the last decade because they'd sold the rights. I was about to say this to Mara when I realised she was no longer with me. Peering back, I saw she'd stopped some distance behind, to stare diagonally across the street. I followed her eyeline to a hand car wash, where a seven-foot inflatable gorilla flailed maniacally from the forecourt.

'Well, well,' Mara murmured as I drew closer. 'A familiar face.'

She wasn't talking about the gorilla. There, wrestling a jet wash hose with a distinct lack of coordination, was a figure I recognised.

Lenny Finch.

His loose-fitting jeans were on the point of falling down, just as they had been on the CCTV footage from Shinetree. The t-shirt he'd paired with them — like the "CREW" shirt at the studios — also appeared a couple of sizes too small. It was already soaked through and clinging unflatteringly, further ballooning the eyes of the yellow Minion figure printed on the front. I don't know who looked to be in more discomfort at their predicament: Lenny Finch or the Minion.

Lenny continued to fumble with the hosepipe's nozzle, sending an erratic spray of water through the open window of a nearby Volvo, to the visible annoyance of its occupants.

'Come on,' said Mara, already stepping off the kerb. 'Let's go and introduce ourselves.'

As we reached the forecourt, the car Lenny had been attempting to clean pulled away, its driver announcing his refusal to pay. Another man exited the car wash's kiosk, grumbling under his breath at Lenny and turning the hose on the next car in the queue.

Lenny looked up as Mara strode towards him, a faint sheen of sweat, or car wash spray, glistening on his forehead. His close-set eyes broadened first in surprise, then something that almost resembled fear. Was this the manner of a guilty man? After witnessing the ham-fisted mess he'd been making of the car wash, I couldn't imagine him being capable of carrying out a plan to kidnap no less than two separate women, and arrange for the first to be killed live on national television in the middle of someone else's magic trick. But then again, maybe he was just a really good actor.

'Lenny Finch?' Mara asked, towering over the man. He was both shorter and chubbier than he'd appeared on the studio footage, or in his Facebook photos. Nevertheless, like his mother, he had a solid build, a build that could easily have overpowered a woman the size of Angel or Katarina.

Lenny dropped the sopping sponge he was still holding, which landed with a wet *thwack* upon the ground. He wiped a sudsy hand on his jeans, smearing soap across the blue denim. 'Uh... yeah?'

'We'd like a quick word, if that's okay,' said Mara.

Lenny didn't reply at first, then stammered, 'Wh— What about? I don't know anything!'

Perhaps he wasn't such a good actor, I thought. If he *was* guilty of having a part in Angel's death, he wasn't doing a great job of hiding it. His body closed up on itself, and he began to scramble away. I was certain we weren't going to get anything out of him at all.

'You like magic?' called Mara to his retreating form, which was fast disappearing through the kiosk doorway.

He froze then, and very slowly shuffled to face us again.

Mara reached into the pocket of her green wool coat and, with a snap of the wrist, produced a single, pristine playing card. The queen of spades.

She moved towards Lenny, who was by now having the kiosk door forcibly closed on him by an irate car wash manager. Lenny's eyes, which had previously darted with confusion between Mara and me, fixed themselves on the card. His jaw slackened.

'Pick a card, any card,' Mara said, her voice taking on a faintly theatrical tone.

Now it was my turn to gaze at Mara in confusion. She was only holding up one card.

Lenny sniggered softly, the card continuing to mesmerise him as though it was a hypnotist's pendulum.

'Queen of spades!' he burbled.

Still holding up the queen of spades, Mara flicked the back of the card and, just like that, it totally transformed into a completely different one.

'No, I'm sorry,' she said, pointing at the new card, 'it was the two of hearts.'

Lenny gasped, a vocalisation of childlike wonder. 'How…

how did you do that?'

'A good magician only reveals their secrets in very, very exceptional circumstances,' replied Mara. 'So I wonder if you could perhaps reveal one of yours for us now?'

The wonder faded from Lenny's face, replaced by a renewed wariness. 'What do you mean?'

'I mean you must be a really good magician,' said Mara. 'One of the best.'

Lenny was obviously intrigued by this, his cheeks colouring slightly.

'You see, you were caught on Shinetree Studios' CCTV cameras last Saturday night,' Mara went on. 'But your mum says you were working at Sonny's off-licence at exactly the same time. That's very impressive. I'd love to know how you did it.'

Lenny paled, his mud-coloured eyes scouring the perimeter of the car wash, as if looking for an escape. He started to fidget, picking at a loose thread on the bottom of his t-shirt. 'I... I don't know what you're talking about.'

Mara left a deliberate pause, but still Lenny wasn't forthcoming, focused instead on unravelling the cotton thread holding up his shirt hem. Mara and I glanced at each other.

'Have you heard of a woman called Katarina Riley?' I took over, remembering the detail that had struck me so forcefully on the way back from the Finches' house.

I think he smelt of cigarettes.

'Someone kidnapped Katarina on Saturday night,' I said, 'and locked her inside a flight case.'

We may not have had any evidence as yet as to whether Lenny had killed Angel, but Katarina's kidnapping by a man who smelt of cigarettes — plus the security footage putting him at the same studio at the same time — seemed too much of a fluke not to mean anything.

'It was lucky Katarina was found,' Mara added. 'If she hadn't been, then whoever put her there would have been responsible for murder.'

No sooner had this last word left Mara's mouth than Lenny's composure crumbled. 'No comment... no comment...' he repeated, his posture that of a cornered animal.

'Come on, Lenny,' Mara encouraged. 'We're not the police. You can tell us.'

'No, no — I can't!' he sputtered. 'Magician's code, I can't! I can't break the magician's code!' He was stiff with panic, reiterating this same phrase, over and over.

It was almost comical, his insistence on maintaining a "magician's code" when he was clearly just a fan. A fan, no less, who lived practically on top of the victim of a murder, and appeared on the verge of confessing something serious.

'I... I can't say anything,' Lenny moaned. 'She'll kill me—'

'Who'll kill you, Lenny?' I breathed, reaching out to him. 'Who—?'

'What the bloody hell is going on here?'

The voice, like flints rattling in a metal bucket, gave me a start. Before I knew it, none other than Jean Finch was bearing down on us. She grabbed hold of her son's arm and proceeded to drag him away. A dog-eared plastic carrier bag displaying the Kwik Save logo swung wildly from her other hand.

Jean looked even more hostile than she had on her doorstep, feet *thwomping* along in her knock-off Ugg boots, her expression thunderous.

'Mum!' squeaked Lenny, recoiling from her as if anticipating a blow.

'Forgot your lunch again, didn't you?' Jean spat. She roughly released her grip on Lenny's arm and pitched the carrier bag towards him. Then she rounded on Mara and me. 'And I thought I told you two where to get off yesterday! Disgusting! You harassing my Lenny when he's trying to earn an honest crust.'

Her tirade was delivered with such gusto that even Mara appeared momentarily taken aback.

'And don't you be telling these vultures anything, you hear me?' Jean barked at her son. 'It's not a crime to be a fan of magic. And the police can't prove anything. Bunch of bleeding amateurs.' She removed a packet of cigarettes from her handbag. 'Light!' Jean clicked her fingers at Lenny, who dug a box of matches out of the pocket of his jeans. He tried again and again to strike one, but the box was too soggy after being drenched by the water from the car wash.

'Useless,' Jean tutted, and struck a match on a nearby wall, before taking a long drag on her cigarette. 'Now bugger off,' she told us, giving an ugly, rasping cough. 'Before I call the coppers myself. Get you two arrested for stalking!'

She stepped in front of her son, shielding him from us, and puffed aggressively, free hand planted firmly on her hip. Behind her, Lenny hugged his sorry-looking packed lunch miserably to his chest.

There was nothing more to be gained, not with Jean Finch standing guard.

Mara and I began to walk away, somewhat defeated. It felt as though we were getting close to something then, with Lenny.

I can't say anything. She'll kill me.

He surely meant Jean?

When we were a good few paces away from the car wash, we heard Jean's grating voice again, a little more muffled now, but still audible.

'Right, I'm off to Iceland for the frozen bits,' she was telling her son. 'You're eating me out of house and home, you big lump. See you at four.'

Mara took hold of my elbow and rapidly steered me down a side street. From here, we watched Jean Finch clomp along the road in the direction of the station.

A slow half-smile spread across Mara's face. 'Well, Clare,' she said, her eyes shining a little unnervingly. 'It seems that opportunity has just knocked. Or rather, nipped out for some frozen peas. How do you fancy popping over to the Finches' house? See what secrets our Lenny is hiding.'

37.

It took us twenty minutes to reach the Finches' on foot, by which point I was convinced there was no time left to glean any clues from the house before Jean returned from the shops. But Mara continued to stride purposefully on until we were at the entrance to the Finches' cul-de-sac.

'Are you sure about this?' I urged, for what felt like the hundredth time since we left the car wash. 'What if Jean's only a few minutes away? What if Lenny comes back, even?'

'You heard his mother, she's not expecting him until four,' said Mara dismissively. 'I doubt he's got the nerve to defy her and leave his post at the car wash early. And even if Jean was quick getting her fish fingers, I doubt she'll be back just yet. There's still enough time for us to take a look around.'

I really didn't like the way she used that word. *Us.*

The terraced house, as we approached, looked more dilapidated than it had on our first visit. The front garden — if you could call it that — was a depressing patch of bald earth, punctuated by a few anaemic weeds and a plant pot clearly in regular use as an ashtray. A tatty plastic windmill had been stuck into this plant pot, doing little to prettify the rumpled, discarded cigarette butts overflowing it and thickly littering the ground.

The Finches' cheap PVC front door was no longer its original white; the lower half densely spotted with mud. The panel surrounding the letterbox was plastered with garish stickers broadcasting various warnings. No junk mail. No flyers. No newspapers. No menus. No charity bags. No cold callers. No Jehovahs.

Jean Finch, it seemed, had all bases covered.

Like the front door, the house's windows were also in need of a clean. Roller blinds had been drawn behind the glass, like firmly closed eyelids, making it impossible to see in.

As I lingered close to the pavement, Mara knelt down before the Finches' front door and thumbed open the letterbox.

'Ordinary hallway,' she remarked. 'Carpet soiled from regular use. Walls stained yellow — by nicotine, presumably. A few bin bags... Coats and shoes... And stacks upon stacks of junk mail, flyers, newspapers and menus.' Mara got to her feet and dusted herself down. 'Jean Finch's door stickers don't appear to be working.'

I couldn't help but stifle a laugh.

It soon died when, much to my dismay, Mara wrapped her fingers around the handle and tried to open the door. 'Locked, as expected.'

'What are you doing?' I hissed. 'Even if it wasn't, there's no way we can go in there.'

Ignoring me, she glided smoothly along the front lower windows, testing them with her fingernails to see if they could be prised outwards.

'Nope,' she said quietly, 'no joy.'

I glanced anxiously around, dreading the sight of one of the neighbours advancing towards us, demanding to know what it was we were up to. Thankfully, the cul-de-sac was quiet.

'Come on,' said Mara, leaving the property and heading back along the road.

The breath I'd been holding gushed out of me. 'Great. Let's go get a coffee. Or some food. Where do you fancy?'

But at the end of the cul-de-sac, Mara didn't continue in the direction of the shops and cafés. She bore sharply off to the right.

'Where are you...?'

'The back alleys are probably down here,' she commented.

'Mara, no!' I half-shouted, half-whispered the words, desperate not to draw anyone's attention.

Mara, however, was undeterred. She proceeded down the street before cutting right again, disappearing down the narrow alleyway that ran parallel to the terraces' back gardens.

I hastily scanned around once more to check that nobody was watching, and stole after her.

The alleyway was rough and unsurfaced, narrowly slicing between the Finches' house and the row of terraces behind it. It wasn't wide enough for a vehicle and was hemmed in on both sides by brick walls into which a variety of gates had been set.

I could vaguely hear Mara up ahead, counting her way along these gates.

'Sixty-three... Sixty-five... Sixty-seven. Aha!' She came to a halt and nodded towards the brown wooden gate in front of her. 'I'm going in.'

I tried to stop her, but again my efforts were in vain. Mara unlatched the gate, which opened onto a relatively small concreted backyard. She crossed the yard, checked the back door of the house, as she had the front, and then started on the windows. The rooms behind these windows, too, were completely obscured. This time by curtains foxed with mould.

Mara pulled a face after the first window didn't budge. But when she tried the second, her expression changed.

'It's open,' she murmured with surprise, as the side-hung window swivelled towards her.

However, instead of merely sticking her head in through the gap for a look around — the thought of which alone gave me serious palpitations — Mara placed her palms onto the sill, and jerked herself upwards with enough momentum to get a knee inside.

'Please don't tell me you're actually *going in*?' I asked her, aghast. 'Mara, that's breaking and entering! You could get us both arrested. I— I've got rent to pay! I could lose my job!'

'Technically, it's trespass, since the window was open,' Mara corrected, as if that made it perfectly acceptable. 'And I'm merely facilitating an investigation.'

'There isn't a chance I'm coming with you,' I insisted, folding my arms.

'I don't want you to. I need you to stay outside and keep watch. Pop your head through this window and shout me if you see anyone coming.'

'Wait—' I attempted to emphasise once more what a dreadful idea this was, but with a flick of her coat hem she vanished behind the curtains.

For a few minutes, I found myself rooted to the spot, praying

Mara wouldn't be long. Eventually, I decided to move around to the front of the house, feign a stroll along the pavement to see if anyone was approaching from the top of the road.

My heart was beating a frantic rhythm against my ribs. But when I reached the cul-de-sac again, the road was clear. There was no sign of anyone.

I took a breath, trying to disguise my nerves. A neighbour could still easily catch sight of me, loitering suspiciously outside the Finches'. One of the neighbours at the back could even have called the police already, having noticed Mara slipping in through the window. Or, for all we knew, Jean Finch might be expecting visitors. What if *they* turned up? Maybe that's why she'd gone shopping in the first place — because she was entertaining. And any second now she'd be back, stomping towards us with a Wall's Viennetta and a couple of cream horns.

The minutes stretched, each one feeling like an eternity. But at least the street remained quiet, save for the hum of traffic from the main road and the occasional *coo* of a pigeon. I lost count of the times I glanced at my watch and then back towards the alley, expecting Mara to reappear, perhaps brandishing some crucial piece of evidence. But there was no movement whatsoever. Just the *tick-tick-tick* of the little ashtray windmill, spinning pathetically.

Four minutes passed. Five.

A knot of anxiety tightened in my stomach. What the hell was she even doing in there?

I hesitated, checked the street yet again. I did a double take, squinted. There was something at the very, very end of it. *Someone.* A stocky figure, making their way determinedly towards me, hands weighted by shopping bags. And that figure was familiar. The woman's booted feet stamped along the pavement, puffs of smoke rising from her at regular intervals, as though her head was the chimney of a steam train.

Oh my God. Jean.

I took off like a hare, fast as I could, racing down the side street and along the alleyway until I located the Finches' gate. I flung the thing open and almost fell right through the still-open window.

'Mara!' I yelled, trying to keep the tremor from my voice.

Silence.

'Mara!' I shouted, louder this time, in the desperate hope she'd hear me, in the desperate hope she'd make it out of the house before Jean Finch arrived.

Nothing.

I carried on crying out, rapping on one of the downstairs windows and then the next.

'Mara!'

All of a sudden, the curtains to the room I was standing directly in front of whipped violently apart. I motioned frantically to Mara to get out, to get out NOW, moving closer to the filthy glass to explain that Jean was coming, that she was almost here.

I found myself peering into a fairly small room, which appeared to be crammed with clutter. Every surface was covered. There was scarcely a spare millimetre of space, especially across the walls. As the clutter coalesced and started to make sense, I realised just what I was staring at.

The walls were populated from floor to ceiling with images

of the Devereauxs. Grainy local press clippings, magic magazine articles, and a whole deluge of photographs; from after-show candids to fuzzier shots, taken on a cheap camera from the back of a theatre. There were even printed-out screen grabs from the Devereauxs' appearances on Talent Quest, tacked up next to screenshots of the online videos of their performances.

This was Lenny's room. And there was no doubt about it. He was, most definitely, a magic super-fan.

In picture after picture was Dex, clad in his trademark tight trousers and unbuttoned shirts, posturing in his leather jackets and heeled shoes. He performed, gestured, bowed, grinned cheesily at the camera in numerous theatre lobbies. And there at his side was Angel.

But as my eyes darted from one image to the next, my blood rushed cold. In nearly every single picture, Angel had been defaced. Jagged, savage swirls of biro had gouged her eyes to black cavities, additional lines of ink obliterating her smile. Onto some of the pictures a dotted line was sketched, across the slender curve of Angel's neck. In one particularly disturbing piece of graffiti, a crude cartoon knife had been drawn, plunged into her heart.

I began to feel sick. These were the kinds of marks made by someone who had taken an intense and perverse pleasure in them, someone with the uncontrollable urge to take pleasure in disfiguring — in *hurting* — women. They were the marks made to a woman's image by a man who had realised he could never have, *would* never have her.

This wasn't just fandom... it was an obscene, murderous obsession.

38. ♠

I screwed my eyes closed, trying to shutter out the sight of that horrific collage. A fresh bolt of panic shot through me. Jean Finch was still on her way. By now, she'd be almost upon us. Throwing caution to the wind, along with my worries that I might be seen by a neighbour, I banged the heel of my hand on the window and gave Mara another frenzied signal.

'She's here!' I shrieked. 'Jean's coming back!'

Ignoring me, Mara had raised her phone and was hurriedly making a stuttering pass of it around the room. She was taking pictures, I realised, documenting the chilling tableaux pinned to the walls.

As soon as Mara had made a dash from the room, I did the same. With trembling hands, I pulled my mobile from my handbag, breathlessly capturing a handful of photos through the grimy glass. I don't know why, just that I wanted a record, proof of the horrible defacements we'd discovered.

No sooner had I done this than Mara rocketed back through the window, shoving it closed behind her. Together we hastily latched the gate and belted our way back down the alley, flattening ourselves against the wall at the end of it to watch Jean Finch clump the last few steps to her door.

I tipped my head back against the cold, damp bricks and emptied my lungs in relief. That was too close a call. And despite what we'd found, I couldn't help but feel a slight stab of annoyance with Mara for almost getting us both arrested. Again.

As I waited for my body to right itself after the surge of adrenaline that had left me shaking, the full implication of what we'd unearthed at the Finches' house hit me. We'd gone there looking for clues about Lenny's involvement in Angel's death. Perhaps hoping to find something to corroborate Katarina's story, and prove that Lenny had been the one to force her into that flight case. But this... this was something else entirely. This was evidence of a violent, all-consuming infatuation. That I'd actually felt sorry for Lenny when we'd spoken to him at the car wash made me shudder.

'We can't pass those photos I just took to the police, of course,' Mara remarked, when we were a few streets away from the Finches'. 'Not given we were in the house when they were taken.'

'*We?*'

'Well... you know what I mean.'

I patted my bag, thinking of the photos on my own phone. 'So, by that token, the ones *I* took are off limits too,' I said. 'Since I took them through the window, and technically we were trespassing by being in the Finches' backyard.'

Mara slowed her steps. '*You* took photos of that stuff as well?' she asked. 'Through the *window*?'

When I confirmed that I had she brought her hands together in a single, gratified clap. 'Perfect! Then we'll pass those on to the police instead.'

'But—?'

'We'll send them an anonymous tip-off. From, say... a window cleaner... A window cleaner who was going about his business when he happened to glance in through the window he was cleaning and see something very disturbing. Send them to me, would you? I'll give you the number now.'

I had to admit it was a good plan. Especially given the state of the windows. And at that moment in time, no other ideas sprang to mind as to how we could inform the police of the darkness Lenny Finch was hiding.

I was just about to tell Mara that I already had her number when she pulled a second mobile from her pocket; a smaller, cheaper model. She dictated the number.

'You think that'll be enough to get them to bring Lenny in?' I asked, sending the photos to Mara's second phone.

'It's certainly more compelling than him being a magic fan who simply happened to be at the studio last Saturday,' she replied. 'A room like that speaks volumes.'

'It's such a shame the police didn't see it when they questioned Lenny. They might have...' My voice faded. Lenny was questioned less than two days ago. It wouldn't have changed anything. Angel Devereaux would still be dead.

'Well, Lenny was never officially arrested for anything,' said Mara. 'It was just a chat. The police didn't even have a warrant.' As she spoke, she pressed a series of buttons on her second phone.

The grotesque images from Lenny's bedroom still burned my mind. 'He has to be involved,' I said after we'd walked several streets in silence. 'Those images... Maybe if Lenny had been hanging around the magic scene for a while, then Dex knew how he felt about Angel, and saw his opportunity. Roped him into helping kidnap Katarina? It would explain how Dex got her inside that case while performing live on television.'

'Maybe,' Mara murmured. 'Or else he was just the kind of naive young man Shane Sinclair knew he could exploit to frame Dex. The order to kidnap Katarina could have come from Sinclair.'

We took a left, the main road swinging into view before us. It was lunchtime now, and alive with activity. An estate agent paced an office window on a call, a brace of pensioners trundled by with wheeled shoppers. Small bands of pigeons scavenged the pavements while construction workers left fast-food restaurants laden with polystyrene containers bulging with chips. It was at once comforting and jarring. To think that ordinary life persisted when, not that many metres away, a young man gouged a woman's face with a biro pen.

'Come on,' said Mara, checking the time. 'I'd say we've earned ourselves a drink.'

Mara and I found a pizza place along the high street. We'd only just given the waitress our orders when the screen of Mara's phone — her primary phone — lit up with a message.

'Dhita,' Mara told me. 'Graham's speaking to Lenny Finch again. Should be interesting.'

Some time later, once our table was a mass of empty glasses and scrunched-up napkins, the tablecloth speckled with crumbs, my lunch began to sit heavy inside me. My thoughts circled back to my earlier conversation with Jeff.

Swirling the juice around in my glass, I tried to choose my moment carefully.

'So... how are you doing?' I asked Mara. 'I hope everything was okay last night? You didn't seem...'

She sighed deeply.

'I'm sorry, I shouldn't have—'

'It's fine,' she replied, taking a long drink. 'Proactive Productions... the various details of this case. It's all hit quite close to home. Suffice to say the past few days have been more... challenging than I expected.'

The cry I'd heard in Mara's house late the previous night. The red mark on her hand, as though it had made contact with a hard surface. I considered again how painful trying to unpick what had happened to Angel Devereaux might be for Mara when, like Angel, Travers had disappeared live on one of Shane's shows. Was Mara now terrified that he, too, would reappear dead?

As strong as my sympathy for Mara was, however, my hand twitched towards my bag, towards the dictaphone still nestling inside of it. I should be taking a note of what she has to say, I thought, recording it. If I was a real journalist, I would even offer to buy her more drinks, try to loosen her tongue into spilling the secrets of what she knew about her husband's disappearance. The inside scoop.

The contents of my stomach rose unpleasantly. Aside from the half-hearted interview with Captain Crater, I hadn't done a stroke of work for Jeff all week. If I didn't hand something in soon, I could kiss goodbye to my job at the Morden Mercury. And with it, my monthly pay packets. Matt's music brought in some money, but not enough to cover our rent and bills.

I readjusted my weight on the restaurant chair and swallowed hard. When my eyes meandered their way guiltily back to Mara's, I saw that she was staring at me intensely—

Suddenly, Mara's phone rang, DI Paulson's name flashing across the screen. Mara pushed the phone away from her, letting it ring out.

'It's Paulson!' I exclaimed, stating the obvious. 'Aren't you curious to see what he wants? He might be ringing to apologise.'

'If there's one thing you should know about Graham,' Mara replied. 'It's that he never apologises.'

The phone rang again, and again Mara ignored it. In fact, she didn't just ignore it; she made a point of letting it ring while she went to the bar to order another drink. I stared at the letters of Paulson's name, illuminating the screen of the mobile, almost tempted to answer his call myself.

When Mara sat back down, she allowed her phone to ring out a further seven times before finally picking up. Though I couldn't hear the details of what Paulson was saying, Mara's responses were clipped, controlled. But with an undeniable note to them that suggested she was enjoying herself.

'Something new has come to light...? A tip-off from a *window cleaner*, you say...?' She paused. 'I don't know if I could fit it in this afternoon, Graham... I'm in the middle of something quite important...' She raised her glass to me, mouthing the word *cheers*.

Paulson's voice burbled incoherently through the receiver.

'You made your feelings very clear last time,' Mara went on. 'I'm not part of this case anymore.' A hint of a smile played on her lips.

Dhita had been right. After firing Mara from the case, Paulson, it seemed, was now back in touch, cap in hand. He evidently needed Mara for something at the station, and she was pretending to want nothing to do with it. I wondered if she was pressing him for an apology...

Mara tapped the screen of her mobile, putting it onto speakerphone.

'I'm... I'm... well,' came Paulson's voice, clearly squirming. 'Yes, about what happened last time. I'm... Okay, okay... I'm sor—'

Just as the man was about to spew the word out, Mara hung up.

'You nearly had him!' I exclaimed. 'He was just about to apologise!'

She put away her phone with a smirk. 'Well, Clare. Lenny Finch has fully clammed up at the station. Some sort of magician's code, apparently. Like last time. So Graham wants me to speak with Lenny myself. See if it'll help draw something out. He's banking on the fact that Lenny will say something to implicate Dex, which will be the final nail in Dex's coffin. Frankly, I doubt it.'

It was Thursday, I realised. Dex had now spent two days in police custody. 'So Paulson's hoping Lenny will reveal something today that will finally see Dex charged with Angel's murder?'

'That's the idea,' Mara replied. 'Or they'll have to let him go.'

39.

Mara texted Paulson to tell him she'd had a change of heart and would help with Lenny. So, an hour later, I again found myself navigating the station corridors, accompanied by DC Taylor. He greeted me with his usual wide smile, which I couldn't help noticing grew a little wider when he saw Mara.

'Funny that new tip-off coming in,' Taylor remarked.

'Wasn't it?' Mara replied.

Something passed between them, and I could have sworn Mara winked.

Taylor turned, a subtle waft of his aftershave catching me as he led us towards the interview suites. We were met there by DI Paulson, whose snack of choice this time was a Jammie Dodger. His cheeks coloured to match the strawberry filling as soon as he saw Mara. Guilty conscience.

'Knight,' he grunted, cramming the biscuit in his mouth and swallowing the little red heart whole.

'Finch is in Interview Room One,' said Taylor, nodding to the door.

'If you can get him to spill what he knows about Devereaux...' garbled Paulson, tiny crumbs of biscuit shooting from his mouth. 'Like I said on the phone, we could get ourselves an arrest. I want Devereaux charged by the end of the day.'

'With the emphasis on *if*,' Mara retorted sceptically, clearly still favouring Shane Sinclair as the prime suspect. 'Perhaps Luke and I should talk to Lenny alone,' she went on. 'You probably make him nervous, Graham.'

Paulson harrumphed at this, self-consciously running a thumb and forefinger over his moustache. But he begrudgingly agreed, escorting me into the darkness of the observation room next door. He flicked on the speakers.

In the brightly lit room on the other side of the glass, I saw Lenny Finch. He was hunched over the pale table, looking even more dishevelled than he had at the car wash. His Minions shirt was rucked, creased in a way that implied it was still damp. Clumps of his hair stuck up in all directions, and his posture was so slumped his nose was nearly touching the table. He didn't bother looking up to see who had entered the room, but continued wringing his hands on the tabletop.

'Hello again, Lenny,' said Mara, as she and Taylor took the seats opposite.

Recalling Mara's voice from earlier, Lenny tilted up his chin a little, eyes nervously flicking to Mara then back to his fists.

'I hear you've not been saying very much,' Mara said.

Lenny picked at a loose scab on his knuckle. 'No,' he mumbled, still avoiding eye contact. 'Magician's code. Can't reveal the secrets.'

Sitting up a little straighter, Mara placed her empty hands on the table. Her palms faced down, the cuffs of her sleeves, raised a few inches up her forearms, showed the bones of her wrists. 'Magicians can reveal secrets to other magicians, Lenny.

Which is why I want to show you this.'

The man's gaze shifted upwards.

Mara curled and uncurled the fingers of her right hand in a rapid snap. A card appeared out of thin air. She held it up and turned its face to Lenny. It was the queen of spades.

'Remember this?' she asked him. She transferred the card to her left hand and gave it a firm flick with the thumb and index finger of her right. Just as it had in the car wash, the queen of spades once again became the two of hearts.

Lenny said nothing and didn't need to, his response to the card trick clear in the set of his face, in the way his posture had seized like a statue. It was obvious he was hanging off Mara's every movement.

'That was what you saw at the car wash,' said Mara. 'What I *allowed* you to see. But what actually happened — how the queen of spades became the two of hearts — is very different.'

She performed the trick again, this time repositioning her hands to reveal exactly how she did it. The two of hearts had been behind the queen of spades all along, and — with a motion of her fingers quicker than the beat of a hummingbird's wing — she'd pulled the queen of spades out from in front of the two of hearts, and secreted it in the curled palm of her right hand.

It was incredible, how Mara could perform a private juggling act with those cards that only she was privy to. And whereas I still wasn't sure I knew how she'd managed to get that card from her fingers to her palm in the matter of a millisecond, it was as though Lenny had understood the manoeuvre perfectly.

'So, will you allow me to see the truth of what happened at Shinetree Studios last Saturday night?' Mara asked Lenny.

Slow seconds passed before Lenny's expression shut itself up once more. 'Still don't know,' he agonised. 'Can't say.'

'I understand,' replied Mara, her tone surprisingly gentle. 'The world of stage magic is built on secrecy, on trust. But sometimes, Lenny, a greater kind of magic is at play. The magic of truth. And sometimes, even the most sacred codes can be overlooked... if it serves a higher purpose.'

Lenny's eyes briefly met Mara's, a kernel of something deep within them – fear, confusion, and also something more obscure. A small sense of release.

I angled myself closer to the glass. At the car wash, I questioned how anyone as bumbling as Lenny Finch could have possibly been involved in a plan to kidnap two women and kill the first. But that was before I saw his bedroom, the hatred in those deep gashes of graffiti across the photos of Angel. Mara, with her psychology background, her newly mellowed voice and sympathetic expression, was trying to get to the truth by playing to Lenny's fears, his pride and insecurities. His obsession. Had he been coerced into helping with Angel's murder and Katarina's kidnap by Dex or Shane? Or had he simply chosen to do it himself?

'Angel Devereaux. Katarina Riley. Those were very dangerous illusions to be involved in, Lenny,' said Mara. 'And we have the evidence you *were* involved. Things are very serious for you.'

The interview room fell silent. Mara didn't draw her gaze away from Lenny and didn't blink. Taylor leant forwards over tightly clasped hands, as though he didn't want to miss the other man so much as breathe. At my side, Paulson chewed loudly. His nails, this time.

After an extended pause, which seemed to last a lifetime, Lenny collapsed forwards onto the table. He started to shake his head from side to side, a movement that gradually became more agitated, more of a thrashing. A noise accompanied it; a strangled, desperate moaning. When Lenny's face jolted up to meet Mara's again, his eyes were wet. 'It wasn't my idea,' he repeated. 'I swear. It wasn't my idea. They said they'd leave a pass and crew shirt for me in the kiosk, so I could get into the studio and help them with the illusion. I was just helping. With the magic.'

'Helping who, Lenny?' Taylor asked, bending further towards him.

Lenny's lower lip quivered.

'It's time to tell us, Lenny,' said Mara. 'Magician's code. This person has already broken it by getting you involved. You say someone left you a pass and crew shirt at Shinetree. Was that person Shane Sinclair, Lenny?'

'For pity's sake, she's bloody leading him!' Paulson snarled, while Taylor darted Mara a cautionary glance.

The low hiss emanating through the speakers in the observation room was the only sound to break the tension. Seconds became minutes.

Eventually, Lenny swiped his cheeks and looked twitchily around, like he was checking there really were just two other people in the interview room with him.

'It was...' he began, shaking. 'It was... Mr Devereaux. He... he messaged me.'

'*Dex Devereaux* messaged you?' asked Mara, failing to mask her surprise.

From next to me came the *chip-chip* sound of Paulson biting his thumbnail.

'On Facebook,' Lenny sniffed, wiping his nose on his shoulder.

'A *private* message?' asked Mara.

Lenny nodded miserably.

'For the purposes of the recording, Mr Finch nodded,' said Taylor.

'A private message. From his official page. Mr Devereaux said he needed my help. For a special new trick he was doing on Talent Quest. A really big one. He said... he said he knew I was a magician, and that he needed someone he could trust. Someone who understood magic.' Lenny's voice cracked with a pathetic pride. 'He said that if I helped, I'd be allowed in the Magic Circle.'

'Well, that's it!' Paulson boomed, his face alight. 'Despite Knight's funny business, we've got Dex Devereaux once and for all! That smarmy bastard will be charged by dinner time.'

So Dex, it seemed, had known Lenny's sordid little secret all along. His obsession with Angel, his violent preoccupation. Dex had seen all this in Lenny and used it to his advantage, taking the other man in on his plan.

He'd had Lenny kidnap Katarina while rigging up that banner to make it look like Angel's death was the work of a deranged serial killer. But it was all a facade, a deception, despite nobody believing Dex had the skill to pull such a deception off. Dex had done it because he wanted to be free to marry Katarina. Though I doubted Katarina would be so keen on a wedding once she knew what Dex had done to his wife.

'Again, ask yourself why Dex didn't do a better job of covering his tracks, Clare,' said Mara, when I raised all this with her. 'I know he's an idiot, but why get in touch with Lenny via his own Facebook page?'

Taylor caught her words. 'You know as well as anyone, Mara, that murderers leave obvious trails all the time,' he said gently. 'People don't always think things through when they're plotting stuff like this. You said it yourself. Logic doesn't always apply.'

I saw his reasoning, but again the investigation — despite just having what was an obvious breakthrough — appeared to have become murkier. Mara had a point about the evidence against Dex. Why was it all so obvious? Unless Shane Sinclair *was* behind it, but rather than him framing Dex, had they actually been working *together*? Was it possible? That Shane had created the perfect, ratings-grabbing content for his show two weeks on the run and, by helping with his scheme, Dex was now free to marry Katarina?

While Lenny was taken to a cell, Taylor and a couple of other detectives went through Dex's and Lenny's Facebook messages. Mara and I hung around the observation room in the meantime. We waited for Dex to be brought back to the interview room, so Paulson could question him about the claims Lenny Finch had just made.

About an hour later, a man was brought in, though I didn't recognise him as Dex Devereaux at first. Almost two days in police custody had given Dex the appearance of a flannel that had spent too long in the tumble dryer. The blond highlights in his hair were now a drab brown and lying flat against his head, which made him look several years older than he had at Shinetree. He wore a polo shirt, which aged him further still, and a demeanour somewhere between outrage and misery.

Dex was accompanied by a sharp-suited woman I *did* happen to recognise. A lawyer. The same lawyer who'd represented Shane Sinclair during his police interview. But who was footing the bill for this woman to represent Dex? I doubted Dex could afford it. So was Shane paying? Maybe I wasn't so far off the mark before. Maybe one of Shane's promises to Dex had been the best legal representation money could buy, in exchange for his collusion?

Since Lenny had confessed to kidnapping Katarina, Paulson had been positively airborne. He was now champing at the bit to start the interview, lips pursing with impatient triumph. I assumed this meant the police had found the Facebook message Dex had sent Lenny.

In the interview room, the lawyer removed some papers from her briefcase and positioned them on the table. Taylor set up the recording, stating the time and date and those present. He'd barely uttered his last syllable when Paulson cut in.

'Well, Mr Devereaux. Some rather interesting new information has come to light in the past hour,' he announced. 'We'd like to put this information to you now.'

'May I remind you that my client has been remarkably patient with these baseless accusations over the last...' The lawyer paused to pointedly examine her watch, 'almost forty-seven hours.'

'*Baseless—?*' Paulson scoffed.

'Which means you have precisely sixty-three minutes to charge or release him,' the lawyer said.

'Let's see about that, shall we?' returned Paulson. 'Mr Devereaux, we have just had a witness come forwards. This witness has made the following statement on record. He states you contacted him via Facebook, instructing him to abduct one Katarina Riley at Shinetree Studios on the night of Saturday, the 22nd of March 2014, and forcibly restrain her inside a locked flight case.'

'Though the message has been deleted from your page,' Taylor added, 'our team has located it in our witness's message folder. We're now taking steps to recover the deleted message from your Facebook account.'

Dex's already fatigued features crumpled in on themselves further. 'What? I never... *Facebook*? I don't even know the bloody password!'

'That's very convenient,' sneered Paulson.

Dex drew his hands roughly across his face in despair. 'Can't you see, even now?' he moaned slowly. 'Someone's clearly trying to set me up—'

'Shane Sinclair,' mouthed Mara.

Before Dex could say any more, the lawyer shuffled her paperwork, uncapping a burnished gold fountain pen. 'DI Paulson, I think it would be helpful if you provided the exact timestamp of this alleged Facebook communication. And confirm from what kind of device it was sent?'

Paulson, momentarily flustered by the lawyer's request,

turned to Taylor.

Taylor took a notebook from his pocket, flipping up the ribbon and consulting the page it marked. 'The message was sent at 14:17 last Friday, the 21st of March. From the official Facebook page of Dex Devereaux. Received by the personal Facebook account of our witness. And the message was sent... from a desktop computer.'

Dex fell quiet, for at least a minute. This was the latest in a slew of evidence against him. None of which, so far, he'd been able to convincingly explain. But to everyone's astonishment, Dex suddenly straightened and slammed down his hand on the tabletop, with enough of a bang to startle even his lawyer.

'Sent fourteen-seventeen last *Friday*? From a *desktop computer*?' he crowed. 'Then I couldn't possibly have sent it!'

'And why might that be?' asked Paulson, a little awkwardly.

Smugness seeped across Dex's face like a spillage. 'Because,' he replied, 'at precisely fourteen-seventeen last Friday, I was having lunch with Miss Riley. In Morden. At the new bistro off the high street.'

Paulson raised his eyebrows. 'Miss Riley?'

'Yes, detective, *Miss Riley*,' Dex repeated mockingly. 'We were discussing our Talent Quest routine. Not only can you ask her to vouch for it, but there were plenty of people who saw us there.' He paused, then broke into an unnatural laugh. 'No, better than that!' he said. 'I did a trick for a girl on the next table. She recorded it for her social media. You'll be able to find the video.'

His laughter continued as he doubled over with the feigned effort of it, even going so far as pretending to wipe tears from his eyes. The lawyer looked wryly on.

'Oh, and detective?' Dex added. 'One more thing. I don't even own a desktop computer.'

Paulson's face didn't just fall; it crashed. 'Check it out,' he muttered to Taylor, and abruptly left the room.

40.♠

Mara and I took a quick walk around the block to stretch our legs and get some fresh air. It was good to have a breather. I'd spent so much time watching people through windows that day I was beginning to feel like a peeping Tom.

A few minutes after we returned to the station, DC Taylor buzzed Mara's phone to tell her Katarina was being brought into Interview Room One. Not waiting for someone to come and get us, Mara let herself into the adjacent observation room, where we again took our places before the glass.

Katarina Riley was led into the room, her appearance and demeanour worlds away from when we'd seen her last. Her long blonde hair had been brushed back into a tight, high ponytail. False lashes fanned from her upper eyelids, and her nails had been freshly manicured. She wore grey jeans and a light-coloured meshy top. Through its fabric, the dark purple blotches of bruising were visible on her arms. The only giveaway as to what had befallen her the previous Saturday.

The two detectives took their places opposite Katarina. DI Paulson's arms were folded high across his chest, and he bore the expression of a bulldog chewing on a particularly stubborn wasp. He let Taylor speak first. I assumed this was a deliberate tactic; that a young, attractive woman might divulge more to an attractive man of a similar age, rather than the grizzled Paulson.

'Miss Riley,' Taylor began, 'thank you for agreeing to come in at such short notice. We just need you to confirm Mr Devereaux's account of his whereabouts last Friday afternoon, the 21st of March. Did you see Mr Devereaux that day at all?'

Katarina narrowed her eyes briefly, then nodded. 'Yes. We met up to discuss our Talent Quest performance. Over lunch.'

'And can you confirm which restaurant you and Mr Devereaux ate at, please?'

'It was the new bistro. In Morden.'

This tallied with Dex's story. Paulson rubbed his palms together in a gesture of minor discomfort as Taylor jotted the information down inside his notebook.

'And do you remember what time you arrived at the bistro? And when you left?' Taylor asked.

'We arrived about one. Left after three,' Katarina replied, pinching the outer corner of her lashes as she recalled the times.

Another match with Dex's account.

'And you can confirm you were with Mr Devereaux for that entire period?' asked Taylor. 'Between one and three?'

Katarina met his gaze without hesitation. 'Yes,' she said. 'We were together the whole time.'

Paulson grunted at this. 'What, you didn't even leave to use the ladies' room?'

From beside me, Mara made a noise. 'Ugh, I hate that term. Anyway, what does Graham think happened while Katarina was in the loo? That Dex pulled a computer out from under the table? A computer he'd smuggled into the bistro with the express intention of messaging Lenny? That's a bit much, even for a magician.'

'Well... yes, I might have,' Katarina returned, from beyond the glass. 'But I wasn't away from the table for long.'

'And do you remember Mr Devereaux performing a trick for someone while you were both in the bistro?' said Taylor.

'I do, yes,' said Katarina. 'A girl. She'd recognised Dex from the telly and asked for his autograph. So he offered to show her a magic trick, suggested the waiter film a video of it for the girl's Instagram.'

Now this was interesting, and I glanced at Mara to gauge her reaction, but she was still gazing through the glass. To me, it was obvious. Dex had offered to show a total stranger a magic trick, suggesting himself that she post it on her social media. It was like he was building a rock-solid alibi, making it appear impossible that he'd sent the message to Lenny. Was the girl even a stranger, I wondered? Could Dex have told her in advance to ask for his autograph?

It seemed like Taylor was about to query this himself when Paulson cut in.

'And what, precisely, did that video show?'

'Well, it showed Dex bending a spoon,' Katarina responded.

'You don't recall what the girl was called, do you?' asked Taylor.

'Yeah, but only because my sister has the same name,' said Katarina. 'She's Khloe as well. Khloe with a "K". And the girl's Instagram handle was something that rhymed. Like, "KhloeLou92" or something.'

Taylor fished his mobile out from inside his jacket and

tapped the screen. After a few moments, he swivelled it to face Katarina. 'For the purposes of the recording, I am showing Miss Riley an Instagram account with the username "KhloeLou92". Is *this* the girl from the restaurant, Miss Riley?'

From our angle, it wasn't easy to see the images Taylor was scrolling through on his phone, but it looked like many of them included a young woman with candy pink hair.

'That's her!' said Katarina.

Taylor tapped the screen, and a video played. Its soundtrack echoed through the speakers in the observation room. Dex Devereaux's voice, issuing a clear instruction to the waiter holding the phone.

'Make sure you get both me and the window in shot.'

Once the interview was finished, Mara pulled out her own mobile and typed Khloe's handle into Instagram, so we could see the video for ourselves.

The slightly wobbly footage showed the decor I remembered from lunch the previous day. The table Katarina and Dex sat at was next to the one Mara and I had occupied, in the bistro's large front window. A view of the road and the shops opposite dominated the backdrop of the shot.

The video started on Katarina, who sat to the left, panning clumsily to Dex on the right. The pink-haired girl — Khloe — occupied a chair next to Dex. So this proved they were both in the bistro together, Dex and Katarina, like they said. But what it hadn't proved so far was *when* they were there. This video could have been filmed at any time.

Dex was holding a silver dessert spoon aloft, offering it out to the girl and grinning. 'Take this... that's right...' he said, guiding the girl's hand to the spoon handle. 'Now, rub the length of it.'

The spoon started to bend.

'Oh look,' Dex went on, mugging at the camera, 'it's going floppy. Bet that doesn't usually happen to you, does it?'

I cringed inwardly.

'What I love about Dex,' remarked Mara, 'is how tasteful his material is.'

Not appearing to mind Dex's double entendres, Khloe shrieked with delight. 'Oh my God, how did you do that?'

Dex winked at her. 'A magician never reveals his secrets, sweetheart. But I think we need a little *viagra-cadabra* to put this right.'

Mara groaned. Though it was a pun Jeff would have admired.

The camera closed in on the spoon as Dex rubbed the handle now. A moment later, the metal had returned to its original shape.

Despite having no clue how Dex had done it, I didn't feel a sense of wonder from watching his trick, as I had from the other magic I'd seen. I was left feeling slightly dirty. Maybe if I'd been several piña coladas into a hen night, I might have felt differently.

Just before the recording ended, the camera panned out again.

'Pause it there!' I blurted to Mara.

The scene on the phone showed Katarina and Dex sitting at

the table, the large bistro window spanning the space behind them. And through it loomed the television shop across the street.

The glare of multiple TV screens cycled through their various trailers, wildlife shows and daytime television programmes. But the television smack bang in the middle of the shop window, in the space between Katarina and Dex, was showing a rolling news channel. The latest headlines looped across it. *Same-sex couples prepare to marry officially in the UK... Fatal stabbing on the Harrowbrook Estate. Police suspect a link to drugs gangs...*

'The news! You can see the news in the background. Which means the video was filmed when Dex said it was!' I exclaimed, disappointed.

'Yes,' said Mara. 'And not just the headlines but the time too. And, of course, there'll most probably be CCTV. It's pretty indisputable that Dex was where he said he was when that Facebook message was sent. Though I suppose the message could have been pre-scheduled. The police will check that next. But I sincerely doubt Dex is that tech-savvy.'

If it could be proven Dex had indeed sent that message to Lenny, then it would be undeniable that he'd also been involved in the events surrounding Angel's death. And yet we *couldn't* prove it, which implied that he was innocent. So why did the words Dex uttered at the start of the video keep rerunning in my head?

Make sure you get both me and the window in shot.

While DC Taylor was arranging for a team to verify the news broadcast in the background of the video, DI Paulson took a call. Mara and I were hovering near the door of the office by then, preparing to leave.

Paulson listened to the details coming through on the other end of the office phone, his face growing progressively grimmer.

'Digital Forensics,' he muttered, slamming down the handset when the call was over. 'They've confirmed the message sent to Lenny Finch from Devereaux's Facebook page was definitely sent at 14:17 last Friday. Meaning it *wasn't* pre-scheduled.'

I glanced at the clock. Two minutes to go until Paulson either had to charge Dex or release him.

'Bugger!' Paulson cursed. 'There's no firm evidence. The CPS will never let us charge as it stands. So we'll have to let him go.'

A few minutes later, as Mara and I exited the office with Paulson, we saw Dex. He and his lawyer were leaving. Though his hair was still flattened and a little greasy, and he was dressed in the same puggy polo shirt he'd been wearing earlier, Dex looked different. There was a new spring in his step, a swagger masking the drabness of his appearance.

As Dex strutted past Paulson, he shot him an exultant look. 'Glad we cleared all that up, Inspector. Just a bit of a misunderstanding, eh?'

Paulson didn't reply. He looked too angry.

'Oh, and by the way,' Dex added, pausing dramatically. 'Don't forget to tune in Saturday night. Shane's invited me back on Talent Quest for the final. The show must go on, and all that. There's a new girl lined up too!'

'So it was Shane Sinclair who paid for his lawyer,' said Mara, once Dex had gone and we were nearing the door ourselves. 'To give him the best chance of not being charged, so Dex could go back on the show for a third time. God help the viewing public.'

'I don't believe it,' I said. 'Not after last weekend. I mean, the man's wife *died* live on air.'

'Which is exactly why Sinclair wants him back,' replied Mara. 'Something has happened every time Dex has appeared on his show. Everyone's talking about it, and everyone wants to see what will happen next. Even more people will tune in this weekend. That scale of publicity — for Sinclair it's a few grand on legal fees well spent. It's what the man's like. He engineers these events on his shows to ensure his ratings stay high. And he couldn't care less how many lives he destroys in the process.'

Dex Devereaux might have walked out of the station a free man, but Lenny Finch wasn't going anywhere. We'd heard before we left that Lenny had been officially charged with the kidnap of Katarina Riley. That his hand size had been positively matched against the bruises on Katarina's arms, and his fingerprints to those on the flight case.

It was late now, and outside the sky was inking over as day tipped into night. Judging by the traffic sounds and the blaring of car horns issuing from the main road, rush hour was already well under way.

Mara and I hadn't spoken since we crossed the station car park, in which time I'd realised I had no real desire to go home, other than to see Jasper. I could hardly believe it had barely been twelve hours since I'd woken up in Mara's house. Twelve hours that had seen us go from Keystone Accountants; to the park to speak to Erin Grant; the car wash to speak to Lenny Finch; Lenny's house to discover those disturbing wall coverings; and finally to the police station, to oversee no less than three separate interviews. It would all be whorling around my head for hours.

So I decided, despite the traffic, to offer Mara a lift home. Or at least part of the way home. But no sooner had I opened my mouth to ask her the question than a stocky figure barrelled right between us, almost knocking me down. The figure left a thick fug of cigarette smoke in its wake as it clumped in the direction of the station without stopping to apologise.

'It's usually polite to say sorry when you bump into someone, *Jean*,' declared Mara.

Jean Finch ground to a slow halt, taking a further few seconds to turn around and face us, not dissimilar to a monster in a horror film. Jean was certainly keeping her son well-fed, as she was clutching a see-through freezer bag in her hand this time. Rattling around inside of it were a sausage roll, a scotch egg, and a packet of Pom-Bears.

When Jean registered who had called out to her, her face curdled.

'You!' she rasped, jabbing a finger in Mara's direction, then mine. 'This is all *your fault*.'

She took one menacing step towards us and then another, the tassels of her fake Ugg boots dancing as she did, a stark contrast to the hostility of their wearer.

'I'm afraid I'm not following,' said Mara.

Jean spluttered a salivary laugh, dripping — quite literally — with sarcasm. 'Well, then... follow *this*. Something very strange has just happened to me. You see, I'm at home, working my fingers to the bone doing my cleaning—'

I doubted this, given what I'd seen of her house.

'If you're going to accuse someone of something,' Mara interrupted, 'then it's best not to begin with a lie.'

She'd clearly had the same thought.

Jean ignored this jibe, continuing her speech without breaking stride. 'When I get a message from a duty solicitor to say my Lenny's been brought back to the police station. Why? I ask. Because, the solicitor says, the window cleaner's just been round to my house, and he's seen something disturbing through the window. And I says to him, well that's odd, cos I don't even have a window cleaner. And then, when I go outside and check the window in question, I know it's definitely all rubbish, cos the window's still dirty.'

'Yes, I see the problem,' said Mara. 'But you said the window cleaner saw something disturbing, which means he probably got frightened off mid-clean.'

'*All* the windows are still dirty,' rasped Jean.

'Probably didn't even get started then,' I added.

'Hold your horses, though, there's more,' Jean persisted. 'Cos then I hear from Mrs Harris at number sixty-four. And she tells me she's seen two women hanging around my house

324

earlier today. A small mousy one with a bob, and a tall dark one with a green coat.' As she said this, she glared deliberately between myself and Mara. 'And what kind of window cleaner opens people's curtains?'

A mild panic gripped me. A panic that, scotch egg aside, Jean might be heading into the station to report us for trespass. Mara, by contrast, remained unruffled.

'That's funny,' she replied. 'The police didn't pick up on any of that stuff about the window cleaner. You should ask them for a job. Is that why you're on your way into the station?'

'Ha ha, bloody ha,' croaked Jean, reaching into her pocket for a cigarette. 'I'm going to give my Lenny his supper. Cos the latest I heard is that he's now been charged! With kidnap, of all things! So, I'm going to tell you once and for all. And you can consider this your final warning.' She took another heavy step forwards until her face was mere inches from ours. 'You two stay away. From me *and* from my Lenny. I can't say I'm not glad Angel's gone, but that was nothing to do with my son. Nothing!'

Jean Finch threw us a final venomous stare and jabbed the unlit cigarette between her lips. She stomped towards the station reception, freezer bag swirling aggressively at her side.

41.

Behind us, Jean Finch's footsteps slowed to a standstill, replaced by the striking of a cigarette lighter.

'What's all this about my son being arrested, and where have you put him?' she demanded, her voice amplified by anger as she launched into a tirade about Lenny's wrongful arrest. When I turned to glance back at her, I saw the man on the receiving end of her fury wasn't even a police officer, not judging by his high vis delivery driver's vest.

'Do you want a lift home?' I asked Mara as we approached the main road, Jean's ranting melding into the intensifying burble of traffic and commuters.

Mara looked surprised at the offer. 'It's quite a way,' she said. 'I'll get a taxi. But thanks.'

'I don't mind. It won't take long to get the car.'

She wavered, her gaze, for a few long moments, fixed towards the shops. 'If you're sure you don't mind?'

We made it to my car just before the heavens opened, and fat rods of rain began lashing down around us. A whole ninety minutes later and we were caught in the dense, endless snarl of west London rush-hour. By that point, I was regretting my decision to drive Mara home.

Mara and I sat for a while listening to the monotonous stop-start chug of the traffic, the pummelling of the rain on the car's metal roof. The details of the Angel Devereaux investigation seesawed through my brain, to the hectic swish of the windscreen wipers. I ran through everything that had happened over the past six days, coming to the conclusion that this whole case was one giant illusion. And we were all still fumbling about in the dark — myself and Mara, Paulson and Taylor — trying to find the trapdoor.

The second woman to go missing during Dex Devereaux's Talent Quest act had been found locked inside a flight case. And we now knew both who'd put her there, and why. Yet we were no closer to uncovering the truth about who'd actually engineered *Angel's* disappearance and death. We had an incriminating video of Shane Sinclair, recorded by Angel on Angel's phone. But after hearing the lengths Dex had gone to on that Instagram video to prove he was in the bistro when the Facebook message was sent to Lenny, my suspicions had swung back to him.

In my opinion, the bulk of the evidence still pointed to Dex. He'd claimed he didn't have time to check those teleportation boxes, that it was Angel's job, when he must have already incapacitated Angel and put her inside. He was jealous of the fact that his wife was a better magician than he was. In short, he'd had opportunity, means and motive. More so than Shane. Yet despite all this, he remained a free man.

I remembered Dex's arrogance and swagger when he was leaving the police station, his crass revelling in the knowledge that he was going to be performing on Talent Quest for the third week running.

Just a bit of a misunderstanding... The show must go on, and all that.

I remembered his ogling the dancers at the studio, just hours after his wife had died, his odious words.

She'd made enough of my money vanish over the years. Bet you're the same...

Bile rose in my throat.

'Even if Shane did have something to do with Angel's death,' I announced, the conviction solidifying with each inch along the road we crawled, 'then Dex must at least have been complicit. Most of the evidence still points to him being involved. And his attitude at Shinetree. It was... well, hateful really, given what'd just happened to his wife.'

Mara stared out of the passenger side window, her profile silhouetted against the rain-drenched glass, the lights of the cityscape blurring beyond. 'But that evidence is still only circumstantial. Compelling, I agree, but not conclusive.'

'Then there *has* to be more,' I pressed, striking my fingers against the steering wheel for emphasis. 'More we just haven't found yet. Like how he sent that Facebook message to Lenny from a desktop computer while he was in the bistro. He chose a table in the window deliberately, knowing those TV screens in the background would show the time. He even asked the waiter to get both him and the window in shot.'

'Only to control the camera angle,' Mara cut back. 'So the method behind his spoon bending wouldn't show up on the recording. You seem to be fixating on that video alibi, Clare.'

This response, a possibility Mara hadn't mentioned before, threw me. And the word "fixating" rankled. I was just trying to analyse all this logically. 'Well...' I flustered, 'then there's the banner he ordered and collected from Presto Print.'

'An awful lot of hassle for Dex to have gone to, just to give the impression there was a misogynistic serial killer at large. Sinclair, however... Well, a banner like that was yet another talking point for his show.'

'Because Dex couldn't have done it any other way,' I said, ignoring her last sentence. 'He had to devise the woman-killer narrative to deflect attention away from himself, to make it look like multiple women were being targeted and stop Katarina from getting into that second box — a box Angel was already inside of.'

Mara didn't miss a beat. 'On one of the highest-profile stages in the country, though?' she countered. 'During what was maybe his last chance at the big time? Dex Devereaux's lazy with his material and not particularly blessed in the intelligence department. His whole supposed plan doesn't seem like anything he'd have the skill to put into practice.'

'Okay then, suppose it was Shane, like you believe. Why would Shane order that banner on Dex's credit card? Something about that doesn't add up.'

Mara glared at me as though I was being wilfully slow. 'To frame Dex, of course.'

'And how did Shane gain access to the Devereauxs' Facebook password to send that message from a desktop computer?'

'Same way he got Dex's credit card details. Presumably from their dressing room at Shinetree.'

I could feel myself growing more exasperated. I could understand why Mara felt the way she did about Shane Sinclair, but because of her prejudice against him, we were going round in circles. Perhaps Paulson was right; Mara did have too much of a bias to be working on this case. 'But you said in the pub that Shane could never have got into the Devereauxs' dressing room unnoticed.'

'An assistant, then.'

I wondered if she'd totally forgotten our conversation of only two days ago. 'Again, you said the more people involved in something like this, the more chance it has of coming out.'

I glanced at Mara, who was frowning at her folded hands. 'Sinclair has a considerable bank of contacts. There's probably an IT specialist on his payroll plenty experienced enough to hack a Facebook account or retrieve a credit card number.'

Another contradiction. And another accomplice for Shane to have to keep quiet, if indeed that was what happened. It all appeared to hinge on the recording on Angel's phone. And that could have been exactly what Shane had claimed it was in his interview: Shane making some sort of pass at Angel, threatening to make her look like a fool on his show if she didn't comply. She'd simply made the recording as proof the encounter had happened, in case Shane followed through with those threats.

Mara's constant rebuttals, which all stemmed from her being dead set that Shane Sinclair was Angel's murderer, made me feel like *I* was floundering, when it seemed logical that all the evidence pointed in the same direction. And they made me feel like I'd been complicating the case so far, rather than helping to solve it.

'You always disagree, don't you?' The words shot out, keener-edged than I'd intended. But at this stage of the proceedings, functioning on little sleep and with the impression we were getting nowhere — literally while crawling along in an endless traffic jam — her attitude grated.

'Not at all.'

'You're doing it right now!' I snorted. 'It's exactly why Paulson wanted you off the case.'

'Graham gets far too het up about everything. It's because I make him nervous.'

'Can I just point out as well,' I went on, 'that it still hasn't been confirmed Dex and Katarina weren't seeing each other, giving Dex an even stronger motive.'

'Oh, they weren't,' Mara returned. 'She was asked about that when she was questioned after being in hospital.'

Another piece of information she hadn't bothered to pass on to me.

'Not for want of trying on Dex's part though, judging by what she said. Probably why he looked so shifty when she was talking to us outside the studio. Didn't want it coming out. But for Katarina, working with Dex was just a job. She wants to get into TV.'

'How'd you know all this?' I asked, incredulous.

'Luke told me. In my opinion, he would have made a much better SIO.'

I experienced a faint and unfamiliar sensation, a thin needling inside my chest. 'Yes, I thought I sensed a bit of a mutual fan club between the two of you.'

Mara affected a laugh. 'I see. *That's* what this is all about.'

I deliberately pushed this remark away. 'If I was a psychologist, I'd say you enjoyed being one step ahead.' I continued, recollecting the previous night. How, after I'd discovered the identity of the second girl in Angel's school photo, I realised Mara hadn't just done the same, she'd gone one better. Finding Erin Grant's job *and* place of work too. And it was me who was meant to be the journalist, uncovering information, filling out gaps. The realisation irritated me anew. 'Because you like being in control. Because it makes up for the fact that you're in a situation at home right now that you have no control over whatsoever. That's why you're obsessed with the idea of Shane Sinclair being Angel's killer. Paulson was right — you're allowing a massive bias to cloud your judgement here.'

The hasty accusations, fuelled by my own deep-seated, simmering insecurities, infected the air between us. I instantly regretted them, knowing, even then, that the remark about Mara having no control over her husband's disappearance was cruel and the jab about Taylor particularly petty.

Mara's face spun from the window. Her light green eyes, usually so enigmatic and assessing, held a mixture of anger and—

'That's what you think, is it? That this is some sort of game to me?' Despite the rapidity of her movements, her speech; her voice was low and cold. 'And if *I* were a psychologist — if I'd become a psychologist, I mean, and not given it all up on a whim — then I would say that you're allowing your massive insecurities to cloud *your* judgement. You project your own feelings onto situations to compensate for your past, to compensate for what you feel are the banalities of your present. And you make assumptions about people of whom you know nothing. People like me.'

Sadness, I recognised then. It was sadness.

A sense of guilt bled through me, though Mara's words stung like hell. Mainly because she was right, of course. My life felt so small, so beige compared to hers. And I'd only started investigating Angel Devereaux in the first place because any woman's disappearance time-machined me straight back to my childhood. To that cold March day when my mother popped out for some milk and never came back.

I knew all this; I did. But hearing it laid bare by Mara was nonetheless crushing.

'Look, what I mean is—' I bumbled.

'You mean you see the surface, the performance. The *misdirection*,' Mara cut in. 'But you don't see what's going on behind it. You think you understand, but you don't.'

I didn't. I didn't understand what had happened two decades ago, even now. I didn't think I could ever understand it. I felt a familiar heat rise in my cheeks, a mixture of embarrassment and impotence. I wanted to apologise, to tell her she was right, but the words wouldn't come.

Instead, feeling like I'd had enough of not speaking my mind, I misguidedly dug in my heels and carried on. 'I understand, alright. I've wanted to make a difference to a story like this ever since...' The statement wilted. I knew what I wanted to say. *Ever since I was ten.* What I said instead was, 'Since I became a journalist. You're only doing this — working on a case like this — because the police pay you—'

At that very second, my phone burst into life from its holder on the dashboard.

"...Two ways to hear my three words."

Bloody Clarey-Bird. Why hadn't I changed that ringtone yet? I muttered a curse, eyes flicking to the screen. It was Jeff.

There was no way I was going to answer the call in front of Mara. After everything that'd just spewed out, all I wanted to do was drop her off as quickly as possible and get back to the flat. But the traffic had begun to move again, and between negotiating the gear stick, a lane change, and my own surging frustration, I swiped clumsily at the phone.

Rather than *rejecting* the call, I mistakenly *answered* it.

With my mobile already connected by Bluetooth, Jeff's voice blasted through the car's speakers. By the time I realised what was about to happen, it was too late.

'Deyes!' Jeff boomed. 'Just following up on earlier. Dug up any dirt on the missing husband yet?'

I cursed again, more frantically now, attempting to keep my eyes on the road *and* fumble with the phone. A gaggle of hooded youths suddenly sprang into the headlights through the sheeting rain. I slammed on my brakes, stopping short of them just in time. They shouted something derogatory, banging on the bonnet of the car.

My nerves were frayed, yet still Jeff's voice rabbited on from my mobile.

'Deyes...? That Travers Knight story could be front page, you know, if you play your cards right. Hey, that's not a bad pun. Cards? Magic—?'

Finally, I managed to hit the right part of the phone, ending the call once and for all. The silence that followed was awful and absolute, blotting out even the throbbing, pelting rain.

I ventured a glance at Mara. She was stiff and unmoving; her face a mask, eyes chips of glinting ice. Her hands were clenched so tightly on her lap her knuckles were bloodless.

'I would tell you to stop the car,' she forced, trying to quell the snag in her voice. 'But seen as we're practically at a standstill, I shall get out here.'

'Mara, I— I'm so sorry, I didn't mean—'

'As I said, here's fine.'

My pulse hammered the same rhythm as the rain, Jeff's words still echoing noxiously. Then Mara grabbed the door handle and clicked free her seatbelt.

'Wait, we're...' I looked around wildly. The street signs were unfamiliar; the architecture grim, imposing. Tower blocks loomed, hemming in the road on either side, their concrete facades streaked with grime. Graffiti screamed from every available surface of every wall, bin, bus stop and bridge.

Then I realised where we were. This was the Harrowbrook Estate, a place notorious for drug gangs. It had been in the news almost constantly for the past month. The police might as well move in they were here so frequently. Breaking up fights so serious they were near fatalities. Investigating stabbings. Carrying out early morning raids. I couldn't let Mara get out here. It would be dodgy enough in the day... but on her own, in the dark?

'...We're not in a very good area,' I finished inadequately. 'Please, let me take you home.'

'I know exactly where we are,' Mara bit out. Paying no heed to my warning, she flung open the door and was out of her seat in a single fluid movement.

'Mara, please!' I cried, leaning across to the passenger door.

'Let me explain. What you just heard, it wasn't what you think—Jeff just—'

She stared at me for a long, discomforting beat, as the cars behind blared their horns impatiently. 'By the way, Clare, you were wrong. The police *don't* pay me. I do all this... for Travers.'

Mara slammed the door and, without looking back, stalked swiftly away, her green coat billowing at her calves. Edging the car slowly forwards, my eyes strained to follow her form until she had vanished completely, dissolving into the ominous shadows of the enormous tower blocks.

I slumped against my seat and brought a hand to my forehead, letting out a growl of despair. I needed to try to find her, find a place to turn around. Taking the next left, I pulled into a gloomy parking area and was faced with a stairwell that gaped before me like a large black void. The place felt menacing, not least since only about a quarter of the car park's lights were still working, the rest of the bulbs smashed on the ground. I had no idea how I would summon the courage to get out and look for Mara.

I took a breath, unlocking the door and willing myself on. Something shifted from the darkness in front of me. It was a figure, a man, coalescing from the chasm of the stairwell. He signalled to someone to my right and broke into a fast walk towards the car. Before I knew it, three young men were closing in on me.

I brought my hand down hard on the door locks, fingers shaking at the ignition as I hastily restarted the engine, tyres spinning back in the direction of the rush hour traffic.

A wave of guilt, so strong it was almost physical, smashed

over me. How could I have been so careless? So thoughtless? All that stuff I'd said to Mara was bad enough, without Jeff's call. Now she thought the only reason I'd spent the past week with her was to exploit her grief, unearth some scandal about her missing husband, and all for a tawdry local newspaper story. Yes, I'd told Jeff I was investigating Travers Knight's disappearance, but only so I could buy myself more time. More time with Mara. More time to try to unravel what exactly had happened to Angel.

The image of Mara melting into the looming tower blocks blazed in my mind. She was alone in a highly dangerous part of London, furious and upset.

And it was all my fault.

In that moment, the certainty that I would never see Mara Knight again was utterly overwhelming. It made another gaping hole. A sudden, aching void where, for a few chaotic and exhilarating days, there had been colour, intrigue, and a strange, unspoken camaraderie.

All that was now left was the still-unsolved case of a murdered woman, and the bitter taste of my own stupidity.

42.♠

The traffic home was horrific; the rain relentless. It was ten by the time I got back to the flat and found somewhere to park. I switched off the ignition, meaning to duck straight inside. But the next thing I knew, thirty minutes had passed. Thirty minutes sitting in the seeping cold, watching the rain runnelling down the windscreen, as my mind turned over every aspect of the argument with Mara until I felt sick.

I eventually summoned the energy to drag my body up the stairs and let myself in. I chucked my bag down by the door, Jasper vaulting towards me from the living room. It had been almost two days since I'd seen him, but it felt like two months. I'd chased one dead end after another, and wrecked a possible friendship with the most interesting person I'd ever met. And when Jeff found out I'd lied to him about the Travers Knight story, who knows whether I would have a job left, either. If that happened, I had no idea what I'd do.

As these thoughts spiralled, my gaze drifted through the open door of the living room. I expected Matt to be in his usual spot on the sofa, guitar in hand. But his guitar lay propped against the coffee table, and the sofa was empty.

'That you, Cla?' came a voice from the bedroom.

When I followed it, I saw Matt was stuffing clothes into a beaten-up rucksack.

'What's all this?' I asked.

'I'm going to my parents for the weekend, remember? Back Sunday.'

'Oh... yes,' I lied, having completely forgotten he'd mentioned it. I couldn't work out whether I was more depressed to be facing the prospect of an entire weekend alone, or pleased I could now wallow in my own self-pity.

'Train's tomorrow morning,' Matt continued. 'Thought I'd pull an all-nighter to get this song finished before I leave. I'll sleep on the train.'

'Right,' I replied, forcing a smile. 'Hope you get it done before you go.'

He pushed a scraggle of blond hair from his forehead with the back of his hand. 'Going great so far. All thanks to that woman you brought here. That new and improved riff's set up the whole album. You should bring her round more often.'

The smile on my face warped into a miserable grimace. It was never going to happen.

'You okay, Cla?' asked Matt, shoving in a last pair of socks and zipping up his bag. 'You seem a bit off. That where you were last night, anyway? Working on that talent show story with her?'

'Er, yeah, I was,' I managed, the words tasting like ash. Off was an understatement. Jasper leapt onto the bed and gave me an encouraging tail wag, as if sensing my anguish. I stroked his paw pathetically.

'Hey, no need to worry about Jaspo,' Matt said, moving beside me to rub the dog's shaggy ears. 'We've been fine, haven't we, boy?'

Matt planted a kiss in the centre of Jasper's head; the genuine affection in the gesture catching me by surprise, as if I was seeing it anew. I'd been off running around for the past week, spending little time with either of them. I'd been entirely consumed by the Angel Devereaux case and Mara's world. To my shame, I'd even felt a spark of jealousy at how well DC Taylor appeared to get on with Mara. And yet here I had a boyfriend who, though he might live like a perpetual student, had a good heart and a genuine love for an animal I'd brought into our home without so much as consulting him first. It made me feel even more wretched than I already did.

'You sure you'll be okay this weekend, Cla?' Matt went on. 'You can come with me if you like? Make a weekend of it. Bring Jasper.'

The dog's tail pounded against the duvet in delight.

I strained another smile. 'That's okay,' I replied, turning away. 'I'll be fine. Might just have a shower and an early night.'

I slept in the next morning, and so did Matt. When I went into the kitchen, he was asleep on the sofa. His guitar lay across his lap, pencil dangling between limp, outstretched fingers. A page of notepaper scrawled with chord sequences had drifted to rest at his feet.

'Hey,' I murmured, nudging him awake. 'Train's in an hour.'

Matt washed his usual Weetabix down with a coffee and

hurriedly gathered up the last of his things. No sooner had the front door closed behind him than a grim and heavy silence descended. The day dragged on in an unremitting haze of self-recrimination. I didn't bother to dress, not even to walk Jasper. I just grabbed his lead and threw a coat on over my pyjamas. The flat curtains remained drawn and, when I could be bothered to switch it on, the radio babbled in the background.

With no energy to shop, I finished what little packet food was left, then ordered in a takeaway. The irony that I was turning into Matt, sans guitar, was not lost on me. But I didn't care. Unwashed crockery piled up on the kitchen worktops, on the living room coffee table. The week's laundry continued to accumulate in mountain-like ranges. Crumbs from the meals I ate off my lap speckled the floor, the sofa cushions, the rugs, even the insides of my slipper-socks.

My phone lay at my side, and every few minutes I picked it up to check I hadn't missed a message from Mara. But there was nothing, only a handful of unread texts from Jeff, which I ignored.

Over the course of that Friday, I pulled Mara's number up on my phone a million times, thumb hovering over the "call" button for endless seconds, before thinking better of it. My drafts folder was full of messages I'd written to her but not summoned the courage to send, all versions of the same thing.

I never intended to write about your husband.

I would never have done it.

I didn't mean the things I said in the car.

I'm sorry.

Despite Jasper's company, the hours passed like molasses,

oozing sickly on. I lay on the sofa, bundled in a duvet, while my gaze stuck, unfocused, on some never-ending box set playing on the television. But seared onto the backs of my eyelids was Mara's face, etched with its cold, wounded fury.

You project your own feelings onto situations to compensate for your past, to compensate for what you feel are the banalities of your present.

To compensate for your past.

The words echoed, the TV's soundtrack fading as the living room of the flat evaporated around me. The neutral paintwork, flat-pack furniture and laminate floors receded, replaced by the green carpets and garish striped wallpaper of the house where I grew up.

Back in that house, that mid-terrace halfway along an unassuming street in Swindon, it was another Friday night in March. Spring was late that year as well, and the old, spongy window frames and single glazing let in fingers of frost, which snaked their way up the insides of the glass.

The dated electric heating did nothing to help, and every morning I could see my breath in the icy bathroom. The pipes froze, the washing machine broke, and when the temperature did start to rise and the rain fall, the roof began to leak.

It only struck me much later that all this must have played a part in what happened next.

That Friday, my mum had come home from her job at the supermarket, my dad from his at a local garage. He'd peeled off his overalls, black with the week's grease, and added them to the pile of clothes waiting for my mum to hand-wash. Then the evening had proceeded as normal. Chicken nuggets, chips, peas. Fruit cocktail and ice cream for afters. The latest episode of *Neighbours* on the little box TV in the kitchen. An hour or two later, Dad sitting on his favourite section of the sofa with a can of beer and *Only Fools and Horses*.

Mum's voice from the hallway was normal, too, even though she never usually went shopping in the evening.

'Just popping out,' she said. 'Get some milk for breakfast.'

'Yep,' Dad replied, still engrossed in his sitcom.

I peered around the front room door and saw Mum hovering in the hall, staring into the mirror. Not realising I was there, she dragged a brush through her chin-length brown hair and swiped some powder across her cheeks. Every time I do the same, even now, my skin creeps a little, the action of it hurling me back to that night in March 1994.

The last night we saw her.

An hour later, when Mum still hadn't returned, I made Dad ring the police. He wasn't keen at first, told me it was nothing, that she'd probably just called in to see one of our neighbours. But I knew there was more to it than that, sensed something was very wrong, even when the police said that as it hadn't been twenty-four hours, there was no cause for concern.

In the days that followed, the missing posters went up. Dad chose the photo, one of Mum taken on a day trip to Bournemouth the previous summer. Her gold clip-on earrings flared like two small suns through her hair, her anorak and skirt licked wildly by the breeze off the sea. But still there were no leads. Nobody had seen her that night, apparently, and nobody had seen her since. She'd never made it to the corner shop, never bought the milk for our Saturday morning cereal. She'd disappeared into the darkness, alone. Just like a woman in a nearby town six months earlier, whose body was eventually found in a wood.

The ensuing years were split asunder by what had happened, a blur of my dad's increasingly shuttered-up despair and my own frantic, childish efforts to find my mum. What had Mara said that first night in her house, when she'd compared a missing person to a magic trick?

When that object doesn't reappear, a state of profound and constant psychological tension is created... In my opinion, there are few things more agonising.

That was it in a nutshell. *Agonising.*

Year after year, I'd scoured local papers, conducted so many of my own interviews in the area that the people whose doors I knocked on went from giving me sympathy and hot Ribena to excuses and a cold shoulder. I drew reams of homemade "missing" posters, walked miles taping them to lampposts and fences, in as large a radius from our house as I could.

When I was sixteen, unable to cope with my dad's remoteness, mood and relationship swings, I finally moved out. A succession of menial jobs and even more menial boyfriends followed, all experienced in the insidious fog of uncertainty.

And then, against an ongoing backdrop of news reports of other missing women, I'd decided, with a new and furious conviction, that journalism was the key. Over the next few years, I worked two, sometimes three jobs at a time to fund a diploma. I was certain it was the answer, the very thing that would furnish me with the skills to find my mother. And with it, I could help other families to solve their own devastating mysteries, like the one that had fractured my life into a "before" and an "after".

And it was the answer. Just not the one I'd expected.

Armed with my brand-new knowledge, I trawled death records, newspaper reports, eyewitness accounts, in a wider and wider circle. Wider in the little car I owned by then than I'd ever managed before.

And then I found her.

But she wasn't a dry pile of bones poking through a damp layer of leaf litter. She was alive and well. Living in a neat semi in Coventry with a primary school headmaster and two children who called her "Mummy". Children who were a similar age to me when Mum disappeared.

So my worst fears were unfounded. My mother hadn't been murdered at all. There was no foul play. There was just a woman who had chosen a different life for herself, a life that didn't include me. And in a way this discovery was much worse, bringing with it a fresh and ringing pain, more bewildering and intense than it had been before.

A shadowy bogeyman hadn't torn my childhood apart; my mother had done it herself. And why? Because the weather was harsh and life difficult at home? Because she was bored with her job, her marriage? Because she had depression, undiagnosed struggles with mental health? My mind had cycled through all of these and more in the years after I found her, but I still didn't understand. I wasn't sure I ever would.

I hadn't really understood until now the wider ripples my mother's actions had created, either. Was Mum walking out on me the reason I was struggling to end things with Matt? Because walking out on him seemed so impossibly cruel, even though, if I was honest with myself, some part of me had questioned whether our relationship was working ever since we'd moved in together?

The ghost of that ten-year-old girl would always live inside me, I realised. Paralysed and confused and desperate for answers. This was just what happened. When someone who should love and protect you unconditionally takes the decision to exorcise you from their life, you will still always be haunted.

The walls of my Morden flat cohered around me again, and I drew Jasper in close. He gave a long, contented groan, proudly displaying the paler fur of his belly. I sobbed out a laugh, scrubbing the wetness from my face and switching off the TV. My self-pity might have soured around me, but a woman had still been murdered. There was still someone out there who had taken Angel Devereaux's life. And they had to be held accountable.

Tomorrow, I resolved. Tomorrow, with or without anyone else's help, I would find out what happened to Angel for myself.

43.♠

The following morning I awoke early, feeling more refreshed than I had in an age. It was the day of the live Talent Quest final. In less than twelve hours, Dex Devereaux would swagger back onto the studio stage to perform once again, as if his wife's death the previous week had been nothing more than an inconvenience. The thought was a grit of annoyance, then a spark, then a flare of outrage. I refused to sit in my flat, stewing in my failure, for another day. It was time to find out what had really happened to Angel.

I took a shower, the hot water sluicing away yesterday's inertia. I dressed in a clean top and jeans. I did the dishes, ran a hoover around the flat, put the washing on. I took Jasper to the park, where we played with his red tomato ball-launcher, and on the way back I stocked up on groceries. Then I opened my laptop and settled myself at the breakfast bar.

Though I wasn't sure why, the remark Mara had made last Sunday night ran through my head.

It's entirely possible that she might have put herself there.

It had since been disproved that Katarina locked herself in the flight case, not least because Lenny had confessed. And he'd put her there because of that Facebook message. But Mara was confident that Dex wasn't capable of masterminding such a complex deception; of crafting himself an alibi so he could contact an accessory, murder his wife live on national television *and* make it all look like the work of a serial killer.

But if Dex hadn't messaged Lenny asking him to kidnap Katarina, then who had? Shane Sinclair? Or someone else? And where to start looking for them?

I cast my mind back to where all this began. Not Angel's disappearance two weeks ago, but the last crazy seven days. It had begun with me finding Mara. Or rather, with Mara finding me. I recalled her methods, her words during the car ride from the prison.

Your social media profiles are public, Clare... I had a little look at your accounts.

It seemed as good a place to start as any. I logged into Facebook, typing Lenny Finch's name into the search bar.

A second later, his profile filled the screen, the main picture still that unnervingly zoomed-in shot of Lenny's fleshy face. I clicked into the "Photos" section of his profile, scrolling through the pictures again, more slowly this time.

I lingered over the shots of him with Dex Devereaux, taken at magic conventions and after shows, in lobbies and corridors and car parks. I reexamined Lenny's wide and desperate smile, as though he was there fulfilling a fantasy, the way his eyes were glued to Angel, who was cropped out on the right-hand edge. I took in the other strange croppings of the pictures, the careless way they'd been framed. And as I did, photos just like them flashed in my mind.

They were the photos those two schoolgirls had taken of

Jasper as we'd walked to Lenny's cul-de-sac. I remembered how the girls had been so focused on taking pictures of my dog, they'd almost cropped themselves out entirely. It was Jasper who remained front and centre. And these pictures on Lenny's Facebook account were the same. Lenny was an afterthought in his own photographs, while Dex was the real focal point. It was as though the person taking the pictures was far more interested in Dex than Lenny.

The person taking the pictures.

I turned my attention from the images to the comments below them, comments that hadn't fully registered initially, since they seemed so easily explained.

My boy! He's definitely got the magic touch!

Gorgeous in this one!

So handsome.

Though a little full-on, they were the sort of comments any proud mother might make about her son. But what if those comments *weren't* about Lenny? What if they were actually... about Dex? Perhaps Lenny *was* fulfilling a fantasy by having his picture taken with Dex. It just wasn't his own.

It was his mother's.

It was *Jean's.*

Unease prickled up my spine as I clicked on Jean Finch's profile.

Fortunately, many of the posts appeared to be public, and I began going back through them all. There was the kind of content you might find on anyone's social media accounts.

Unflattering selfies, photographs of meals out, complaints about the council. And in between all these were photos of Dex, posted with keen regularity. There were screenshots, pictures of him performing. There were candids taken backstage. Yet the tone of the text that accompanied the pictures was odd. While many of the captions gushed about Dex's charisma, or his incredible talent for magic, others took a much darker tone. They veered wildly between heartsore infatuation and a boiling, venomous resentment.

King of my Heart!

I will never stop loving you.

Traitor.

You broke my heart.

Why her when you had me?

Bitch.

My stomach tightened. Jean was furious, furious with both Dex *and* Angel. But despite many of the comments reading like those written by an unstable and obsessive fan, one in particular stood out.

Why her when you had me?

When you *had* me?

I dragged the scroll bar to the top of Jean's profile. Was her date of birth here somewhere? Clicking on the "About" section, I found it. Jean was born on the 22nd of January 1964. So she was fifty years old. The same age as Dex. And her hometown was listed as Cleethorpes, Lincolnshire.

Lincolnshire. The same county that Dex was from. Was it simply a coincidence?

I navigated back to midway down Jean's profile and continued to study the content, coming across a photo posted several years ago. Judging by the clothing and the picture quality, it looked like it'd been taken in the very early eighties.

The photo showed a couple who couldn't have been more than nineteen years old. They were smiling widely, posing below a sign that read "Pier Pavilion" in a bowing, mid-century font. For sale behind them were seaside mementoes: buckets of familiar plastic windmills. The young woman was blonde, her full hourglass figure emphasised by a cinching, spangly leotard. The man was stocky, brown-haired, a fan of playing cards spread between his fingers. Yet, despite the age of the photograph and the fresh faces of the couple, I recognised them both. They were Dex and Jean.

So, Dexter Dodd and Jean Finch had known each other since they were teenagers. And judging by her outfit, Jean must have been Dex's assistant in those earliest days of his career. His *original* assistant.

You broke my heart.

What was it Erin had said? That when Dex and Angel had met in Edinburgh, Dex was already in a relationship. A relationship with Jean.

I scrolled down the page faster, a sense of nausea rising, together with the conviction that there was still more to find.

Then, there it was, the image that made everything align into a new and horrifying understanding. A photo from about a decade ago, taken from a local newspaper. In this photo, Dex stood beside Angel, their poses not dissimilar to the older photo of Dex and Jean. Angel's hands were angled showily towards Dex, who was again fanning out a deck of playing cards. Her slim form was sheathed in its usual sequinned stage gear, legs glossed by stockings and lengthened by heels.

At least I assumed that woman was Angel. It was impossible to be sure, because pasted over her head was another woman's head. It had been taken from a different photograph altogether, the mismatched face illuminated by a much harsher light. The cut-out head was also a little too large for the body it was stuck to, and was glued on at an unnatural slant. If the resulting image wasn't so disturbing, it could almost have been comical. Underneath was a caption, written in capitals and boldly underlined.

THE REAL DEVEREAUX

At first I assumed the image had been crudely made in Photoshop, before realising this was an actual paper collage. Somebody had cut and pasted it together, photographed it, and finally posted it online. And that somebody, of course, was Jean.

My pulse quickened as everything reframed itself before me. That room Mara and I had discovered at the Finches' house, with its grotesque walls plastered with Angel's defaced photographs. The gouged-out eyes, the hand-drawn knife in Angel's heart. Mara had assumed this was Lenny's room, Lenny's handiwork. We both had.

But it wasn't Lenny's room. It was Jean's.

Jean, who seethed with jealousy for Angel. Jean, who still loved Dex and believed she should still be with him. Jean, who had taken this belief to its most twisted, literal conclusion.

She'll kill me.

Lenny had indeed been referring to his mother that day at the car wash; it was Jean he was afraid of. Was it Jean who sent Lenny that Facebook message, having somehow hacked the Devereauxs' page? Was she trying to cover her tracks, make it look like the message had come from Dex? Perhaps Jean had later revealed to her son that she was behind the plan and sworn him to secrecy. Hence, *she'll kill me.*

I sat staring at the screen for a while, processing everything. After a few minutes had passed, I distractedly scrolled back to the top of Jean Finch's profile. I was about to click away from it when my gaze hooked on a post that hadn't been there before. A brand new photo posted only three minutes ago.

It was a selfie of Jean, heavily made up. Her lips were an asymmetrical gash of red, accentuating the downwards turn of her mouth. Her short bleached hair had been teased and lacquered into a stiff, precarious bouffant. She was wearing a low-cut sequinned top that looked suspiciously like an assistant's leotard.

Then I turned my attention to the caption below the selfie, and ice coursed through my veins.

It's showtime! All glammed up and off to the studios, where someone's gonna get what they deserve. #TalentQuestFinal #KingofHearts #JusticeForDex

I glanced at the time. I'd no idea it was so late, the afternoon having evaporated as I'd sat rooted to my laptop, trawling the world of Dex, Angel and Jean. It was after five now. The Talent

Quest final would be going live in under three hours.

Mara's voice ran once more through my head.

Something has happened every time Dex has appeared on the show. Everyone's talking about it, and everyone wants to see what will happen next.

Whatever was going to happen next, whatever Jean had planned, I had to stop it.

44.♠

My first instinct was to ring Mara and tell her what I'd found. I leapt from the breakfast bar, seizing my phone and dialling her number. When there was no answer, I decided to call the police.

But who to call?

I didn't have DI Paulson's or DC Taylor's number and, despite my fears about what Jean might do at Shinetree, it wasn't technically an emergency. So I rang 101, waiting to be connected for what seemed like forever before explaining what I'd found.

'Please, pass what I'm telling you on to DI Paulson... on the Angel Devereaux investigation,' I pleaded.

'You know for certain this Jean Pinch is about to harm someone?' the operator asked, in a tone that suggested I stop wasting her time. 'Cos if we sent an officer out every time someone said something stupid on Facebook... You'd be better off reporting this online—'

Growling in frustration, I hung up and tried calling Mara again as I prepared to leave, phone jammed under my chin as I hastily refilled Jasper's bowls.

I tried again as I fumbled into my jacket and grabbed my car keys.

Still nothing.

Either she didn't want to speak to me or... The image of those looming tower blocks returned, of Mara swallowed by their shadows. I snatched my handbag up from where I'd dropped it earlier after walking Jasper. Shrugging it onto my shoulder, I typed out a message to Mara, recalling the words of our argument, which had been swimming around my head since Thursday.

> **What's going on: I'm on my way to Shinetree. I think something bad will happen at the final. What's really going on: I would never have written some cheap story about your husband, I just let Jeff think that to buy myself some time. I wasn't investigating Angel Devereaux because of Travers. I was doing it because of my mother. To compensate for my past. The profound and constant psychological tension, like you said. I didn't mean those things I said in the car. I'm sorry. Even if we never see each other again, I hope you understand. Cx**

My thumb hovered over the send button for the briefest moment before I pressed it and tore down the stairs. I had to get to Shinetree.

The drive north took an eternity, every speed limit interminable, every red light torture. Whenever I ground to another standstill, I tapped my phone and tried Mara's number. There was still no reply. My stomach churned harder each time it rang out, until I was certain something awful really had happened to her in the Harrowbrook Estate, and I was overwhelmed by guilt anew. Jeff's call slipping through to speakerphone. My stupid words. They had driven her right into danger.

My mind raced, veering from thoughts of Mara late on Thursday night — alone and bloodied, or worse — to what I had uncovered about Jean. That she and Dex had known each other since they were teenagers. That Jean was his original assistant. That the bedroom was *hers*, not her son's, and with it all those obliterated pictures of Angel.

Ignoring the Shane Sinclair recording on Angel's phone, did everything else we'd found fit with Jean being Angel's killer? Firstly, there was the banner. Jean could have ordered that to detract attention away from herself, and also from Dex. Perhaps she got hold of Dex's credit card details at a magic show, somehow? She could then have placed the order by phone and sent Lenny into Presto Print to collect it. After all, the shop was local to the Finches, plus this all tallied with what Mr Chen had told us.

Next, there were the objects found at the Devereauxs' house. The hair, the rings, the love letter. I couldn't explain the hair or letter, and it was unlikely they were from Jean. But if Jean had discovered that Dex was hoping to marry Katarina — as proven by the rings — then she had more reason to want Katarina out of the picture too. Either by having Katarina kidnapped mid-show to frighten her off, or by locking her away before killing her, as she had killed Angel. Could Jean have even framed Dex in anger?

But Angel had left Shinetree in disguise. Had Jean duped her into doing this? Had Angel been kept at the Finches' house the week she was missing, guarded by Lenny? It was possible.

What had Jean told us outside the police station?

I can't say I'm not glad Angel's gone.

So, who did Jean Finch plan to harm this week? Dex's latest assistant?

Finally, the slick chrome lettering of the studio entrance veered into view up ahead. Only then did the practicalities of coming to Shinetree hit me. What to do now? I'd been so consumed by my thoughts of Mara and Jean on the way here, I hadn't formulated a plan. How the hell was I even going to get past the security guard's kiosk? I could already see the barrier was down and, unlike that barrier at HMP Ferndon, there was no way around it.

A cold sweat nettled my forearms. *Think*, I told myself. *There must be a way.*

I brought to mind the last time I'd driven to Shinetree. I had been with Mara then, as she'd flashed her police pass at the man in the kiosk. But that same morning, Mara had also given me a security pass. My gaze landed on the passenger seat, where my bulging handbag lay. And inside of it, I hoped, was the Proactive Productions pass for a woman named Cece Sutherland.

I drew the car to a halt at the barrier and dived a hand into my bag, relief flooding through me as my fingers closed around my press pass lanyard, into which Cece's pass was still fixed. For once I was glad I never bothered to clear my bag out. I offered the security guard both the pass and my friendliest smile, hoping they'd be enough.

The man narrowed his eyes, examining the pass and then me, in a way that was somewhat uncertain. I caught my reflection in the wing mirror. My smile had seized on my face, making me look more than a little unhinged. I quickly readjusted my expression and gave myself an internal pep talk. I had to bluff it tonight, pretend I had every right to be here, just as Mara had done at the prison. It was the only way to stop whatever was about to happen, whatever Jean Finch had in store.

After a few seconds, the guard gave a shrug and returned the pass to me. The barrier rose, and I accelerated towards the studio without looking back.

Parking up, I spent what few rushed seconds I could making myself slightly more presentable. I fished out the bits of makeup I had in my bag and used Cece's photo as a reference. I would probably have to show that pass again, and I currently looked as much like Cece Sutherland as the dodgy tribute act in the Swindon Working Men's Club looked like Elvis. Though, on second thoughts, I looked as much like Cece Sutherland as Kelly Keogan looked like Mara, and that had been enough to fool me.

I looped the pass around my neck and fluffed up my hair, attempting a pout in the mirror. It would have to do. Taking a breath, I left the car, and hurried in the direction of the Talent Quest studio.

There was a queue at the entrance, and I realised the people waiting were members of the public, the last of the studio audience to go inside. They were having their names checked against a list of seat bookings, and they were having their bags checked too. The queue wasn't exactly moving quickly, but I couldn't see any alternative than to join it. By attempting to find another door, I might only draw more attention to myself, and I didn't want to risk being chucked out of Shinetree before I'd even had the chance to find Jean.

Ahead of me, a security guard was confiscating a bottle of water from a woman's handbag.

'No liquids, I'm afraid,' he said when she began to grumble.

My hand flew to my own bag, as I tried to recall whether *I* had any liquids. I remembered I did. The perfume Mara had given me. The first and only time someone had gifted me a decent bottle of perfume and I would have to relinquish it. Typical.

I unzipped my handbag and peeped inside, wondering if I could hide the bottle. But the first thing I saw wasn't the perfume; it was Jasper's extendable ball-launcher, cradling his favourite tomato ball. I could save up for another bottle of Luxe Lumina's perfume — over the next twenty years or so, maybe — but my dog's toy, scented over months of park playtimes, was irreplaceable. No way was I losing *that*.

'God, this queue's taking ages,' the woman in front of me moaned. 'I hope we don't miss Josie.'

Having somehow made it through to the Talent Quest final, Josie the Chihuahua was performing again tonight. Suddenly, I knew what to do.

I reached into my bag and removed the ball-launcher. Then, summoning the same sense of authority as Mara when she'd checked my bag at the prison, I marched around the queue and smartly up to the security guard.

'Excuse me, Cece Sutherland, member of the production team,' I announced in my most commanding voice as I lifted the pass. 'Important prop here for Josie Chihuahua, I must get this backstage immediately.'

The woman who'd been in front of me cooed admiringly at the mention of Josie's name. Though I tried not to let it show, my pulse thudded in my neck. The guard, however, seemed to accept my fib, and directed me down an alleyway to a backstage entrance.

I returned the ball-launcher to my bag, feeling even more anxious as I neared the door to the studio's backstage area. It was open, and the corridor beyond it was a furious mass of activity. Feverish threads of people wearing the same "CREW" t-shirt Lenny had worn buzzed about, shouting instructions into walkie-talkies. Others sported headsets and brandished cue cards and papers. More still bore plates of sandwiches and bottles of wine. Speakers bracketed to the walls pumped out synth-rock music.

A woman with a clipboard was stationed at this backstage entrance.

'Cece Sutherland,' I said, showing her my pass. 'Proactive Productions.'

She looked me up and down for several long seconds. 'Oh,' she said at last. 'Hi Cece. You look different this evening.'

'I've... I've cut my hair,' I blurted.

'You look a lot shorter without your heels,' she countered.

Glancing down at my Converse, I strained a smile. 'Yeah. In flats tonight.' I shrugged. 'Bunion's been playing me up.'

Why I'd suddenly started to channel an eighty-year-old woman, I wasn't entirely sure. I couldn't imagine Cece Sutherland wearing Converse, let alone admitting to having a bunion.

The woman gave an awkward laugh, as though she'd found the bunion revelation embarrassing. 'Go ahead,' she said, waving me away. 'Shane's expecting you. He's in his dressing room.'

I didn't like the sound of this. If Shane was expecting Cece, then—

Behind me, a car slowed ominously.

'Thanks so much!' I called to the woman, shoving through the throng of people and down the corridor as if my life depended on it. I hadn't got far when her voice cut back at me through the hubbub.

'Hey, you... come here!'

I ventured the smallest glance back at the woman. She was red-faced now, shaking her clipboard in an effort to get me to stop. And she'd been joined by a second woman. A woman who'd become very familiar to me over the past half an hour. Cece Sutherland.

'I'm calling Shane,' Cece declared loudly, prodding the woman with the clipboard. 'And I suggest you call security.'

I broke into a run, praying I wasn't inadvertently heading towards Shane Sinclair's dressing room. After all the time it had taken to get inside, I needed to find a way into the studio audience. I needed to find Jean. And quickly.

It dawned on me then that what was coming through the corridor's speakers was actually the sound of what was happening inside the Talent Quest studio. The synth-rock had stopped, and a man was warming up the audience, running through the order of the acts. Dex Devereaux, he said, would kick off the show, preceded by a specially recorded video tribute to Angel. And it would all be going live in less than five minutes.

As the audience whooped with anticipation at this news, I ducked into a doorway, snatching a few seconds to think. Could

Mara already be here? I pulled out my phone, hoping to see a message from her, telling me she was indeed at Shinetree, that she knew what Jean was about to do. But there was still nothing. I tipped back my head in frustration, and a jumble of signs hanging from the ceiling caught my attention.

Green Rooms

Gallery

Audience

The Talent Quest theme music began blasting along the corridor as I followed the last of these signs. The final was starting.

45.

At last, I reached the door I wanted, and pushed through it to find myself at the left-hand edge of the audience. A blazing, dancing kaleidoscope of lights above the crowd momentarily dazzled me, and I shaded my eyes to frantically scour the raked rows of seating, searching for Jean.

In doing so, my gaze absentmindedly passed across a fair head in the very front row. I distantly recognised this head, its half-profile flaring in and out of the pulsating blackness. But it wasn't Jean.

Continuing to scan upwards through the rows of the audience, there, on an aisle seat not too far from the back, I eventually found her. Jean's bouffant stood starkly out from the crowd, the colour of pale custard. Her face was tight and intense.

As I climbed the steps to the back of the audience, the Talent Quest theme music drew to a close and the studio was suddenly submerged by darkness. I floundered to Jean's aisle, and when the stage lights reignited, I saw I was only a few feet behind her.

I could hear my heart hammering even above the swell of applause from the crowd. What would I say? I wished Mara was here; she'd know exactly what to do. But she wasn't. It was up to me. The presenter began his introduction.

Jean's focus on the stage was so all-consuming she didn't notice when I crouched down next to her. Was she anticipating a cue? Had she already rigged something up in advance? Was it now just a case of waiting?

'Jean?' I whispered.

I would ask her to quietly step outside, I decided. I would try to get her to see sense, and then I would call the police.

Jean remained motionless, hands tightly guarding the leopard-print bag on her lap, her concentration unbroken. The thought struck me she might be holding the bag so tightly because there was a weapon inside. But that didn't make sense. How had she got it through the bag check?

'Jean?' I repeated, this time patting her arm.

She turned towards me then, in a distracted double take. Her thickly layered makeup became a mask first of shock, and then anger. 'You!' she breathed. 'I thought I'd told you already. Leave. Me. Alone.'

She angled herself away from me and fixed her eyes back on the stage.

'Would you come and speak to me outside, please?' I asked, resting a hand on her forearm. 'Just for a moment.'

Jean shook me off hotly. 'No, I bloody won't. You must be mad.'

It was no use; she wasn't going anywhere. What would Mara do if she was here? I recollected all those things I'd unearthed on Jean's Facebook. The bitterness, the anger, the unrequited love. That was it. I needed to tap into her psychology. Show Jean I understood.

'I know you're planning something, Jean,' I said, my voice becoming more urgent. 'And I know how you feel. I know how hard it is when someone rejects you. But, take it from me, wreaking revenge isn't the answer.'

Her face puckered sourly, and she dragged her gaze from the stage. 'I was wrong.'

A small draft of relief whistled through me. 'That's good to hear. Please, come and—'

'No, I was wrong about *you*,' Jean cut in. 'Mad isn't the word for you, you're totally insane. Now piss off.'

The curse caught the attention of the people closest to us. They tutted, hissing for us to keep quiet.

'I saw your Facebook post,' I told Jean, lowering my voice again. 'Whatever you're intending to do tonight, please don't. Just come with me now, and we'll go to the police together. Explain everything.'

Jean's eyes beaded darkly. 'What I'm intending to *do*?'

'What you said. On your latest post,' I replied. '*Someone's going to get what they deserve.*'

She mulled the sentence over a beat before her expression re-hardened. 'God, I was right! You're insane. And you're a bloody stalker, to boot!' She jabbed a finger into my arm, emphasising her words. 'I was talking about *Dex*, you silly cow. His appearance tonight. He deserves to be famous, for people to see the talent I've always known him to be. He deserves his own show. *That's* what I meant.'

The response threw me a little, as more shushing erupted from the rows around us. Was this really what Jean had meant? Or was she concealing the actual reason she was here by trying to re-contextualise what she'd written?

'The talent you've always known him to be?' I pressed, ignoring the increasing irritation of the crowd. I had come this far and wasn't about to give up. I was certain Jean was dangerous, that Angel's death was just the beginning. 'From when you were teenagers? Childhood sweethearts? You were his assistant back then, weren't you? You want to be his assistant again, rekindle the relationship you had all those years ago.'

A flicker of something between pain and fury crossed her face.

On stage, the presenter adopted a cloying, falsely sympathetic voice as he started to introduce the video tribute to Angel. 'And now, after the incredibly sad events of last Saturday — and before Dex Devereaux returns to the stage — let's take a very special look back at the incredible talent and beauty of the unforgettable magician's wife... Angel Devereaux!'

The giant screen at the back of the stage burst into life, spilling over with Angel's blinding smile. Several members of the audience gasped, some drew hands to their chests, others dabbed their eyes. I could even hear one person, from somewhere close to the stage, utter a sob.

I looked back at Jean. Her body had tensed, attention steeled to the stage, to the tribute to Angel, as her hand crept deeper inside the handbag on her lap.

She was reaching for a weapon.

'No, Jean!' I cried, grasping at the bag too.

Jean swore and batted me roughly away, causing me to stumble backwards. Like her son, she was solid and stocky, immovable. Dead set on whatever she was about to do.

Her hand emerged from the handbag as if in slow motion. And her fingers were firmly curled around something silver. Something that looked scarily like a gun.

Because it was a gun.

I had to do something.

A vision of Mara's PAVA spray loomed large in my mind, and I wished desperately that I had kept it, taken it from the hallway of her house. It would have incapacitated Jean as it had the prison wardens, stopped her in her tracks.

I didn't have the PAVA spray in my bag, but I did have the next best thing. Or rather, the only thing. My Parma Violet perfume.

Adrenaline surged, and without a second thought, I drew the perfume out and lunged towards Jean Finch.

'No!' I yelled, uncapping the bottle and aiming the nozzle directly at her head.

Jean, gun still in hand, startled, swirling to face me just as I depressed the sprayer.

A dense cloud of floral scent was released into the air. Jean shrieked, recoiled, her hands flying to her eyes as the gun spun out of her grip to plop back inside her bag. 'Argh, what the—!'

The man behind Jean coughed and sprang to his feet. 'Security!'

Chaos broke out then, much of the furore drowned by the Angel Devereaux tribute video, still playing on the giant screen. People fanned the air furiously, assuming that, given Jean's reaction, the spray was something toxic.

'Over there!' I heard a man exclaim.

I wheeled around to see two burly security guards heading

straight for me.

To my right, Jean was still thrashing, her face puce, her lurid red lipstick now a slash across her cheek. 'You crazy bitch!'

One of the security guards clenched hold of Jean, the other me.

'She has a weapon!' I declared as the man guided me to the door. 'You should be removing her, not me!'

In the fracas of my remonstrations; Jean's coughing; the surrounding audience's confusion; and the security guards' descent; Jean's handbag tumbled to the floor, its contents spilling across the aisle. Lipstick, cigarettes, a crumpled packet of tissues, loose change... and the gun.

'There it is!' I shouted, waving at the floor.

It was over. I had managed to do it. Jean had been stopped.

Rubbing her eyes, Jean recovered herself enough to take in the object I was pointing at. 'That's a bloody fag lighter!' she wheezed. 'And you're a bloody mental case! I was only trying to get my phone out for a picture.'

My stomach plummeted as the realisation sank in. It *was* a cigarette lighter. It was so obvious now. How could I not have seen it before? I cast my mind back to when Mara and I had stood on Jean's doorstep, the flash of silver between her fingers as she'd turned to light a fresh cigarette.

The security guard holding Jean proceeded to lead her to the door, with me steered by the other man in the same direction.

'There's a hole in my handbag lining,' Jean protested, hands raised in supplication. 'Look, I know I shouldn't have that lighter in here, but I need my fags. I have a medical condition!'

That's why she was guarding her bag so tightly. Not to protect a concealed weapon. But because it contained her precious cigarettes.

'Get your hands off me!' Jean screamed. 'Let me stay! I'm only here for the next act. He's the love of my life — we've been together since we were sixteen! That Angel was never his real wife, their marriage was nothing but a sham... a *sham*!'

Jean's voice faded as she disappeared through the door ahead of me, but her words rang loudly, clearly in my head.

The love of my life...

Together since we were sixteen...

Jean had said these things about her and Dex, but it might have been two other people she was talking about.

Never his real wife...

The marriage was a sham...

And that was when the dead ends, the distractions and the deceptions of the past seven days finally made sense. That was when it all suddenly aligned, like the finely fitting components of an illusion.

A long blonde hair, a new pair of wedding rings, a love letter. Two sixteen-year-old girls in school uniform. One charismatic, vivacious. The second quieter, an unmistakable trace of admiration for the first girl animating her expression. The sun shining down on them both, hazing the scene, holding it as if in amber.

A woman on a park bench, voice papery and hoarse, eyes red like she'd been crying. *She's been feeling a little off this week.* But it wasn't hay fever.

The video tribute to Angel drew to a close. A stills image of her, resplendent in her sequins and bouffant, faded to black and, as it did, the entire studio was once again plunged into darkness. A few seconds passed, and then the opening bars of Dex Devereaux's intro music started to pound.

The audience cheered as the stage lights once again flared. There, already in the centre of the stage, not striding out from the wings, but slap bang in his spotlight, was Dex.

Only he wasn't posing as if ready to begin his act. And he certainly wasn't smiling. He was frozen in a static, unnatural posture, chest rising and falling heavily, head strained stiffly back.

And Dex wasn't alone.

Someone was on stage with him. Not his new assistant, nor any of the production team. Someone who shouldn't have been on stage at all.

And that person was pressing a knife to Dex's throat.

The woman's hair was loose now, fair and sheeted across her shoulders, her startling blue eyes wide, her body taut, set to purpose.

It was Erin Grant.

46.

As the audience gave a collective gasp, the security guard's grip slackened on my arm, then fell away entirely. I half-noticed the guard hesitate a second behind me, questioning whether the scene now unfolding on Talent Quest was part of the show, his voice fogged by confusion. I didn't turn or answer him. My gaze was too fixed on the stage. On Dex Devereaux, held in the blanching white spotlight, fear set deep in his face. The wide, glinting knife digging perilously into the flesh of his throat. And holding that knife was Erin Grant.

Her blonde hair, which had been so neatly chignoned the last time I'd seen her, now hung loose and wild about her shoulders. The same height as Dex, one of her hands tightly gripped the knife, the other Dex's arm, clamping him in place. Erin's expression was a swirl of wrath and anguish, her pale eyes blazing, her cheeks wet. Of course, the familiar fair head I'd seen in the row near the front, the sob that had erupted from the crowd during Angel's video tribute. It was her.

The audience had fallen quiet, a silence so heavy I could feel it pressing against my skin. I was alone, I realised. The security guards were nowhere to be seen. The judges and camera operators were statues at the edge of the stage. The shell-shocked audience was stuck to their seats. And none of them understood what was happening before them, what had led to this moment. A woman was about to commit murder live on national television, and only I knew why.

That meant only I could stop her. My legs were lead, but I willed them into motion, stumbling down the aisle towards the stage. What could I possibly do? I wasn't a police officer, a negotiator or a counsellor. I was Clare Deyes, a junior reporter at a local newspaper.

My mind screamed for Mara. Mara would know what to say, what to do, how to defuse this. But Mara was gone, driven away by my own misguided actions. I had no idea whether she was even dead or alive.

Midway down the aisle, I skidded to a standstill and pulled out my mobile, intending this time to call 999. On stage, Dex emitted a small, gurgling whimper. Erin's hand, holding the knife, had raised. She was preparing to do it, preparing to kill him.

'No, Erin!' I shouted from the aisle. 'Please, stop!'

Mute, astonished heads spun to face me. The silence in the studio was thicker than ever, broken only by the hum of that blinding spotlight, by the pounding of my heart against my ribs.

I wracked my brain for the right thing to say next. I opened my mouth in the hope that something would come, when a sudden noise shattered the silence. A sound so ordinary, yet so hideously inappropriate, that a wave of unadulterated mortification washed over me.

I looked down at the object in my hand, mouth still open. My phone was ringing. That same bloody ringtone that I'd been meaning to change for the past week but never had. *"One way to fly, my Clarey-Bird. But two ways to hear my three words."* It was like my nightmare of being on Talent Quest all over again, but this time it was humiliatingly, undeniably real.

Heat flooded my cheeks. And then the caller's name on the phone screen registered.

Mara Knight.

Of all the times for her to call me back. Matt's ardent folk-pop song continued, an excruciating counterpoint to the life-or-death drama on stage. I didn't know what to do. I stared at my phone. Should I answer it? I stared at the stage, where Dex and Erin were locked together. From somewhere in the audience, a girl whispered, 'What's a Clarey-Bird?'

'Aren't you going to answer it?' Erin Grant spat from the stage, causing Dex to flinch. Her voice was sore and unwieldy.

'There's no need!' a voice announced from the wings, and my phone stopped ringing.

Suddenly, a figure moved into the spotlight. A tall form, dark coat billowing, a familiar silhouette against the glare.

It was Mara. She was here.

Relief broke over me. But on stage, Erin's resolve had not wavered. I was sure I could even see the narrowest rivulet of blood trickling down Dex's throat.

Mara slowed a few feet in front of Dex and Erin, the entire studio centred on her. Cameras swung into position, and I wondered why. Surely, given what was going on, the channel had taken Talent Quest off air, had cut to a test card and some nice classical music? By now they must even be showing another programme.

'Hello, Erin,' said Mara. Her voice was soft, sympathetic.

'Go away,' Erin croaked back.

'I just came to say I understand what has happened. I understand what you're going through.'

Erin snorted bitterly. 'What I'm going through? You don't know a thing.'

'I know that none of this is what it seems. It never has been.'

Erin's eyes narrowed.

'Not what it seems!' Dex blurted. 'There's a knife at my jugular. For God's sake, do something!'

Erin's grip on Dex became even more of a vice, and the man bleated a moan.

'You just heard it for yourself,' Mara went on, nodding at me. 'Courtesy of my friend down there. "Two ways to hear three words." Three words. The Magician's Wife.'

Murmurs rippled through the audience.

'The presenter said it, too, when he introduced that tribute. It's how everyone's been referring to her for the past fortnight. On the news, in the papers. The Magician's Wife... Angel Devereaux. But that isn't quite correct, is it, Erin? I'm sure you'll agree, that is selling Angel's talents rather short. After all, she was a skilled magician in her own right, wasn't she? Not merely the wife of one.' Mara's voice resonated with a calm authority as she articulated those puzzle pieces which had begun to slide into place since my confrontation with Jean.

'So there *are* two ways to hear those three words — "The Magician's Wife". Because Angel was the magician. And her wife...' Mara let the sentence hang there. 'Well, like I said, I understand. You wore matching wedding rings, you and Angel...'

The strangely flimsy, shabbyish rings both women wore. I recalled seeing Erin's in the park, and Angel's in the online video of her making the boy's pen disappear.

Those two rings matched.

'I think it's probably best if we spoke about the rest of this somewhere more private,' Mara added.

Erin's determination seemed to splinter for the slimmest moment as she weighed Mara's words. Then she made a visible effort to focus again on the task at hand, fingers recurling around the handle of the knife. 'Say what you need to here,' she tore back. 'I have nothing to hide anymore. I'm sick of hiding. And I'm not going anywhere. *He* deserves to be punished for what he's done.'

Dex's eyes flew desperately to the ceiling.

'Very well,' replied Mara, palms lifted in appeasement. 'Several items were found at the Devereauxs' house this week. In a chest containing both Dex's *and* Angel's clothes. Those items were assumed to have been hidden there by Dex. A letter. Two brand new wedding bands. Items from a secret life, a love affair. But it wasn't Dex's affair, was it?'

'It wasn't an *affair*!' Erin shot, the last word laden with scorn. 'We were in love. We were planning to marry, but this bastard wouldn't agree to a divorce!' She shook Dex as she said this, and he flinched in pain.

It wasn't Angel who wouldn't consent to a divorce. It was Dex.

'I agree,' said Mara. 'It wasn't an affair, that's far too cheap a word for it. It was a secret life though, wasn't it?'

A secret life. Tucked away in a secret compartment inside a

chest of drawers. The letter hidden in that compartment wasn't from Katarina Riley to Dex. It was from Erin Grant to Angel.

My heart, always...

It doesn't seem like your divorce will ever happen...

When we can finally be together... properly, legally...

The first legal same-sex marriages had finally taken place in London earlier today. Saturday, the 29th of March 2014. An entire fourteen years into the twenty-first century. The passing of the Same-Sex Couples Marriage Act had been in and out of the news for the last year. And in the headlines all week.

I remembered the images on Angel's phone – the "couple photos" of meals, theatre tickets, drinks, funfair tokens. But Angel hadn't taken those photos on days out with Dex; she'd taken them on dates with Erin. If I looked again at the picture of those takeaway hot chocolate cups, would I see the pillars of a bandstand in the background? *Nice view of the bandstand,* Mara had said to Erin in the park. Only it wasn't a random remark at all.

'Of course it was a secret life,' Erin hissed. 'What else could it be?' She forced the next part out. 'Look, Angela... Angela was bisexual.'

'Let's do this offstage,' said Mara.

'What's the point? It's too late. She's dead, isn't she?' Erin cut back. 'I'm sick of having to live my life in the wings.' She held Dex tighter still. 'When they met in Edinburgh, maybe this moron did turn her head. But mainly because of what he represented. He was doing the thing she was most passionate about. Living a life she wanted. I told you, Angela was obsessed with magic. She thought marrying *him* was the only way to make it in his world. She also thought that if people found out about us, she wouldn't be able to keep performing. I hated her being his... his *wife*. Hated it. But how could I have got in the way of her doing what she loved the most?'

Never his real wife. The marriage was a sham.

'I know you're angry with Dex,' said Mara, her voice mellowing a little, though her gaze remained sharp. 'You think, as the police do, that it was Dex who killed Angel. But I promise you, it wasn't. Killing him tonight isn't the way to deal with this. Because if you did kill him, it would be the only murder in this whole case.'

There was a stunned exhalation from the crowd. I realised I was holding my breath, too, my chest taut. The objects found at the Devereauxs' house, Angel and Erin's relationship. I'd worked all this out for myself, but what did Mara mean now? *The only murder in this whole case.*

'This whole elaborate case,' Mara continued, 'has been nothing but a tragic piece of misdirection.'

'Instigated by him!' Erin declared, readjusting the blade so the point of it gouged Dex's neck.

'You're giving him too much credit, Erin,' said Mara. 'You've seen the standard of his work compared to Angel's.'

Dex struggled to swallow, his lips parting as if he was about to object to the insult, before thinking better of it.

'What happened on this show last week,' Mara explained. 'It wasn't some master plan of Dex's. It was *Angel's* plan. *Angel's* intricate misdirection.'

Erin's reaction was a tangle of emotions: outrage, guilt, disbelief. But she set her brow and shook her head defiantly. 'No.

He wanted Angela dead,' she countered, still unable to say Dex's name. 'He had done for years. He was jealous of everything she was that he wasn't. She'd been begging him for a divorce for ages, but he refused. And why? Because if they did divorce, he'd have lost the royalty payments from his most lucrative illusion. An illusion he didn't even invent.'

So, that paperwork in Erin's office did relate to Angel's accounts. And it was folded exactly the same way as Erin's letter, the love letter we'd first believed to have been written by Katarina.

She'd made enough of my money vanish over the years.

That money will set us free.

Erin angled her mouth to Dex's ear, expression contorted with rage. 'Tell them!' she screamed as he shied and screwed his face. 'Tell them who *really* invented Fire and Water!'

Dex, trembling, could only manage three choked syllables. 'A... Angel.'

It was as Mara had surmised. That dazzling, dangerous illusion had Angel's brilliance stamped all over it. Not Dex's mediocrity.

'I don't know what happened last Saturday,' said Erin, her voice strangled, her grip on the knife unyielding. 'All I know is I lost the one person I've ever loved. And whichever way you look at it *he* was involved. So now I'm going to finish what Angela started. By killing him.'

47.♠

The studio was a vacuum. The hum of every light; the strained focus of the crowd. Everything was sucked towards the vortex of the spot where Dex's breathing was ragged. Where the sinews showed in Erin's wrist from the force with which she was gripping the knife.

'I understand.' Mara addressed Erin again, her presence steadying amidst the turmoil. 'I understand what you're going through, Erin. The grief, the anger. The most important person in your life has disappeared.' Here, she paused, her lips tightening a moment as she shot Shane Sinclair a look. 'You feel as though the world has tilted on its axis and nothing makes sense any more.'

She was describing her own life, of course. She was describing mine.

Erin's hand wobbled slightly. 'I told you, you don't know anything. You can't possibly know what the last week has been like. It's been hell—'

'Hell on earth?' Mara finished for her. 'Like living on a boat that's taking on water, and all you have is a thimble. So, you use that thimble to scoop as much water from your boat as you can. At first, it feels completely impossible. But then you do it, you finally make some progress emptying the water, when another wave catches you and throws in even more. Absence is the opposite of what you'd expect. It's not a gap, it's a burden. A weight unlike anything you've ever known. Like wearing a backpack of bricks you can never take off. Some days you can bear it better than others. But no matter how tired you get, the weight is always there.' Mara took a long blink, the only time she'd broken eye contact with Erin for more than a millisecond. 'Believe me, I know what it's like.'

My throat constricted painfully, and the scene before me blurred.

'Angel wasn't murdered last week, Erin, and her plan wasn't to kill Dex, or die herself,' said Mara. 'But you knew what she *was* planning, didn't you? Just like you knew what her plan was two weeks ago, when she disappeared. Angel laid low with you the week she was missing, didn't she?'

Erin gave a minute, almost imperceptible nod. So she had known all along that Angel hadn't been kidnapped. Might that also explain why there were so few of Angel's personal possessions at the Devereauxs' house... because they were at Erin's?

'Angel wanted to embarrass Dex two weeks ago, by disappearing on Talent Quest,' Mara went on. 'Embarrass him by vanishing in the middle of one of the biggest performances of his career. She was trying to force his hand, to finally get him to agree to a divorce, so that you and she could be together. *Legally.*'

The word from Erin's letter hung in the air, an acknowledgement of the milestone reached earlier that day: the

UK's first same-sex marriages.

'But then Shane Sinclair — seeing how everyone was talking about Angel's disappearance and thinking only of his ratings — invited Dex back on the show. Which neither Angel nor Dex expected. Is that right, Erin?'

Erin nodded stiffly again. 'Angela came up with the plan of not reappearing in that second box two weeks ago,' she said, with effort. 'She purposefully never got inside it, so when the box opened it would be empty and *he* would look like a fool.' She rattled Dex's arm.

Dex grimaced, though whether through annoyance or alarm it was difficult to tell.

'She thought she'd wait a few days, then make contact with Dex, ask him again for the divorce. She thought that by then he'd have begun to be implicated in her disappearance, and so be willing to agree to anything.'

'But when Angel heard Dex had been invited back on the show, she devised a new scheme, didn't she?' Mara asked. 'A more elaborate one. She needed to up the ante. Instead of disappearing last week, she planned to *reappear*. In that second box, in her stage outfit. During the show. And she wanted to make the spectacle bigger, more shocking than the previous week. To humiliate Dex even more. To ask him again for a divorce, live on air this time.'

Erin's chin quivered. 'I told her it was a stupid idea. Begged her just to leave him, to move in with me. But she was adamant. She had the proof that she'd invented Fire and Water herself and, with the right divorce lawyer, she was certain she'd be entitled to the bulk of the royalties.' Her voice faltered. 'Once

Angela had an idea in her head, there was no stopping her.'

'And so the first thing she did...' Mara began.

The first thing she did. What had been the first thing we'd discovered back on Monday? That a telephone order had been placed at Presto Print, using Dex's credit card.

'The banner,' I whispered, the details clicking into place.

'The first thing she did was order a banner from a print shop in south London. She did this under Dex's name, using his credit card, as it was placed during the week she was supposed to be missing. It read, "I heart hurting women." But it was really just a calculated piece of theatre. It didn't mean Dex was some sadist with mummy issues, but a chauvinist who was drawing out his marriage for his own gain, and in doing so denying the happiness of two women.'

So the banner was yet another element of the story that hadn't at all been what it seemed. It was only by reframing those superficially murderous words that it made sense. This story hadn't been about perverse psychopathic desires; it had been about a thwarted happy ever after. I thought back over what Mr Chen had told us, reframing that too.

'Angel had probably made a note of Dex's credit card details in advance,' Mara confirmed. 'She had Lenny Finch collect the banner last Saturday morning. And in the afternoon, just before the props were collected for that night's show, she went to the lock-up. She set the banner up in the second box. Then she put on her wig and stage clothes — which is when she must have dropped her phone — before concealing herself in the secret compartment in the box's base, in order to be smuggled into the studio without drawing attention to herself.'

Which is also how Angel had left the studio that first Saturday, I realised. By disguising herself as a member of the production crew, to hide in plain sight.

Erin's grasp on the knife loosened a little. She was fixed on what Mara was saying, exhaling in shallow gasps.

'The box, with Angel still hidden inside it, was loaded onto a van and transported here, to the studio. But we saw the CCTV footage, Erin. We saw that same box being *un*loaded.' Mara's gaze was locked intensely on Erin's, eyebrows oblique, sympathetic, her voice lowered. 'And that's where the plan went tragically, irrevocably wrong. The props team was careless. The box slipped, rolled out of control, colliding with a wall. When it did, Angel was sadly knocked unconscious.'

That's why Angel's blood had been found inside the base of the second box. The wound hadn't been caused by a blow to her head inflicted by Dex, Shane, Lenny or Jean. It had been the result of a sloppy, accidental mishandling. A terrible coming together of ingredients.

A smattering of murmurs rose and died in the audience. Onstage, the spotlight braced Erin and Dex in a tableau of dawning realisation.

'Unfortunately, Dex was late arriving at the studio last Saturday. He never examined the box in advance. It was usually Angel's job. He was telling the truth about that.'

Dex attempted to nod in agreement, but with the knife still pressed against him, all he could muster was a frantic twinge.

'Dex had no idea that Angel was inside the box, unconscious. So, when the sides of the box fell away live on air...'

Mara didn't need to finish the sentence. We'd all seen it.

Angel, plummeting limply to the stage, unconscious and unable to break her fall. And due to the way she was positioned in the base of that box — the way she'd *always* positioned herself inside it — the angle at which she fell was fatal.

'It was a terrible, tragic accident, Erin,' Mara finished. 'An illusion of sorts, gone catastrophically wrong. But it wasn't murder.'

Erin stared at Mara, her arm sagging, space opening up between the blade and the skin of Dex's neck. 'An... accident?' she repeated, her voice hollow.

'I'm sorry,' replied Mara. 'I really am. Come with me now. There are people who can help.'

Erin blinked quickly. 'Twenty-four years,' she murmured, confused. 'I loved her for nearly a quarter of a century. Most of it wasted because we never... just...' The words ruptured, tears now streaming freely down her face. The regret in her voice was crushing. Regret that they hadn't spent every minute of that time together. 'We were going to get married,' she said. 'Properly, this time. It's what we always wanted. And with the new laws...'

'Properly, *this time*,' Mara echoed.

Erin uttered a distracted noise, as though re-conjuring the moment in her mind. 'We had a wedding ceremony. At university. Just a silly homemade thing. We came up with our own vows. Bought the rings from a charity shop in Lincoln.'

Erin's ring finger, with its humble, paper-thin band, twitched on Dex's arm.

'Finally,' Erin continued, her voice growing more anguished, 'the chance opened up for us to do it properly. Get legally married. That's why I moved back to the area. Because Angela told me she was certain this time. She was going to leave, ask for a divorce. She had the previous royalty payments from Fire and Water to keep her going. All we needed was for *him*,' Erin jutted her chin contemptuously at Dex, 'to agree to it. But he wouldn't, would he?'

'I know,' said Mara, taking a careful step closer as she sensed Erin's agitation rising again. 'But Angel loved you very much, Erin. Everything she did, all these elaborate plans, it was all for you. For your future together.'

Erin shook her head furiously, evaporated tear tracks bisecting her cheeks in two jagged lines. 'All we wanted was a second chance to be together. *He's* had plenty, chance after chance on this stupid show. He didn't deserve any of them!'

Mara took another tentative step closer. 'Pass me the knife, Erin.'

'No!' Erin yelled, the word tearing from her throat. '*He* needs to pay. If he'd agreed to the divorce when she asked, then Angela... Angela would still be here today!' She choked it out, the vowels peeled raw by anger, and examined the blade in her hand as though seeing it anew. 'He has to pay!'

My heart stopped as two things happened together: Mara moving forwards to intervene as Erin Grant swung her arm high, knife arcing dangerously as she prepared to thrust it downwards into Dex's neck.

There was no time to think. Before adrenaline had the chance to take hold, or my brain to catch up with what my body was doing, I unsheathed Jasper's ball-launcher from my handbag and, in one smooth motion, extended the handle. I drew back my arm, gave a forceful flick of the wrist, and discharged the missile.

Time seemed to collapse as the ball propelled itself towards the stage. Faces turned, mouths gaped, and the bright red orb whistled overhead, reaching its target and connecting squarely with Erin's hand.

The unexpected impact caused the knife to fly clean from her grasp, clattering to the floor. The tomato-shaped ball bounced with a series of ridiculous, cartoonish squeaks before coming to rest beside it.

Several beats of astounded silence passed. Then Mara swept towards the weapon, scooping it into the air. She moved downstage, holding the knife up theatrically to the audience, to the cameras. Surely, I thought, with a sickening lurch, they couldn't *still* be rolling?

'As I said,' Mara announced, 'this has all been a case of misdirection. As you can see, this knife...' She pressed the blade against the palm of her hand and it buckled harmlessly. 'Is *fake.*'

A ripple of uncertain relief travelled through the audience. I couldn't believe what I was seeing. The knife had been fake all along. Rubber, just like the knife in Mara's kitchen.

'Everyone, take note that Erin Grant never intended to harm Dex Devereaux tonight. She just wanted to make a point, if you'll pardon the pun. Please...' She gestured to the wings, from where two figures in dark suits stepped out.

Erin Grant, her face set in exhausted, bewildered grief, allowed herself to be led quietly away.

The breath collapsed from Dex in a great gush, and he fell to his knees and wept for the first time since his wife's death. The blinding white spotlight lingered on him for a second longer than it should have, and then went out.

48.

I stood alone in the studio car park, waiting to give a statement to the police. It had grown dark in the time I'd been inside, and a heavy shower of rain had fallen. The tarmac was shining with puddles, flashing blue lights strobing across the surface of the water. Ambulances and police cars had arrived, to park hastily and aslant across the studio doors. Dazed-looking members of the public lingered in clumps, production and emergency personnel moving between the studio buildings, managing the crowd.

Although the Angel Devereaux case now finally made sense, I felt as disoriented as many of the people around me looked. It was difficult to comprehend what had just happened, that an accountant had held a magician at knifepoint live on one of the most popular TV shows in the country. An accountant and a magician who had been players in a drama gone dreadfully, accidentally wrong. A tragic love story, ultimately.

I brought my handbag to my front in order to retrieve my phone. I might be here for some time, and I was curious to know what was being said online about what had just happened on Talent Quest. I opened the mouth of my bag wide, and was about to remove my phone when a brightly coloured projectile whizzed towards me, landing directly inside the bag with a squeak.

I fished it out. A familiar, worn red shape.

Jasper's ball.

'I knew you were a decent shot, Clare,' a voice said. 'But that really was outstanding.'

I looked up. It was Mara, slightly paler than usual but as commanding as ever, shrouded in the deep green folds of her coat.

She was trailed by a paramedic, who was attempting to drape a foil blanket across her shoulders "for shock". Mara shrugged the woman off, insisting she wasn't in shock and that if the woman really wanted to help, she could bring her a vodka.

I wanted to laugh, a heady relief coursing through me as Mara came closer. Not only had nothing bad befallen her at the Harrowbrook Estate, but she'd made a triumphant reappearance at Shinetree to solve a potential murder and prevent another. And she'd lost none of her strange, prickly charisma.

Mara drew to a halt opposite me. 'I think it's fair to say you saved a life tonight.'

'You too,' I replied. 'Good job Erin didn't just cut Dex's throat when she had the knife pressed against it, or I'd never have been able to get in a clean shot, to knock the ball away.'

Yet the knife had been fake, despite the blood on Dex's neck...

Mara, not mentioning this, shrugged. 'Dex nearly died on stage. It's something he's used to.'

I smiled, despite — or perhaps because of — the crassness of the remark. It was classic Mara, even though hundreds of people had just seen her handle Erin's rampant grief with such empathy and understanding. Or maybe it was her ability to articulate the pain of Erin's experience that made her so cynical. Her cynicism was the crust that had formed as she navigated the same pain on a daily basis. It was the way she'd evolved to bear the weight of that backpack of bricks.

'You could probably say the same about nearly being hit by a tomato,' I offered. 'Dex'll be used to that as well.'

Mara stifled one of her single syllable laughs. 'A rotten tomato, definitely. Though actually I didn't mean you saved Dex's life,' she said. 'I meant you saved Erin's.'

I paused a moment, taking this in. How Erin could hopefully now get some help to deal with Angel's loss and try to rebuild her life. How it was likely that, given she'd been stopped before causing anyone physical harm, no charges would be brought against her. Though again, since the knife wasn't real, surely no physical harm would have been caused anyway...? The thought dwindled.

'Thanks,' I managed finally, the word feeling insufficient. 'All those things you said on stage. They were... well, pretty amazing really. How you were with Erin, how you worked it all out, about Angel's plan. I knew you would.'

Mara's lips lifted into a small smile, and she glanced away.

'Oh, and your pun was pretty good too,' I added. 'Someone with a knife, just wanting to "make a point".'

'One for Jeff Tych, I think,' Mara replied, the ghost of a smile still playing on her lips. 'I've no doubt he'll want to cover the story, especially given the Morden connection. The least he could do is allow you to write it. Seen as you were fundamental to the outcome.'

My stomach shifted as I recalled all the unread texts and unplayed voicemail messages from Jeff piled up on my phone. 'I... I doubt I have a job at the Mercury anymore,' I mumbled. 'And even if I did...'

Even if I did what? The truth was, after the past week, I wasn't sure I was best suited to a life of local news reporting. Or any news reporting, come to that. I didn't have an ounce of Jeff's pushiness or lack of scruples, for a start.

I'd become a journalist to make a difference and, in this last week, I had. I'd made a difference to the Angel Devereaux case by finding Katarina, linking the banner back to Presto Print. By finding Angel's phone and helping to solve what had happened to her. But none of that had been achieved by writing about cats stuck up Christmas trees or gnomes in potholes.

I decided to keep this to myself.

'Even if I did still have a job, I doubt Jeff would let me write the story,' I said, finishing the sentence. 'I'm just a junior reporter.'

'You're not *just* a junior reporter, Clare.'

I frowned at the ball in my hand and slid it into my bag, so I didn't have to meet Mara's gaze.

'Mara, about what happened in the car—' I began.

'Here we are!' The paramedic was back, and this time she was brandishing a styrofoam cup, pushing it into Mara's hand.

'What's this?' Mara asked, staring at the cup as though it was the most peculiar thing she'd ever seen.

'Hot sweet tea,' the woman answered. 'Just the thing for shock.'

'I told you, I'm not in shock,' Mara replied dismissively,

then reexamined the liquid in her hand. 'Does it contain any vodka—?'

The woman, who had already begun to walk away, didn't reply.

Mara took a sip from the cup and pulled a face. 'The answer is no,' she confirmed.

I gave a low laugh, then the words tumbled out. 'Mara, about what happened Thursday night. I'm so sorry. I wasn't lying in my text when I said I really never intended to write about Travers. I just let Jeff think that to buy myself some more time on the case. I didn't mean any of the things I said in the car.'

Mara's expression hazed slightly, becoming unreadable. 'You were right, I was letting my bias against Sinclair affect the investigation...' She hesitated. 'Those things you said... you actually got scarily close to the truth.'

A pregnant pause.

'Well, you do always like to disagree,' I added, breaking it.

'Not at all.'

'Also—' I took a breath, the memory of the pettiness of the next part making my cheeks burn. 'I didn't mean what I said. About you and DC Taylor. I had no business insinuating that.'

She harrumphed kindly, waving this away. 'Don't worry about Taylor,' she said. 'That's another thing that wasn't quite what it seemed. I've known Luke since he was fourteen. Since Dhita and Jake started seeing each other, in fact. He's Jake's younger brother.'

'Dhita's partner... Jake,' I murmured, bringing to mind the similarity between the two men, the way Jake had reminded me of someone when we'd met. The way Dhita always had the latest info on the investigation. 'Oh. I'm sorry.'

'It's alright, Clare,' said Mara, depositing her barely touched cup of tea on the bonnet of a nearby police car. 'Anyway, it's certainly not as bad as your ringtone. Though that did sort of turn out to be relevant, I'll grant you.'

A reluctant laugh escaped me. '"Two ways to hear my three words." Thanks to Matt, it was staring us in the face all along.' I didn't mention that when I'd asked him what the two meanings were, he hadn't known, saying poetry was so deep it didn't have to mean anything. I wondered if the three words were even "I love you". I didn't ask, in case Matt didn't know the answer to that either.

'The Magician's Wife,' Mara nodded. 'Or, more accurately, the magician and her wife.'

We stood in a momentary pocket of quiet amidst the surrounding tumult, the blue lights throwing fleeting patterns across Mara's face. Now she'd put down the cup, she was shaking, I noticed, a fine tremor running through her hands. The paramedic was right. She was in shock.

'So, how did you work it all out?' I asked, eager to understand the final turns of the illusion. 'That it was Angel's plan? A tragic accident?'

'Once it sunk in that you were right about my being fixated with Sinclair,' said Mara, 'I took stock of the things that didn't quite add up about Dex being the one who sent that Facebook message to Lenny. And rather than Dex having crafted an alibi that was, to be blunt, well beyond his capabilities, it was a question of who the next most likely person was to have access to that Facebook account. That person wasn't one of Sinclair's

IT guys. That person was Angel.'

Dex *had* told DI Paulson that he left all his social media updates to Angel.

'But to have sent the message, Angel must still have been alive the week after her disappearance,' I remarked. 'It was a pretty big leap to assume that she was, even with the CCTV footage of her leaving the studio.'

Mara raised an eyebrow. 'Once you eliminate the impossible, whatever remains—'

'No matter how improbable, must be the truth,' I finished for her.

'After that,' she went on, 'it was just a matter of psychology. Why would Angel have wanted Katarina out of the way last Saturday? For the same reason she engineered her own disappearance mid-trick the week before. To embarrass Dex into granting the divorce she wanted to marry Erin.'

'And the blonde hair Lindi found was one of Erin's?'

'Most likely.'

'But how did you know that Angel and Erin wanted to marry?' I asked, still a little confused. 'You noticed their matching wedding rings and presumed that, with the changing laws, they might want to make it official?'

'The Fire and Water trick,' Mara continued. 'A large-scale illusion was the key to this whole... well, large-scale illusion. Angel invented it. Not just as an illusion, but as a *tribute*. Fire and water. Their star signs. Angel was a Leo, a fire sign. We saw the framed print on her dressing table. And Erin—'

'A Pisces,' I cut in, recollecting our conversation with her in the park. 'Of course. And Angel's lock screen, on her phone... that swirling pattern of blue waves and orange flames.' Something so generic, so totally unremarkable in Dex's lock-up, now seemed so poignant. As did those new wedding rings in their box, set with their blue and orange stones. 'And obviously, Erin was dealing with Angel's accounts. Her royalty payments from Fire and Water.'

Mara nodded. 'It's one of the reasons they felt they had to keep everything so secret. Like Erin said, if Dex had discovered their relationship, any divorce settlement would have been far more contentious. He'd have fought harder to keep a larger share of those royalties.'

I thought how sad it was that Angel had felt the need to reduce a love that'd endured since childhood to a series of such generic photos on a mobile phone: two meals, two drinks, the stubs of two tickets. Though maybe "reduce" was the wrong word. However, there wasn't a sense of restraint in those pictures so much as constraint.

'I suppose Angel also thought she had to keep her relationship with Erin under wraps because she worried that coming out would ruin her career. I know it's the twenty-first century and everything, but people can be very unforgiving.'

'Indeed,' agreed Mara. 'Especially audiences, bookers, et cetera, who've perceived Angel as Dex's wife for so long. That... *partnership* was part of the magic,' she added distantly.

A sense of admiration tinged with sadness passed over me. 'Angel was brilliant, wasn't she? To come up with such an intricate plan, all those layers of deception. I mean, it was crazy in a way, and because Angel wasn't around to let Katarina out of that flight case, Katarina could have died. But Angel could never have foreseen it would all go wrong because a box was carelessly unloaded.'

'She had a mind perfectly attuned to cause and effect, to misdirection,' Mara replied. 'And she knew how to play them all. She was, of course, wasted in a double act.'

Misdirection. How had that Arden Lake blog article described Angel's talents? *An uncanny ability for clever misdirection.*

I remembered the way Angel had left Shinetree disguised as one of the crew. She must have smuggled that outfit into the studio in a bag, putting it on over her leotard so she could leave Shinetree quickly. And I was willing to bet money that the bulge beneath her t-shirt that disguised her figure was the empty bag.

'And is there proof of all this, do you think?' I asked Mara. 'Aside from what Erin admitted? That it was Angel who got Lenny to kidnap Katarina?'

'My guess is the Facebook message was sent from Erin's desktop,' Mara said. 'So I imagine the IP address will trace back to her house.'

As well as getting Lenny to kidnap Katarina, Angel had also tasked him with collecting that banner from Presto Print. I doubted Jean was aware of any of it.

I felt a little sorry for Lenny then, living with a domineering and slightly unhinged mother, albeit one who kept him well supplied with packed lunches. But he was a naive and lonely young man who'd become entangled in a kidnapping just so he could join the Magic Circle.

'I wonder what will happen to Lenny?' I asked Mara. 'He'll be released fairly soon, surely? It seems like he was just a pawn.'

'I would have thought so. It can be proven that it wasn't his idea. I suppose it all depends on whether Katarina Riley wants to press charges.'

I brought to mind the childlike desperation in Lenny's eyes, his talk of the "magician's code". He had only done what he'd done as he genuinely believed he was helping his hero, Dex Devereaux. A new thought struck me.

'Oh my God,' I started, 'it's a bit of a leap, but... you don't think Lenny could be Dex's son? Jean and Dex were a couple when he met Angel — the timing would fit. Do you think that's why Jean half-bullies, half-smothers her son, because he reminds her of his father, a man who left her for another woman?'

Mara mulled this over for a second. 'Let's just say it wouldn't surprise me. And that's a good psychological assessment, though physically Lenny's almost his mother's double. If he is Dex's son, then Dex's genes didn't even get a look-in. Which, given Jean Finch's personality, doesn't actually surprise me.'

I laughed. 'I really thought she was behind it all. That horrible room of hers, her Facebook page...'

'When I saw those posts, I thought exactly the same,' Mara confessed. 'Graham assured me he'd already checked her out.'

I remembered the scene I'd unleashed. Jean Finch, wheezing and flailing in that sweet cloud of perfume, as soft-focus photographs of Angel faded in and out on the giant screen behind her. 'I even confronted Jean about it, you know. At the studio, during Angel's video tribute.'

Mara's lips twitched. 'I thought I heard a bit of a fracas in the audience. It was the perfect distraction, as it happened. Allowed me to slip into the wings unnoticed. Seems like you were inspired by those women at the prison.'

She meant the two prisoners at HMP Ferndon fighting over the vape. Though their scratching and hair-pulling was a lot less pleasant than a couple of sprays of Parma Violet.

That all seemed like a lifetime ago now, not the seven days it was. So much had happened since. It was strange to think that while Mara had been plotting her prison break in north London, Angel had been in the south, planning an escape of her own. But whereas Mara had escaped from a physical prison, Angel had attempted to free herself from the confines of a life she'd chosen, a marriage she'd endured in pursuit of a dream. There had been no foul play behind the mystery of her disappearance. She had chosen the path herself.

It's entirely possible that she might have put herself there.

'Angel Devereaux reminds me of my mother,' I blurted, the words out before I could stop them. 'I mean… my mother wasn't murdered, as I thought for so long. She took matters into her own hands, like Angel. Chose a different path, a different life.' I waited for the gut punch that usually followed when I thought about Mum leaving, but for the first time it didn't come.

Mara held my gaze, a new softness to her pale green eyes, a flicker of understanding that went beyond the case. The noise of the car park receded, the flashing lights dimmed. For a moment, it was just the two of us. Two women who understood the weight of absence, and what it meant for a life to be irrevocably altered.

Without us noticing, the paramedic returned, slipping a foil blanket around Mara's shoulders. She didn't shake it off this time, but pulled it more tightly around her, turning to the woman.

'We'll have one of these for Clare too,' Mara said.

49.

It was afternoon of the following day when I finally caught up with what people were saying online. Matt had already messaged to tell me he hoped I was okay, and he'd be back in a couple of hours. He also said I needed to watch the latest episode of Talent Quest online, because the woman I knew in the green coat had been on it, trying to save a magician from having his head cut off.

I was at Talent Quest too, I wrote back.

No way! he replied. *I thought that tomato looked like Jasper's. And the Clarey-Bird song's famous!*

I considered what Matt had said about Mara being on the show. Despite the studio cameras appearing to continue filming, I knew the official broadcast of the Talent Quest final had cut away the moment Erin had appeared with the knife. Before Mara even took to the stage. I asked Matt how he'd seen the rest.

Mobile phone footage from the crowd, just like a gig! It's all over the internet!!

I grabbed my laptop, nestled myself next to Jasper on the sofa, and navigated to Clipster.

Matt had been right: the site was awash with footage of the

previous night's show. It turned out that once Erin produced the knife, a good portion of the audience hadn't been so frozen with anticipation as I'd assumed.

There were clips of it all. Of Mara attempting to calm Erin, of Erin telling her story, of Mara presenting the fake knife to the crowd, of Dex dropping to his knees. There were even videos of my own cameo, as Jasper's red ball hurtled through the air to connect with Erin's hand.

Talent Quest may have officially pulled the broadcast prior to all the drama, but Shane Sinclair must still be delighted. Ironically, these videos — a number of which had already started going viral — would send his show's popularity into the stratosphere. Everyone would be talking about it for months to come. And he wouldn't have to part with a penny for the publicity. Given what had happened to Travers, I wondered how Mara felt about that.

I watched one clip after another and then began to scroll through the comments. There were literally thousands.

The magician and her wife. Mind. Blown. Such a tragic story. #LGBT

Erin is a hero. Standing up for the woman she loved. Even if the knife was fake, her pain was real.

I cried when Erin was talking about their university wedding. So sad that Angel felt she had to hide who she was for her career. #LoveisLove

From hostage situation to dog toy intervention! LMAO Talent Quest, you never fail to surprise. #TomatoSavesTheDay

I need to know more about Ball-Launcher Lady. Is she friends with Green Coat Lady? #DynamicDuo

But it wasn't just the tragedy of what had happened to Angel and Erin, or even my ball-launching skills, that most people seemed to be talking about.

It was Mara.

The story of the Talent Quest final had been picked up by several online news channels, their headlines blazing from the recommended videos in the sidebar.

Mysterious Woman in Green Coat Defuses Knifepoint Hostage Situation

Who is Talent Quest's Unlikely Heroine?

Mara Knight: The Real Magic on Saturday's Talent Quest

The headlines were sensational; the videos' comment sections even more so. Everyone was discussing what Mara had done, how she'd calmly faced Erin down, her voice a steady anchor in the storm of chaos.

That woman in the green coat is an actual superhero. She just appeared and took control. No panic, just pure focus. #Fearless

Talent Quest needs to hire that woman as a permanent judge. She'd see through all the acts in a second!

I want her to solve all my life problems. She'd probably do it in 5 minutes with a perfectly arched

eyebrow.

That coat. That voice. That presence. #Obsessed

Some of the comments were even directing people to the Mara Knight fan pages that were already springing up.

I clicked on the video of the Talent Quest final that had the most views. It was possibly the clearest recording of them all, filmed on a phone by someone fairly close to the stage.

Pressing play, I watched the whole thing again. I witnessed Mara stride out from the wings, a dark, assertive figure under the spotlight's unrelenting glare. I heard her voice, calm and measured, cutting through Erin's anguish. I saw her hold up the knife, revealing it to be fake.

Moving down the page to the comments section, one comment in particular caught my attention.

Pretty sure the woman in the green coat switched the knives. Watch @8:13 when she picks the knife up. Classic sleight of hand. Erin had a REAL blade.

My breath hitched. I hastily scrolled back up to the player and jumped to the eight-minute thirteen-second mark, my eyes glued to the screen. But it was only when I'd replayed the same few seconds of footage several more times that I actually saw it.

When Mara rose after stooping to retrieve the knife Erin had dropped, she gave an almost undetectable flick of her wrist.

The commenter was right. Mara *had* switched those knives. The rubber version must still have been in her coat after she made it disappear that day in her kitchen. Erin Grant had been holding a real blade to Dex's throat. How the hell had I not seen it before?

Mara had not only put herself in incredible danger by walking onto that stage, but she'd also, with astonishing coolness, executed a perfect magic trick in order to protect Erin, to minimise the consequences for her. It was reckless. It was audacious. It was...

Well, it was Mara.

Late in the afternoon, I eventually closed my laptop. Matt would be home soon. After my cleaning marathon yesterday, the flat was looking impressive. The only hint of clutter was in the hall, where my handbag sat disgorging its contents onto the floor. Contents minus the ball-launcher, which Jasper had already reclaimed.

I scooped the bag up. After a week of it being a mobile office-cum-toolkit, it was in an even sorrier state than when Mara had checked it at the prison. Crumpled food receipts, a semi-eaten packet of Haribo, half a dozen pens with their ends chewed, a notebook. And right at the bottom of all this, my dictaphone.

I hadn't used it since that day at HMP Ferndon, when I'd interviewed Kelly Keogan, the woman I'd assumed was Mara. I remembered the ungodly burp she gave when I asked her to test the sound levels, Mara's subsequent amusement when I'd told her about it. A smile touched my lips.

On a whim, I rewound the dictaphone recording and pressed play. Kelly's burp echoed around the flat. I listened to my own flustered questions as the prison interview drew to its unproductive close. Then, just as I was about to switch the dictaphone off, a new voice sounded. A voice that hadn't been there before.

It was Mara.

I dropped to the floor, stunned, the dictaphone still in my hand. When had she done this? Despite Mara and I having spent pretty much the whole of the past week together, I'd barely let my handbag out of my sight.

And yet, the things she was saying... about my job, about Travers, about what I said when I spoke to Kelly. I realised Mara could only have made this recording the previous night. I shook my head in amazement and continued to listen, the smile on my face spreading across my entire body.

'Couple of things, Clare,' Mara's voice said. 'Firstly, your job. If you're certain it's time to move on from the Mercury, then I might have something for you. It transpires I'm in need of an assistant. The job's yours if you want it. A fresh start for you, perhaps? Think about it.'

Mara had seen through my lie in the studio car park, recognising what I really meant. That, even if I did still have a job left with Jeff, I wasn't sure I wanted it.

But there was more.

'Secondly, I presume you'll have listened to the whole of your dictaphone recording before getting this far, so you'll remember what you said to me — or rather, to Kelly — one week ago.'

It was about her husband; I knew instantly. I'd offered to help find Travers.

'And the answer is yes. I'd appreciate that. Very much.'

EPILOGUE

Jasper and I stood facing the building's vast facade, exactly two weeks after it had all begun. I guessed that, given the job I'd just accepted, I would be seeing a lot more of this bizarre, bewitching place from now on. *A fresh start.* But why Jasper had been invited along this evening, especially given the owner's aversion to dogs, I really couldn't work out.

We stepped through the stone pillars and into the porch as one of the great pairs of double doors swung inwards.

'Welcome back,' said Mara, eyeing Jasper a little less warily than she had the last time she'd seen him. Perhaps she was making some progress.

Jasper and I followed Mara across the chequerboard tiles of her hallway, which were bathed in the last hazy rays of the day. It would be dusk soon, and the falling light imbued the place with even more of a magical quality, a momentary sense of suspension between the old and the new.

Ahead of me, Mara opened the door to her living room and, as soon as I entered, my jaw dropped.

'Mara!' I exclaimed, for there, hanging high from the carved wooden wall that had once formed the church's old altar, was a gigantic pet birthday banner. A pet birthday banner complete with an enormous likeness of Jasper, posing endearingly for the camera, one paw raised. A polka-dot party hat had been photoshopped onto his head, and huge words above and below him read: "Happy BARK-day, Jasper! It's PAW-ty Time, let's raise the WOOF!"

'Are you sure this banner came from Mr Chen and not Jeff Tych?' I asked.

Mara gave a hum of amusement from the other side of the room, where she was busy with her drinks cabinet.

An additional line of text had been printed at the bottom of the banner. "I ♥ HAPPY DOGS." Words that had taken me full circle in two weeks: from a junior job at a local paper and a missing woman, to this.

I smiled. 'Mara, this is... I don't know what to say.'

'Drink?' she asked airily, as if having a ten-foot banner in her house to wish a dog a happy birthday was an everyday occurrence. 'There's food out in the kitchen too, if you want any. Including...' she grimaced, 'dog-friendly cupcakes and something called *Paw*-secco.'

I laughed. 'So all that party inspiration saved to Instagram came in handy?'

She approached me with a glass of wine. 'It would seem so.'

I put my arms around her. Felt her tense and then relax. 'Thank you,' I murmured.

An hour or so later, Pawsecco gratefully demolished by Jasper

— and several glasses of human wine gratefully demolished by me — and my dog and I were comfortably nestled on Mara's squashy velvet sofa. The night was chilly, and a log fire had been lit in the hearth to crackle soothingly in the background.

Mara had switched on her huge, wall-mounted television as we waited for the re-scheduled final of Talent Quest to start. This time, Dex Devereaux would not be performing.

'How's it been this week, then?' I asked Mara. I hadn't seen her since we'd stood in the car park at Shinetree the previous Saturday. I'd spent the week speaking to Jeff and handing in my notice, tying up the last loose ends and local stories at the Mercury. 'Your new celebrity status keeping you busy?'

'I've had one hundred and forty-two emails,' Mara replied. 'If that's what you mean by "keeping me busy".'

'That's a lot for a week,' I agreed.

'That was just today,' said Mara. 'And that's without the letters sent to Travers's management. Thankfully, no one's tracked down my home address yet.' She shook her head. 'People apparently want my help with everything from poisoned pets to poison pen letters.'

'You're the nation's new favourite detective,' I remarked, stretching contentedly. 'Like Sherlock, only in a much better coat.'

Mara raised her eyebrows. 'There's also my work with the police... the magic props hire... I've a feeling we're going to be kept very busy.'

'Can't wait,' I said, though it was an understatement. The thought of working alongside Mara, delving into the intricacies of human deception, was far more exciting than any pun-laced local newspaper headline. 'Though I'm not sure my ball-launching skills will be required on every case.'

Mara's lips twitched. 'You never know.'

On the television screen before us, the adverts ended and Talent Quest's opening titles began, its theme music erupting from the speakers. Mara groaned, mentally preparing herself for another performance from Josie the Chihuahua. Then, suddenly, the programme cut out.

The garish, light-saturated studio was gone, the TV screen we were now looking at having split into eight. Eight monochrome and slightly grainy videos. I realised they were the views from Mara's security cameras.

Mara straightened in her wingback. 'Somebody must be out there,' she said, putting down her glass. 'So much for no one tracking down my home address.'

As we continued to watch, a dark form moved into shot at the front door, cast in the eerie, flat glow of the building's outdoor lights. The figure was skinny and dressed in a dark tracksuit; the hood pulled low, face obscured. It moved with a furtive, uneasy energy, stopping to check about itself before creeping closer to the door.

Mara and I exchanged a glance.

Then the figure on screen jabbed at the doorbell, and the CCTV feed on Mara's television switched. This time, it showed the close-up from the doorbell camera, a face filling the screen. Strands of lank, dark hair trailed the person's pale cheeks, which looked like they hadn't seen daylight in months.

The face was instantly familiar.

Kelly Keogan.

'Shouldn't she be...?' I began.

'Yes,' Mara answered. 'Serving a five-year sentence for grievous bodily harm.'

Then Kelly spoke. 'Mara Knight?' she asked urgently. 'I need your help. It's about little Tayte.'

Kelly paused, like what she was about to say next was too unbelievable to utter aloud.

'He's started having visions of the future. Visions that are coming true. Thing is, he's now saying... He's saying a man is going to *kill* him. Please... Please help me stop it.'

As Kelly's voice reverberated around the room, a fresh wave of exhilaration buzzed through me. The Angel Devereaux investigation might be over, but our next case had just arrived.

**Clare and Mara will
return in *Second Sight*.
Coming early 2026.**

AUTHOR'S AFTERWORD

Thank you so much for reading *The Magician's Wife*. In this noisy, busy world, I really do appreciate that you took the time both to choose and read my book in particular, and I very much hope you enjoyed it. If you did, I would be so grateful if you'd consider leaving it a nice review.

Here's a little more about me...

After studying English Literature at Durham University, I moved to London to work in the TV industry. There I wrote factual programme content and comedy material for companies like the BBC and Channel 4. And there, while working at one of these companies, I met my husband. Writing this book has been a complete passion project for me — a story I've wanted to tell for six years — since I am a real-life magician's wife. My husband, Barry Jones, was once part of a magic double act and, as a result, I spent the decade or so after we met working behind the scenes with him on his tricks and illusions, everywhere from back rooms at comedy clubs to the huge studio stages of prime time TV shows. As a result, I've been able to surreptitiously glean all sorts of top-secret industry info and forbidden knowledge along the way. Though sadly, I'm nowhere near as good at magic tricks as Mara...

Together, Barry and I are the co-creators and co-hosts of a popular fortnightly podcast, also called *The Magician's Wife*. In it, we break down a baffling, real-life mystery into an Effect and a Method and — just like a magic trick — try to work out how it might have been done.

You can listen to all our episodes here if you're curious: **themagicianswife.co.uk**

The Magician's Wife is my second novel. My debut, a historical mystery, sold to big-five publishers in the UK and US in major deals within twenty-four hours of going on submission. It was also published in a further five languages.

And to end with a few thank yous…

Firstly, a big thanks to the following people for their help in bringing this book to publication: Barry Jones, Abigail Fenton, Paula Gadd and the team at Vanish Publishing, plus all the authors who kindly offered quotes.

With a million more thanks to you, my reader. I had huge fun writing this novel and I hope you love it — and the world I've created — as much as I do.

Lora x

(A well-wisher)

I really hope you enjoyed reading *The Magician's Wife*.

If you did, please consider becoming a part of my Readers' Club for a FREE EBOOK, plus FREE MONTHLY MYSTERIES, all set in the impossible crime world of Clare Deyes and Mara Knight.

I love to connect with readers through my Readers' Club, and this is where I also share other exclusive tidbits, plus all the latest news about upcoming book releases, live events, giveaways and more!

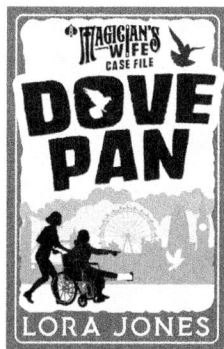

Sign up to receive your FREE ebook,
Dove Pan: A Magician's Wife Case File!

fiction.lorajones.com

Printed in Dunstable, United Kingdom